Hoodwink

Lt. Jake Chase has a jinx – trouble just naturally comes his way – but he's used to it. He's annoyed when he's taken off his Big Case to investigate what looks like an ordinary mugging, but the new assignment looks easy.

Then he meets the beautiful but zany Casey Hewson – and suddenly Jake's jinx starts working full time. He finds out the dead man was an ex-convict about to publish the awful truth about a certain local gangster and a missing socialite. There's also a drunk who isn't a drunk, a mysterious desk that keeps disappearing, a politician with an old grudge, a cack-handed bunch of hoods who can't get anything right, and The Man Who Keeps Buying Hats. His Captain never told him there'd be cases like *this*. As poor Jake trips, falls and is dragged from one disaster to another, he realises his first mistake was getting out of bed, and his next mistake might be his last.

Hoodwink is a merry-go-round of mayhem, mobsters, and misapprehensions as everybody tries to fool everyone else and only the killer means business.

Paula Gosling, author of many exciting and witty crime novels, including *Monkey Puzzle* – which won the coveted Gold Dagger – will keep you in wild-eyed suspense until the very end. You'll love being hoodwinked.

HOODWINK

Paula Gosling

**MACMILLAN
LONDON**

First published in 1988 by
MACMILLAN LONDON LIMITED
4 Little Essex Street London WC2R 3LF
and Basingstoke

Associated companies in Auckland, Delhi, Dublin, Gaborone,
Hamburg, Harare, Hong Kong, Johannesburg, Kuala
Lumpur, Lagos, Manzini, Melbourne, Mexico City, Nairobi,
New York, Singapore and Tokyo

British Library Cataloguing in Publication Data

Gosling, Paula
    Hoodwink.
    I. Title
    813'.54[F]   PR6057.075

    ISBN 0-333-46298-X

Typeset by Columns of Reading

Printed and bound in England by Anchor Brendon Ltd, Essex

This book is for all the actors on my private stage, without whom there would be no characters—

and for Kay Hall, without whom there would be no stage, no time, and no books.

ONE

Don't run, *don't run*!

People stare at you if you run.

He forced himself to walk, but in his chest his heart still ran, thudding and galloping behind his ribs, threatening to rise up and choke him as he struggled to slow his breathing, his steps, his racing mind.

Don't look back.

Other people may look that way, too.

Face in neutral, eyes ahead, pretend to blow your nose and wipe the sweat from your face, replace the handkerchief, casually, slowly – and feel what else lies in that pocket.

Get rid of it, *get rid of it!*

He started toward a litter bin standing by the curb, but there was a shout behind him, so he kept on walking. Involuntarily his steps quickened again.

Suddenly, a woman screamed – loud enough to be heard all this distance away – so it could only mean one thing.

She'd found him.

Now somebody *was* running – footsteps behind him, many footsteps, everyone running, running. My God! Get off the street!

He turned in the next doorway he came to, not noticing, not caring what the establishment was, just to get away, to breathe, to think – or not to think – about what he'd done.

What he'd had to do.

'May I help you, sir?'

His eyes focused abruptly on the person who stood before him, blocking his way. A woman, all teeth and expectations, dark dress, bright inquiring expression, silly smile. He wanted to slap her silly smile right off her silly face.

'No thank you, just looking.'

Her disappointment pleased him. Old bat. 'Anything in particular?' she asked.

He wanted to scream 'DON'T PUSH ME!' but he shook his head and managed, 'No – just browsing, thanks,' and moved on into the huge room, seeing it for the first time.

Furniture everywhere. Old furniture – antiques, obviously. Casually, as he moved between the ormulu bureaus and the bow-fronted secretaires, he glanced back at the glass window facing the Avenue. The letters were backwards and it took him a moment to reassemble them in his chaotic mind. Lecomber Galleries. Of course, he'd passed it hundreds of times, even paused on occasion for a longer view of something special. Idle moments, slow afternoons. Not this one. Not now.

As a policeman in uniform ran past the window, he turned away quickly. He began to examine a table, its surface carved, inlaid, gilded and in every way obliterated by bad taste and fine workmanship.

'This is French, of course, late eighteenth century.' That damned woman again, beaming, full of information and eager to please. 'Lovely, isn't it?'

'Lovely – but a little out of my range.' The price tag read, unbelievably, eight thousand dollars. Whoever would spend that amount of money on such a gross object obviously deserved it. He moved away, toward the back of the room. Behind him the door to the street opened and the saleswoman turned toward the fresh prey, like a small patrolling shark.

There were several doors at the back of the room. He went through the first one he came to, marked 'Exit' in very small, worn letters, and found himself in a narrow stairwell of unpainted gray concrete walls and dusty metal steps.

It was very quiet here.

He started down, hoping for a back entrance, something, anything. He was only halfway when someone came through the door above him and also started down. *Don't run!*

It was a woman, and she was hurrying. He could hear the clack of the high heels. He made himself hold onto the railing, made himself move slowly and deliberately. She came behind him, beside him, and he looked up. Not the saleswoman. Another woman, gray-haired and birdlike. She bustled past, then paused and looked back.

'Are you looking for someone?'

This, then, was not a public stairway, damn the luck. 'Mr Winters?'

She frowned. 'We don't have – could you mean Mr Frost?'

People were so helpful. 'Oh, yes, of course – Mr Frost. Stupid of me, I'm very bad about names.' Had he said the wrong thing? She was still frowning.

'I'm afraid he's not in today. Was it about anything in particular? Could someone else help perhaps?'

'A – a desk. Just a desk.'

Her face cleared. 'Ah, well – you've taken the wrong stairway. Come on – I'll show you.'

Dutifully, still listening for accusing shouts of alarm from above, he followed her down the stairs. She opened a door at the foot of the stairwell, and the enclosed silence was shattered by a cacophony of typewriters, calculators, telephone bells and people. A windowless room, full of activity, messy, undecorated, a small hive of worker bees, supporting the honeycomb above. Several of the people looked up as they entered, saw the woman, saw him, looked away.

Briskly she led him past the counter at the front of the room, down a short hallway, through another door. 'Here you are, then. Take your pick.' She gave a small giggle and disappeared, leaving him to face a room nearly as large as the gallery above, but without the elegant decor. It, too, was filled with furniture, but this was different. No gleam of mahogany, no glow of gilt – just solid, workmanlike secondhand stuff, good quality, but nothing special. The cheap seats.

It would do, he supposed. Anything would do, he was desperate, he could feel panic rising and he fought, fought, fought it down. He began to move quickly between the items. There was less space here, everything was crowded together without pretension, sofas next to bookcases, dressing tables next to easy chairs and, over in the corner, a vista of blank tops – desks.

He went to them, machine-like, because he'd said 'desk' and because his mind was beginning to fray at the edges. He felt a sudden impulse to vomit but controlled it. A shudder shook him, reaction setting in now, the adrenalin of flight washing through him, an overdose, making his teeth chatter, his hands shake and his heart pound, trapped, within him. Someone came into the room. He started at the sound of footsteps, voices.

Don't run! *Don't run!*

He glanced over, and then away. It was more than one person – a young couple, talking softly together, looking at the bookcases. A woman, not with them, moving away toward

9

dining tables. And a man, thumping the back of a leather chair with casual curiosity. Just testing.

He came to a desk – or rather, it came to him, at about thigh level – and painfully. This would do. This would do. The place was filling up, he had to get on, get away, *get rid of it!* Copying the businesslike attitude of the chair-thumper, he crouched and began to inspect the desk. Small, rather old and battered, but solidly built and cheap at the price – seventy-five dollars.

He slid out the bottom drawer and felt in the well – a gap at the back. Perfect. Hunched over, he slipped the thing from his pocket and quickly shoved it deep into the rear well of the drawer. As he had hoped, there was plenty of room, and the drawer slid into place without difficulty. The relief made his throat relax and he felt the acid rising again from his stomach, burning and bitter.

'May I help you?'

He jumped – he couldn't help it – and straightened up, turning his gag into a cough, turning his fear into annoyance, turning his attention onto this young man who hung over him like a vulture, eyes bright with curiosity.

'I'd like to buy this desk.' He was amazed to hear how ordinary his voice sounded. Hardly a sign in it that he was on the verge of a scream. Had been, since that terrible moment when he felt the cloth of jacket and shirt split beneath the blade, the momentary resistance of flesh, the hard resistance of bone. And the shock on the face, the staring eyes, the open mouth—

'Certainly. A nice, solid little piece.' The bland face of the young salesman had been transformed by the prospect of a quick sale before closing. 'Would you just come this way?'

He couldn't give them a check or use his credit card – no sense leaving his name lying around so close to what had happened up the street. He knew how thorough the police could be, once they got the bit between their teeth. Fortunately, he had sufficient cash on him – just.

Then there was the problem of an address for delivery – equally dangerous. He made up some story about deciding between two offices to rent, and said he'd ring them in the morning with the address. That was fine – they were in a hurry to close, anyway. In three minutes he found himself out on the street again.

There was a knot of police cars down the street to his right, and a crowd had gathered. More people were coming from every direction, drawn by the possibility of drama. He had been out of sight for no more than twenty minutes. There was still a possibility that he might be recognized, stopped, questioned. He turned back to the shop – but saw that the doors had been locked behind him.

The traffic in the street had been halted by the police activity. The cars, taxis and trucks were full of red-faced men leaning out of the windows, blowing horns, cursing the delay and one another. The sky was darkening early – there would be rain later. A chill breath of wind made him shiver suddenly. He hesitated, then turned left and began to walk away.

Don't run, don't run, *don't run*!

People stare at you if you run.

TWO

'It's yours, Chase.'

'Yeah, but I don't want to do it!'

Jake Chase glowered around at the crowded lobby of the apartment building, stuck his hands in his trouser pockets and took a tour of the place. He ducked the drooping rubber plant, inspected the pictures on the walls, gazed at the fingerprint men with their brushes, the photographer flashing the body, the gaping elevator man, the crush of people outside the double glass doors and the jammed and honking traffic in the street beyond. He examined the edge of the carpet, the battered board that listed the occupants of the building, his own shoes.

Anything to keep from hitting Captain Leo Klotzman in the chops.

His circuit ended, he came face to face with his boss again. Klotzman hadn't moved, but had stood watching Chase go round. It wasn't the first time Chase had proved a pain in the neck and it probably wouldn't be the last. Lieutenant Jake Chase was not a legend in his own time – more of a cautionary tale. He was energetic, good-looking, kind-natured, very intelligent – and accident-prone. He had the X-rays to prove it. There was, however, another side to what some called 'Jake's Jinx'. He also tripped over leads that looked hopeless to everyone else, backed into blind alleys that had a way of opening up and fell over previously invisible clues. Thus does Nature delude us into thinking she is occasionally kind.

He was fatalistic about this – it had been his lot since childhood. His mother had taken him to doctors, psychologists, psychiatrists – and they had said that the boy was maybe a little sideways in his thinking, but basically a good boy. They liked Jake. Everybody liked Jake. (His mother was crazy about him.) Nevertheless, disaster followed him – and not only him, but everyone around him.

In the end, it was a shoe salesman who had revealed the truth. Jake was left-handed and right-footed. Maybe it was his brain, the salesman said – or maybe he just needed new shoes? Either way Jake had learned to live with it. That was the way things were, and he accepted that if he tried to change them, he probably would have knocked someone down or broken a leg.

So everybody liked him, but it was a watchful affection they felt. There was never any warning with Jake, and everyone had their own story to tell as a result. It took a patient man to stay with him. Fortunately Klotzman was a patient man.

'I got no alternatives, Jake,' he said.

'And I got a real line on the Corelli case,' Jake told him. 'I tell you, Leo, I'm close – real close.'

'You're off,' Klotzman said. 'As of ten minutes ago, you're off. Deeds, Stryker, Weinburger – *they're* on the Corelli case.'

'Oh, come on, this is maybe a quick in-and-out mugging, Leo,' Jake persisted. He tried to extricate his hand from his pocket to wave around at the general scene, but got his thumb stuck in the lining.

Klotzman looked down. 'Didn't your father tell you that could stunt your growth?' he growled.

There was a clatter of change as Jake pulled the pocket inside out and freed his thumb. 'Listen, Leo—' he began. The short, round man shook his head and headed for the door. Jake followed him, stepping over a scene-of-crime technician who was crawling past on the floor.

'I got no time to listen,' Klotzman snapped, his patience at an end. 'And you got no time to argue. If it was a mugging, fine, you'll get through it quick and then you can go back on the Corelli thing. But whatever it is, you do it, Chase, or you go back to Criminal Records again.'

Chase stopped dead. 'You wouldn't,' he said, aghast.

Klotzman would have to have been pushed a lot further to do it, considering what had happened last time and how long it had taken to clear up, but his expression gave nothing away. 'I got a Division to run, and you are not helping me,' he said in an even voice.

'Oh, shit, Leo—' Jake said.

Klotzman almost smiled. 'Maybe,' he conceded. 'Just don't get any on your shoes this time.'

Jake sighed and watched Klotzman push his way through the crowd to his car at the curb. A voice came from behind him.

'I got the feeling maybe we're on this case,' Joe Kaminsky said lugubriously. Jake turned to look at him.

'That's what I like about you, Joe – your instant grasp of the obvious,' he said in a morose voice.

His partner regarded him blandly. 'Somebody has to do it,' he said. They stared at one another for a full minute, and then Jake grinned.

'All right, already.' They turned to face the lobby, and one of the scene-of-crime men shouted the announcement. Or perhaps it was a warning.

'It's gonna be the Joe and Jake Show, folks.'

Joe and Jake struck a buck-and-wing attitude, but were booed down. Jake ducked as somebody threw a balled-up record sheet at them. 'Come on, you guys, let's get serious,' he said sternly. 'This is a dead person here, and you're playing games? I am deeply shocked at this display of irreverence.'

'So's your old man,' somebody said.

Jake stepped over a pair of white-gloved men who were scraping the carpet for loose fibers, and squatted down beside Carter, the artist, who was sketching the scene. 'I love your use of chiaroscuro,' he said. 'It gives the whole concept a feeling of depth and meaning that other brands lack.'

'Uh-huh,' Carter said, spitting on his finger and rubbing out a line. 'That comes from my rich inner store of philosophic reflections, as well as the chapter in my coloring book on how to impress smart-ass Homicide lieutenants who were hoping to dazzle the promotions board by solving the Corelli case and are now bitter and twisted at being taken off it.'

'Shows that much, huh?' Jake asked.

Carter glanced at him. 'Only to those who know how to see,' he said solemnly.

'Where's Hack?'

'Over there, behind the rubber plant.' Carter added a fresh line and regarded it sourly. 'He's either communing with God or thinking up a new form for us to fill in – hard to tell from here.'

'Don't forget to send me a ticket to your next exhibition,' Jake said, standing up and stepping on a packet of new pencils, all of which shattered under his weight. Carter looked down at them and then up at Jake.

'You'll be the first to know,' he said, through clenched teeth.

'Sorry about the—'

'I'm used to it,' Carter said resignedly. 'We're *all* used to it, Jake.'

14

'Right,' Jake said, walking carefully around Carter and bumping into a fingerprint man. 'Sorry.' The fingerprint man sighed and began to brush powder off his suit jacket. 'Sorry, really.' He edged his way over to Hack, the senior forensic man.

Hack looked up from his paperwork and groaned. 'What did you break?' he asked bleakly.

'Nothing, nothing,' Jake said casually. 'A few pencils is all.'

Hack turned over a page in his notebook, wrote 'Chase' at the top, and then added 'pencils'. He was planning to present a paper on Jake to the Forensic Society one day, entitled 'Hazards to Efficient Investigation'. The thought of it was the only thing that kept him going some days. He was about to speak again when one of his men came up. 'Well, what have you got?'

The man was excited. 'I think there's a Mafia connection,' he said eagerly, holding out a plastic bag. 'There's four Italian coins in here. I found them over there about ten feet from the body.'

They all examined the coins in the bag. 'Maybe it's something to do with the Corelli thing,' Jake said, happy at last. 'There were coins like that found near *his* body, too. I went to the bank and got some duplicates . . .' He reached for his pocket and encountered the lining which was still projecting from it. He looked down. Hack looked down. The junior forensic man looked down. Hack sighed and wrote 'Coins' in his notebook. The junior forensic man handed the plastic bag to Jake, gave him a disgusted look and returned to his labors. Jake put the plastic bag into his jacket pocket and pushed the lining back into his trousers.

Joe came over and looked at them. There was a distant expression in his eyes. 'The woman who found the body has been taken to a private clinic. She's a Mrs Ethel G. Potzheimer, and her doctor says we can't talk to her until she's had a chance to recover from her Terribly Traumatic Experience. He talks with capitals. Her poodle is also in a private clinic. The vet says we can talk to it if we like, but he doesn't think the dog saw much, because it is very short and, anyway, its bow fell over its eyes in the excitement. I said we'd send it a get-well bone.'

Jake looked up at the ceiling. 'I want to become a plumber!' he shouted. 'God, make me a plumber, or a shoe salesman, or a brain surgeon.'

Hack shivered. 'Jeez, not a brain surgeon, Jake. Have a heart.'

Jake shouted the amendment. 'A heart surgeon, God! Come on, anything but this!'

Kaminsky and Hack ignored him. 'I got here male, middle-to-late sixties, stabbed in the chest one time,' Kaminsky said, checking his notebook. 'I got no weapon found, I got positive ID of Fred Norris, resident of this building, I got keys to his place, which is Apartment Four-B, I got no witnesses to the actual crime, but the elevator man who brought him down went up, came down again and found the woman screaming over him and the poodle running around in circles. That's the elevator man trying to look around the screens for an excuse to throw up so he can go outside for fresh air and tell everybody all about it. He's waiting to make his statement. I got unofficial time of death about four forty-five p.m., I got possible evidence of robbery. Norris has no wallet on him, but his credit cards are still there in another case. Check so far?'

Hack scanned his own rough notes. 'Check.'

'Anything else?' Kaminsky asked.

'Maybe a sugar-beet farmer, God,' Jake was muttering now. 'Or a welder.'

'He's got a mark around his neck, like maybe he had a gold chain or something there that got snatched off,' Hack said. 'Watch taken, too.' He ticked off something on his list. 'You going up to the apartment?'

'I thought maybe a quick look around before we go,' Kaminsky said.

Hack glanced at Jake. 'You taking him?'

'He's my partner,' Kaminsky pointed out. 'Also he's in charge of the damn case, remember?'

'Do me a favor,' Hack said in a low voice. 'Keep him around the edges, OK?'

'I'll do my best,' Kaminsky promised. 'Come on, Jake.'

'Maybe a short-order cook,' Jake said, following Kaminsky obediently. They stepped carefully over the corpse, edged around the makeshift screens and entered the elevator.

'Four,' Kaminsky told the still gaping elevator operator. He turned to his partner. 'You wouldn't like being a cook, Jake.'

'Why not?' Jake wanted to know.

16

The doors closed on the partially-hidden scene of a man stabbed viciously to death, his lifeblood spreading around him, his chest laid open by the blade, his gray-white face turned up blindly to the ceiling.

'No laughs,' Kaminsky said.

THREE

The Lightfoot family had always lived over the shop.

When Gregory 'Digger' Lightfoot had made his first few grand as a bootlegger, he had bought an old hotel on Federal Avenue. The owner, a nervous little man named Tump, had been glad to sell cheap, because what with one thing and another the hotel business had fallen off in Federal Street.

The one thing and another had been a series of affrays and deaths at the Magnolia Hotel down the block, owned by Digger's biggest rival, Red Ned Porter. Ned was a big carrot-haired man with a huge appetite for life, which he bit off in chunks, spitting out what he didn't like.

The story was, he definitely didn't like Digger Lightfoot, and the feeling was mutual. Their rivalry was good for business – it kept their respective gangs sharp and on their toes, and gave visitors to Federal Street a little frisson of possible danger. Would this be the night Digger and Red Ned shot it out? Would blood instead of booze run in the gutters?

During Prohibition, Ned Porter and Digger Lightfoot pretended to run their hotels, but everyone knew they were just glorified speakeasys with hot-and-cold running girls upstairs. And they did well – until Prohibition folded.

Digger Lightfoot had come from sensible stock, and had put a lot of the money he made from bootlegging liquor into more traditional investments – bookies, extortion, numbers and other historically sound activities. Upon Repeal, he simply converted his hotel into an office building for his many concerns, known collectively as Lightfoot Enterprises, retaining the top two floors for his family. And there they remained to this day.

Ned Porter was not so lucky. He'd laughed loud, loved freely and spent lavishly. With Prohibition over, he was left with a big empty hotel, huge debts and many enemies. The Magnolia went downhill rapidly, and Ned . . . Ned Porter just disappeared one day, without a word to anyone.

Everybody said – well, everybody was sure it was true – that Digger had him bumped off. It was true that Digger was found to have purchased the Magnolia Hotel and other Porter properties, but no one could ever prove that the contracts were signed under duress. No one could ever prove anything.

The funny thing was, Digger seemed to miss his old rival.

After Ned went, Digger Lightfoot grew old rapidly. Life just didn't have the old zip without Ned somehow. When Digger passed away, his son, Gurney Lightfoot, took over. Gurney ran Lightfoot Enterprises with flair and style and hardly killed anyone at all. He used the threat of violence like the craftsman he was, repaying loyalty, punishing traitors and closing deals with snakelike speed.

But now he, too, was growing old. The only thing that kept him going was the old rivalry with the Porter family who, through judicious marriages, had resurfaced on the right side of society. Red Ned's son, Charley, was every bit as smart as Gurney. He had worked hard, become a successful lawyer, married the mayor's daughter, become mayor himself in time and retired rich. And now Ned Porter's grandson Tony was, at twenty-eight, the youngest city planner Grantham had ever had. What's more, he was slowly – very slowly – closing in on the Lightfoot organization. Not with the law, but with bulldozers.

Young Tony Porter had a plan for downtown Grantham. A plan which involved the redevelopment of two square miles of ghetto. Right through the middle of this ghetto ran Federal Street. And right in the middle of Federal Street stood Gurney Lightfoot – metaphorically speaking.

Month by month the bulldozers chewed their way closer and closer, crunching through the reams of lawsuits that the Lightfoot lawyers threw in their path, laying waste to block after block of old buildings and coming closer, ever closer. Now the last complete block of Federal Street stood like a ghost town in the middle of a vast plain of mud, holes and construction huts.

The buildings still standing on this lonely block of Federal Street consisted of several small office buildings (mostly empty), a grocery store and a drugstore (both run by Lightfoot Enterprises), an old movie house that alternated bingo nights with old Humphrey Bogart and Edward G. Robinson films, the old Magnolia Hotel (long since condemned as unsafe) and the Lightfoot Building itself.

Gurney Lightfoot owned it all, and he was not giving it up without a fight – no matter what his son, Rocky, said about the leafy attractions of the suburbs and the increased profits that lay in diversification.

'Hell with 'em all,' mumbled Gurney, who was presently propped up for his dinner, pillows massed behind his head, a shawl over his neck and shoulders, a napkin tucked in under his prominent Adam's apple. Once a large and meaty man, Gurney had been shriveled and diminished by illness. He glared at his hands, a stranger's hands, his father's hands, stringy and bony. The knuckles showed white through the translucent skin as he clutched the soup spoon, and the spoon, thus regarded, trembled slightly. He grunted in annoyance and thrust it into the thick soup he didn't want. 'Take it away.'

'You must eat, Mr Lightfoot. The doctor said—'

'The doctor can eat it, then.'

'You'll have to be put back on a drip if you don't behave, Mr Lightfoot, and you know how you hate—'

'All right, all *right*!' he said. He conveyed a spoonful of soup to his mouth, drank it and dropped the spoon back into the bowl. 'There.'

'Now, now,' the nurse clucked in a childish tone. 'You must eat it all up like a good boy.'

'I'll eat it if you show me your tits,' he said maliciously.

'That's quite enough,' she said, standing up. 'I shall go out now. When I come back I expect to see the soup gone, and I do *not* expect to find it under your pillow like last time. You're a wicked old man and I'm cross with you.'

He watched her go out and sighed. He'd only said that to shock her – he had no more interest in her body than he did in the soup. It was all academic as far as he was concerned.

All memories. Memories of mammaries. His eyes closed and his head drooped.

'I think he's asleep,' said Littlewood.

'I'm damn well not asleep,' Gurney said, lifting his head and glaring at the two men who'd come in after the nurse had left and were now standing quietly beside his bed. 'Here, eat this goddamn soup before she comes back.'

'You're supposed to eat it,' Littlewood protested.

'Eat the goddamn soup!' Gurney demanded.

Littlewood glanced at his companion for instructions.

'Eat the goddamn soup,' Rocky Lightfoot said softly. He was small and spindly, with a large head and huge, dark eyes, but he was his father's son, and Littlewood looked away.

'There's a problem,' Rocky told his father, as Littlewood picked up the bowl and started to drink the soup.

'So?'

'Norris is dead.'

The old man smiled, then frowned. 'That was dumb, Rocky. You should have got hold of the proof first, then killed him.'

Rocky sighed – this was the bad part. 'We didn't kill Norris.'

'No?' The old man was startled.

'No. Somebody stabbed him in the lobby of his apartment house.'

'Who?'

'We don't know.'

A light appeared in Gurney's eye. 'Could we pin this on Porter?'

'I don't see how. It was probably a junkie, looking for quick money.'

The old man closed his eyes and considered the possibilities. After a while he opened his eyes and looked at his son, who he could see was very nervous. That was good. It made him feel good when they were still nervous in his presence. 'No – Norris was a bastard. Whoever killed him meant to do it.'

Rocky sighed again. 'Does it matter? He's dead now – he can't hurt you.'

'Norris doesn't matter. It's the proof about the Finch woman we have to get hold of now. Try the girl. Maybe he told the girl.'

'We'll have to wait for an opportunity—'

The old man struggled up onto his elbows, his dark eyes sunken in their sockets but still blazing. 'I haven't got a lot of time to wait for opportunities,' he snarled.

'Of course you have,' Littlewood said quickly.

'Don't play games,' Rocky said. 'He's right.'

'You're a good boy,' said Gurney. 'You tell your father the truth, like the mean little shit you are.'

'I learned all I know at my father's knee,' Rocky said.

Gurney laughed – it was like paper crackling in a slow fire. 'So, you're making your move at last, are you, boy? I been waiting for it, did you know that? Waiting until I was about to give up.' He saw by the momentary flare of light in Rocky's eyes that this was a surprise – but in another moment the light was gone. Gurney approved. 'I tell you one thing, Rocky, I'll die happy knowing you're coming after me with a big hammer and a small mind. What they call a winning combination in our business.'

'And I intend to stick to business,' Rocky said.

'Then find out who killed Norris,' Gurney said fretfully, as Littlewood placed the empty soup bowl on the tray. 'You find out about that, boy, and we'll get somewhere. Me, I smell Porter.'

'You've got Porter on the brain,' Rocky said dismissively. 'Whatever happens, whatever goes wrong, you say "Porter".'

'And I'm usually right, you little smart-ass,' Gurney spat.

'This Norris killing is out of left field, Gurney,' Littlewood said, eager to please. 'Like a bolt of lightning, you might say.'

'*You* might say. You've got soup on your chin,' Gurney said. 'Where are the police on this?'

'I'm glad *they're* not on my chin,' Littlewood chuckled.

'My contacts say nothing doing yet,' Rocky said, ignoring Littlewood's spaniel attempts at humor. 'All they got is that it was a man. The elevator operator says Norris met the guy in the lobby of his apartment building. They were standing there talking when he got a call and went up to answer it. When he came back down, Norris was sitting on a bench with a surprised look on his face, blood dripping down his shirt and some dame screaming her facelift off. Says the guy talking to Norris was well dressed, wearing a hat, but had his back to the elevator, so he didn't see his face. The police said thanks a lot and sealed off Norris's apartment.'

'You got someone in there.' It wasn't a question – Gurney knew his boy too well.

'We had two guys on Norris full time. But they were outside the apartment building, didn't know what had happened until the woman started screaming. They were only told to follow Norris. A dozen guys came and went that afternoon. Could have been any of them.' He wasn't apologizing – just explaining. 'As soon as they realized what had happened, they took the stairs straight up. They were in and out of the building before the detectives even got there.'

'Which guys did we have on him?'

'This was Fritz and Knapp.'

Gurney shrugged, then winced as if the movement had been

painful, which it had. 'They're not our best boys. They are just muscle and they are impulsive. You should have sent our best boys, Rocky. This is important.'

'I didn't expect Norris to get killed, did I? Only wanted to keep an eye on him – they were up to that all right. They found nothing. In my opinion Norris had the proof on him, or if it was too big to carry maybe something to say where it is, and the guy who killed him got it. That's my thinking.'

'Then we got to find the guy before the police. You figure maybe he was being blackmailed, too?'

'I figure maybe.'

'Who could that be?'

'Anybody,' Littlewood said. 'That Norris, he wasn't proud, you know. He'd blackmail anybody.'

Gurney met his son's eyes. 'Even me, hey?'

Rocky allowed himself a small smile. 'Even you.'

Gurney nodded. 'Norris was always trouble. That's why I had him framed for the numbers thing. OK. Maybe I should have killed the little bastard instead. I see that now. That was my big mistake. OK. He came out hating my guts and started up with this thing about Ariadne Finch. Believe me, if he said he had the goods, then he had the goods, and we got to *find* the goods. Picking up the guy who killed him, that's one way. The girl is maybe another.' He looked at his son. 'Busy days, boy.'

'You always told me an active life is a healthy life,' Rocky said.

Gurney grimaced. 'Yeah, and look where it got me.'

'You've had a good run,' Rocky said.

'I'm not through yet,' the old man snarled. 'I'm still the boss here, you little snot-nosed twerp. And don't you forget it.'

'Would I forget it?' Rocky asked Littlewood in an innocent voice.

'He wouldn't forget it,' Littlewood said loyally.

'No matter how hard I try,' Rocky concluded, and this time the smile was wide and wolfish. He gestured to Littlewood and they went out. Gurney stared after them. His expression was bitter. The nurse returned and looked at the empty soup bowl with enthusiastic approval.

'Why, that's wonderful, Mr Lightfoot, you've eaten it all up! What a good boy you are.'

'I'd rather be a bad boy,' he leered at her.

'Don't be naughty.' Her tone was arch – she was forty-five going on fourteen. 'I'll slap your face if you don't stop talking like a nasty man.'

'And I'll have acid thrown in yours if you don't stop talking like Goldilocks,' he snarled. 'Take this goddamn tray away!'

She took the tray away.

FOUR

Molly Pemberton was a perfectly lovely old lady.

Everybody thought so.

'Damn fools,' Molly would say to herself, and go on smiling. She was a librarian – such a suitable occupation for a widow of a certain age – and conducted her life and her duties with exemplary professionalism and kindness. Over the years, Molly Pemberton had become an expert on all kinds of subjects. Whenever anyone needed specialized information they asked Molly. If she didn't know, she knew where and how to find out.

Her late husband had been a police sergeant. He had been shot during a scuffle with a drug addict brought in for questioning. Perhaps because of this, plus the fact that the Reference Library was just up the avenue from Police Headquarters, she was often called upon for special information during investigations.

As a result, there was nothing Molly loved so much as a good crime, real or imagined. Her current preoccupation was with the Corelli case. Neither the evening newspapers nor the television news had produced any further developments, much to her disappointment. After washing the dinner dishes she had settled down with her first book and her coffee and announced her day's meager findings concerning the crime to her companion, Mr Braithwaite.

'You mark my words, it was that wife of his, that Vita Corelli, with her big blue eyes full of tears. She never loved him. She was after his money all along, but she was afraid he was going to divorce her and marry this little tootsie he'd been carrying on with, so she had to act fast. You'll see – they'll get her in the end,' she told Mr Braithwaite.

He made no comment on the subject.

Mr Braithwaite was a perfectly lovely old cat.

Everybody said so.

But he was no intellectual.

Molly sighed and opened her book. She read at least six books a week, and many of them had to do with crime, fictional and/or factual. Whether she'd been asked to look up something concerning them or not, she kept up on all the current crimes in the city and solved most of them – from her armchair, of course. It gave her a great deal of satisfaction to be right, but it never occurred to her to actually *do* anything about it, like a Maud Silver or a Miss Marple. Absolutely *not*.

It was dangerous out there.

Casey Hewson looked up from the manuscript pages on her desk, stretched, sighed and rubbed her aching back. Enough was enough. She glanced at her watch and then out the window at the spindly tree that was trying valiantly to bring nature back to the city. Its branches were whipping themselves into a frenzy, and as she looked there was a flicker of lightning in the sky, outlining the roofs of the buildings opposite. 'It was a dark and stormy night,' she said aloud. Her voice sounded odd and flat in the small office. 'Lady,' she told herself, 'go home.'

Instead, she leaned back in her chair and looked round with some satisfaction at the long, narrow, newly decorated office that was her pride and joy. Done in deep rose with white woodwork, with the desk and bookshelves built in to her own specification, it was both feminine and practical, like its owner. It wasn't much, she supposed, in the great scheme of things – but she had earned it. By God, she had. And while being an editor at the small family publishing firm of Augustus Millington Inc. was also pretty small beer, she had earned that, too. Funny, when you thought about it – but she decided not to think about it. No sense in scaring herself to death.

She gathered her things together, switched off her desk light and went out into the corridor. It was dark and silent, and her heels clattered on the worn linoleum.

The old brownstone had once been the Millington family home, she knew, but fortunes had turned, and it was now almost all offices. Her boss, Eustace Millington, had managed to retain the top floor as an apartment. She supposed he was up there now, and glanced edgily up the stairs at the back of the hall before letting herself out the front. She just wasn't up to an encounter with Eustace just then. He'd only propose again.

It was getting to be a problem.

She hesitated at the top of the steps leading down to the sidewalk. Although rain had not yet begun to fall, its damp message was in the blustering wind that rocked the trees and buffeted passing cars. There was a distant rumbling of meteorological indigestion. Clouds were massing in the darkness overhead.

Casey regretted lingering as long as she had over the manuscript she had been editing almost as much as she regretted leaving her umbrella in her office – but there was no sense in going back for it, unless she grew another arm. She went down the steps cautiously and turned left, hoping to find a taxi on Washington Avenue.

However, burdened with review copies of three books, her new briefcase and an armful of magazines, she found making headway against the unpredictable wind was hard work. The flapping cover of *Passion's Child* kept catching under her chin, and three loose pages of *The Case of the Bloodstained Burberry* flew away to dance and curvet above the rather unfashionable environs of Park Street.

Perhaps that was why she didn't hear the footsteps behind her.

Not at first.

It wasn't until she reached the long dark patch where several streetlights were out that she was aware of someone moving in the shadows behind her.

Dismissing it at first as a trick of the intermittent wind, she continued toward the safe bright lights of Washington Avenue. She began to walk a little faster.

So did the person behind her.

Faster, still.

Likewise.

'Oh, damn,' she gasped, and broke into a trot. The magazines, an unwieldy and unreliable burden from the beginning, slid away and cascaded under her running feet. She hopped over one, kicked another and with a shriek skidded two feet on the shiny cover of a third.

The footsteps were gaining on her – no doubt about them now.

She was being pursued.

'Oh, *God*!' she shouted. 'Why me? Why *now*, all of a sudden?'

Panic gripped her, and she broke into an unashamed and frantic run. Four steps into it her left heel broke off. She cannoned into the boarded-up front of an old candy store, cursing. Regaining her stride – one high, one low – she lurched on toward the lighted avenue ahead, panting, terrified, hating herself for getting into this in the first place, running, running, running—

A figure suddenly emerged from behind a parked car on her right. Desperately she shuddered to a halt before him.

'Oh, listen,' she gasped. 'Somebody is following me—'

The figure, a small, broad man with a cap pulled down over his forehead, shrugged his shoulders. 'Shame,' he said, and grabbed her briefcase.

Casey, after a frozen moment of astonishment, grabbed it back. 'How dare you?' she demanded.

The small, broad man glared up at her and snatched it back again, irritably this time. 'Piss off,' he said.

'No!' Casey said, reaching for it again.

The man stepped back quickly. 'Yes,' he echoed.

'But it's *mine*!' She had momentarily forgotten about being followed. Her adrenalin had surged from fear to outrage. Who did this little nerd think he was, anyway? '*MINE!*' she announced firmly, and went for him.

'She's the possessive type,' the small man announced, as he hopped back with the briefcase clutched protectively to his chest.

'Why, that's very selfish, isn't it?' said a soft voice behind her. It had an odd, lilting accent which Casey could not readily place and did not feel she had the time to research in the circumstances. She glanced over her shoulder and saw a black man in a dark overcoat and Homburg standing close by, watching. He was a very *large* man, but as Casey was rapidly becoming more annoyed than frightened she chose to ignore his stature. Perhaps that was another mistake.

'Give me back my briefcase *now*,' she said, in her very best recently acquired editorial tones. 'There is nothing in it that could possibly interest *you*—'

On the last word she lunged for it and got her fingers around the edges. The small man began to back away, moving in a circle, and she followed, not letting go of the briefcase. After a moment the black man joined the dance, trying to insinuate himself between them, his long powerful fingers also grasping the case. This terpsichorean activity continued in silence for some seconds as they struggled for possession of the briefcase, first one then another gaining the firmer hold, but no one winning. Then the black man let go and spoke in a voice of bored resignation.

'Oh, the shit with it,' he said, feeling in his overcoat pocket. He withdrew a small black object and, taking quick aim, struck Casey on the side of the head.

Stunned, she let go of the briefcase.

She reeled away from the two of them, hovered open-mouthed for a moment in the dark doorway of the once popular and now deserted Starlight Bar and Grill, tried to speak, failed and then went down.

She was aware of landing on something large that thrashed and moved beneath her, a soft and unexpected tangle of arms and legs, accompanied by shrieks of outrage, curses and the sound of breaking glass. Vaguely she saw her two attackers watching her. The little one was still holding her beautiful new briefcase.

Then her eyes crossed and she slid into darkness.

She awoke to the howl of the wind, a strong smell of gin and the low grumbling of a person with whom she lay in intimate and intricate contact.

'Damned women,' said a blurred voice somewhere beneath her right elbow. 'Never look where they're going.'

Casey moved gingerly, testing arms and legs. There was pain in her head, in one knee and one elbow. Her face was wet. She wiped at it awkwardly, then licked experimentally at one corner of her mouth. Blood and gin in approximately equal parts were apparently dripping down her nose and off her chin. The voice beneath her elbow continued sadly and reflectively to complain, and she edged to one side, peering down.

It was an old man, face like a shrunken apple, eyes like two bright pips sunk into a network of wrinkles and grime, nose running, gap-toothed mouth working over its disastrous litany of outrages. Their bodies were entwined like lovers' as they lay on the gritty marble. The wind blew old papers past the mouth of the entry, and in the distance a car engine revved and then roared away.

It seemed to Casey she should get up and do something constructive, but she was afraid to move too quickly, lest a limb might suddenly snap from one or the other of them.

'Busted Maggie's bottle,' the old man muttered at her, pulling himself upright with a huffy jerk and settling the outermost of his several coats over his thin shanks. 'She's gone to get another one.' He reached over himself and thrust her handbag at her. 'Took the money from here. Just what she needed, of course,' he added, with defensive belligerence. '*We* ain't no thieves.'

'I never thought you were,' Casey croaked. 'Those men—'

'Gone,' the old man said tersely. He had been patting himself experimentally, and brightened. 'Not all is lost,' he announced with sudden and unexpected dignity, and extracted his prize. 'You broke Maggie's bottle, but not mine.' He unscrewed the top of the Johnny Walker Red Label with relish. 'We're OK, sweetie. Hell with Maggie. You stick with me.' He tilted the bottle upright and took a deep gulp, then lowered it and wiped his mouth with the back of his hand.

Casey watched in fascination, still dizzy and disoriented from the blow on her head and the crash landing afterward. She decided, woozily, that she was not all *that* uncomfortable, lying there. Maybe it would be better if she rested a while at that. Everything seemed so blurred – events, reasons, logic and the end of her nose. Without warning, she belched. 'Oh, dear. Pardon me,' she said politely. (After all, whatever her present position, she *had* been properly brought up.)

The old man's elbow nudged her companionably. 'Here,' he said. 'Have a belt. It'll settle you right down.'

'No, really . . . I must be going,' she said, struggling to rise.

'So soon?' the old man inquired in a disappointed voice.

'Yes – I'm sorry – ouch!' Her right knee was not cooperating at all. She sat back down again abruptly and waited for the street to stop spinning.

The nudge came again, and the old man gave her a snaggle-toothed grin. 'Take a belt,' he said in a friendly tone. 'It'll kill the pain.'

'Well . . .' She took the bottle gingerly, started to wipe the neck, then realized this probably would be bad form on the basis of whatever manners applied in doorway acquaintanceships. Oh, well, alcohol killed germs, didn't it? Killed something or other anyway. Tilting her head back, she held the bottleneck just above her open mouth and let a small amount of the whiskey trickle down her throat, choked and then swallowed again. Giddy and not a little confused, she wiped her chin on her coat sleeve and spoke.

'Good,' she said hoarsely.

'You betcha,' she old man said with growing enthusiasm, looking her over from top to toe – no mean feat under the circumstances. He joggled her leg with his own. 'You take another belt, and then you and me, we'll go on someplace before Maggie gets back, how about it?'

Casey obediently took another swallow, tipping up the bottle with growing expertise. 'Well . . .' she said, coughing. 'The thing is . . .'

'Casey? Is that you?'

A tall, angular figure stood in the doorway, peering down at the two people entwined intimately in the doorway with the bottle of Johnny Walker and one another. Casey looked up through her tangled hair and felt her companion stiffen in alcoholic possessiveness. 'Move on, buster,' the old man growled 'Find one of your own.'

Casey tried to focus her eyes, and then regretted it as a car passed, momentarily illuminating the aristocratic features of her employer, Eustace Millington.

He seemed upset.

'Hello, Eustace,' she croaked.

Beside her, the old man scowled, then sighed hugely in resignation. He extricated the bottle of whiskey (with some difficulty) from her convulsive grip and extended it upward.

'Any friend of hers is a friend of mine,' he said cheerfully. 'Here, Eustace – have a snort.'

FIVE

The Porter mansion was a magnificent graystone edifice on the western outskirts of the city. Its grounds covered several acres which were carefully landscaped to give the illusion of a country estate. One could have been forgiven for forgetting that the city itself flowed busily around all four sides, beyond the high stone walls.

Charles Edward Porter was also, in his way, a magnificent edifice. A large fair-skinned man, some might even have said a fat man, he carried his bulk well and gave the impression of solid muscle rather than excess flesh. He was tall and tanned, with a rim of curling gray hair around his bald head, and sharp blue eyes. He had been accounted extremely handsome in his youth.

But Charley Porter had no fond memories of those early years, for they had been years of suffering and shame. He had been only six when his father disappeared. Until then, unaware of how his father made all the money that bought little Charley so many toys, he had thought only how wonderful he was. Big and warm and laughing, Red Ned Porter would come home and toss the boy in the air until he hiccuped with giggles, then catch him and hold him close. Little Charley would press his face against the rough tweed shoulder, inhale the sweet smell of good cigars and whiskey and know security.

And then, suddenly, his father was gone. Just – gone. Something in his mother died, too – she became a thin woman in black, sitting silent for hours in the kitchens of ever smaller and bleaker cold-water apartments. As Charley grew older, he heard her curse the name of Lightfoot – but it was not until he was fourteen that he found out why. Found out on the playground, through taunts and fights, that his father had been a criminal.

The shame had nearly destroyed him.

But Red Ned's energy lived on in his son, and shame transmuted it into a hunger for achievement. A firm believer in the maxim 'Success is the best revenge', Charley became a brilliant student. He might not have good trousers, but he had a fine mind, and he got himself scholarships to both university and law school, coming top of his class in everything.

There was one thing his mother had never let him forget while she lived, and that was the name of the man she held responsible for Red Ned's disappearance – Digger Lightfoot, his old competitor. It was a name Charley never forgot. When he joined the public prosecutor's staff, he began stalking the Lightfoot organization whenever and wherever he could. He soon learned that his enemy was both clever and resourceful – not an easy prey. Gurney Lightfoot had inherited all his father's guile as well as his kingdom, and had added to both. Gurney Lightfoot was the most powerful man in Grantham. If Charley wanted to destroy him, he required more fire power. So he had looked around.

It wasn't long before, in the social event of the year, amid pomp, circumstance and ten thousand dollars' worth of hot-house orchids, Charley Porter married the mayor's daughter. Sybil Westwood wasn't beautiful or sexy. On the contrary, she was rather plain, solidly built and without imagination. But she was sweet-natured and placid, and she absolutely adored Charley Porter. Her father was very, very, very rich – and very, very grateful to have found such a brilliant son-in-law.

From his fortress, Gurney Lightfoot watched the progress of Charley Porter and hated him for it. He envied the constant sycophantic publicity he got in all the newspapers – handsome Charley Porter, clever Charley Porter.

And it got worse. After Charley came his son. Tony Porter was about the same age as Gurney's own son, Rocky. They had even attended the same expensive private high school in Grantham.

But there the resemblance ended.

Tony Porter went to Harvard and majored in architecture and city planning. When he came back from Harvard he, too, became visible in the media – handsome Tony Porter, clever Tony Porter, handsome clever Charley Porter's son.

The only time Gurney Lightfoot got into the papers was in fighting off lawsuits – rotten Gurney Lightfoot, terrible Gurney Lightfoot. The only time Rocky Lightfoot got into the papers was when his Junior Achievement badge was taken away after they discovered he'd cooked the books of his company.

Therefore, when Charley was finally elected mayor, Gurney

33

Lightfoot had soon made it known that whenever he could make it difficult for Charley Porter in their mutual town, he would. That was fine with Charley.

Both were deadly in their fashion.

Every year, Gurney Lightfoot caused trouble in Grantham. Through his union connections he achieved slowdowns, scandals and strikes. And every year, in return, Charley lopped a tentacle or two off the Lightfoot octopus. But he never succeeded in putting Gurney Lightfoot behind bars, and this rankled with him. When he retired from the mayor's office, Charley went into private legal practice and did very well. But always, in the back of his mind, was the dream of total destruction for the Lightfoot clan.

Fred Norris had given him a chance at that destruction.

Now Norris was dead.

Charley switched off the television set and glowered at his brandy, trying to decide on his next move.

'Good evening, Father.'

Charley looked up and the scowl disappeared. Tony had come into the room looking, as always, like the young god he was – blond, athletic, intelligent, charming. Charley beamed at him. 'And where are you off to this evening?'

Tony Porter returned the smile and poured out a whiskey for himself. 'Smelly and I are taking the girls to see *King Lear*, and then we're going to the Balmoral Club for a late supper.'

Charley scowled. 'Is it absolutely necessary to refer to the son and heir of Aaron Smeltzer as "Smelly"? You're past that sort of thing, aren't you?'

'Nope. Smelly doesn't mind. They call me all kinds of things.' Tony grinned. 'Didn't you have a nickname when you were young?'

Charley flushed slightly. 'No, of course not.'

'Yes, you did. Mother told me once. They called you Curley, she said.' His gaze rested fondly on his father's gleaming scalp. 'I guess you grew out of that one.'

'Indeed.' Charley's tone was wry.

'Where were you this afternoon?' Tony asked. 'I tried to call you several times, but Beecher said you were out.'

'So I was,' Charley said. 'I had an appointment with Stanley Quiddick to discuss some business – didn't I mention it at breakfast?'

34

'No.'

'Sorry. Why did you want me?'

'Oh – just to say I think we've got a breakthrough on that last block of Federal Avenue – through the condemnation order on the Magnolia Hotel. Lightfoot's lawyer has fired his last shot and missed. We'll be able to execute the demolition order any day now. I suppose you'll be sorry to see it go.'

Charley smiled. 'Not really – it's not exactly a source of pride to know my father ran a speakeasy, you know.'

Tony grinned. 'I think it's great having a grandfather like Red Ned Porter, King of the Bootleggers. You have no sense of historical romance, Dad.'

'I'm not sure I like my childhood memories coming into the category of "historical" anything,' Charley said. 'I'm feeling my years as it is.'

'You doing anything tonight?' Tony asked idly. He sat down opposite his father, but his position on the edge of the cushion made it clear that this was merely a polite concession to the older man. He was impatient to be off.

'Oh, not really. Stanley is coming around for dinner and a game of chess, that's all.'

'Oh. Great.' Tony tossed off his drink and stood up. 'Well, don't wait up for me.'

'I wouldn't dream of it,' Charley said demurely. He answered Tony's breezy wave with a raised finger, watched him go out and wondered who 'the girl' was tonight. Tony never lacked for female company. From the age of sixteen he had been able to pick and choose from the girls – and women – who found him attractive. If only he would marry and settle down. His money, looks and position made him a very eligible bachelor – and he seemed content to reap the many benefits without getting tied down. Ah well – perhaps it would come eventually. For the present it was enough that Tony respected his father's opinion and followed his suggestions on the best ways to improve the city.

So useful. So practical. So profitable.

Now that Tony had been appointed city planner, and was pushing this thing through with the downtown development, Charley had another weapon against the Lightfoot family. Of course, Tony knew very little of the old feud – he only saw Lightfoot as a common, garden-variety crook. Charley had never shared with his son the deep loathing he had for the Lightfoot name and empire. Tony was too good, too gifted and creative and brilliant, to be shackled with that.

But if improving Grantham destroyed Lightfoot, so much the better.

Tony Porter climbed into his car and sat for a moment staring up at the house, his keys held loosely in his hands. Then he shook his head and started the engine.

After all these years he still hadn't decided whether it was a compliment or an insult for his father to think that he could do all the things he'd done without his wife or his son knowing. The man was far from a fool, and yet he had this one blind spot. Perhaps it was a case of self-preservation, perhaps Charley needed to think that someone believed the public persona he had worked so hard all his adult life to maintain.

As he reversed out of the garage, Tony saw in his rear-view mirror the remains of the little garden house where his late mother had spent so many happy afternoons sitting doing her petit point and getting quietly, placidly stoned. Until he was ten he had connected the smell of gin with gardens, and his mother's inner glow with what could only be a deeply spiritual nature.

About the time he was ten he had overheard the first rumours about his father – that Mayor Porter was corrupt, that he destroyed the lives and careers of men who opposed him, that he was power-mad and ruthless. He saw a story in the newspaper about a man who had killed himself because Charley had fired him from an important position in the city government.

Deeply troubled about this, Tony had sought his mother's counsel. She had been in bed, he remembered, surrounded by satin, lace, ruffles, flounces and the faint aroma of gin. Tony had poured out his tale of woe, cuddled to her ample and comforting bosom. Was it true? Was Charley a bad man?

His mother considered her answer carefully. Despite everything, she still adored Charley Porter, who had been a kind, generous and really quite loving husband over the years. But she was a politician's daughter and, while not overintelligent, had become wise in the ways of the species. She knew her husband was a powerful man – and that in some ways having power had corrupted him. She knew of his deep and abiding hate for the Lightfoots, and the reason for it. Never having known Red Ned

Porter, she couldn't know the depth of loss Charley felt for him – but she could see how it ate at him from within.

She also was aware that her son was unusually bright and beautiful. Was it not too soon to bring down such a lovely little bird with a shot to the heart?

In the end she had told him that, as the mayor, his father had a responsibility to the people who had elected him, and if he had to be ruthless sometimes, it was because it was necessary, and not because it was fun. The man in the newspaper story had been breaking the law, stealing money from the city funds. Charley had known him and liked him, but in the end he had ordered his prosecution. Yes, the man had killed himself, but that wasn't Charley's fault. The man had been weak, and Charley had been strong.

Tony had gone back to his room and thought about what his mother had said. After a while he thought about what his mother *hadn't* said. He looked at his room. He looked out the window at the gardens and the wall around them and the city beyond.

He hadn't told his mother the real reason he had been so upset – that only a few nights previous to the man's death, he had heard Charley telling Stanley Quiddick, over a game of chess, that the man must be 'dealt with'.

Now he thought he understood. Charley had done a bad thing. But this man had, apparently, also done bad things. The man was now dead, and his father was still alive. The man's family was now poor, and his family was rich. The dead man was labeled a crook, and his father was still a very important man.

The lesson seemed clear – there was good bad, and there was bad bad. What was important was not which was which, but which won. As he grew older, and learned more of the truth, and more of the details, the lesson became even clearer.

What did not become clear was what he could do about it.

Or with it.

He still wondered – but not as often.

Halfway down the drive, he slowed the car as it passed the ornamental fountain he had built when he was eighteen. It was the summer after his mother had died, the summer before he went away to college. He'd designed and built the fountain himself, as a memorial to his dear, silly, lovely mother. It had been his first real architectural project. He'd done all the work himself, every bit of it. The memory was so clear. It had been a long, hot summer – in many ways the most important summer of his life. How he'd labored over that fountain on all the hot afternoons, how glad he'd been when the cool nights came, how relieved he'd been when it was finished.

It was dry now and filled with leaves, but still graceful. He always thought of her when he passed it.

He put his foot down and picked up speed again, heading toward the closed gates in the wall. He knew exactly when to activate the electronic opening device, and judged his exit perfectly. As he roared into the stream of traffic, the gates swung gently closed behind him.

In the house, Charley Porter frowned. He must tell Tony to drive more carefully. The boy was precious to him. He was all he had left, and he didn't want him to be hurt. Also, the car was an expensive one.

And the Porters had a public image to maintain.

SIX

'I still don't see why we had to come down *here*,' Eustace complained, looking around him with deep distaste. The Washington Avenue Police Station was one of the more elderly in the city. The reception area – where they sat on a bench like three owls – was filled with street people, who ignored them, and policemen, who typed and filed and talked and took people away and brought people back and told jokes between themselves, and also ignored them.

Eustace Millington was not accustomed to being ignored. He ran a highly prestigious publishing business, had a wide circle of very respectable and cultured friends and many social and charitable interests. One of his current interests was Casey Hewson, whom he had employed as an editor for their new paperback imprint, Phoenix Books. Casey was clever, attractive and ambitious. He was biding his time, bringing her along nicely, and – when he'd established the propriety of her upbringing – he planned to marry her.

Or had planned, until now.

'This whole episode has been deeply unsavory and very unsettling. I would rather have forgotten it entirely and gone home. You should do the same.'

Casey settled herself on the bench and leaned her head back against the wall. 'I'm sorry, Eustace. You needn't have come, you know.'

Eustace Millington drew himself up. 'It was my duty to accompany and protect you against further molestation,' he said, glaring past her at the old man who sat on her other side. The old man leered at him and winked, offering the bottle yet again. When Millington shook his head impatiently, the old man shrugged and took another drink.

'You should stop that for a while, Sylvester,' Casey said. Although her eyes were closed she could hear the convulsive swallowing noises in the old man's scrawny throat. 'You'll probably have to look at some pictures, you know.'

'I know, I know,' Sylvester muttered. 'I see better with

a little bag on, you know?'

'You'd certainly *look* better with a bag on,' Eustace grumbled. 'Preferably a large one.'

Sylvester sneered. 'Puerile poof,' he observed, wiping his nose with his sleeve and belching quietly.

Casey opened her eyes and looked from one to the other in amazement.

'The opinions of a common drunk do not concern me,' Eustace said, gazing at the ceiling with imperious concentration.

'Not drunk,' Sylvester corrected him. 'Not yet. More merry than drunk.'

Eustace sniffed. 'Merry, indeed.'

Sylvester leaned forward and scowled at him. 'There is nothing wrong with seeking a little ease and respite from this maddened and frustricated world,' he said, sententiously and very, very carefully.

'That's not the point—'

'That *is* the point.' Sylvester imitated him in a prissy voice.

'And stop scratching,' Eustace snapped, as the old man began to scrape at his belly yet again.

'I've got a disease,' Sylvester whined.

'A thorough bath would cure it,' Eustace sniffed.

'I'd like to wash *you* off, that's for sure,' Sylvester muttered, clutching his bottle to himself to cover yet another surreptitious scratch.

'Now, boys, don't quarrel,' Casey murmured, wiping her nose on the back of her sleeve. Absently she, too, scratched her stomach and hiccuped.

'Casey, darling, don't move. I want to remember you just like this.'

She opened her eyes at the familiar voice. 'Oh, no,' she groaned. 'Not *you*.'

The man in the rain-spangled coat grinned. 'You were expecting maybe Gary Cooper?'

'I was expecting a little kindness in a cruel and heartless world,' she moaned, and closed her eyes again.

'I can be kind,' the man said. 'I can be brave, clean and reverent, too. You just have to give me a chance.'

'No, thank you, I'll pass,' she said.

The last time she'd given Jake Chase a chance, the pass had been his. He had an apartment in the same building as her own, and made a habit of asking her out whenever their entry or exit chanced to coincide. He was good-looking, well dressed, had an engagingly crooked smile and very nice eyes, but she couldn't stand him.

He was so . . . damn . . . jaunty.

Now he gazed down at her, at Eustace Millington and at the drunken Sylvester. 'Good party?' he asked cheerfully.

Eustace Millington stood, and was annoyed to discover that although he had always considered himself a tall man he still had to look up to this police person who addressed one of his personally chosen employees so familiarly. 'Miss Hewson has been through a deeply traumatic experience,' he announced imperiously. 'She has been assaulted, robbed and left to lie unconscious among drunkards and perverts.'

Sylvester drew himself up. 'Hey! you old poop, knock off that pervert stuff!' Unfortunately, his resentment was insufficient to maintain his balance, and he fell back onto the bench.

Millington ignored him. 'Instead of being given due care and attention she has been left sitting here, exposed to the eyes of the curious and forced to bear the company of . . .' He gestured disdainfully at the old man.

Jake glanced down. 'Hello, Sylvester,' he said.

'Lieutenant Chase,' Sylvester said, raising the bottle in a salute. He glanced over at Millington and spoke in a confidential whisper. 'Don't mind old Eustace there – he can't help being an asshole.'

Casey had opened her eyes again and was staring at Chase. 'Oh, my God,' she moaned. 'I don't believe this.'

'A lack of faith is a sad thing,' Chase said solemnly. He reached down and took her hand, pulling her to her feet. 'Come here for a minute.' He drew her a few steps away. 'Did I get the story right from the duty sergeant?' he asked in a low voice. 'You were found lying drunk in a doorway with Sylvester over there?'

She was still gaping at him. 'You're not . . . you're not a . . . *cop*?'

He looked at her in mock amazement. 'I'm *not*? Oh, hell – the captain is going to be *real* annoyed when he hears that. He's been giving me assignments for years now, real dangerous stuff, too. I guess I must just be a brave civilian.'

'Oh, my God, you *are* a cop,' she groaned.

'I wish you'd make up your mind,' he said. 'First you say I'm not, then you say I am – it's *very* unsettling.' He crossed his arms and leaned against the wall, grinning at her. 'Maybe I'd better have it tattooed on my forehead. Now that you know I am a reliable, responsible member of society, how about dinner tomorrow night?'

Casey fixed him with a baleful if bloodshot eye and felt her anger automatically rising to the bait. Damn the man anyway! 'I am not *that* drunk,' she said firmly. 'And I wasn't lying around in the doorway for fun,' she added.

'No, I'm sure you were perfectly serious about the whole thing,' Jake agreed supportively. 'You can't help it if it *looked* like fun, can you? Some people just don't understand these things.' He sniffed, then sniffed again. 'Comparative research on gin, was it? Domestic versus imported? I always think that—'

Eustace Millington, left fretting by the bench, finally snapped. He drew a deep breath and addressed the uncaring world in his best Aggrieved Monarch tones. 'Can We Not Have A Little *Privacy*?' he bellowed.

Instantly, all activity in the place ceased, and in the silence everyone turned to stare at them. This being exactly the opposite of what Eustace had demanded, he began to turn purple with indignation and embarrassment. Chase looked at him for a moment and then glanced at Casey.

'My boss,' Casey murmured.

'We all have them,' Jake said sympathetically, and went over to the duty sergeant for a quick word. A few minutes later they were in an interrogation room. Jake Chase closed the door and waited.

'I demand to see a lawyer,' Eustace said.

'You ain't been charged with anything, Eustace, my dear,' Sylvester said, with another discreet belch. He settled himself in a chair and put his feet up on the table, pulling his disreputable hat down over his eyes. 'You may wake me when required,' he informed them with a casual wave of his hand, and almost immediately lapsed into peaceful, regular snores.

Millington took a step toward him with undisclosed intent, but Chase reached out and took hold of his sleeve. 'Let him be,' he said quietly but firmly. 'Sit down and relax.' Although Chase's grip seemed to be light, Eustace Millington found himself inexorably drawn down into a chair and held there. He opened his mouth like a fish, closed it, opened it again, cleared his throat and lapsed into a sulk. Only then did Chase let go.

'Now, then – tell me from the beginning,' he instructed Casey.

With a sigh, she did as she was told. Jake Chase listened to every word without a sneer or even the raising of an eyebrow. He seemed, for the moment, almost human. This in itself was highly suspicious. She decided it was part of a larger plan and remained wary.

When she was finished, Chase leaned back in his chair and regarded her with curiosity. 'What was in the briefcase?' he asked.

'Nothing,' Casey said quickly. 'Just a manuscript I'm editing and my notes. Scribbles, really. Nothing that would interest a thief. Certainly nothing to interest *two* thieves.'

'Something,' Chase said, watching her face. 'There was something in it.'

'Well—' She flushed pink.

'Go on – what was it – copy of *Playgirl*?' he teased.

'Don't be stupid.'

'Well, then?'

'The remains of my lunch.'

He was disappointed. 'You didn't finish your lunch? That's terrible – a girl needs to keep up her strength.'

'Oh, shut up.'

Sylvester opened his eyes and pushed back his hat. He looked over at Casey's rather modest curves with proprietary pleasure and nodded. 'The sweetest meat is closest to the bone,' he observed. Millington began to growl.

Chase reached over and held Eustace down, all the while keeping his eyes on Casey. 'And that's it? That's *everything*?'

'Everything. They never even touched my handbag. I had credit cards, checkbook, about eighty dollars in cash—'

'Seventy,' Sylvester murmured, replacing his hat on the bridge of his nose. 'Maggie took ten for the bottle of gin you busted when you fell on her.'

'That was after,' Casey said. 'Before, when they were grabbing for me, there was eighty.'

Sylvester waved a grimy hand. 'Details,' he said, 'details.'

Casey did not feel she was performing at her best. She had a headache, needed a bath to get the gin out of her hair and had torn her tights. She had an overwhelming impulse to smack the skeptical smile off Jake Chase's face, but supposed that under the circumstances she had better behave herself. If she'd known he was a cop, and that she risked running into him here, she'd have followed Eustace Millington's first suggestion and just forgotten the whole thing. The briefcase had been new and beautiful and expensive – but not worth the risk of facing Charley Smart-ass here. And she could hardly say anything else – at least not until she'd spoken to Richard. She'd rung him as soon as they arrived at the station. Why hadn't he answered his phone? Where was he?

'Somebody said something about some pictures?' she said wearily. 'About our looking at some pictures to identify these two men who attacked me?'

Chase, who had called into the station rather furtively to see someone about the Corelli case he was no longer officially interested in, hadn't slept for the past thirty-six hours. He knew he should have walked right on by Casey Hewson. It would have been the act of a sensible man, something he occasionally aspired to be. But no – he'd had to stop, stick his nose in, and now he was stuck. Why didn't he ever learn? he asked himself. He'd asked this girl out a few times, she'd made it damned clear she wasn't interested, and he had better things to do with his time than hang around here on a simple mugging case, right? He worked out of Headquarters, he was a highly trained officer, not a local precinct man. On the other hand, she was obviously upset, and he couldn't just desert her. Could he?

He stood up. 'I'll get the books,' he said.

An hour later Casey pointed a finger. 'That's one of them,' she said. Sylvester jumped up and peered.

'That's one of them,' he agreed, then looked suddenly worried. 'Where's the john?' he inquired with some urgency, and tried to get his feet organized. His subsequent frenzied struggles with his chair, which eventually gave way with a crash, woke Eustace Millington, who had been lulled into a doze by the swish of turning pages. He sat upright with a jerk that nearly broke his own neck. Over his involuntary cry of pain, Sylvester's voice rose sadly.

'Never mind,' he said, and sat down again.

Millington, massaging his neck, looked at Sylvester in horror.

He took a breath, grimaced, raised his eyes to the ceiling and stood up. 'I must make a telephone call,' he announced. 'My man will be worried.'

'I knew he was a fag,' Sylvester said with deep satisfaction, and began to shake his wet foot to dry it.

'My *servant* will be waiting up for me,' Eustace snarled.

'Phone right down the hall, on the left,' Jake Chase said. He had been staring at the photograph Casey had identified, and did not look up as Millington left. 'You're certain that's the man?'

'Yes,' Casey said.

Sylvester was attempting to focus on the words below the picture. 'Obe-di-ah Smith,' he said triumphantly, and beamed at them both. 'That's the big one, all right, all right.'

Jake Chase moved the book away and replaced it with another one. 'Go on,' he said encouragingly. 'Try this.'

It was only four pages in. 'Him,' Casey said. She pointed again. 'That's the other one.'

Sylvester, full of excitement, jumped up, nearly fell over the table and with crossed eyes regarded the page which was virtually under his dripping nose. He drew his sleeve up over his wrist and wiped the page. 'Yup, that's the little one, that is. Right there. Lessee his name. Jones, Tanker Jones.' He grinned. 'Smith and Jones,' he said. And then, as he heard his own words, the smile dropped away from his face. After a moment he began to cry.

Casey regarded him in some dismay. She leaned forward to look again at the page, but Jake closed the book with a thud. 'What's the matter?' she asked.

Chase looked unhappy, too. 'It's nothing,' he said. 'Think nothing of it, really. Too much gin, that's all.'

'We're dead, my dear,' Sylvester sniveled. 'We're dead as doornails, even while we're walking around.'

'Shut up, Sylvester,' Jake snapped, stacking the books and pushing them aside.

'I don't understand,' Casey said, looking from one to the other. 'Are they dangerous or something?'

Jake looked uneasy as he stacked the books. 'They're professional criminals,' he told her. 'I must admit, simple mugging isn't usually in their line—'

'They're contract killers,' Sylvester said. 'Everybody in town knows those names. Smith and Jones will get you if you don't

45

watch out, that's what they say.' He began to sing to himself, in a morose voice. 'They know if you've been bad or good, so be good for—'

She stared at Chase. 'Is that true?'

'Well – they've never actually been *convicted* in this state,' Jake said reluctantly. 'Out-of-town boys – we've only had them in on suspicion a few times.'

Eustace Millington returned from making his phone call. 'There seems to be a good deal of excitement out there,' he said, closing the door on the sounds of cheering. 'I could hardly make myself heard over all the shouting.'

'Oh, yeah?' Jake said, without much interest.

'Seems there's been some kind of arrest – some woman named Vita Corelli?' Eustace said. 'They seem quite overjoyed about it.'

Jake Chase sank into his chair with a thump. 'Oh, great,' he said morosely. 'That's just great.'

Millington looked around and was puzzled at the misery evident on the three faces around the table. 'Well, then – have you identified the men who took your briefcase, my dear?' he asked.

'Yes,' Casey said glumly.

'Splendid. And can we go now?'

'No,' Sylvester said bleakly.

'I don't understand,' Eustace Millington said crossly. 'Surely that's what you wanted – an identification? Miss Hewson will sign a complaint and that will be an end to it.'

'Not quite,' Jake said.

'More like an end to us,' Sylvester said, and began to cry again, the tears running from one grimy wrinkle to the next and soaking into his bedraggled muffler. 'My mother will be so *upset*.'

SEVEN

Rocky Lightfoot took a deep breath, turned the doorknob and entered his father's bedroom. It was softly lit, but the bed itself was in shadows, cornered by high posts and drapes. The old man who lay on the pillows was almost as pale as the linen itself, and only the naturally sallow cast of his skin gave color to his face. The nurse, who sat dozing beside the bed, did not stir when the young man approached the bed, but the old man's eyes flew open, sudden and black and sharp, and nearly startled the young man to death.

'What?' the old man asked, his voice weak and scratchy.

'Trouble, Father,' Rocky whispered.

'So. Tell.' The old man preferred to save his energy for living rather than talking. He waited while his son chose his words – as if words mattered anymore. Breathing mattered, pain mattered, revenge mattered. Words – he didn't give a damn for words.

'The men you sent got the manuscript.'

The old man nodded. 'Good.'

Rocky sighed. This was the bad part. 'They didn't get the girl.'

'No?' The old man was startled. He almost sat up.

'No.'

'Why not?'

'There were – complications.'

'Complications?' The old man sneered. 'They know how to deal with complications, those two.'

'Well, not this time. But don't worry about it,' Rocky said. He was forming his own plan to deal with the 'complications'. 'The girl is with the police.'

'Can she identify Smith and Jones?'

'I don't know,' Rocky admitted. 'But if she can, they may make a connection with us. If they haven't already. You should have sent someone else – someone we'd never used before.'

'There wasn't time,' Gurney snapped.

'Another day—'

'There wasn't time for *me*!' Gurney hissed. He sank back and

47

closed his eyes. 'Did you look at the manuscript?'

'Yes – but it was only a carbon copy, and it was incomplete. They probably won't publish now anyway.' Rocky Lightfoot held his irritation down and tried to speak calmly. Tonight's fiasco was just further evidence of his father's waning ability to handle the business. He resented having to clean up after other people's idiocy. It hadn't been *his* decision to get the girl. His father had been using Smith and Jones on another matter and had switched them to her. The trouble with Smith and Jones, in Rocky's opinion, was that they thought for themselves. He didn't like that. Leaving the girl alive had been a bad mistake on their part. Still – it might prove to have its advantages.

'Find the proof,' Gurney said stubbornly, closing his eyes.

'Where should we look?' Rocky asked.

The old man scowled. 'I told you. Get the girl.'

'I don't think—'

The old man struggled up onto his elbows, his dark eyes sunken in their sockets but still blazing. 'Then maybe you should start thinking, you little asshole. Or do I have to get up and do it myself?'

The nurse woke up and jumped to her feet. 'You shouldn't be in here,' she snapped, coming around the bed and taking Rocky's arm to push him toward the door. 'You know the doctor said he mustn't get excited.'

'Get the girl!' came Gurney Lightfoot's cracked voice from the shadows of the bed. There was a thump and a rustle as he fell back onto the pillows.

The nurse glanced over her shoulder and practically shoved the young man out the door. 'You stupid boy, you could have killed him!'

The door closed and the young man stood there staring at it. 'Don't I wish!' he muttered, but it lacked a certain conviction. He still loved his father, a feeling which annoyed him deeply but which he could not overcome. He was, however, trying.

Perhaps this was the last evidence needed to prove that it was time he took over completely. Maybe his moment had come at last.

As he turned and walked down the hall to his own suite, Rocky Lightfoot was miffed. It was not a new sensation. He had been continually miffed since the age of fifteen, when he had realized that somehow, in the cosmic order of things, he had been victimized. Whether it was by accident or design, someone, somewhere, was walking around in his body.

He only had to look in a full-length mirror to see it. His head was huge, his body puny. It was a blatant mismatch, and he had been looking for a culprit to blame for years. It affected his relationship with his parents (not good), women (worse) and friends (he had none).

During his pre-adolescent years he had entertained fantasies of Martians having come down to the hospital where he had been born and doing a head transplant in the darkness of the night nursery, leaving no seam to show where their evil work had been done. He constantly gazed at the night sky, waiting for some signal to reveal that they knew he was here and were coming to claim him for Mars, where, as its rightful ruler, he would dispense mercy and cruelty in unequal measure.

However, under the constant and unremitting onslaught of reality, his cherished Martian fantasies slowly eroded away to expose a sullen bedrock of suspicion crisscrossed by deep veins of obsession. The strongest of these was his historical research into the lives of Great Men, especially Great Men with Big Heads and Little Bodies.

Einstein was one of his favorites, of course, but there were others. He had spent a long time researching the hat sizes of Napoleon and Ghengis Khan, and frequently wrote articles with titles like 'Famous Crowned Heads' and 'Great Heads of State' for minor scientific journals. He was currently engaged in correspondence with several anthropologists concerning The Largest Skull Ever Measured and the relationship between brain-power and cranial capacity.

Most of these learned men never answered his letters, which were thick with amateur theory and heavy with the weight of his suppressed rage. This refusal of the scientific world to acknowledge what to him seemed obvious only served to further fuel his sense of being cruelly passed over by Destiny.

As his general appearance was childlike, women invariably tried to mother him. His own mother had been large but small-headed (many said pin-headed for marrying the likes of Gurney Lightfoot). She had named him Ronald, after her favorite movie star. He had used his proper name, Ronald R. Lightfoot, at college and in all his correspondence, and he had tried to get the men to call him Ronald, but it was no use.

For after one look at his puny son, Gurney had quickly nicknamed him Rocky in an effort to make him 'tough', and Rocky he remained. He had borne this further burden with difficulty, for tough he was not. He'd tried to be tough, God knows he'd tried. He'd hung out with a wild bunch in high school and gotten into as many scrapes as he could manage, but his heart hadn't been in them. When the moment came to take the final step – whatever it might be – he always found a way to avoid it. It was an exhausting existence.

Perhaps that was why, when it came to matters of love, Rocky liked the luxurious comfort of big blonde women. Unfortunately, all the big blonde women he approached thought he was cute and wanted to pat him. This tended either to enrage him or to inflame his passion, depending on where they chose to pat, and he was unfortunately quick in his responses. As a result, he had been repeatedly in trouble over women during his late adolescence. As this was not the kind of 'tough' he had envisaged when nicknaming his son, it was with some relief and considerable exasperation that his father sent him off to college. It was less expensive than constantly paying off irate fathers and/or husbands.

As he grew older, Rocky learned that what he really wanted was a woman who would think he was big and strong and wonderful, and would say so all the time, especially in bed. He'd had a brief marriage of compromise, to a medium-sized redhead who thought he was both cute and a fool. This opinion she had eventually blurted out while drunk, after a party at which Rocky had argued with everyone. He had put her out of the car immediately and had made a determined effort to run over her while pulling away. After that he had found it easier to have big blonde mistresses who would say what he wanted to hear and also allow him to boss them around. The current incumbent was a dim-witted but pretty girl named Evelyn, ash-blonde, billowy of bust and thighs, who really did think he was terrific, especially in the matter of paying her clothing bills. She'd also developed a wonderful ability to cringe, ever so subtly, when he came into the room, and so looked like being a stayer.

When he'd finished college (a double degree in business administration and anthropology from Fripp – a small college in northern South Dakota) he'd come home and looked around to see what the world had to offer. It wasn't long before he discovered that, because of his father's line of work, there were plenty of men hanging round the house who would now obey his orders, however perverse, without question. With his great brain, therefore, it did not take Rocky long to realize that his natural inclination in business matters matched his father's – he liked running things. He had a lot of plans and ideas for improving the organization, and he was happy as long as people did what he told them to do. If they didn't, he sulked and they suffered.

By the age of twenty-eight, then, Rocky Lightfoot had become a thoroughly miffed, obsessive, calculating little son-of-a-gangster, and heir to a kingdom.

When his father died.

Marvin Littlewood was Rocky's personal assistant. One look at Rocky's face when he walked into the office was message enough for him. There was only one thing to do.

Because of his obsession with his head, Rocky collected hats. He had an arrangement with a hat scout who was always on the lookout for something special, and a new shipment had arrived that afternoon. Littlewood had opened the box and left it ready for just such a moment. Trying on hats was the best way to calm Rocky down, and Littlewood leapt into action beside the mirror.

His first offering from the box was a brown derby with a rainbow-striped band. Rocky placed it at a jaunty angle and regarded the result. Not bad. He took a deep breath and relaxed a little.

'We have to find the stuff Norris had,' he said to Littlewood, who stood ready with the next offering – a swooping musketeer's hat imported from France complete with ostrich feathers.

'And when we find it, we'll burn it,' Littlewood said enthusiastically, handing over the feathered creation and selecting the next hat from the box – a replica of Uncle Sam's topper. It said 'Made in Japan' inside the hatband.

'We will not burn it,' said Rocky with a grimace. The musketeer's hat was not a success. He took it off and threw it on the floor. 'We will use it for our own purposes.'

'We will?' Littlewood asked, amazed.

'We will.' The topper was more satisfactory – it added inches to his height, as well as diminishing the airfoil effect of his ears.

He smiled wolfishly at his reflection. 'I think the old bastard may be right this time about Porter. Remember, he first got the word about this book from somebody we have placed in Porter's office. Maybe Norris found out that Dad paid his lawyer to lose the case and get Norris put away.'

'Did he do that?'

'I don't know for certain – I was still in college at the time. I've been thinking about it though, and I think maybe Dad found out Norris had been in Porter's pocket. I don't know why Dad didn't just have him removed – somebody knocked the lawyer off a year or so later.'

'That wasn't us,' Littlewood said.

Rocky's eyes met his in the mirror, and he accepted the statement. Littlewood would always know what action had been taken, even if he didn't know why – and he was too stupid to lie. 'Wasn't it?' Rocky mused. 'Anyway – what's the result? As soon as Norris comes out, he starts up with this book business, which for some reason scares the hell out my old man. If you ask me, Norris was bluffing. He never intended to publish the book – it was simple blackmail. But Dad wouldn't play or pay, because he's old and sick and stubborn.'

'And he hated Norris,' Littlewood added.

'Well, OK. The way I see it, if my father is going to be blackmailed, it would be better to keep it all in the family, don't you agree?'

'You'd blackmail your own father?' Littlewood said. It didn't sound right to him somehow. Not the done thing.

'I've been wanting to get something solid on him for years,' Rocky said. 'I've made a lot of improvements to the business – but he doesn't appreciate them. He doesn't seem to realize that when he goes it will be my responsibility to keep the family firm running smoothly. I've been trying to run it for the past year and a half, since he's been sick, but he keeps meddling, even from his bed, asking questions and changing my orders. If I didn't keep on top of things, the whole setup would fall apart – or be taken over.'

'That would be bad.' Littlewood nodded, handing over the next hat – a flattish straw cone from the paddy fields. It was a disaster. Rocky tore it off and threw it on the floor. It had made him look like a charity appeal poster for the Boat People. 'Damn that Nubbins, he should know better!' he shouted. He jumped up and down on the hat a few times, pretending it was Nubbins, then went to sulk behind his desk.

'Dad should never have sent Smith and Jones after the girl, it was like using a cannon to knock over a pigeon,' he grumbled. 'I'm going to put Fritz and Knapp on the girl. If she knows anything, I want to hear it before Dad does. From now on, he only knows what he's told. The time has come for me to take charge once and for all. You tell everyone – especially that godawful nurse – that nobody sees dear old Dad without seeing me first. Tell them he's too sick and tired to be bothered. From now on, you and I are the only ones that get in there. Right?'

'Oh, right.' Littlewood frowned. 'What if he hears about that?'

'How can he hear about it if nobody gets in there to tell him?'

'Oh, right.' Littlewood nodded happily.

Rocky opened a drawer and took out his embroidered Chinese smoking cap. He always felt better in it – toying with the long tassel had a soothing effect on his nerves. 'Meanwhile we'll keep Smith and Jones off the street. Rest them up.'

'They won't like that – they're freelance, remember.'

Rocky scowled. 'We will keep them out of sight. Explain to them it's for their own good.' He sighed. '*Pay* them.'

'Oh, yeah. Right. What do they care, as long as the money's good, right?'

'Not exactly,' Rocky said. 'Smith may get restless – in which case we'll have to find something for him to kill or maim a little. Meanwhile he stays low.'

'Low. Right.' Littlewood made a note.

Rocky smiled. 'Tell them I'm saving them for a special occasion.'

Littlewood regarded his boss with mixed feelings. Rocky had picked him from the lowest ranks of the organization and he was pathetically grateful for that. Nobody else had ever thought him good for anything except bashing people. Rocky gave him all kinds of things to do – interesting things (sometimes rather odd things), but he never questioned them. He knew Rocky had a wonderful brain, while he himself had practically none, and he was deeply loyal to him. Lately, however, he had become worried. So had the other men on the Lightfoot staff.

It seemed that since Gurney had gotten sick and Rocky had started taking a hand, there hadn't been so much for them to do, and they were getting bored. Of course, being as they were getting on in years, there wasn't much they *could* do, but they liked to keep their hands in. Gurney had always kept them on the run, here and there. Now, under Rocky's control, nothing seemed to move except the little lights on his computers. The money came in, but nobody went out and busted heads anymore. Nobody leaned. Nobody collected. It was strange.

Some of them had started playing bridge in the afternoons. Kretzmer and Cyril were repainting the staff dining room, and Bumbo Perkiss had taken up the saxophone. Its mournful tones often echoed down the long, dark halls in the evenings and made Thrushwood, the garage man, cry because he remembered the old days, before he lost his lip and the first two fingers of his left hand. Also, apparently, there had been a girl who had done him wrong.

'Would you tell me something?' Littlewood asked after a while.

Rocky looked at him in surprise – Littlewood almost never initiated a train of thought, even more rarely expressed any. 'What?' he asked suspiciously.

'Did you kill Norris?' Littlewood blurted out.

Rocky started. A series of expressions flashed across his ferret-like features – anger, belligerence, speculation, amusement and finally a kind of furtive smugness. 'I might have,' he murmured, playing with the tassel of his cap.

Littlewood looked at him in awe. He certainly worked for a deep one, all right. 'Gosh,' he breathed. 'I never would have guessed.'

'No,' Rocky agreed. 'Nobody would.'

EIGHT

Sense prevailed around the interrogation table, if only temporarily.

'Is there any reason why someone should want you killed?' Jake asked.

'No – of course not,' Casey said very firmly.

He shrugged. 'OK. So it must have been some kind of mistake, right? If they'd wanted to murder you, they would have murdered you,' Jake said, in what he hoped was a totally reasonable tone.

'Too many witnesses,' Casey snapped back.

'I would have sprang to her defense,' Sylvester stated. 'Maybe Maggie also, but I'm not too sure of that, as she was wearing a new dress somebody had thrown out hardly worn.' He considered this and decided it was unfair. 'No, Maggie, too. She's a good woman, if a trifle on the bony side. She could still bite.'

'My God,' Eustace said, glaring at Sylvester in exasperation. 'How much more of this do we have to put up with?'

'I thought you were a publisher, she told me,' Sylvester said, eyeing him in kind.

'And so I am.'

'Well, you should know better than to end sentences with a preposition,' Sylvester said smugly.

Casey, who found Sylvester quite delightful, hygienic considerations aside, seconded the observation. 'So there,' she said. Eustace looked startled and seemed about to protest this treachery, when Jake broke in.

'I think the best thing would be for you all to just go home and get some sleep,' Jake said, determinedly ignoring all the linguistic ebb and flow. 'For myself, it is what one might call a necessity.'

The statements had been dictated, typed and signed, but both Casey and Sylvester showed a great reluctance to emerge from the relatively secure confines of the police station. Casey kept asking questions and looking out the window, as if waiting for the dawn.

'Come on – let's go home,' Jake said, standing up and taking Casey's arm.

'I *beg* your pardon?' Eustace demanded, outraged.

'We live in the same apartment building, Eustace,' Casey said wearily. 'It makes good sense really. A police escort, so to speak.'

'Exactly,' Jake agreed. He wished he weren't so damn tired, or he would be enjoying the prospect more. 'Can we drop you two anywhere?'

'My man is on his way over with the limousine,' Eustace said huffily.

'Perhaps you can give Sylvester a lift, then,' Jake suggested.

Neither Eustace nor Sylvester himself seemed enamored of this idea. 'I think you should arrest me,' Sylvester said, breaking the uncomfortable silence. 'If you like, I'll zonk Eustace here in the chops for it.'

Eustace stepped back hurriedly. 'You serious?' Jake asked the old man.

'Well, it's a nasty night and I'm kind of tired. They know me here, they'll let me have a shower and stuff like that,' Sylvester said.

'Don't you want to go home?' Casey asked.

Both Sylvester and Jake looked at her in amazement. Sylvester even seemed a bit insulted. 'Sylvester is a street person,' Jake explained. 'It's only late September – too early to hole up.'

'You got it,' Sylvester said. 'Do I zonk old eagle-beak here or not?'

'No, that's all right,' Jake said. 'I'll tell Sergeant Phillips to put you down as a vagrant D-and-I – that will be good for twenty-four hours.'

'Sounds fine to me. Private cell?'

Jake eyed him. 'Don't push your luck.'

'I saved her life, didn't I?' Sylvester was hurt.

'We don't give medals for acting as a crash mattress,' Jake said. 'But I'll ask Phillips to see if there's a space outside the tank.'

'I could have robbed her,' Sylvester protested as they emerged into the outer room. 'She was out like a light, you know. I could have even ra—' He paused and looked at Casey. For a moment an old and mischievous light flared in his eyes, and then he grinned ruefully. 'Well, I could have robbed you anyway,' he said.

The bulky form of Sergeant Phillips loomed up, and he took the old man's arm, not ungently. 'Come on, Sylvester. I've got a real good cell with a view of the river, and only one roommate, an uptown pickpocket, straight, no lice, no vice.'

Sylvester looked up at him as they went away. 'Luxury stuff, hey?'

'The best,' Phillips assured him. 'Absolutely the best.'

Casey sat primly in the front seat of Chase's car, knees together, staring out the window at the passing streets, her vision blurred by exhaustion and the rain streaking the glass.

'Sorry about all this,' Chase said.

'Not your fault.'

'Guardian of justice, protector of the innocent—'

'One of those things.'

'Well, not nice for you anyway.'

She turned to look at him. 'Those are really nasty men – the ones who took my case. Aren't they?'

'Really, really nasty,' he agreed, negotiating a sharp turn and letting the wheel slide back through his hands, against regulations. What a rebel, he thought. I'll be wearing unpolished shoes next. 'About as nasty as they come. Smith, he specializes in slow torture, used to be a Ton Ton Macoute in Haiti—'

'I don't want to hear about it,' she said quickly.

'Then stop asking me about it,' he said. 'Forget it. Just one of those things, like you said. Momentary aberration on their part probably. Maybe they thought you had the payroll in there or something.'

'Only a manuscript, I told you.'

'Love story, was it?'

She turned away again and regarded the bleary streets. 'No, one of those books that rehash old crimes. This one was about a woman named Ariadne Finch who disappeared about ten years ago. You know – kind of an X-dunnit.'

'And who's X?' When she didn't answer, he glanced at her. 'Well?'

'According to the author, some old gangster named Gurney Lightfoot – hey!'

'Damn!' He had swerved and been forced to slam on the

57

brakes to avoid a cat. They were stalled in the middle of the wet street, in between lights. 'Did you say Lightfoot?'

'Yes.'

'And that doesn't mean anything to you?'

'Should it?'

'Did you grow up in this town?'

She looked stonily out the window. 'What difference would that make?'

He restarted the engine and they moved slowly on. 'Oh, none, I don't suppose. Except maybe if you had you'd realize that the word "boring" doesn't really apply to Gurney Lightfoot. Corrupt, yes. Dangerous, sneaky, powerful, slippery as hell, yes. Boring – I don't think so. That could be why your briefcase was stolen, you know. Who was doing the accusing, by the way?'

'A nasty little man named Fred Norris – hey!'

They'd swerved again, this time nearly into the side of a large refrigerated truck with the name 'Merrythought Ice Cream' painted on the side. The snowman waving the banner which bore this strange device beamed down at them in blank cheeriness. The engine had stalled again.

'I must say, it's a good thing it's three in the morning, the way you drive,' Casey said, pushing herself back onto the seat. Jake Chase had his head down on the wheel and was slowly and gently pounding his knees. 'Are you all right?'

'Fine, fine, fine. Why didn't you mention this before?'

Casey shrugged. 'I didn't think it was relevant.'

'I see.'

'I mean, for heaven's sake, it wasn't even the original. And it wasn't complete either – we were still working on it. Well, arguing over it. People with obsessions aren't very flexible.'

Jake had finished his drum act, and was staring out the window – rather grimly, Casey thought. 'Heard from Norris lately?' he asked.

'No. As a matter of fact, he was due to come into the office this afternoon, but he never arrived for his appointment. He's not very reliable, but usually he calls if – *now* what?'

Jake had turned to face her now, and his expression was very peculiar indeed. 'I want you to keep quite, quite calm.'

There was something in his voice that warned her. 'Oh, God!' she wailed.

'Let me rephrase that,' Jake said quickly. 'Don't worry about it.'

'About what?'

'The murder.'

'*Murder?*' Her voice cracked.

'Probably just a coincidence.'

'*MURDER?*'

'Probably just one of those things. Big city, lots going on, all kinds of people running around, things happen, coincidences, stuff like that . . .' He shrugged. 'And . . . stuff like that. You know. Things.'

'Murder is not a thing.'

'It's a *kind* of a thing.'

'Tell me. Just – tell me.'

'Well, the reason this Norris didn't make his appointment is, he was—'

'Murdered.'

'Well . . .'

'Was he murdered or wasn't he murdered?'

'He was . . . yes . . . a little bit . . . stabbed. To death. In the lobby of his apartment building. About five o'clock this afternoon. Maybe a little earlier. Maybe four thirty. Or even—'

'By Obediah Smith?'

'I didn't say that.'

'But you think it. He killed Norris, and then he came looking for me—'

'Oh? And why should he come after you?' he asked curiously. 'How would he *know* about you?'

'Maybe Norris told him. To stop them. But they didn't stop. And now – and now—'

'And now what? Is there something you're not telling me about all this?' he asked, suddenly suspicious.

'No, of course not,' she said quickly.

'Something in that manuscript, say?'

'No – really. I was just being silly.' She took a deep breath and got herself under control. The last thing she wanted or needed was Jake Chase getting involved.

He looked at her for a long while, then restarted the car and drove carefully the rest of the way home. He pulled up in front of their mutual apartment building, turned off the engine and faced her. Over the past months he'd watched her coming and going from the building. On her way to work she would wear sensible suits and large-lensed glasses, her hair neatly styled and her makeup impeccable – the sophisticated career girl. On weekends she would wear jeans and old sweatshirts, her hair would often be standing on end, and without makeup she would look ten years younger. At this moment, despite the mess she was in and the reek of gin that overlaid the expensive perfume, she was wearing her prim manners – but they didn't fool him for a minute. She was definitely gorgeous, he decided, even in a bad mood. He kissed her.

'Stop that!' she said, pulling away.

'Sorry – irresistible impulse.'

'I thought the police could be trusted.'

'Oh, we can be. Absolutely. That's why I've decided to take you into protective custody, until we get this whole thing sorted out. Starting now.'

'You what?'

He smiled down at her. 'I think I should look after you night and day, day and night, in the roaring traffic's boom, in the silence of your lonely room I'll look after you, night—'

She glared at him and pulled away. 'Don't be stupid.'

'I'm not stupid. I may *look* stupid . . .' He glanced at her and waited for a denial which didn't come, so he cleared his throat and continued. 'But really, I'm very smart. I don't claim to be a genius, but on the other hand, I did come third from top in my graduating class at the academy and I have two citations for bravery – hey, come back!' He got out of the car and ran after her.

'I don't appreciate your kind of humor, Mr Chase,' she said irritably when he caught up with her in the foyer. She was scrabbling in her handbag for her key, as usual. It was a very large handbag and a very small key ring. 'I'm sure nothing else is going to happen to me – it was all just bad luck or something.' She felt like crying, but she was damned if she was going to let him see her do it. What she needed was a good hot bath, a good hard cry and then some sleep. Everything would look better in the morning. She hoped. If she could just make him go *away*! '*Damn*, where's my *key*?' Her voice shot up shrilly, and she bit her lip.

Gently he took her handbag from her and slung it over

his own shoulder. Then he put his hands on her arms and gave her a small shake. 'Listen, I'm not making jokes. Or at least, I'm not *trying* to make them. If I sounded like an idiot in the car, I'm sorry, it's just that this thing has knocked me back a little. I'd been working on another case for the past week, and only was handed the Norris killing a few hours ago. The next thing I know, you tell me he's writing a book directly accusing Gurney Lightfoot of murder, you're editing it, and somebody has stolen the manuscript – or part of it – from you. There's a connection, there has to be. You can't really believe all that is just coincidence? Come on.'

'Coincidences happen all the time,' she insisted.

'Yes, I know, especially to me. But probably not to you. I think you're in danger, I really do.'

She looked up at him. Really looked at him this time, and saw that he wasn't being in the least jaunty, or smart-aleck. He looked honestly worried about her. 'Really?' she asked in a small voice.

'Well, no, actually I made the whole thing up, to scare you into bed. Ouch! OK, OK, I deserved that. Listen—'

'Give me my handbag.'

He looked down. 'Oh, come on – I think it looks really nice with this jacket, don't you? All right, all right.' He handed it over, then got his own key out and let them both into the inner hall. She marched ahead angrily, and he trailed after her. 'Look, we're going to have to work together on this thing.'

'No, we're not. There's no "thing" to work on anyway.'

They had reached the third floor, and both were panting. In deference to the other residents, he called out in a loud stage whisper to her. 'I think there is. I think there's a mystery here, and that you're in danger until we figure it out.'

She glared at him, and began rummaging in her handbag again. 'Leave me alone,' she snapped. 'There's no mystery, there's just a ridiculous little bit of a coincidence, that's all. If you didn't happen to know me already, and hadn't happened to come into the station this evening—'

'And you didn't *happen* to be working on the manuscript written by the man whose death I'm supposed to be investigating, and didn't *happen* to have been chased and mugged by two men who are known killers, and they didn't *happen* to be occasionally employed by the man Norris was writing about—'

'Are they?' She looked up suddenly. 'You mean they've worked for him before?'

'Oh, yes. Frequently.'

'How long have they worked for him? Ten years? More than ten years?'

'I don't know – I'd have to check the records. Why?' Her sudden and seemingly irrational interest threw him momentarily.

'It doesn't matter.' She turned away and began to search once again for her key ring. 'Thank you for seeing me home. Good night.'

'Not even going to invite me in for a cup of coffee, after all we've meant to one another?' he asked, leaning against her apartment door. It swung inward, and he nearly landed on the floor. Regaining his balance, he pushed her against the far wall and drew his gun from its shoulder holster. While she stared at him open-mouthed, he entered the apartment, gun at the ready, turned on the lights and made a thorough and efficient search of the rooms. When he returned to the door, she was still propped against the wall. Her mouth was still open.

'I think you'd better come in here,' he said quietly.

'No.'

He reached over and took her hand, pulling her gently but irresistibly through into her own living room. 'Take a look.'

There, in the middle of the carpet, was her briefcase.

He put the gun away, got out a handkerchief and picked up the case. Carrying it to the desk, he clicked open the two gold locks, still using his handkerchief. He lifted the lid.

It was empty.

'It's empty,' Casey said.

He turned to look at her. 'Keen eyes. I like that.'

'But why . . . why . . .?'

'Are you asking me why? Don't hesitate, come right out with it. Why did they return your case, which I notice has neither your name nor address on it?' He smiled grimly when she nodded, and closed the case. 'They returned it to let *you* know that *they* know who you are and where you live. In case they want to find you again.'

She leapt into his arms with a small, terrified screech. He

patted her shoulder and looked at himself in the mirror over the desk. Chase, you bastard, he thought. You were just trying to scare her to start with. And now look what's happened.

Now you're *both* scared.

NINE

'Yeah, that's right, and I'm staying right here in her apartment,' Jake said into the telephone.

'That's convenient,' Joe Kaminsky said blandly.

'Very funny. She's asleep in her own bed and I am lying on a very lumpy sofa in the living room pretending I like it. Listen, we've got to go over to Norris's place and take another look around, Joe. In the morning, pick up the PM and forensic reports, get his keys out of Property and come over here, OK?'

'OK, OK, stop nagging,' Joe mumbled. 'Did you hear about the Corelli arrest, by the way?'

Jake scowled. 'Yeah, yeah, I heard about it. I told you it was the wife from the beginning, didn't I? Nobody ever listens to me. Why doesn't anybody ever listen to me?'

'They don't listen because you talk too much.'

'I see. Thank you for sharing that with me, Joe,' he said sourly. He tried to settle his spine more comfortably against cushions that seemed to be stuffed with someone's old orange rinds, and succeeded only in spilling coffee onto his stomach. 'Ouch! Listen, what do you think? I know it's a hell of a coincidence, but once you've made all those "gee-what-a-hell-of-a-coincidence" noises, you're still left with it, right?'

'Is that supposed to impress me?' Joe growled.

Jake shrugged. 'I requested an APB on Smith and Jones.'

'For all the good it will do.'

'Don't you think they're after the girl?'

'I do not. I think you're just trying to get next to her.'

'What an evil mind you have.'

'Comes from working with you. Listen, Becky is going to wake up and give me hell in a minute. Is there anything else I can do for you, O master?'

'The manuscript of Norris's that was in her briefcase was a hatchet job on Gurney Lightfoot,' Jake said in a flat voice. There was a silence. 'You still there?'

'Son of a bitch.'

'I thought you'd be pleased. She tells me the book was

supposed to be an account of an old murder case – and accused Lightfoot of being involved. Norris claimed he had proof – was heading for a real good libel suit if he didn't.'

'And Norris knew where the body is buried, so to speak?'

'Maybe. Trouble is, he's now qualified for the Buried Body Club himself, so we've got no leads to follow up. At least, nothing on paper. What we have got is the girl. Still think I'm making it up as I go along?'

Another silence indicated that Joe was thinking about it. 'I can see how they might think she knows something, yeah, but what the hell difference does it make? Lightfoot's a sick man – what can she do to him, for crying out loud? Cure him? For this we should knock her off ourselves.'

'Very funny. He's sick, yes, dying even, but the sting is still there – and it will be even after he kicks the bucket. When he goes, that noodle-necked son of his is ready to take over. In fact I hear he can hardly wait. Little Rocky's not much to look at, but his mind goes clickety-click just like his old man's, so we aren't going to gain much either way. The Lightfoot clan are an ever-present joy, so to speak. Which is what worries me. Do you understand now?'

'It's the middle of the night, Jake. I don't understand *anything* in the middle of the night.'

'OK, OK, we'll discuss it in the morning.' A thought struck him. 'Who got the Corelli woman, by the way?'

'A triple play – Neilson to Pinsky to Stryker.'

Jake scowled. 'Lucky bastards. I *thought* they were getting there ahead of me. And I'd just gotten onto that new lead, too.'

'C'est la vie, my friend. We need to resole our Reboks, I guess.' Kaminsky was the philosophical type. With five kids, he needed to be. 'Is there anything else I can bring tomorrow? Beer, pretzels, my old copy of Masters and Johnson?'

'Must be falling apart by now. No, thanks. Just the Norris file. We may have a case of protective custody here, you know.'

'You hope.'

Jake cleared his throat. 'She's not such a big deal.'

'Uh-huh. This *is* the blonde in Number Six you've been trying to pin down to a steak and a beer for the last two months, isn't it? Or have I got it wrong?'

'No, that's the one.' He could hear Joe's chuckle far down the line, and felt defensive. 'So? Can I help it if she's gotten into trouble?'

'Of course you can't,' Joe said with deep sincerity.

'Oh, go back to sleep.' He could still hear Joe chuckling as he hung up.

Casey lay back on her bed, after hanging up her extension. The phone's brief 'ting' when Jake had started his call a few minutes before had woken her from her shallow sleep. She had picked it up while it was still ringing at the other end, and had listened with interest to the ensuing conversation.

So he'd talked about her, had he? Made comments around the coffee machine about the 'little blonde' he'd been trying to date? Maybe had a few bets on how soon he'd break down her resistance? The rat, the stinker, the monster!

Attractive monster, though.

It was so damned annoying. She could not deny that Jake Chase was attractive, and that his brief kiss in the car had been stimulating. As had the other two or three in her apartment, before she'd made herself go into the bedroom and lock the door between them.

Letting him kiss her was probably a mistake under the circumstances, she decided. On the other hand, she *had* been upset, more upset than he knew actually – and where was the sense in trying to bite the lip that soothes you? she asked herself. She turned over and punched the pillow around a little.

She tried to forget him and to concentrate on what she had to do – which was wait until Jake was asleep and then call Richard. The trouble was, she kept slipping off to sleep while she was waiting, and that would never do.

She tried to stay angry at Jake in order to keep her adrenalin flowing, but it was difficult. She could hear him humming to himself in the kitchen now. He sounded happy. She pinched herself in the stomach.

Listen, she told herself, get your act together. All right – so Jake was nice. And so you've got glands like anyone else. Big deal. Maybe there *had* been times in her life when she would have been more than delighted to have an attractive man worried about her, having him make passes at her even.

But this was *not* one of those times.

She had a job to do and she was going to do it, no matter what

Jake or her own common sense told her to do. She had an obligation and she had a job.

She also had a terrible headache.

Perhaps if she just closed her eyes for a minute . . .

The relief was incredible.

Norris was dead, and he was off the hook.

Nobody would ever know what had happened to Ariadne Finch now. Nobody had guessed for ten years, nobody had even suspected.

He wasn't proud of killing her. Hell, he'd loved her. Maybe he'd loved her too much – that was why he'd gone berserk when she'd laughed at him that night. He'd never let a woman get that close to him again, never, never. No sense taking chances, and no need either. Caring made you vulnerable.

Well, he wasn't vulnerable anymore.

He was strong, he was safe, he was all right.

In the morning, all he had to do was find a furnished apartment or a little office somewhere, pay a month's rent and tell Lecomber Galleries to deliver the desk to him under the false name he'd given them – B. Pilkington.

Then he'd take out the knife and get rid of it, use the key to – the key! It was still in his jacket pocket! He went over to the closet and felt in the dark for the little brass acorn with the key attached. He'd only caught a glimpse of it as he yanked it from Norris's neck, but he was pretty certain it was the key to a safe deposit box. In the box had to be the proof. All he had to do was – was—

There was no key in his pocket.

He turned the lights on and looked again, pulled out every pocket. He found the one stained with blood, where he'd shoved the knife and the handkerchief and the key in those awful seconds when he'd started to run. The lining of the pocket was stiff and sticky with blood.

Sticky with blood.

The key had stuck to the handkerchief or the knife when he'd pulled them out and shoved them into the back of the desk! Of course, that had to be it. My God! What if it fell out when they were delivering it? What if – what if—?

Calm down, he ordered himself. Just calm down. Panic is

what got you into trouble ten years ago and again this afternoon. No more panic. And no problem. If the key stuck to the handkerchief, then it's still stuck to it. He sat on the edge of the bed and forced himself to breathe slowly, evenly.

Nothing has changed, he told himself.

There's no problem.

The desk will be delivered, and I will retrieve the key and get rid of the knife and the handkerchief and the jacket with the bloodstained pocket and nobody will ever know.

Just as nobody has ever known the real me.

Except Ariadne, of course.

And look what happened to her.

He lay down on the bed and stared into the dark.

It would have been wonderful, Ariadne.

If you hadn't found out about the real me.

TEN

Casey turned her shower on full blast and then crept back to her bedside table. She could hear Jake talking to his partner in the kitchen, giving her the first chance she had had to get to a phone without being overheard. She dialed slowly and carefully, and waited. Eventually, after the various clicks, burps and pings to which she had become accustomed, it was answered.

'Armbruster.'

The relief made her knees go weak, and she sank onto the edge of the bed. 'Richard – it's Casey.'

'My God, where are you? I've been calling you all night!' Concern was evident in his voice. 'Have you seen the morning papers?'

'No, I've been sort of—'

'He's dead! Somebody killed him! And whoever it was must have gotten the key!'

'Yes, I know. There was a mark on his neck where the chain was pulled off.'

'How did you know that?'

'Jake told me on the way home from the police station.'

'The *police* station?' There was a pause. 'What were you doing at a police station?'

'I was mugged when I left the office. That's why I wasn't here when you called. First I was lying in a doorway with a nice old drunk named Sylvester. You'd like him. Eustace didn't. He found us lying there and was very snide about it. Sylvester kicked him, and Eustace started yelling, and a patrol car came by just then, so we went to the police station to make a statement about the muggers, and then Jake took me home and stayed with me all night. That is—'

'And who is Jake?' Richard's voice was dangerously quiet, and Casey smiled.

'He is the police lieutenant who is in charge of investigating the murder of Fred Norris. He is in my kitchen right now, looking over the post mortem and forensic reports on Mr Norris. His partner is here, too. They think my life is in danger,' she explained, rather too brightly. In the pause that followed she could hear him breathing – in fact she could practically hear him thinking. Finally he sighed. 'I'd better come over.'

'No – I think you should just let me get on with it.'

'But my darling girl, if someone's trying to kill you—'

'I have police protection. I'll be fine.'

'I don't like it. You'll have to stop—'

'There's no need for me to stop. I'll keep in touch, I promise.'

'That's not good enough, Casey. You'll have to tell them—'

'No!'

'Why not?'

She bit her lip. 'Because it means a lot to me to do it myself, in my own way. Personal reasons, Richard.'

'That's not good enough.'

'It will have to be. You must let me finish what I started.'

'I don't have to do any such thing,' he snapped. 'I admit it might take some time, but I can get someone else in there—'

'Please, Richard. Don't spoil this now, just because of some silly chauvinistic ideas about protecting the little woman and all that. I'm fine. If it gets too bad, I'll get out. I'm not a complete fool, you know.'

'I don't like it. Zane won't like it either.'

'Then you and Zane can lump it. I'm warning you, Richard, let me run on this, or the whole thing will go down the drain. I can handle it, I promise you.' She hung up the phone before he could argue anymore, and went in to have her shower and make her plans.

In the sitting room Jake Chase replaced the receiver of the desk phone and looked at Joe with raised eyebrows. 'Was I right, or was I right?'

Joe sighed. 'Jesus Christ, Jake. How do you do it?'

'It's a real gift, isn't it?' Jake said sadly.

They had breakfast – Kaminsky and Casey at the little table in the kitchen, Jake walking around with the Norris file in one hand, alternating toast and coffee in the other.

'Been in this place long?' Joe asked, glancing around.

'Seven months,' Casey said. She knew how the place must look to a stranger – sometimes it looked peculiar to her, too. When she had first moved in, she had brought some things with her from her old apartment. Good things, but lived-in. Most of them were in the bedroom. She had painted all the walls in the place white, so it was fresh and clean. Then, over the subsequent months, she had gradually assembled an incredibly motley collection of odd furniture and junkshop finds. Pictures with broken glass or chipped frames leaned against the wall at floor level waiting to be repaired, regilded and hung (Metropolitan Framing, Fire Sale, Damaged Goods Half Price), and there were two more packing cases of books in the corners with lace tablecloths (Lost and Found Sale, the Bus Station) thrown over them. There was a pair of huge vases and a dragon-printed screen (Bernstein Brothers, Theatrical Suppliers, Moving to New Premises). There was a glass dome with a stuffed owl sitting in the broken seat of an old dentist's chair (Marjory's Muddle Shop, Come In and Look), and two rather splendid but fake oriental rugs (Bring 'n Buy, St Elmo's Episcopalian Church) were laid over a worn and dismal buff carpet. The drapes that hung from huge brass rods were actually Indian saris (Baghoosh Importing, Going Out of Business, Everything Half Price). Each of them was of a different pattern – although all were in the same blending colors.

'Norris was a juvenile offender,' Jake called from the front room. There was a small thud and a grunt as he walked into the carved ebony coffee table (garage sale in River Heights). 'Damn.'

'Got some . . . interesting stuff here,' Joe said carefully.

'You mean my junk collection?' Casey chuckled. 'I promise you, I have a vision.'

'Got into a little light extortion in high school,' said Jake, his nose still in the file.

'You see, I'm going to classes on upholstering and refinishing furniture at night school,' Casey went on. 'All these things are—'

'Moved over to numbers after taking a one-three fall for assault, out in eighteen months for good behavior. Became a runner, then a bagman for the Lightfoot organization in 'fifty-eight,' Jake droned on.

'. . . basically of sound construction – they just need doing up or refinishing. When I'm ready, I'll do the whole thing at once, during my vacation.' Casey looked as if she enjoyed the prospect.

'Some vacation,' Joe murmured.

'Then – and only then – will I rip up this terrible carpet so I can sand down and polish—'

Jake appeared in the doorway, 'Did you hear me? The Lightfoot bunch. In 'fifty-eight. So Norris put in over twenty years with Gurney Lightfoot before he got sent down in 'eighty-one.'

'I heard you,' Joe said.

'Everybody in the building probably heard you,' Casey said, not turning around.

'Lightfoot is a big man in local crime,' Joe said.

'Yes, I know,' Casey said.

'Old now.'

'Yes, I know,' Casey said. 'And sick, too. Jake told me.'

'Norris got around.' Jake waved the police file, and then bent down to pick up the papers that fell out. 'So, what was a Terribly Nice Publisher like your Eustace doing with a jailbird like Norris?'

'Trying to survive,' Casey snapped. 'There are two kinds of books in this world. One improves the mind, the other the bank balance. Sometimes they're the same – but not often. Most publishers find combining the two is the only way to stay afloat. You might say Mr Norris's book would pay for five others that would not have gotten published otherwise.'

'All right, all right, I only asked a simple question,' Jake said, rearing back in mock alarm.

'In other words, you didn't think much of the book either,' Joe said to Casey.

'I could see it had potential,' Casey said carefully. 'But it wasn't my kind of book.'

'Yet you agreed to work with Norris?'

'Yes. An editorship went with it. I'd have been a fool to turn it down.'

'Are you ambitious?' Jake asked.

'Certainly. Aren't you?'

'Jake is very ambitious,' Joe answered for him. 'The trouble is, he keeps falling off the ladder of success.'

Jake scowled at him. 'Only because you keep greasing the rungs.'

Joe just laughed and winked at Casey. He was a mild-looking man with a slow, quiet voice. His ordinary appearance was in marked contrast to the dark good looks of Jake Chase, his laid-back manner the perfect foil to Jake's rapid-fire delivery and motion. At times Jake seemed like a man ignited, trying to outrun his fuse. Joe Kaminsky just sat there, watching, listening, weighing things up.

'This business with the Norris book and all. I assume the copy stolen from your briefcase was the only one?' he asked idly.

'No,' she said. 'Of course not. That was the carbon – and not even a complete one at that. The original is still at the photocopiers around the corner from the office.'

Jake reappeared in the doorway. 'But that's great! Let's go get it!'

'It's only eight thirty,' Joe pointed out. 'They won't be open yet.'

'Nobody wants to work anymore,' Jake said irritably. He leaned against the doorpost, went back to perusing the file on Norris, then looked up again at Joe. 'This case that Norris was raking up – the Ariadne Finch thing. Do you remember it? We were rookies then, on the other side of town, but everybody had an opinion.'

'I remember,' Joe said. 'She disappeared the day before you broke your leg going after that bald Nigerian dwarf in the bowling alley.'

'Yeah. Everybody else thought his head was a ball in the rack, waiting to be rolled, but bowling balls don't sweat,' Jake confided to Casey. 'I jumped him and he tried to knife me, so I decided if he wanted to be a bowling ball, that was fine with me. I rolled him straight down the alley.'

'And forgot to let go,' Joe said dryly. 'Only made a spare. Left three pins standing. We caught the dwarf in the gutter all right, but Jake snagged his leg in the automatic pin-changer and set it off. Took us ten minutes to get him down. It was while we were in the emergency room waiting for his X-rays to come back that the call came through about the Finch woman. We had to let it go, because they decided to put Jake in traction.'

'Totally unnecessary,' Jake growled.

'They said it would give us all a rest to know where he'd be for a week or two. He's been in there so often, he's got his own monogramed bedpan,' Joe grinned.

'I thought about Ariadne Finch a lot in hospital,' Jake said. 'Nothing else to do, really. I think she's dead, always did. They never found a body though. I figure somebody ground her up and fed her to the pigs. Or put her on a concrete pedestal and used her to decorate the bottom of the river. Or used acid—'

Apparently unaccustomed to the black humor of the police world, Casey had gone pale. 'Please – do you mind?'

Jake shrugged. 'In the end, nobody got convicted,' he finished.

'Yes,' Casey said. 'I don't remember reading about your leg in the manuscript though. Shame he missed that – it would have made the whole thing come to life.'

Jake gave her a glance but said nothing. Joe quickly stuffed some bacon and toast into his mouth. Casey continued. 'The book was going to be a problem because Norris insisted on accusing Lightfoot outright, which would have been actionable, of course. We had to change it or be prepared to go to court, but he kept arguing and arguing.' She frowned. 'I was beginning to think Norris either *wanted* to be sued or *didn't* want to be published after all. He was a very difficult man to reason with – very bitter. Very vindictive. He blamed Lightfoot for his last spell in prison, you know. He said he was framed. Well, I guess they all say that, but he—'

'Did Norris say he could actually *prove* Lightfoot ordered the death of Ariadne Finch?' Jake interrupted, coming over to the table to put down his coffee.

'No,' Casey said.

'Oh.' Jake was disappointed, and picked up his coffee again.

'What he said was he could prove Lightfoot *himself* killed Mrs Finch.' She looked sideways at them. 'He kept going on about having this mysterious "evidence", but to be perfectly frank, I think he was just bragging.'

Jake met Joe's eyes across the top of her head.

'Do you suppose it was *true* – that he *had* proof?' Casey asked, wide-eyed. When there was silence, she turned in her chair to look up at Jake. 'Do you suppose that was why Lightfoot had Norris killed? And took my briefcase? And then searched this apartment?'

Jake stared at her. 'This apartment was searched? It was as neat as a pin when we came in here last night.'

'Yes, I know. But it was a mess when I left yesterday morning,' Casey said. 'That's how I knew.'

'Do I assume from Jake's open mouth that you didn't mention this before?' Joe asked gently, not wanting to startle her but very much wishing to strangle her.

She shrugged. 'I was upset last night. And then this morning I was busy making the breakfast,' she said. 'I was going to mention it when I got the chance. Well, I just did, didn't I?'

Joe sighed and stood up. He took out his notebook. 'Do you want to call Hack in to look it over, or should I?' he asked Jake.

'I'll do it,' Jake said, feeling that distance between himself and Casey Hewson would probably be a sensible thing at present. 'You two start making a list of the things we've touched since we came in here, and of anything that might be missing.' He went out and picked up the phone. 'Like her brains, for instance,' he muttered into the receiver.

ELEVEN

The elevator man gave them an odd look as he took them up.

'Somebody was here already' he finally said.

'And somebody will be here again later,' Joe said quickly. 'Just keep your eyes on the road.'

'You people sure are thorough,' the elevator man said, shaking his head. 'He was only a guy, you know? Lousy tipper, too.'

'A common failing,' Jake said, ignoring the hint as they stepped out and went down the hall to the apartment of the late and apparently unlamented Fred Norris.

'I feel funny about this,' Casey said, glancing back at the elevator man, whose scowl was slowly obliterated by the closing doors.

Jake glanced at her as Joe unlocked the Norris apartment. 'Why? You're with us, aren't you?'

'Exactly,' she said, looking around edgily. She caught a glimpse of the three of them in a wall mirror. Three very suspicious characters. 'And anyway, I should be at the office.'

'You'll *be* at the office, dammit, as soon as we finish here. How are we supposed to recognize what we're looking for without you?'

'Well, I thought you *knew*! Everything in this place that's important has a little red whistle on it, and when you come close the little red whistle goes "phweeeeeeeet" and then you—'

'Jesus, ouch, save us,' Jake said, turning away in exasperation and bumping into a footstool.

'That was unkind,' Joe said to her. 'He's only doing his best.'

'Is that what it is?' Casey asked wryly. 'I wondered.'

'Now, we'll be systematic about things,' Jake said, full of serious purpose. 'Yesterday we only took a quick look. Today is Get Serious Time. I'll take the bedroom, Casey can take the kitchen and the bathroom, and Joe, you do the living room.'

'What am I going to find in the kitchen?' wailed Casey.

'Crumbs and little bits of rotten food and maybe a mouse or two,' Jake said repressively. 'Go.'

'I never heard anything so absolutely stupid in all my life,' Casey muttered, eyeing Joe who was headed toward the desk in the living room. Nevertheless, she went into the kitchen and began to clatter things around.

'That should keep her out of trouble,' Jake said quietly to Joe, and went into the bedroom. A moment or two later there was a thud. Joe turned toward the open bedroom door, where, after a moment, Jake appeared, wearing what seemed to be the entire stock of a rather racy ladies' lingerie department draped over his head, shoulders and arms. 'I don't want any remarks,' he told Joe.

'There isn't a single one that could do you justice,' Joe agreed.

'It would appear that Norris liked to dress up in ladies' underwear, which he kept in a large, loosely covered box on the top shelf of the closet, I just discovered,' Jake went on, speaking between the cups of the brassiere that hung over one eye. 'Either that or he was planning a big Christmas surprise for his sweet little old white-haired mother.'

'White-haired old mothers don't usually go in for that kind of thing,' Joe observed. 'Especially not in those colours. Maybe a mistress?'

'He was nearly seventy,' Jake protested.

'That doesn't stop *my* old man, and I sure as hell don't intend for it to stop me,' Joe said.

Jake pouted and smoothed down a magenta slip over his hip. 'You Kaminskys, you're all alike,' he said, and disappeared back into the bedroom. 'Animals,' he called from within. 'Just *animals!*' There was a pause. 'Doesn't your little old mother have white hair?'

'Not unless the beauty parlor burnt down,' Joe said.

'What?' Casey asked, from the kitchen.

'Nothing. Keep looking.'

An hour later they sat in the living room, gazing at a pile of objects on the coffee table. 'There really doesn't seem to be anything here,' Casey observed. 'Just junk.'

'One man's junk is another man's treasure,' Jake said brightly. The other two just looked at him. 'I am not the obscure object of desire here,' he went on. 'Eyes down for a win, folks.'

They peered at the table. Inventory: three odd buttons that didn't match any clothes in the place; two laundry tickets; four dry-cleaning tickets; a scrapbook containing old photographs of Lightfoot gang members taken during friendlier days; a box full of embroidery equipment plus a half-finished cushion cover with a design of butterflies; three birth certificates for three different people; a book on *How to Become a Touch-Typist in Twenty-One Days*; a pair of ballet slippers; a woman's makeup kit (not much used); and a set of chest expanders.

'You know what's funny about this place, don't you?' Jake said.

'Funny?' Casey said, glancing around at the functional and rather bleak decor. 'It isn't even faintly amusing.'

'What's funny is, what *isn't* here,' Jake told her. 'We came up here yesterday, right after the murder, and had a look around. Only quick, figuring to come back today, like this, because it was late and Joe had to get home.'

'Not me,' Joe protested. 'You said you had a date with Marylou.'

'Who's Marylou?' Casey asked Jake.

'Nobody.' He cleared his throat. 'We looked around—'

'She must be somebody, if you had a date with her. People don't have dates with people who don't exist,' Casey persisted.

'We came up here yesterday—' Jake said doggedly.

'Is she blonde or brunette?' Casey asked Joe.

'She's a redhead,' Joe said, with a lascivious leer. 'She's a waitress at the Hands Off Club.'

'But they don't wear clothes at that place,' Casey said, shocked.

'Of *course* they wear clothes,' Jake snapped. '*Some* clothes, anyway, they wear.' He ran his hands through his hair and began again. 'We came up here and—'

'Does he often have dates with topless waitresses?' Casey asked Joe.

'She's had the hots for him for months,' Joe said helpfully. 'He feels sorry for her, so he takes her out now and again.'

'Charity,' Jake said. 'Just charity, that's all.' He sighed heavily. 'We came up here yesterday and what we didn't find—'

'I think topless waitresses are disgusting,' Casey said.

'She's a very respectable girl,' Jake said, stung at last. 'She has a degree in home economics from Purdue. Anyway, last night she had a cold, so we canceled.'

'I'm not surprised she had a cold,' Casey said. 'What surprises me is that she didn't have pleurisy. Or pneumonia, letting her bare chest hang out over the ice cubes in all those drinks. Why doesn't she work for Betty Crocker or someone if she's so respectable with a degree in home economics?'

'What we didn't find here is anything,' Jake said loudly. 'No address books, no private papers, nothing. I figured we didn't look in the right places. Now I don't know.'

'He gets it from his father,' Joe said informatively. 'His mother is a sweetie, but his old man is *wild*. Used to be a lumberjack, he tells you, used to be a pony express rider, all that stuff. Been in insurance all his life, but to hear him tell it . . .' He caught Jake's eye and trailed off.

'I hope he doesn't insure any topless waitresses,' Casey said. 'Bad risks, what with pneumon—'

'He is a marine insurer, which doesn't mean he insures marines, it means he insures boats,' Jake said clearly, loudly and repressively. 'It's a highly skilled business, and he is very successful at it. My mother is a retired schoolteacher.'

'Home economics?' Casey asked brightly.

'Mathematics and technical drawing.'

There was a minute of silence.

Joe took a deep breath. 'Well, looking at this collection of stuff, *I* reckon Norris was a transvestite with ambitions for either a gold medal in weightlifting or the lead in *Swan Lake*, and had an identity problem.'

'Oh, no,' Casey said. 'He was a skilled needleperson with an identity problem. He was fascinated by the creative challenge of cushion covers, but what he *really* wanted was to date a topless waitress he met while—'

'You're both wrong,' Jake said firmly. 'He was an old lag who had learned to embroider in jail, liked to hire prostitutes and dress them up (all that underwear is in different sizes), learned to type in order to write his damn book, tried to keep his clothes clean and his body in shape . . . and had an identity problem.' He picked up the three birth certificates and read them aloud. 'Number one, Feldman, Bernard, born in 1949, Chicago, Illinois; number two, Glock, Theodore, born in 1947, Detroit, Michigan; number three, Clancy, James, born in 1938, Brooklyn, New York.' He considered them for a while.

'But he . . .' Casey began.

'Was in his late sixties,' Joe said.

79

'And looked it,' Jake concluded. 'So he couldn't have used them for false passports or driver's licenses. Not an identity problem at all.' He sat in silence for a moment, then glanced at Joe. 'But still a problem.'

'Oh, God,' Joe said. 'You've got an idea.'

'Yeah,' Jake said, ignoring Joe's sudden look of apprehension. 'Check the mothers out with Detroit, Chicago and Brooklyn.'

'Uh-huh.' Joe was briefly silent, then turned to Casey. 'Did Norris have a lawyer, by the way?'

'I guess so,' Casey said. 'I remember he took the contract away to have someone look at it before he'd sign.'

'What contract?' Joe asked.

'For the book.'

'Oh, yeah, the book.' Joe nodded. He was making notes gloomily, and glowered at Jake, who beamed back in a friendly, supportive fashion that made absolutely no impact whatsoever. 'So you want all this checked out, right?'

'Right,' Jake said firmly. He turned to Casey. 'Did you tear up the bread, pour out the milk and put a knife through the flour and sugar and stuff in the kitchen?'

'I wasn't that hungry,' Casey said.

'No, sometimes people put things *in* things, you know. Don't you ever watch television?'

Casey stood up. 'Oh, well, they have to be thrown out anyway, I suppose.' She went back into the kitchen.

Jake turned to Joe. 'Thanks for your support – I'll wear it to the next Policeman's Ball.'

Joe indicated his notebook and the birth certificates. 'You've thanked me enough already.' He glanced toward the kitchen. 'Aren't you going to watch her? What if she finds something out there?'

Jake smiled. 'While his boys were going over her apartment, Hack was going over this one. It was Hack who set that trap for me in the closet. Along with all the underwear there was a note. He left a few things for us to find. We've got all but one of them here. Let's see what happens.'

'You're a sneaky bastard, Jake,' Joe told him.

Casey returned from the kitchen. 'Norris was too old to cut the mustard,' she said. 'There was nothing in any of the jars, or stuck in the cheese, or whatever. I threw the rest of the food out – here are some empty bags for the stuff we've collected.'

'Nothing else?' Jake asked.

Reluctantly, Casey produced a Chubb key on a tag marked '474'. 'Just this,' she said.

'Ah – good girl.' Jake took it. 'Where was it?'

'In a canister of sugar. What do you think it is?'

'Definitely a key,' Jake said.

Casey looked at Joe. 'Is he always this smart?'

'Oh, yeah,' Joe said. 'Smart Jake, we call him. Here comes Smart Jake, how are you today, Smart Jake? Stuff like that.'

Jake handed him the key. 'You can check this out, too, Smart Joe,' he said.

Joe took the key and glared at him. 'This and the birth certificates is going to keep me and everybody else down there busy all damn day.'

'It's my contribution to your personal mental health program. You know you get twitchy when you're bored,' Jake said, standing up and stretching. 'And now, on to the higher things in life.'

'Such as?' Joe growled.

'Such as escorting this absolutely charming, gorgeous and delightful lady to work,' Jake said.

'Oh, go jump into a topless waitress,' Casey said. 'I don't need any damn escort, and if I did I certainly wouldn't want you.'

Jake tapped Joe on the shoulder. 'See what being in publishing can do for your manners?' he asked.

Casey glared at him. 'Fathead.'

'*And* your vocabulary?' Jake added.

They watched Casey as she stormed out. 'You're rough on her, Jake,' Joe said. 'She gave you the key, didn't she?'

Jake nodded. 'Sure. But according to Hack's note, there were *two* keys on that ring.'

Joe stared after Casey. 'You mean she palmed the other one?'

Jake grinned. 'Yeah. Right now she's the proud possessor of Hack's spare garage key. I wonder what she's going to do with it?'

TWELVE

They drove crosstown with Casey protesting loudly and continuously that this whole protection thing was unnecessary and a farce, that he was an imbecile and an opportunist, that she didn't like him *or* his necktie, and she was going to complain to someone the first chance she got, who did he think he was anyway?

Jake, keeping an eye on the rear-view mirror, kept going 'Uh-huh' at appropriate moments, until she was on the verge of striking him forcibly. He parked close to the brownstone, locked up and followed her up the steps, through the entry and down the hall. Before they had reached her office, however, a door at the far end opened, and Eustace Millington stepped out.

'Ah, Casey – there you are,' he said, pointedly ignoring Jake. He came toward them. 'I rang your home, but some man told me you had left. Who might that have been?'

Casey sighed. 'Probably one of the technicians looking for fingerprints.'

Eustace took Casey's arm and propelled her toward his office. 'Fingerprints? In your apartment?'

'Yes – it was searched last night while we were at the police station.'

'Searched?' Eustace was horrified. 'Your own apartment? By the police?'

'No, not the police.'

'Then by whom? Was it a burglary?'

'Not exactly. It's very complicated, Eustace, and has to do with the Norris book. For all I know they searched my office, too. I haven't had a chance to look yet.' Casey was beginning to feel like an old hand.

Eustace froze in the doorway of his office. 'What do you mean, they might have searched the office? Who? What for?'

'Just *my* office, Eustace. Looking for the Norris manuscript, or anything to do with it, I imagine. You know about Fred Norris being murdered, I take it?'

'Yes, it was in the morning papers. That's why I was so eager to talk to you. We must decide what to do about it.' He glanced back at Jake.

'Hello,' Jake said in a friendly tone.

'What *is* this person doing here?' Eustace asked Casey. He had moved her into his office and attempted to close the door, but Jake came in after them, still smiling. He looked around with approval.

Eustace's office was very luxurious. Dark red walls, white paintwork and draperies and a very old Persian carpet centered on the dark polished floorboards made the room seem not so much an office as a gentleman's study. Books were little in evidence – surprising for a publisher – although the walls of the hall outside were lined with bookcases filled floor to ceiling. Here there seemed little connection with the world of print.

Instead, paintings took pride of place. Well placed and well lit, they glowed from the walls like jewels, a mixture of old and new, with Pre-Raphaelites predominating. The only concession to business was a beautifully carved desk set at an angle in one corner on which sat a telephone, a leather blotter and a highly polished brass inkstand. Next to the blotter was a matching leather folder, within which was a thin collection of business papers.

That was all.

For the rest, the room had a deeply buttoned leather sofa with four matching armchairs, set around a low mahogany table.

'He says he's guarding me. I've told him to go away, but he won't,' Casey said. 'He's annoying me.'

'Then why don't you call the police?' Jake beamed at her. 'Nice place you've got here, Eustace. Classy.'

'Look, Casey is perfectly safe with me,' Eustace began. 'Why don't you go away and beat up a few juvenile delinquents or something?'

Jake raised an eyebrow, then sank down onto one of the leather sofas. 'You carry a gun, Eustace?' he asked.

'Of course not.'

'Then I'll stay. You just do whatever it is you want to do. I have an open mind – nothing shocks me. I'm fine right here. If you're serving coffee, mine's white, no sugar.' He smiled cheerfully at them both.

Joe stood by a bench in the forensic laboratory. 'What is it?' Joe asked Hack.

'It's a key,' Hack said.

Joe grinned. 'You always this smart?' he asked, borrowing Casey's line.

Hack looked at him. 'You want a knuckle sandwich for lunch?' he snarled.

Joe swallowed. 'Just kidding.'

'Yeah.' Hack glared at him, then returned his small, ball-bearing eyes to the little key which he had taken from the Norris apartment and for which he had substituted his own. 'It's a safe key, see? Maker's mark here, number here.'

'Can you find the safe from the number?'

'Sure, I could do that,' Hack said lugubriously.

'Great!' Joe said.

'If the safe company was still in business,' Hack went on. 'See, Priory Safes, they went out of business in the 'fifties.' He laughed suddenly. 'Somebody broke into their strong room and stole all their assets!'

'You're kidding,' Joe said.

Hack nodded. 'Yeah, I'm kidding,' he agreed. 'Now, this other key, the Chubb, we got more possibilities with this. Since Jake wanted me to leave it where it was, I took an impression, see—' Something occurred to him. 'How long is this dame going to keep my garage key, by the way?'

'I don't know,' Joe said. 'I think Jake wants to see what she does with it.'

'He sure comes up with some lulus,' Hack said. 'That was the only key I had with me which was approximately the right size – in case she'd seen it before. But I got to mow the lawn this weekend and that's the only key—'

'We'll get it back to you as soon as we can,' Joe said. 'What about the Chubb?'

'Well, it's a door key, obviously, maybe a house, maybe an apartment – not his apartment, by the way, I checked it before I put it back into the sugar canister. One thing we know for sure.'

'Oh, yeah?' Joe was encouraged. 'What?'

'It's the key to number four-seven-four,' Hack said. 'Now all we got to do is find out four hundred and seventy-four whats.'

Joe sighed. 'Let me know when you do.'

Hack nodded. 'I will run to·the nearest phone, believe me. I got nothing better to do anyway, have I?' He indicated the forensic lab and the stack of work at the end of his bench. 'I just *live* for Chase's Challenges. We all do. Why, it makes the life of a scientist—'

But Joe was gone. Hack gave a short laugh and tossed the wax key impression to one of his assistants. 'Start the machine,' he said.

'Lecomber Galleries.'

'Good morning. My name is Pilkington. I purchased a desk from your secondhand department—'

'I'm putting you through.'

'Furniture Department, Mr Szambecki speaking.'

'Good morning. My name is Pilkington, I purchased a desk from you yesterday afternoon and—'

'Couldn't have been me, I wasn't on yesterday afternoon. It must have been Roberto.'

'I see. Well, could I speak to Roberto, please?'

'It's his day off. Or so he *said*. Personally, I—'

'Could I speak to someone in the office, then?'

'They're useless in the office here. Can't keep track of anything – days off, vacation pay, the whole—'

'Then could you help me?'

'Oh. Well. All right, then. What is the problem?'

'Oh, no problem at all. I paid for the desk yesterday and told them I would ring through with an address for delivery today.'

'Yes?'

'And – I have the address.'

'Oh. Well, you'd better give it to me, then, I suppose.'

'Four-one-six Elmhurst Avenue, Apartment Three.'

'. . . hurst, Apartment Three. Got it. OK, Mr Pendleton, I'll pass the information along. A desk, was it?'

'That's right. And it's Pilkington . . . hello? Hello?'

'Are you really going to hang around me all day?' Casey demanded as they entered her small office.

'Sure. Why not?'

'It's not necessary,' she said, sitting down in her chair and glaring at her desk.

'Oh, I don't know,' Jake said, edging past her and going over to look out the narrow window that overlooked the street. 'Anyway, I want to read the manuscript.'

'You can do that anywhere. Go on – take one.'

Jake had finished glaring out at the street – only a few pedestrians, and taxis taking shortcuts. It was not a very busy street just then. Most of the old houses that lined either side of it had been subdivided into offices for accountants, architects, lawyers, tax advisors, etc. A white-collar ghetto. This house was one of the few given over entirely to one company, and that was only by virtue of the fact that it had originally been the Millington family residence, and Eustace Millington had kept the top floor as a private apartment after his father had died. There had been no money to maintain both this house and expensive office premises downtown, so compromise had to be reached. Eustace was, apparently, good at compromise.

'OK.' He took the top photocopy. 'I'll just read this manuscript which you and Eustace have just stupidly decided to publish after all.'

'It's a perfectly sound business decision,' Casey said.

'It's taking advantage of the publicity over the murder, pandering to ghouls, and you know it. I wonder why Eustace is so determined to do it – don't you? Maybe the book will tell me. Maybe it's a good book, maybe that was it,' Jake murmured. He turned her visitor's chair so that he could keep watch on both the street outside and her office door, loosened his tie and began to read.

Casey regarded him with some amazement before she was able to speak. 'Are you just going to . . . to . . . sit there?'

'Sure.' He turned a page.

'But—'

He looked up. 'But what?'

'I have *work* to do.'

He shrugged. 'So do it. Won't bother me.' He went back to his reading.

'How much do you earn?' she finally asked.

'Enough to keep you in the manner to which you have allowed yourself to descend,' he said calmly. 'You must admit, my apartment is in better shape than yours. And my drapes are nicer, too. When you marry me, of course, I will allow you to change them. I'm not stubborn about small details.'

She chose to ignore that. 'Surely as a lieutenant you must earn too much to waste your time sitting here reading and getting in my way?'

'I'm not getting in your way,' he said mildly, turning another page. 'I am getting in *their* way.'

'Whose way?'

'The two men in the car that's gone by this place four times already and looks like it's turning the corner for another run past. They slow down, look up at this window and then go on by. I can stand it as long as they can.'

He turned another page.

Inside the car in question, the two men were getting restive. 'He's just sitting there,' the heavy-set one groused. 'I think he's gonna sit there all day.'

'Bagels,' the skinny one said.

The heavy-set one was working on A Plan. 'If he has to go to the john, it might give us enough time. But there's other people in there. We'd have to get past them, convince her and get her out again. It would be better if we waited until maybe lunch time.'

They made another circuit, held up for a few extra minutes by a truck making a delivery to the Piggy Wiggy Wondermart, and an ambulance going by on Washington which caused them to miss the light. Going past again, the heavy-set one gave a quick glance out the window.

'Still there.'

'Blintzes and sour cream,' the skinny one said.

The heavy-set one became reflective. 'I recognize him from a bust maybe three, four years ago. Chase, his name is. Looks dumb, acts dumb, but dumb he isn't. Sent Marty Delawitz up for eight to ten for fencing the goddamn Feeney diamonds when Marty was just doing a *favor* for a guy, for crying out loud. Chase was offered a real good deal to unloosen Marty, but he wouldn't unloosen. Maybe he *is* dumb, at that.'

They had to brake abruptly for an old bag lady crossing the street, and the heavy-set one banged his head slightly on the windshield. 'Watch it, for Chrissakes, you could have marked me like that.' They came abreast of the Millington house and he looked up past his hand as he rubbed his forehead. 'Still there,' he growled.

'Knishes,' the skinny one said.

The heavy-set one sighed. 'Me, too. Pull in at that deli up ahead. We'll have a snack, call Rocky, see what he says. Me, I'd like to pull off a good one, like the old days. You and me, we haven't pulled off a good one in years, right? We deserve a little action.'

'And coffee.'

Thirty minutes later the telephone on Casey's desk rang. She was deeply engrossed in her copy of the Norris manuscript, and reached for the phone without looking at it.

'Hello,' she said absently.

'Hello, pretty lady,' said a thin, strange voice, reminiscent of Peter Lorre without the accent. 'How would you like your throat cut from ear to ear with a dull knife?'

She stared at the phone and then thrust it away from her as if the instrument itself was about to attack. She made a small whimpering sound that made Jake look up. He dropped the manuscript and reached for the phone, getting it to his ear in time to hear the rest of the threat.

'If you don't hand over everything you've got from Fred Norris, you'll be splayed, flayed and salted, my dear. And then the acid – have you ever seen what acid can do to—?'

'Good morning,' Jake said in a loud cheerful voice. 'And how is the Bear of Very Little Brain this morning?'

The telephone hissed into his ear, and Jake smiled.

'Leave the lady alone already. She knows nothing, has nothing and wouldn't give it to you if she did. But if there is anything interesting lying around, *we* will find it, and *we* will use it, in court. In the meantime, piss off.'

There was another hiss, and then a crash, which made Jake jerk his head back. He replaced the phone and smiled at Casey.

'Wrong number,' he said.

THIRTEEN

'I don't care, I *need* things!' Casey said, marching through the automatic doors of the Piggy Wiggy Wondermart and catching hold of a cart.

She was furious with him. He had stayed beside her every second of the day, like an over-cheerful barnacle. During a brief visit to the powder room, she had finally had a moment to slip the key she had found in the sugar canister at Norris's apartment from her bra and inspect it. It was only a small key, and she was certain it must be the duplicate of the one Norris had worn around his neck on a gold chain. The one that would open the whole can of worms at last. She was sure Richard would know what to do with it.

If she could only get it to him.

But Jake had watched her writing every letter and sealing every envelope. He had followed her out when she spoke to her secretary. And, as chance would have it, each time she'd gone to the powder room she'd been in there alone, and so had no opportunity to ask one of the girls to mail it to Richard either. All in all, Jake Chase had become a distinct liability, and she could gladly have strangled him.

Now he'd followed her into the supermarket. As she stomped down the aisle, the background music which was a constant presence in all Piggy Wiggy Wondermarts went with her, as did Jake. As they moved past canned soups to canned vegetables, a rather robust interpretation of 'Ebb Tide' played on the Hammond organ gave way to a mariachi band playing a rollicking version of 'Yes, We Have No Bananas'. Neither of them noticed it, but both walked more quickly in an unconscious response to the new rhythm.

'We have to eat, don't we?' Casey demanded. 'You won't let me go into a restaurant, so I have to stock up. Especially if you're going to be hanging around all the time, like a fretting grandmother. Bread, milk, eggs, butter, jam, pickles . . .'

'I don't eat many pickles,' Jake sid, marching grumpily alongside her. He looked over his shoulder at the door but saw only a short, fat woman with an ugly child following them into the small supermarket.

Jake had intended to take Casey straight back to her flat when she'd finished work. He had told Joe to pick them up in front of the office, and they had been standing at the top of the steps waiting for the car to arrive when she had suddenly pulled away from him, darted down the street and shot into this supermarket. Torn between waiting for Joe and leaving her on her own, he had hesitated on the curb. Just then the patrolling car containing the two men who had turned the far corner and made up his mind for him. He was here among the broccoli and canned soup, following her up and down the aisles, and he didn't like it one bit.

'How about peanut butter?' Casey asked, reaching up to a shelf and extracting a couple of jars.

'The hell with it,' Jake snapped, trying to look between the special-offer banners on the plate glass window to see if Joe had arrived yet. 'Come on, come on, get a move on, will you?'

As they went around a small mountain of stacked bags of flour on 'extra-special offer' the two men who had been watching her office all morning entered the market cautiously.

'They're down there,' said the big one, whose name was Fritz.

'I don't like this,' said the skinny one, whose name was Knapp.

'What – tomato soup?' Fritz asked, as they passed the ranks of red-and-white cans.

'No – coming in here like this.'

'We got a right to shop,' Fritz said, judiciously selecting a tall, narrow can of asparagus. 'We got a right to be here.'

'We got no chance of grabbing her in here.'

'It doesn't hurt to look around,' Fritz said. 'That's what supermarkets are for, isn't it? So look around. Notice, for instance, the exit to the loading bay at the back. Notice how high the shelves are, so you can't see from one aisle to the other. Notice how there's hardly anybody in here at the moment, except a fat woman and a kid, that fruity-looking twerp stacking melons and a blonde bimbo at the checkout. Notice how many little corners there are to take out a dumb cop and grab a girl. Shove him between the cornflakes, put a gun in her ribs and out she comes. Like pimento from out of an olive. You got to look around, Knapp. That's what supermarket shopping is all about.'

Knapp scowled and hunched over the cart he was pushing. 'I don't like asparagus,' he muttered.

'This can of asparagus is not for eating,' Fritz told him genially. 'It's for busting Chase's head. But you go on grouching and maybe I change my target.' He beamed at his reluctant partner. 'Think how impressed Rocky will be when we bring her back, hey? I'm sick of him thinking we're so dumb and maybe no use anymore.'

Knapp scowled even more – to the point where it was questionable whether or not he could actually see where he was going – and belched. 'My stomach is all acid. I think we should go home.'

'We don't go home without we make a shot at this, I'm telling you. We are still good stuff. Shut up and push.'

'What do you figure made Norris decide to write this book all of a sudden?' Jake asked as they paused before the canned fish shelves. 'Did he take a creative writing course in jail? Was he smitten by religion? A thirst for revenge? What?'

'All three, sort of,' Casey said. 'He told me too many people had gotten away with too much for too long, and it was time somebody blew the whistle on them.'

'Sounds like his conversation was on about the same level as his writing ability,' Jake said, selecting a can of king crab meat.

'I can't afford that,' Casey protested.

'I can,' he said. 'Groceries we'll split fifty-fifty until the first kids come along. Then I'll pay the bills while you—'

But she was gone, pushing the cart with a determinedly quick step around the far end of the aisle. He had to move fast to catch up with her, a second can of crab meat in one hand and a can of sardines in the other.

She had stopped in front of the toilet paper. In the background, pouring from the dusty speaker near the ceiling, the mariachi band swung into a Beatles number. 'It didn't ring true,' she said reflectively.

He gazed at the stacked rolls. 'Pardon?'

'Fred Norris. He was full of pompous judgments, but they didn't sound like his own. More like he'd memorized them. He only really came alive when he talked about the money side of it – how much he might make, whether somebody would buy it for a film, that sort of thing. He wasn't really a very nice man, you know.'

'Really? I thought he was the salt of the earth, old Fred,' Jake said sarcastically. 'He wasn't really a criminal when he extorted money from old people and small businessmen – more of a social worker trying to redistribute the nation's wealth.'

'I don't like you.'

'Yes, you do. You just don't like admitting it,' Jake said, dropping his two cans of fish into the cart and gazing at the shelves beside them. He put his head on one side, then the other, considering. 'I think the pink is kind of cute – let's have pink toilet paper this week.' He selected a couple of rolls and dropped them beside the cans.

'You know what you can do with that toilet paper?'

'Surprise me.'

She pressed her mouth into a thin line and marched on. He loped along behind her, seemingly eager to please. But his eyes were everywhere – and in the aisle they'd just left he could hear a cart invisibly keeping pace with them. It had a squeaking wheel. Was it the fat lady with the kid?

'How come Eustace took Norris on, anyway?' he asked when they came around the end of the next aisle and approached the cheese display.

'He had an idea for a new imprint, sort of a platform for inspiration – people rising from the ashes of defeat, that sort of thing. That's why he called it "Phoenix" Books,' Casey said grimly. 'You know, Eustace is really quite a person when you get to know him. He cares a lot about . . . things. He does a lot of charity work, and is connected with all kinds of committees. And he heads up the Millington Foundation – they give grants for various cultural projects. You mustn't judge him by the way he behaved at the station last night, or at the office today. He's just worried about me. He's very sweet, really.'

'A darling man,' Jake said. 'I love him already.'

Casey sighed in exasperation. She reached into the dairy case for some cheese and, as she did so, Fritz and Knapp rounded the far end of the aisle, heading straight for her. Jake stiffened and his hand began to go toward the shoulder holster under his jacket. His eyes met Fritz's and held. As Casey rummaged in the cheeses, the two heavies drew closer and closer. They were nearly level with them. Knapp lifted his hands from the push bar of his cart as Casey straightened up with two wrapped portions of dolcelatte.

92

She didn't see Knapp, who was behind her. Knapp was about to grab her when his eyes went past and focused at the far end of the aisle.

'I wanna popsicle!' It was the ugly, whining child with his fat mother, entering from the opposite direction.

'Do you like this a lot or just a little?' Casey asked.

Jake's eyes remained locked with Fritz's. Knapp took hold of his cart again. They passed by slowly, went on down the aisle, passed the fat woman and the child and turned around a stack of olive oil cans.

'Well?'

'Not much,' Jake said, dropping his hand from his holster and straightening his jacket. 'I prefer something milder.'

'Kraft American?' Casey asked.

'Fine, fine, whatever you like.' He was listening to the squeak of Knapp's cart, passing in the next aisle. It stopped. 'Look, have you got much more to get?'

'Tons,' Casey said.

'Jesus wept,' Jake muttered. 'Well, get on with it, will you?'

'*I'm* not the one who couldn't make up his mind about which color toilet paper,' Casey said, tossing the dolcelatte into the cart along with the processed cheese. She decided to do her entire week's shopping, instead of picking up the few things she had intended to get. He was so damned annoying. It wasn't just because he hadn't left her office for a minute, all afternoon. Every time she managed to concentrate, he would interrupt with some facetious remark about redecorating his apartment when she moved in, or questions about whether she slept with the window open or closed, and how many children they should have when this was all over.

As far as she was concerned, it was over already.

Admittedly, the phone call at the office has been nasty. She still felt sick when she thought about it. Jake had answered the phone all the rest of the day after that. She guessed she was grateful. And he had intercepted a package that her secretary had brought in. He hadn't let her see what was in it, but it was clear from the expression on his face that it was *not* a diamond necklace or a small but perfect Utrillo. He had sent for a squad car to have the package taken away for examination, and had refused to discuss it, going back to his facile comments about their future lives together, her favorite flavor ice cream, her childhood memories – ridiculous man. He really was.

And the way her secretary and the other girls had kept coming in and out of the office all day long. All freshly made up and everything. She could hear them giggling and whispering in the hall, and then bouncing in with the most unnecessary papers and problems.

It had been just *pathetic*.

'Salt,' she announced. 'And toothpaste and mayonnaise and detergent and—'

'Wait a minute,' Jake said. 'You said just a few things.'

'Well, if you're going to keep me trapped like this, I have to stock up. You never know when the Indians will attack, do you?' she asked archly.

'Come here,' he said, grabbing her arm and dragging her along the aisle to the back of the store. There was a phone on the wall, and he made her stand next to him while he punched the numbers grimly.

'I'll just—'

'Shut up and stand still,' he growled, pushing her against the wall with his body, inadvertently striking her on the forehead with the telephone receiver.

'Ouch!'

He commenced a series of short, incomprehensible exchanges with people at the other end of the line, finally achieving a connection with his partner. 'Joe? Where the hell are you?'

She was close enough to hear Joe's reply. 'Me? Where the hell are *you*? I've circled the block four times already.'

'We're in the goddamned Piggy Wiggy Wondermart.' From the Muzak speaker over their heads the mariachi band could be heard doing enthusiastic and ethnic things to 'Eleanor Rigby'. Casey felt sorry for the poor girl.

'What are you doing in there?' Joe's voice sounded like he was shouting.

'Dancing,' Casey said to the phone receiver which Jake was holding just over her nose. Somehow the cord had gotten around her neck.

'What?' Joe asked. 'Just a minute, wait until I pull over, I thought she said dancing.'

'He's dancing, I'm strangling,' Casey said, trying to get the cord over her chin.

'Oh, for Christ's sake,' Jake snarled into the phone. 'Park the damn car. I think I need some backup in here, fast. Those two goons are planning to make a move, they're in here shopping.'

'What two goons?' Casey asked, peering under his upraised arm. 'There's only a lady and her little boy.'

'They're shopping?' Joe asked incredulously.

'They're *pretending* to shop, they're planning to take home about a hundred and ten pounds of Casey Hewson, I can see it in their eyes. Get your ass in here, we're back beside the potatoes.' He hung up the phone and glared down at her. 'We wait for Joe.'

'What, just stand here like this?'

'It's not so bad.' In fact, from where he stood, with his body pressed up against hers as she squirmed rebelliously against the wall, it was damned good. He gazed down at her benignly.

'Hey, listen, that's not a public phone, mister.' It was the kid who had been stacking melons. 'That's Mr Dibney's phone. He's the manager, and he doesn't let anyone—'

Jake turned. 'And where is this Dibney?' he asked in a dangerous voice.

'He – he's gone to the bank.'

'The best place for him,' Jake said. 'Let's hope he stays there.'

'No, listen, you can't—'

Jake reached into an inner pocket and produced his ID and badge. 'Yes, I can. Go stack your melons, kid.'

'Oh, shit – is this a bust?' the boy quavered.

'Why – should it be?' Jake asked with real interest.

'No. No, of course not.' The boy looked around nervously.

'Got a stash in here, have you? Been selling a few "herbs" on the side, between the melons and the apples?'

'I don't know what you mean,' the boy said, his hand going involuntarily to his jacket pocket.

'Of course you don't,' Jake agreed. 'Just a nice kid working his way through school, right?'

'This man is trying to strangle me,' Casey said, finally managing to remove the cord from her throat. 'He is a menace to society.'

'You're telling me,' the stockboy said, edging toward the rear entrance.

'Here's Joe,' Jake said, spotting his partner coming down the aisle toward them. 'Let's go.'

'I haven't finished my shopping,' Casey wailed, pulling away from him and reaching for her cart.

As Joe came toward them, Fritz and Knapp appeared abruptly from behind a stack of spice boxes, out of Joe's line of sight and moving fast. They were beside Casey in a moment, and each took one of her arms in a firm grasp, shouldering a startled Jake to one side.

'Just a damn minute!' Jake shouted, reaching for his gun. But the telephone cord was still around his arm, and as he went to help her the cord jerked taut and snatched him backward, pulling him off balance.

'Come on, sweetheart, somebody wants to talk to you,' Fritz said in Casey's ear.

'Let me go!' Casey shouted.

'Uh – listen, guys . . .' the supermarket boy said hesitantly. 'Let's not—'

Joe, coming around the stack, took in the situation quickly and went for his gun. Knapp went for his, too. Jake, struggling to free himself from the phone cord, went for *his* gun with his left hand, but couldn't free it at that angle. He gave a great heave of his shoulders and pulled the phone off the wall. The telephone crashed to the floor and began to ring as he dragged it behind him. The supermarket boy, seeing the guns waving about, started to shout 'Call the cops!' to the girl in the front, and then realized the cops were already here. He followed up with 'Never mind, they're already here!'

'No, call the cops, call the cops!' Jake and Joe chorused in unison.

It looked like a standoff. Everybody had a plan in mind but nobody wanted to die. They stared at one another as the chirpy strains of 'The Mexican Hat Dance' flowed over them, suddenly loud. Knapp began to sweat profusely. Fritz, who had been filling himself full of bravado and Diet Pepsi all afternoon, wished he'd had the foresight to go to the toilet before making their Big Move.

'Maybe another time?' Knapp suggested, leaning forward to see past Casey and catch his partner's eye.

'Maybe never,' Jake snapped. 'You're under arrest.'

Fritz drew himself up. 'We thought the lady was going to fall over – we only tried to save her from hurting herself.'

'It's a free country,' Knapp added nervously.

'Let go of her then,' Jake said grimly.

'Maybe she needs some fresh air after nearly falling down,' Fritz mused. 'It's kind of stuffy in here.'

'I feel fine,' Casey said, trying to get her arms back. The three of them rocked gently from side to side, but neither Fritz nor Knapp would let go. 'I don't *want* to go outside.'

'Drop the guns, gentlemen,' Joe said, stepping toward them.

'He's taking this very seriously,' Knapp said thinly.

'Don't let it get to you,' Fritz told him. He could see Knapp was on the verge of cracking.

Making his mind up suddenly and without warning, Fritz let go of Casey and pushed her to one side. Knapp, caught off guard and still holding on, went with her. Together, they cannoned into the stack of spice boxes, Fritz firing involuntarily as they did so. His bullet went high and hit the tower of canned tomatoes. A great spurt of juice squirted out and hit Jake in the side of the face.

'He's been shot! He's been shot!' the stockboy screamed, pointing at the red flood pouring down Jake's face.

Jake wiped his face and stared in horror at his dripping red hand.

'You bastard!' Joe shouted, and took a wild shot at Knapp, which missed and hit one of the toppling spice boxes, causing it to split and emit a cloud of chili powder.

Knapp, sneezing, squeezed off two more shots, which went wide and hit, respectively, a jar of mustard and a large gallon can of unrefined Greek olive oil. Most of the mustard flew over the top of the shelf and landed on the head of the fat woman and her child, who were crouching beside a display of Twinkies. The child began to cry, and the woman took a packet of Twinkies, unwrapped it and stuffed one into the child's mouth. Slowly, with mustard coagulating in her hair, she stuffed the other Twinkie into her own mouth and resolved for the third time that month to move to a better neighbourhood.

Meanwhile, back on the other side of the shelf, the can of olive oil had collapsed and folded under the impact of the bullet. Mortally wounded, it began to drool green liquid onto the floor.

'Oh, Jake, darling!' Casey shouted, pulling free at last from Knapp's convulsive grip and running toward her reeling protector. She hit the pool of olive oil and skidded, managing to catch the sleeve of the stockboy as she sailed past. Impelled by her forward motion, he took a step after her, hit the oil and began to skid, too.

Together they rammed into Jake, who was wiping the tomato goo from his face with disgust, having abruptly realized what it was, and they all fell together into the pool of olive oil.

Fritz, meanwhile, was holding his gun on Joe.

Joe, who was still covering the by now hysterically hyped-up Knapp, told him to drop it.

'Forget it, copper,' Fritz snarled in his best movie voice, impressing himself considerably.

'Yeah,' said Knapp shrilly. 'You can't get both of us.'

Jake, who had finally managed to get out his own gun, pushed it between the stockboy and Casey, who were both struggling to get up. 'But we can each take one of you,' he shouted, trying to see between the crisscrossing elbows as he released the safety catch.

Unfortunately Casey, when nearly upright, slipped again. Her flailing hand struck the barrel and whipped Jake's gun out of his grasp. It hit the stack of flour bags and went off.

Fritz, Knapp and Joe all pivoted and fired at the sound, and in an instant the air was filled with a swirling cloud of flour.

From the front of the store came the wail of the blonde on checkout duty, rising plaintively above the echoes of the gunshots. 'Mr Dibney, Mr Dibney, quick, quick, we're being robbed, we're being robbed!'

After a second or two's pause she began to wail even louder. 'Mr Dibney – come back! COME BAAAAAAAACK!'

Coughing and sneezing, Jake tried to stand up, slipped in the oil and went down again. Joe, coming toward him, hit the edge of the constantly widening pool and began a strangely elegant dance as he tried to keep his balance, his gun waving wildly at the end of one outstretched arm. His other arm struck the stack of melons that the boy had been carefully arranging, dislodging the bottom-most front row.

Slowly at first, then with eager acceleration, the melons began to roll down from the slanted display counter. The first few hit the floor and split, but the ones coming after, meeting the soft cushion of their fallen brothers, stayed whole and provided a nicely rounded takeoff surface for the rest.

Fritz and Knapp, trying to see through the flour fog, felt the first impact around their ankles. Knapp fired downwards at the assailants he couldn't see, and was showered with flying melon seeds.

'Midgets! Now they got midgets helping them!' Fritz yelled as the invisible melons began to thud against his knees. He fired downward, too. Knapp, moving forward blindly, caught Fritz's last bullet in his left foot and screamed.

Fritz, startled by Knapp's scream, which was practically in his ear, screamed too. Casey, startled by these two virtually simultaneous screams, also screamed. This combined and unexpected outburst made the stockboy shriek in sudden panic, and he started to crawl away at speed, knocking blindly into things at knee level, thereby reinforcing Knapp's panicky conviction that they had been suddenly and inexplicably surrounded by little people. Joe and Jake, trying to make sense of the noise and movement within the billowing clouds of flour, also started to yell.

'Shut up! Stand still! Sit still! Shut up!'

'One of them midgets shot me!' Knapp bellowed in shocked tones, hopping on one foot and trying to grab the other. 'Little bastards, little bastards!' Enraged by his pain, he fired his last bullet downward, hoping to hit one of his imagined miniature assailants. Instead, he hit the steel support of the fruit display stand. The bullet ricocheted and whined past Fritz's ear from a new and totally unexpected direction.

'Reinforcements!' Fritz shouted. 'Let's get the hell out of here!' In the flour fog he managed to make out Knapp's hopping figure, grabbed his arm and yanked him down the aisle. Every time Knapp's injured foot hit the floor he howled 'Damn!'

The girl at the checkout had remained frozen beside her cash register during the sudden cacophony of shouting, shooting and screaming that had erupted in the distance, its source invisible beyond the barrier of the long, narrow aisles. Open-mouthed, she had watched the billowing clouds of flour rising up at the far end of the store, swirling and obliterating the red and green arrows pointing to various bargains.

Now, still transfixed, she saw two white figures coming toward her, one limping and cursing, the other waving a gun. Alone and unarmed, deserted by Mr Dibney, she did the only thing a girl could do under the circumstances.

She shut her cash drawer firmly, and fainted.

Fritz and Knapp, running and limping past, never noticed her.

Little puffs of flour and chili powder rose from their clothing as they moved. Sweat made rivers down their coated faces, clotting here and there into a pinkish paste. Their trousers were spattered with melon seeds. The automatic doors swished open for them and they burst out into the street, heading toward their car. A dog began to run after them, barking. In the distance there was a rising shriek of sirens coming their way.

At the back of the store there was silence.

The Muzak speaker, mortally wounded by the last ricochet, hung disconsolately askew from the scarred ceiling. Aside from an occasional strangled crackle, it was mute.

Nobody spoke.

Nobody moved.

The cloud of flour slowly settled onto the heads and shoulders of Jake, Joe, Casey and the stockboy, all of whom now sat in the pool of olive oil, spices, melon pulp and tomato juice.

Finally, Joe sighed. He lifted a dripping hand and rubbed his forehead where some chili powder had gotten into a scratch and started to burn. A trickle of liquid slid down his cheek and into the corner of his mouth. Absently, he licked it.

'Needs salt,' he said.

FOURTEEN

'Ah, Mizz Pemberton, I was waiting for you!'

Molly Pemberton turned from the stairs. 'Were you, Mr Niforos?'

'They have delivered today.' The round, cheerful countenance of Mr Niforos gleamed with perspiration and the brilliance of his eyes and teeth. 'I have let them in, and I have put it under the window, like you said, but it does not look good there, so I have put it under the other window, and also there it does not look good, and this is because it is needing a stripping and a cleaning and so I say to myself, Niforos, what better thing to do than rub it down and refinish it yourself in the basement, as this is your work before coming to this country and caretaking the apartments, so I announce this to them. They are not pleased, but I tell them to shut their faces, and I make them a tip on your behalf, that you leave for me to do, and finally they take it downstairs for me. Muttering, it is true, but they do it. This is all right?'

Molly Pemberton was touched. 'But this is wonderful, Mr Niforos! And quite unnecessary – I had simply planned to paint it some cheerful color—'

The look of horror on Mr Niforos's face stopped her. '*Paint?*' he gasped. 'But this is beautiful wood, this is cherry wood, Mizz Pemberton, did you not know? Lovely grain under the terrible varnish, some vandal had it before, to varnish it like that, cheap and thick, to chip off.'

'It did seem to have something about it,' Molly acknowledged, delighted with this expert verification of her intuitive good taste. 'Sort of a secret glow . . .'

'Exactly so, exactly so, you have the touch, Mizz Pemberton, you have the eye!' And she also had the heart of Victor Niforos, if she but knew it, pulsing warmly and hopefully under his plaid shirt.

His was a passionate nature, unfulfilled by the placid calm of his kind but bovine wife, who at the moment was away in Cleveland visiting their daughter Sofia, who was having her first baby. He would be a grandfather when this baby arrived. He was too young to be an old man and felt betrayed by this rush of events.

Always, from the first time he had seen her, he had cherished secret yearnings for Molly Pemberton. She was, to him, a creature of mystery. What did she *do* up there, all alone every night save for that cat? It was true she was a woman of a certain age, but she had a youthful figure yet, and dressed so beautifully, so fashionably, with her silvery gray hair cut in the latest style, like in the magazines at his dentist's office. He felt she must be a witch at least. She seemed so quiet, so elegant. And yet those eyes – dark and burning!

Molly, thinking only about the luxury of getting into her old chenille robe and out of her tight shoes and contact lenses, smiled at Mr Niforos. 'It's very kind of you, Mr Niforos – I will pay you, of course.'

He scowled. 'No – this I do for friendship. For the wood, you understand, for it to live again.' He thought for a moment. To be smitten was one thing, to be foolish another. 'You may pay for the materials I must buy,' he conceded with dignity.

'Of course. And I beg your pardon – I should have realized that for a craftsman to see something poorly treated must be painful.'

You see? his heart sang. You see how she understands? This offer of money, this was but a mistake, she did not know how to accept the gift. Well, this was America, the women were uneasy here, not knowing their place. He had to allow for such things. 'Exactly. For you, for pleasure I do this.'

'I can't wait to see it!' she said, easing one foot and then the other up onto the stairs. 'And when it is finished, you must tell me where it would look best in the apartment.'

He stared up at her. Was this, at last, the invitation he had been dreaming about, all these years? He felt himself flush and then pale. He made a small, stiff bow. 'I will do this, of course,' he said in a strangled voice, suddenly formal under the press of his great emotion.

'Thank you, Mr Niforos. You are really a very, very nice man. We are lucky to have you looking after all of us here.' Molly beamed at him in what she hoped was an acceptable way – he was such a strange, unpredictable man – and continued upstairs.

Victor Niforos watched her go up the stairs, listening raptly to her light, quick footsteps. It was only when he heard her apartment door shut, two floors above him, that he remembered what he had found wedged at the back of the bottom drawer of the desk. It puzzled and worried him still. A filthy handkerchief, sticky and stained. A kitchen knife with a splintered handle, its blade also darkly stained. And, tangled around the broken handle, a key ring strung on a thin gold chain. He had quickly thrown the knife into the incinerator, for it gave him a strange, uneasy feeling to handle it.

But the key ring that had been with it, this he had washed and kept, thinking the small key it contained belonged to the desk. It was only later, when he had tried it in the lock, that he realized it was the wrong kind of key, rather odd and unlike any he had ever seen. Probably it had belonged to someone who had owned the desk before and had thought it long since lost. And the knife had slipped down there sometime, too. Perhaps many, many years ago.

He knew Mrs Pemberton had bought the desk secondhand, so surely, if she had bought the desk, she had bought the key, too? He felt disinclined to mention the knife to her – such a disgusting object wasn't a matter for discussion with such a fine woman. But the little key ring with the delightful golden acorn attached? He patted the pocket of his shirt for a moment and felt it there. The key ring he would present to her with the desk, when it was finished.

She would be so pleased.

FIFTEEN

Joe and Jake sat side by side on Casey's couch, listening to the shower running in the bathroom. Jake had cleaned up and changed, but none of his clothes fit Joe, so Joe was wearing Jake's bathrobe. Joe's clothes were standing in Casey's kitchen sink, stiff in their vegetable varnish and probably beyond saving.

They were still feeling stunned and bruised from the explosive reaction of Captain Klotzman to the scene that had greeted him upon his arrival at the Piggy Wiggy Wondermart. Klotzman's rage had reached new heights of invective, and he finally had to be led away by Sergeant Pinsky, who had been a paramedic in 'Nam and feared Klotzman was going to have a stroke.

Jake felt deeply unappreciated.

Joe felt they had gotten off lightly.

And there were other problems.

'Becky's going to kill me,' Joe said.

'Yeah,' Jake agreed.

'She gave me that jacket for my birthday last year.'

'I know. I helped her pick it out.'

Joe sighed. 'And those were my favorite shoes.'

'Yeah. You said.'

They listened to the shower for a little while.

'I got the listing for that license number you phoned in, by the way,' Joe said.

'Oh?'

'Surprise, surprise. Registered to Marvin Littlewood. On the record, Littlewood runs a car-lease agency. But he only leases to Ronald Lightfoot.'

'Tax dodge.'

'Yeah, I guess. We couldn't find a make or want on that "Richard Armbruster", though. Phone company has no listing. We came up with an Agatha Armbruster out in Hill Crest, but she's a spinster of seventy-four.'

'He didn't sound like a spinster,' Jake said. 'What about the IRS? FBI?'

104

'Nothing yet.'

The shower stopped. After a few minutes, Casey came out of her bedroom wearing a cotton kimono. Her feet were bare. Her hair was wet and hung around her face in dripping tendrils. She was halfheartedly rubbing it with a towel. Her face was free of makeup, and there were shadows under her eyes.

Jake thought she looked wonderful, and said so.

She just glanced at him grimly and went into the kitchen. After a moment she came back in and sat down. She looked at them both with a kind of blankness. 'Those men were trying to kidnap me,' she observed distantly.

'Uh-huh,' Jake said.

'They weren't going to kill me.'

'No. Not right away anyhow.'

'Why?'

Jake sighed. 'I don't know, not for sure. They were Lightfoot's boys. I don't know if it was Daddy Lightfoot or Baby Lightfoot who sicced them on you. Not yet anyway. I'm working on it.'

'Who's Baby Lightfoot?'

'You talked to him on the phone earlier.'

'Oh. Ronald.'

'That's the one – except they call him "Rocky".'

She seemed astonished. 'Do they?'

Joe grimaced. 'They try – but it's hard going. Hey, maybe that's why they call him that, because . . . it's . . . never mind.'

They sat there for a while.

'We made an awful mess of the supermarket,' Casey said eventually. She'd rubbed her hair up into a halo that surrounded her face and made her look even smaller than before.

'I think the stockboy and the manager were dealing out of the back,' Jake said to Joe. Joe nodded.

'Dealing?' Casey asked.

'Dope,' Joe said.

'Good heavens,' Casey murmured. 'And they have such good fruit and vegetables there.'

'They *did*,' Jake corrected her.

Joe looked at her speculatively. 'I looked through that manuscript you sent over this afternoon,' he said. 'Didn't your boss realize that if he published it Lightfoot would have hit him and Norris with a libel suit a mile high and a mile wide?'

'Of course. That's what I was supposed to be preventing. As I told Jake, it wasn't easy to make Norris back down.'

'You mean you were weaseling it so nobody could make a case?' Jake asked. 'That's a lawyer's job.'

'Yes, well – I am a lawyer,' Casey said somewhat defensively. 'That is, I have a law degree, although I've never practiced in this state.'

'Good heavens, one of Them,' Jake said to Joe in mock alarm. He looked back at Casey. 'Why aren't you out there getting poor undefended rapists and mass murderers out of the clutches of the wicked cops?'

'There are too many lawyers doing that already,' Casey snapped. She got up and went back into the kitchen.

'Did you hear that?' Joe said thoughtfully. 'She *could* be saved.'

Casey returned bearing cups of coffee. 'Besides, I didn't really like the law. I only took the degree to please my father and he's dead now, so what's the point? I find publishing much more challenging.'

'Maybe a little too challenging?' Joe asked.

Her chin came up. 'I don't think we can count the present situation as normal,' she said. 'As a rule, lawyers get mugged far more often than publishers.'

'Is that a fact?' Jake asked.

'It stands to reason.' She sat down.

There was a silence. Jake sat back with his coffee and reassessed Miss Casey Hewson. There had to be *some* explanation for her attitude and actions in all this.

Apparently she was not the brainless blonde she pretended to be. To achieve a degree in law presupposes some form of logical thinking. Perhaps *that* was why, instead of screaming and howling for protection after the events of the past twenty-four hours, she had seemed more peevish and annoyed than afraid.

Mind you, she said she didn't like *him*, and that was very illogical, as he was a delightful human being. His mother had told him so.

'So you're not scared?' he asked her. 'Even now?'

Her chin stayed up. 'If anybody wanted to kill me they could have done so several times today. They didn't. Therefore, my death isn't what they're after. They're after something else.'

'Simple,' Jake said. 'They think you have the proof that Norris had.'

'But I don't. Why can't we just tell them that?'

'They won't believe you,' Joe said sadly. 'Maybe after a little starvation, a little pushing around, some torture—'

She'd gone a little paler. 'But surely – AAAAAAH!' Her scream would have galvanized both the men if the sound that had caused it hadn't already brought them to their feet, reaching for their guns.

Somebody had knocked on the bedroom window.

'See?' Jake said irritably. 'You *are* in danger.'

The knock came again.

'People who come to do harm don't usually knock,' Casey said, but her voice had a slight quaver. She was watching Joe scrabble for his gun in the deep pockets of Jake's robe.

The knock came a third time – more insistently now.

'You know what? I think somebody should answer that,' Joe said. He had located his gun between the sofa cushions. He headed toward the bedroom door, and Jake came after him. They stood on either side of the door, guns held high. There was a muffled shout from outside the window, something about it being cold out there.

'Oh, for heaven's sake,' Casey said in exasperation, and marched between the two men before they even realized she had left her chair. Jake made a grab for her, but she was too quick for him. She went across the bedroom and opened the curtains. Then she unlocked the window and raised it.

'Hello, my dear,' said Sylvester. 'How are you?'

'I been doing your job for you,' Sylvester said, around a sandwich Casey had hastily assembled from the remnants of the food the deli had delivered. She had put on a fresh pot of coffee and was listening from the kitchen. 'I been watching the Lightfoot place,' Sylvester went on. He wiped his fingers elaborately on a paper napkin, cleaning the tips and leaving the knuckles as grimy as ever.

'Why the hell did you do that?' Jake demanded.

'I lay in my cell all last night, thinking things over,' Sylvester said. 'At first I was afraid. Then gradually—'

'As the booze wore off,' Jake put in.

Sylvester ignored that. 'Then gradually I began to see that the best form of defense was attack. After all, I was slighted last night. I resent it.'

'How were you slighted, for God's sake?' Jake asked.

Sylvester sniffed. 'They ignored me. They thought I was an old drunk and didn't count. I take that badly, I really do. I wish to show them there are teeth in the old shark yet. I have not had a drink all day, nor do I intend to have one. I am reforming until I have gotten my revenge.' He looked around. 'I do, however, require a place to sleep, as the weather has deteriorated and a cold front has moved in from the north.'

'Well, you're not moving in here,' Jake said.

'You're very welcome to stay, Sylvester,' Casey said quickly as she came back from the kitchen. 'But I don't think you should get involved in any violence at your age.'

He looked at her reproachfully. 'I am only twenty-eight – I have led a hard life.'

'You're fifty-six,' Joe corrected him. 'Your name is James Sylvester Crump, and you used to be a cop.'

They all stared at Sylvester.

'I cannot deny it,' he said with great dignity. 'But it was in a far place, long ago, where the sun was warm and—'

'You went to Columbia University and graduated with honors. You taught school for a while, got bored with it and volunteered for Korea. You went into Intelligence, and then into the Military Police. It wasn't a good move – according to your personnel file, you got pretty shot up during an "argument" with some non-coms who were stealing drugs and selling them on the black market. You were sent back, and when they figured you were fit to walk the streets you decided to do it officially. Your injuries kept you out of metropolitan work, so you worked in several small towns in the South as a deputy sheriff. Another bad choice. This time you went on the booze,' Joe went on quietly. 'You did a spell as a private dick—'

'Always was fond of Chandler,' Sylvester murmured, examining his shoes with an air of modesty.

'. . . then moved to another state and conned your way into teaching at a private school for the rich and stupid, but they were smart enough to finally count up the bottles in your garbage can. Another state, a less choosy school, and so on down the line.

You have been drifting ever since, but have lived here for the past six years, God knows why.'

'Lovely town,' Sylvester said, apparently unperturbed by these revelations. 'Big enough to hide in, small enough to know. A sufficient supply of fools and knaves to keep things interesting, enough kindness to make things bearable and plenty of quick exits.'

Joe continued calmly. 'You have had four arrests for Drunk and Incapable, but have otherwise led a reasonably straight life while here. The local winos speak highly of you, as does Father McClary down at the Fourth Street Mission where, I gather, you often help out with odd jobs. He sends his regards.'

'Dear man,' Sylvester said. 'I was not a very good police officer, you know. Long on brains, of course, but short on brawn, and a truly deplorable shot. I detest loud noises. I have a sensitive nature, hence my move to more cultural pursuits.'

'I don't believe he was a cop,' Jake said. 'He couldn't have been a cop with a mouth like that.'

Sylvester gave him a look. 'I believe that is a case of the pot calling the kettle black,' he said. 'I, too, was once like you, cynical and sure of my welcome. Look on me and despair, O ye of—'

'Oh, for Pete's sake, I liked you better drunk,' Jake said, getting up and walking around the room in agitation. 'How did you know about Lightfoot?' he asked suspiciously.

'I asked around,' Sylvester said. 'As soon as I was released this morning, I went over to Lightfoot's place. Weird – one block of buildings standing alone in the middle of a barren plain. Like something out of T. S. Eliot. Anyway, I found a good flop by the garbage cans in the basement entry and pretended to be drunk.'

'Practice makes perfect,' Jake said.

'I not only watched, I listened to them coming out, all his little men. They kept talking about how Lightfoot wanted the man who killed Norris. He's offering benefits to them for fingering the guy.'

'I hear Lightfoot has a *real* good dental plan going,' Jake said to Joe.

'And a chiropodist comes in every other Wednesday,' Joe nodded.

Sylvester pretended they were furniture. 'I also saw the two who attacked young Casey last night. The big one was looking very put out indeed. I think he got told off, myself. Serves him right, pushing a lovely young thing around that way. How is your head this evening, my dear?'

'Fine, thank you,' Casey smiled. 'Why ever did you risk going to that place?'

'We don't want any more people involved in this than there already are,' Jake grumbled.

'I was involved before you were, smart-ass,' Sylvester said with sudden sharpness. He took a breath and returned to his chocolate-brown voice. 'You might say I was involved before you were *born*, which was apparently yesterday. I gather you are here annoying this delightful young woman because a man named Norris, who was taken out yesterday afternoon by a person or persons unknown, was writing a book about Lightfoot, and that book was going to be published by her employer. How is Eustace today, my dear?'

'Fine,' Casey smiled.

'How the hell did you know *that*?' Jake demanded.

'I have my sources,' Sylvester said grandly. 'Anyway, it's my considered opinion that Gurney Lightfoot does not give a bowl of cold macaroni for this book of Norris's. Just writing a book is nothing. Newspapers print things all the time. There had to be something else, something real, something heavy. *I* reckon Norris had some kind of proof to back up his story.'

Jake looked at Joe. 'He worked it out.'

'Don't let it worry you. People do it all the time,' Joe reassured him. 'My mother figures things out, my wife does, and my four-year-old is a regular whiz on—'

Sylvester was leaning closer and closer to Casey. 'I think that whoever bumped off Norris now has whatever evidence *Norris* had on Gurney Lightfoot.'

'Do you *really* think so?' Casey asked earnestly.

Sylvester looked into the middle distance. Joe looked at Jake. Jake looked at Casey. Casey looked at the floor.

'If I'm right,' Sylvester continued reflectively, 'our friend will probably be putting the bite on Lightfoot any time now. Could be for money. Could be for a favor. Could be for anything – but the bite will come.' He sat back and smiled at Casey in triumph. He spared a sideways glance for the other two. A large drip

110

gathered on the end of his nose, and he wiped it off with his sleeve.

'Now,' he said, leaning back and putting his feet up on the coffee table. 'Tell me why you were all on television twenty minutes ago.'

SIXTEEN

He'd waited all day.

Of course, he'd been unable to stay at the apartment. He had other obligations – people would have wondered where he was. He checked back several times, morning and afternoon. The caretaker had been instructed to admit the men with the desk.

But every time he unlocked the door the apartment had been the same: utilitarian, neutral, without personality – and without the desk.

He'd started calling Lecomber Galleries at four. Again at four thirty. Again at ten to five.

The first time they said it definitely had been on the list for delivery, and no doubt it would be along any minute.

The second time they suggested that some holdup may have led to its being held over until the morning – they would check with the delivery men when the truck returned.

The third time they told him categorically that the desk had been delivered. Well, perhaps it had.

But it hadn't been delivered to him.

They said they were sorry.

They said they would check.

They said they would straighten it out, Mr Petherton.

'Pilkington!' he'd shouted down the line.

But the line was dead.

And when he called back, nobody would answer.

After all, it was 4:58.

And it had been such a long day.

He glared at the phone and his own white knuckles.

Well, they might have closed to the general public, but they would open up for him – whether they knew it or not.

Somebody, somewhere, had his desk.

All he had to do was get a look at the delivery list.

But it had better be later.

After dinner.

When it was dark.

*   *   *

Dinner was rarely a formal affair at the Porter residence.

Charley was often asked out – he still was considered a very eligible widower – and Tony frequently worked late or had a date. When either was home, they made do with a tray in front of the television set.

This is where they were when the story of the "Affray at the Piggy Wiggy Wondermart" was televised, and Tony nearly choked on a fishbone.

'My God, no wonder they call him Jake the Jinx,' he gasped, reaching for his wine. 'Will you look at that *mess*!'

Charley was staring at the screen. 'That girl works for Eustace Millington,' he said, half to himself.

'Does she? How did you recognize her under all that?'

'I didn't – the name just rang a bell. You know Millington, don't you?'

'He's a fraternity brother, if that's what you mean, but he has a good fifteen years on me. Why?'

Charley shrugged. 'His father was a good friend to me once.'

'That would be Augustus?'

'Yes. Augustus the Great, they called him. Rather an eccentric character, full of what they now call "charisma". He and Red Ned used to run booze together from Canada – just for the hell of it.'

'Old Augustus Millington was a *bootlegger*?'

'Well – in a manner of speaking. He had a fast boat and liked to take chances. I don't suppose they did it more than two or three times – for special parties or some such. Your grandmother told me about it. I gather they were nearly caught once and had to sink the boat and swim for it. Fortunately they were both fit and strong – but it was a near thing.' Charley smiled to himself.

'And how was he a friend to you?' Tony had one eye on the television. This was a new Red Ned story – but he had heard so many.

'He paid my way through law school,' Charley said. 'Said it was an investment. He was always making investments in things and in people. Still does, in a manner of speaking – through his Foundation.'

'I've heard rumors that the Foundation isn't exactly as charitable as it's made out to be,' Tony said, putting his tray aside.

113

Charley turned to stare at him. 'What is that supposed to mean?'

'Only rumors, Dad. Apparently the IRS have been trying to get a full accounting, but the Foundation has some kind of immunity – something about the way it was set up?'

'Stanley Quiddick set it up, years ago, just before old Augustus died.'

'I guess that would explain it all right,' Tony said wryly.

'Am I to deduce that you think Stanley Quiddick is dishonest?' Charley asked rather coldly.

Tony raised a hand to defend himself. 'Hey – would I say a thing like that? Why, the man's a genius, you've said so yourself dozens of times. A genius at weaseling, that is.'

'I never said *that*.' Charley was hurt.

'No, but plenty of people have. I don't know why you still stick to him. Does he have something on you?'

Charley's face went white. 'That's a terrible thing to say!'

Tony was disconcerted at the degree to which he'd upset his father. 'Dad – I was only joking. I'd hardly say it if I thought it was really true, would I?' He watched his father in dismay. 'Are you all right?'

Charley wiped his mouth with his napkin and pushed his tray away. 'I'm fine. Don't fuss, Tony – of course I'm all right.' Charley got up. 'I'm going to have a brandy with my coffee. How about you?'

'Sure – why not?' Tony said. He watched his father pouring out the brandies and was surprised to see Charley's hand tremble slightly. He'd never seen that before.

It was very disturbing.

And rather interesting.

SEVENTEEN

'What do you suppose the old bastard is up to?' Jake asked edgily, peering around the bedroom door at Sylvester and Casey, who were in deep conversation on the sofa.

'Maybe just what he says,' Joe said, peering over Jake's head. Jake straightened suddenly, and his head connected with Joe's jaw. 'Ouch! Damn, that hurt!'

'Sorry.' Jake began to pace around the room, while Joe rubbed his chin, prodding it to see if there were any chips of bone floating loose under the skin. 'I just don't get it.'

'Unlike me,' Joe complained, going over to the mirror and tilting his head back to take a look. 'Your head comes to a point, you know that? I got the mark here to prove it.'

'He's a bum, a drunk, a flophouse failure – why the hell should he suddenly give a damn about anything?'

'Why should anybody?' Joe asked. 'Maybe it's her.'

'Who?'

'Casey. Maybe she's inspired him or something, brought out the father in him.'

Jake was back at the door. 'Or the wolf.'

'Jesus, you're not jealous of an old poop like *that*, are you?' Joe asked.

'OF COURSE NOT!' Jake shouted. When he looked back through the crack in the door, Sylvester and Casey were both staring at it. He moved quickly away and paused suddenly, halfway between the bed and the bureau. 'You don't suppose he got out of danger by offering to kill her for Lightfoot, do you?'

Joe stared at him. 'Let me take a look at your head, old buddy,' he said soothingly. 'Maybe my chin is harder than I thought.'

'Well, what do we know? He could have – admit it – he could have figured that was his best chance at survival, couldn't he? She's a stranger to him, for crying out loud, what's it to him whether she's dead or not?' He was beginning to sweat now, and went back to the door to peer around it again. 'Jesus, she's patting him on the knee,' he whispered.

'So she was watched, so she was threatened,' Joe said. 'She was right about one thing – they could have killed her anytime today. A good marksman with a rifle on the roof opposite her office—'

'Shut up!' Jake snapped.

'Well, I'm right, aren't I? You aren't a sheet of steel, my friend. Hanging around her like this isn't going to change anything. We're good, but we're not that good, Jake.'

'We did all right at the market.'

'Come on – we got lucky. Those guys were pathetic. Tomorrow, the next day – they'll use their A-team. If they really want her, they'll get her, unless she's in total protective custody. And Klotzman wiill never go for that – especially after he gets the bill from Mr Piggy Wiggy.'

'He's used to it.'

'He's pissed off, Jake. He was bad enough when he left, but if what Sylvester says is true, and that roving TV bunch that came up got us onto the six o'clock news, he's going to be kicking butt tomorrow morning. You know what they're like about adverse publicity these days. We'll be directing traffic in Blueberry Hills by noon tomorrow. Who will look after Little Miss Problem Child then?'

'Is he still watching us?' Sylvester asked Casey.

'No. At least, I can't see his little beady eyes glinting in the crack like before.'

'He's sweet on you, my dear,' Sylvester said.

'He's an idiot,' Casey grumbled, smoothing her hair back behind her ears. 'I never heard anyone babble so much nonsense in my life. How he made the grade of lieutenant I'll never know.'

Sylvester smiled. 'Well, they don't hand out those ranks like peanuts, you know. The man must have something.'

'He does – a big mouth.' She turned to face the old man more squarely and was surprised at the change in him. In fact, looking at him closely for the first time since he'd arrived via the fire escape, she saw quite a few changes. 'You're clean,' she said.

Sylvester chuckled. 'Apart from the hands and face, which are decorated for camouflage purposes, I am, as you say, clean. It's a most peculiar sensation – it makes me feel very unprotected and vulnerable. I haven't decided whether I like it or not. There is a certain degree of sordid solace in grime, you know. One rather gets used to it.'

'You're a strange man.'

'I take pleasure in that distinction,' Sylvester nodded.

'Last night, when you were dru—' She cleared her throat. 'Last night you sounded very different than you do now, for example. I suppose after hearing your history, I shouldn't be surprised, but . . .'

'Ah, in Johnny Walker veritas,' Sylvester said. 'I tend to revert to my street persona when under the influence. Like grime, sloppy language has a comforting quality. Similar to a woman taking off her girdle and getting into an old flannel wrapper and slippers, I would imagine.'

Casey laughed. 'And that's just when the doorbell rings.'

The doorbell rang. Two shorts and a long.

'How did you do that?' Sylvester asked with some interest, turning to look at the door. 'Remote control?'

Casey stood up, glancing uncertainly at the bedroom door. It opened, and Jake strode out. 'Leave it,' he said briskly.

'It's *my* doorbell,' Casey said, moving quickly. It was a dead heat to the buzzer, but Casey's hand was the first to land on the control, with Jake's on top of it.

'Now that was really dumb!' Jake exploded. 'That could be anybody – including those two goons.'

'They wouldn't ring the doorbell,' Casey said.

'Why not?' Jake countered. 'They have to get in somehow, don't they?'

'They could get in through the fire escape,' Sylvester said.

'Yeah – especially the way she keeps opening it up for anybody who wants to drop by,' Jake said.

'I'm not—'

'He's not just anybody,' Casey said.

'He *could* have been anybody,' Jake snapped. 'He could have been a gorilla with a machine gun.'

'Sure – or a giraffe with a peanut-butter-and-banana sandwich,' Casey snapped back. 'But I recognized his voice.'

'The hell you did,' Jake snarled.

'The hell I didn't.'

There was a peremptory knock on the door, startling them into breaking off their confrontation. Casey, with difficulty, pulled her hand out from under Jake's and opened the door.

'Well, hello!' she said brightly.

The man in the doorway was in his forties, tall and neatly made, with a pleasant, bony face and large, dark eyes behind hornrim glasses. His beige hair was showing an occasional fleck of gray and needed a trim. He was wearing a tweed suit, a button-down Oxford cloth shirt and a dark maroon tie.

He smiled rather anxiously at Casey – and then his eyes traveled past her to take in the rest of the company: Jake, scowling, one hand frozen in the act of reaching under his jacket for his gun, Joe Kaminsky standing in a bathrobe beside the bedroom door, reaching into his empty armpit and looking puzzled, and Sylvester, very disreputable and dirty on the sofa, reaching for his coffee.

The newcomer looked at Casey, and Casey looked at him. Then she reached up, planted a kiss on his cheek and drew him inside. 'Everybody – this is Richard Armbruster. My fiancé. Say hello to everybody, Richard.'

'Hello, everybody,' said Richard.

EIGHTEEN

'Fiancé?' Jake shouted.

'Yes. You are my fiancé, aren't you, Richard?'

Armbruster looked down at her in a bemused fashion, then smiled. 'Of course, darling. Although, having seen you in action on television tonight, I'm not so certain I want to go through with it.'

'Oh, dear – you saw it, too,' Casey said.

'And I came right over to see if you were all right,' Richard said firmly. 'Getting tangled up in something like that must have been a terrible—'

'How come we haven't heard about you before?' Jake interrupted.

'I beg your pardon?' Richard Armbruster turned to face him. 'I don't believe I know—'

'This is Lieutenant Jake Chase, Richard,' Casey said. 'He's protecting mc against any further attack by maddened melons.'

'I beg your pardon?'

'Your girlfriend was mugged last night,' Jake said, coming forward and looking Richard Armbruster up and down speculatively. 'How come she didn't call for you to come and look after her instead of hanging around with Eustace Millington, who also thinks he's engaged to her?'

'He doesn't!' Casey said, horrified.

'I was out of town yesterday and last night,' Richard Armbruster said in a shocked voice. 'My God, Casey, why didn't you have someone from head office try to get in touch with me? They had my full itinerary. Are you all right?'

'I'm fine, Richard,' Casey said, patting his arm.

'But being mugged – that's dreadful.' Armbruster looked seriously concerned. 'What was taken?'

'Only my briefcase – and my dignity.'

Jake was watching all this with a degree of admiration. No doubt about it, the man gave the distinct impression of hearing all this for the first time. A very polished performance – almost professional. He cleared his throat. 'A lot of people plan to marry your so-called fiancée,' Jake said. 'I know I do. Do you?'

Richard looked at him for a long moment, his head back and his eyes seeming to add up a long column of invisible figures. Eventually he seemed to reach a total. 'I should have thought it was up to her,' he said mildly. He glanced at Sylvester and then at Casey. His eyes crinkled behind his spectacles. 'Is this another suitor, Casey?'

'No, this is Sylvester,' Casey said.

Sylvester stood up. 'Don't dismiss me so lightly, Casey, my dear, I should be delighted to marry you at a moment's notice. I would even remain sober for the event – a singular offer, if you but knew it.'

'Sylvester was there when I was attacked,' Casey said.

'I protected her,' Sylvester said with heavy drama. 'If I hadn't been there, God knows what would have happened.'

'Then I'm most grateful to you, sir,' Armbruster said, and came forward to shake Sylvester's hand, not even flinching at the grime. This was appreciated by Sylvester, who prided himself on being a good judge of men. It was a conviction that had not been bolstered by much proof over the years, but Sylvester's was a forgiving nature.

'I congratulate you on your good fortune, Mr Armbruster.'

'Good fortune?'

'He means me,' Casey said. 'Say thank you, Richard.'

'Thank you,' Richard said with a slow smile. 'Indeed.'

'And this is Joe. He has five children.'

Richard looked at Joe and at the bathrobe he was wearing. Joe looked down and smiled weakly. 'My clothes are in Casey's sink.'

'We're planning to have them for dinner,' Casey said. 'How did I look on television, Richard?'

'Soggy,' Richard said. 'Very soggy.'

'Where do you live?' Jake suddenly demanded.

Richard looked at him and took off his glasses. He removed a handkerchief from his pocket and slowly began to polish the lenses. 'I live at the Metropolitan Vista Motel at the moment,' he said quietly. 'I have been sent here by my company to set up a branch office, and I am still looking for an apartment. Or a house. If Casey prefers a house, that is.' He put his glasses back on and his handkerchief back in his pocket. 'Where do *you* live?'

'Downstairs, in Apartment Two-C,' Jake said. His eyes

narrowed. 'How come I've never seen you coming in here or going out?'

'I have a cloak of invisibility, given to me by elves,' Richard said.

'I've always wanted one of those,' Sylvester said wistfully.

'I'll see what I can do,' Richard told him. 'Casey, are you sure you're all right?'

'I'm fine, really. Richard—'

'What's the name of your company?' Jake demanded.

Armbruster sighed, reached into his jacket and produced a card. 'Washington General Life and Accident. We cover all risks.'

'Forget it, Jake – you couldn't afford the premiums,' Joe snorted.

The doorbell rang.

'Now who can that be?' Casey asked. 'Everybody I know is here.'

'Why don't you just press your magic twanger, Froggy, and let him in?' Jake inquired sweetly. 'With any luck it will be our friendly neighborhood psychiatrist, answering my telepathic call.'

'He must have a good receiver to pick up such a weak signal,' Casey observed. There was only the briefest of knocks on the door before she flung it open, saying, 'Duck, they've got you covered!'

'I beg your pardon?' Eustace Millington stood blinking in the doorway. 'Am I intruding?'

'Norris was sent to me by a mutual acquaintance,' Eustace said defensively, staring around at all the faces. Due to the crowded conditions now pertaining in the tiny apartment, he had been forced to sit on the dentist's chair and looked so apprehensive it might have been the real thing. 'A lawyer whose late partner had defended Norris – unsuccessfully – at his last trial. He said that Norris had "seen the light", whatever that meant, and that he had an interesting story to tell.'

'Sell, was that?' Sylvester asked, cupping his hand behind an ear.

'No, tell. *Tell*,' Eustace enunciated, somehow building a sneer into his clarification.

Sylvester nodded. 'And you fell for it.'

Eustace turned to Casey. 'Why are all these *people* here?' he asked irritably.

'Protection,' Joe and Jake chorused.

'You got a suspicious way about you, Eustace,' Sylvester added. 'Minute we knew it was you at the door, we all ran right over,' he cackled. 'Isn't that right, boys?'

'Actually—' Joe began.

'The fact is—' Jake said, at the same time.

'It's not quite like that—' Richard's voice was drowned out by the others.

Armbruster was new to Millington – he already knew he hated all the others. Having had him introduced as Casey's fiancé, however, was reason enough to add him to the list of undesirables. 'Why should you need protecting, Casey?' Eustace asked.

'Well, apparently someone is trying to kidnap me,' Casey said in a disgusted tone. 'We had a gunfight with them in the Piggy Wiggy, and we all fell into the olive oil, and Jake's clothes don't fit Joe, so Joe's wife is going to bring some clean ones over as soon as she can find a babysitter. I just had a shower, and Sylvester came in through the window to tell us about the men who attacked me—'

'In the Piggy Wiggy?' Eustace asked weakly.

'No, last night, where you found me.'

'He admits he knows them?' Eustace's eyes widened as he turned to look at Sylvester.

'Not personally,' Sylvester said.

'You surprise me,' Eustace said, and turned back to Casey.

'The men last night didn't come to the Piggy Wiggy,' Casey said patiently. 'They were *new* men at the Piggy Wiggy.'

'Uh-huh,' Eustace said mesmerized.

'*They* didn't get me, because Joe arrived in the nick of time – he's Joe—'

'In the bathrobe.'

'Yes.'

'I could have handled it,' Jake protested. 'It wasn't all Joe, you know.'

'Mostly it was the melons,' Joe said modestly.

Casey indicated Jake. His shower had been a bit hasty and there was still a little dried tomato juice in his left ear. '*This* one is still in charge. I'd feel safer if it was Mortimer Snerd.'

'You shouldn't be disloyal to your future husband,' Jake said. 'My mother won't like that.'

'Future husband? I thought Mr Anstruther here—' Eustace was floundering.

'Armbruster,' Richard said rather sharply.

Casey patted Richard's arm and tried again to explain the situation to Eustace. 'They think that the men who stole my briefcase were after the Norris manuscript. By the way, I forgot to tell you this morning, they returned it because they realized it was a carbon copy.'

'No, it was the original briefcase,' Jake put in. 'I saw it. Not *my* taste in small hand luggage but, of its sort, quite genuine.' He looked at his watch. 'Isn't it a bit late for you to be out, Eustace? Why don't you call around at the station tomorrow, and we can go into all this—'

'Tell them some more about Fred Norris,' Casey interrupted. Jake made a face at her. She ignored him and possessively put her arm through Richard Armbruster's, snuggling up to him on the couch. Sliding her hand into his, she pressed the key she had stolen from the Norris apartment into his palm. The key was almost hot because she had been holding it for so long in her fist. Armbruster's face didn't change, but his hand closed very, very slowly around the key, as Casey urged Eustace on. 'Tell them about his reason for writing the book.'

'Money,' Sylvester said promptly. 'Why does anyone write a book? Dickens wouldn't pen a word without cash on the nail. And as for Shakespeare—'

'It was simple enough,' Eustace said, deciding to deal with one thing at a time. 'Norris did it for revenge – he hated Gurney Lightfoot, because he knew Lightfoot had betrayed him nine years ago and got him sent to jail.' He looked at them all. 'Do you wish me to continue?'

'Not if you're in a hurry. We'd hate to detain you,' Jake said pointedly.

'I'm not in a hurry,' Eustace said. Slowly and deliberately, he took cigarettes and lighter out of his pocket, lit up and looked around the cluttered sitting room. His eye fell on the oval oak drop-leaf dining table standing against the far wall. He spoke in a deliberate way. 'Is that new, Casey? I don't think I remember your having a dining table like that.'

'It was probably covered up last time you were here,' Casey

said, with a quick glance at Richard. 'It took me a long time to refinish it. Now I've finally found the right chairs to match.'

'Last time he was here?' Jake asked, through gritted teeth.

Eustace regarded Jake with a certain degree of smugness. 'Casey and I frequently work late together. I don't believe there is a law against a woman offering to cook a meal for an unmarried male acquaintance, is there?'

'I don't know,' Jake said. 'What do you think, Armbruster?'

'I think it's time Casey got out of the publishing business,' Richard Armbruster said. He stood up, pulling Casey up beside him. 'Come on, my dear – let's leave these gentlemen to their interrogation. How about some coffee?'

'Of course, darling,' Casey said.

They went out into the kitchen. Jake started to follow them, but Joe caught hold of his sleeve and shook his head. Then he turned to Eustace. 'What proof did Norris have that Lightfoot had done away with Ariadne Finch?'

'He wasn't very specific,' Millington said with a shrug. 'Just that he had proof – I couldn't draw him out any further than that. Sorry.'

'Why didn't he come to us with this proof?' Joe asked.

Eustace smiled. 'He hated the police – would have nothing to do with them.'

'He could have gone to the newspapers,' Joe suggested.

Millington nodded. 'I agree. As a matter of fact, we were negotiating for newspaper serialization of the text – or a condensed version anyway. To be honest, I think he thought there was some kind of cachet connected to a book – that simply selling straight to the newspapers wasn't prestigious enough. He was a strange and complex man, full of bitterness and a need for what he called "justice". He said the case of Ariadne Finch's disappearance had never been explained, just "scabbed over", in his colorful phrase, and that he meant the whole wound to be opened up again before Lightfoot died. He wanted the old man to go down in shame, it seemed. An entirely vengeful aim, I am sorry to say.'

'And you were willing to be a party to that sort of thing?' Joe asked. He ignored Jake's pointed look at the kitchen.

Millington looked uncomfortable. 'Despite appearances, which I struggle to maintain, I am not personally a rich man. Most of Father's money went into the Millington Foundation

124

when he died. I got a small annuity and the family publishing business. Unfortunately, publishing is a high-risk proposition, and I seem to lack my late father's unique flair for discovering and encouraging bankable authors. It was a matter of the company changing direction or going under – as simple as that. Sordid commerce.' His tone was self-mocking. 'One must indulge, or die.'

'I see,' said Jake, who didn't. 'Why not just close down Millington Inc. as a dead loss, or sell it off and go to work for Doubleday or one of the other big boys?'

Eustace was shocked. 'The company was entrusted to me by my father.'

'Doubleday wouldn't hire you, hey?' Jake said sympathetically. 'Rough one.'

'I resent that remark,' Eustace huffed. 'I never for a moment considered working for anyone else.'

'Yeah, yeah, sorry,' Jake said in a distracted tone. There had been a burst of laughter from the kitchen. 'So how far along was this book toward coming out, then?'

'Miss Hewson had nearly completed the copyediting of the first half, I believe, but was having difficulty convincing Norris to make changes in the second half,' Eustace said. 'I did know Norris was being difficult – Casey even told me she didn't think he was serious about the project, but I told her that was just nerves. I don't know the details concerning his refusal, of course. Once contracts are signed, I leave it to my staff to carry out projects.'

'Back to the opera, hey?'

'I beg your pardon?' Eustace asked, puzzled.

Casey and Richard came back from the kitchen. Richard was bearing a tray of coffee cups, milk, sugar and the percolator.

'Casey knew what was in the original manuscript,' Jake said, the words coming out rather oddly from between his clenched teeth as he watched Richard and Casey standing close together handing out the coffee. They worked well as a team.

'Well, so did I,' Eustace said, stubbing out his cigarette. 'I did read it, you know. Just quickly, once over, before offering Norris the contract. So did two of our regular manuscript readers. Plus, presumably, the woman who typed it. Why not kill one of them? Or me?'

'Don't tempt me,' Jake muttered. 'I don't know, Mr

125

Millington,' he added in a more normal tone. 'All we know is that it was Casey who was attacked, Casey whose apartment and office were searched, Casey who has been followed all day and Casey they tried to kidnap in the supermarket. Of course, if they can't get her, they may turn to you – I don't know.'

Millington paled slightly. 'My God, you can't be serious!' His hand shook as he took his cup of coffee from Casey.

'Glad to see that possibility makes *somebody* nervous,' Jake said. 'Casey still thinks we're making all this up.'

'Well – not since the Piggy Wiggy I don't,' Casey conceded. 'But I still don't see why you have to stay right here in my apartment with ketchup in your ears.'

'I don't have ketchup in my ears,' Jake said. He looked at Joe. Joe smiled and handed him his handkerchief.

'Of course it's not necessary,' Richard said. 'Casey will come to my motel tonight. I'm quite capable of protecting her.'

'And I shall take out a large advertisement in the newspapers, saying that we no longer intend to publish the Norris book,' Eustace said. 'I shall offer to burn every copy of the manuscript and swear an oath to reveal nothing.'

Sylvester laughed. 'That should bring the big boys running,' he said.

'He's right, Eustace,' Casey said. 'The more fuss you make, the more fuss everyone else will make.'

Millington looked desperate. 'A small announcement in the trade press, then. Say it was in his will that we had to burn everything if he died.'

'Was it?' Jake asked, interested.

'Was it what?' Eustace asked.

'In his will.'

'*I* don't know what was in his will. I don't know if he had a will. I don't know anything about anything.' Millington gulped down his coffee and turned to Casey. 'The project is finished,' he said. 'We aren't publishing the Norris book, and neither is anyone else. Surely word could be gotten to Lightfoot telling him that, couldn't it? Good God, I'll write him a letter myself with my personal guarantee.' He looked at Jake. 'That should settle everything, shouldn't it?'

'It might, but I doubt it,' Jake said.

Casey was looking at Eustace with a certain air of disappointment, as if she had hoped for a slightly better show of backbone.

126

'But – what shall I be working on, then, Eustace?'

He looked at her blankly for a moment and then seemed to come to himself. 'Oh, there are several things in the pipeline, my dear. Always something to do.'

'Perhaps I could help you with all that extra Foundation work you said had been piling up. Until we find another promising manuscript, that is,' she said in a bright voice.

'I don't think you should plan on doing anything for a while,' Jake said severely. He glanced at Armbruster. 'Or on going to any motel. I want you where I can keep an eye on you.'

She set her jaw and glared at him. 'Oh, really? And who are you, exactly – God?'

'Yes. Shut up.'

'*What?*'

'Uh – Jake—' Joe said warningly.

But it was too late. Miss Casey Hewson had had enough. She went up to him and shouted into his face. 'I will do what I want when I want and with whom I want, and if it was up to me I can guarantee none of it would be with you.' She took Joe's handkerchief and held it up in front of Jake's mouth.

'Spit.'

He spat.

She rubbed the last bit of dried tomato juice from his left ear. 'You seem to have a deep inner desire to be a salad. So be it. I wish you every success with your endeavor.' She gave Joe back his handkerchief. 'Now please go somewhere else and look for your ideal radish. I am not it.'

'Now, don't be hasty,' Sylvester said. 'He means well.'

'If you want to stay alive, you'll do what I say,' Jake warned her. 'Even radishes have a right to police protection.'

Casey took a deep breath, screamed and went for him. Richard grabbed her from behind, but she managed to kick Jake on the leg before she was dragged back onto the sofa. Richard held her there, while Sylvester sat on her other side. She looked from one to the other, took a deep breath, then put her face into her hands and began to cry.

'Now look what you've done,' Joe said.

Richard and Sylvester each put an arm around Casey, jostling for elbow room on her slender shoulders. She glanced at Jake through her fingers and wailed even louder.

Jake was standing on one foot, rubbing the shin of his other leg where she'd caught him right on the bone. 'She'll be fine,' he said in a loud voice. 'Let her cry – it's good for her – just what she needs. I've been trying to get her to do that all day.' He kept his watering eyes on Millington. 'What was the name of the lawyer who sent Norris to you?'

'What's that got to do with it?' Eustace looked as if he, too, wanted to comfort Casey, but there didn't seem to be room on the sofa.

'Perhaps nothing,' Jake said. He was still rubbing his shin, lost his balance abruptly and began to lurch around the room. 'Perhaps everything.'

'I don't understand,' Eustace complained, torn between watching the sobbing girl and the hopping man.

Jake banged into the doorway of the kitchen, put his foot down and began to rub his elbow. 'Damn. Look, it's simple. You signed a contract with Norris, which he showed to a lawyer. If he had a lawyer, maybe he had a will. And if he had a will, it means he had an heir or heirs. *They* might have something to say about publication. I could consult Professor Kingsfield, but it's my understanding that contracts work both ways.'

Millington looked suddenly older. 'My God, I never thought of that,' he whispered. 'He never mentioned a wife, or relatives, or a family of any kind. I thought he was entirely alone in the world.'

'So,' Jake persisted, 'who was the lawyer? Was he in this city?'

'Oh, yes, he's very well known,' Eustace said. 'His name is Stanley Quiddick.'

NINETEEN

'What do you mean, some old guy climbed up the fire escape and she let him in?' demanded Rocky Lightfoot.

Arthur Burpee shrugged. He and Nipsy Friedlander had been dispatched to watch Casey's apartment building after the ignominious events in the Piggy Wiggy Wondermart had been reported by a dripping and downcast Fritz and Knapp. The latter now sat side by side in the corner, listening morosely and pondering their future. Rocky Lightfoot was less than delighted with them.

Burpee was reporting the subsequent night's events. If anything, he and Friedlander were more stupid than their predecessors, but they were all that Rocky had on hand at present. It seemed as if the good men were always at the dentist getting new dentures, and those with healthy teeth were chronically incompetent. 'Well?' he demanded waspishly.

'That's what happened, what can I tell you? He was like a tramp. He clumb up, he banged on the window a few times, and she lets him in, shuts the window, pulls down the blind, and that's it.'

'No, that's not it,' Rocky said. He turned to Fritz and Knapp and spoke through clenched teeth. 'Tell me again, from the beginning.'

Fritz brightened momentarily at this opportunity to show what great efforts they had made during the day to get hold of the girl. 'In the morning we're waiting outside the girl's apartment building, like you said, for her to come out so's we can grab her, but she doesn't come. About eight o'clock Chase's partner shows up, he's in there about an hour. Then they come out and they go over to the Norris place.'

Rocky sat up with a jerk that nearly sent his Chinese embroidered smoking cap over his nose. 'You didn't tell me that before!'

Fritz looked startled, then puzzled, then ashamed. 'I forgot. What with all the trouble—'

'Never mind the trouble, go on about them going to the

Norris place,' Rocky snapped. Burpee and Friedlander smirked at one another over Fritz and Knapp's obvious discomfort. This could mean their moving up in the hierarchy – this could lead to big stuff.

Fritz shifted uncomfortably in his chair – there was still a little tomato juice here and there in his underwear. 'They was only there maybe forty minutes or so. They come out, and Chase's partner, he puts a brown bag of stuff in the trunk, then he takes them to her office. They was always with her – we never got close. We didn't follow Chase's partner when he split. You told us to stay with her, so we stayed with her, like you told us.'

Rocky moaned. 'Go on, go on. They went to her office—'

'Yeah. Like I said.'

'And?'

'Annnnndddd . . . they stayed there all day. I called you, and you said—'

'To stay with her, yes, I know. Go on.'

'Well, they was in there until four o'clock, and then they come out and stand around for a minute, and then the girl, she goes into the market. At first I figure it's because we were spotted, then I figure it's because they was hungry, right?' Fritz laughed for a while. Then, getting no response, he cleared his throat. 'You know what happened next,' he finished lamely. 'We tried for her and ran into a little trouble.'

'A little trouble,' Rocky echoed. 'You call drawing the attention of four squad cars, a fire engine, an ambulance, plus two roving television reporters who happened to be in the neighborhood and got the whole thing on video tape in time for the six o'clock news "a little trouble", do you?'

'Well . . .' Fritz waggled a hand. 'On the TV they said it was a robbery attempt.'

'And I would like to know the reason Lieutenant Jake Chase told *that* little story,' Rocky muttered. He turned his attention back to Burpee. 'Go on about the tramp.'

'On the fire escape?' Burpee asked, just to be sure.

'No, the one dangling from the television aerial,' Rocky said, exasperated.

'I din' see no—' Friedlander began.

'The tramp climbed up the fire escape, like I said,' Burpee said hurriedly, with a repressive grimace at his partner. 'At first I figured he was a snitch, reporting to Chase on the quiet, like.'

He was growing unnerved by Rocky's glare.

Rocky had leaned back in his chair again and was cleaning his nails with a large paper knife. 'What *time* was this exactly?'

Burpee and Friedlander looked at one another. Friedlander shrugged and stared down at his shoes. 'Maybe about eight o'clock.'

'And what did this old man look like? Exactly?'

'Like an old man. Kind of dirty and wearing old clothes – lots of old clothes – and his hair was gray and kind of hung down from under his hat.'

Rocky looked up quickly. 'What kind of hat?'

'Just an old black hat with a big brim. You know, like gangsters wear.'

Rocky regarded the two of them. Burpee was wearing a narrow-brimmed tweed hat that barely covered the top of his large bald head, and Friedlander was wearing a knitted stocking cap with a large red bobble on the top, which his mother had made for him. 'Like gangsters wear,' he echoed faintly, as if seeking clarification.

'Yeah, like in the movies. *You* know. Like Sidney Greenstreet and them. Floppy, so's you can't see their mean little eyes.'

'Ah, yes. A gangster's hat,' Rocky nodded, with his eyes closed. 'Do you think he was a gangster, Burpee?'

'Nah, I think he was a slob,' Burpee said. 'He probably stole the hat.'

'From a gangster?'

Burpee began to feel a little uncomfortable. 'Well . . .'

'Go on.'

In some relief – because Rocky's voice sounded so odd and because Rocky was so odd and Burpee wished to hell he could talk to Gurney instead of Rocky because Rocky gave him the goddamn creeps – Burpee continued. 'And then a little later, this fag turns up.'

'Fag?' Rocky's eyes opened again. 'How do you know he was a fag?'

Friedlander looked up slyly. 'Because he had a fag's hat on?'

'Nah, he had on one of them hamburger hats,' Burpee said to Friedlander. 'Like rich guys in the movies wear. You saw him yourself, dummy.' Friedlander looked back at his shoes, and a small smile played about his mouth.

'A Homburg,' Rocky said coldly. He owned several.

'Like I said,' Burpee agreed.

'And did this elegant gentleman *also* climb up the fire escape?' Rocky asked. He sounded as if he *really* wanted to know.

'No,' Burpee said, in a wounded voice. 'He rang the bell and went in just like an ordinary person would go in. He stayed about an hour and came out to where this old limousine was waiting for him—'

'License plate?'

'Personalized. ALM 1,' Friedlander supplied eagerly. 'It was an old Heron, black, with door panels lacquered in dark red, one of the big straight-eights, with independent suspension and tubular—'

'Thank you,' Rocky interrupted, making a note of the license number. 'And when did the old man in the gangster hat come out?'

Burpee and Friedlander looked at one another again.

'He didn't,' Burpee finally said. 'When Sam and Ernie come to relieve us at midnight, he was still in there.'

TWENTY

Stanley Quiddick's office was in the Tower, a new skyscraper built four years previously, overlooking the riverfront and a vast expanse of downtown Grantham. His was a corner office on the floor retained by Quiddick, Rauscher and Trimm for themselves and their many subordinates. QRT was one of the leading firms of attorneys in the city. Rauscher and his team of junior partners specialized in commercial litigation, Trimm and his flock took the criminal cases, and Quiddick . . . kept busy.

As senior partner he took an active interest only in selected cases, primarily those of old and favored clients, such as the Westwoods, the Finches, the Bullstarkes, the Nitneys, the Rasmussens and/or their estates. Even with his client list limited to friends and favorites, his personal assistants were ever busy, coming and going, toing and froing, bustling between Stanley and his mysterious dealings in the world outside. It was accepted that Stanley had 'connections', and made use of them.

Aside from progress reports on cases in hand during partners' meetings, Rauscher and Trimm never asked Stanley how things were going – because they were always going Stanley's way. As this was often advantageous to them, they left well enough alone.

After all, the Millington Foundation retainer alone was enough to justify his participation in company profits.

It was not easy to get in to see Stanley Quiddick if you were an ordinary mortal, nor was it particularly easy if you were a police lieutenant. However, by simple persistence and, eventually, a few subdued threats, Jake managed to gain the inner sanctum. He had seen many photographs of Stanley Quiddick at public functions, so he was not surprised by the high, bald forehead, the piercing black eyes behind their gold-rimmed glasses or the unexpectedly sensuous mouth beneath the ascetic high-bridged nose.

What the photos had cleverly disguised was Mr Quiddick's stature – or lack of it. Had he not had a special chair perched on a carpeted plinth that ran behind his desk, he would have been barely visible above the gleaming expanse of mahogany, which was itself raised above floor level, thus placing Stanley Quiddick at center stage in his own office. This being the case, his glare was at eye level with the two policemen who had penetrated his domain, and above them when they were seated.

'Who?' he squeaked.

'Frederick Norris,' Jake repeated. 'I believe you sent him to a publisher named Millington with—'

'Oh, yes, I remember now. A legacy from my late partner, Miles Archer.' He gave a little laugh. 'When your partner dies you're supposed to do something about it.' He peered at Jake expectantly.

'I didn't come here to get the Maltese Falcon, Mr Quiddick,' Jake said patiently.

Stanley Quiddick leaned back in his chair, apparently gratified. 'I like games,' he said. 'Do you?'

'Is the guy nuts or what?' Joe muttered out the corner of his mouth.

'No, I am not nuts, young man – what did you say your name was, by the way?'

'His name is Luchinsky,' Jake said, stepping on Joe's foot. Quiddick could mean trouble and he didn't want Joe's name stuck anywhere in the lawyer's legendary memory for those who had offended or blocked him. 'I assume you know that Fred Norris is dead, sir. He was stabbed in the lobby of his apartment building. We're attempting to locate his attorney.'

'Your attempts have been successful – I am, or was, Mr Norris's attorney of record,' Quiddick said. He gave Joe a sharp look, then apparently dismissed him from conscious consideration and kept his eyes on Jake. 'What can I do for you, Lieutenant? The will, I suppose? That sort of thing?'

'Yes, that sort of thing. Does Norris have any family?'

Quiddick smiled. 'He has several families – take your pick.'

'Who inherits?'

'His eldest son, James Clancy, of Brooklyn, New York. He didn't much care for the other two.'

Jake consulted his notebook. 'That would be Theodore Glock and Bernard Feldman?'

Quiddick was surprised. 'Now, where did you get those names, I wonder?'

'From their birth certificates, which we found in Mr Norris's apartment. They were about *all* we found there, by the way. Mr Norris seems to have been a very peculiar man. He had a telephone but no book or list of personal numbers, he had a desk but no appointments diary or calendar, he had a book on how to type but no typewriter, he presumably had an income and bills but no checkbook and no records of expenditure.'

Quiddick smiled. 'As you say – a peculiar man.'

'Have you any suggestion as to why his life was so devoid of detail?'

'None whatsoever, unless it was because he hadn't been out of jail for many months. I have his will in my safe, of course, and one of my people will put it through for probate. Will the coroner be releasing the body for interment soon?'

'I have no idea, you'll have to ask him,' Jake said.

'Someone will do so.'

'I'd like to see the will,' Jake said.

'I'm sure you would,' Quiddick agreed.

Jake sighed. 'May I please see the will, Mr Quiddick?' When the attorney seemed to hesitate, he added, 'I can get a court order.'

Quiddick shook his head. 'You needn't bother. You may see the will if you wish. But aside from leaving everything to Clancy – an honest, hard-working carpenter who will be grateful for the money, by the way – the document contains very little of interest.'

'What money?'

'Why, Mr Norris's money, of course. He made careful investments before entering jail and resisted the temptation of tinkering with them while "away" – so when he returned, quite a fortune had been amassed for him. Mr Clancy should realize something in the order of a hundred thousand, after expenses.'

'Does he know it?'

'Absolutely not. None of the boys knew that Fred Norris was their father. Or rather, they may have known his name but nothing else. That was the condition on which maintenance was agreed with their various mothers. I gather Mr Norris was fair, in his fashion, but not sentimental. He followed their progress, of course, but from a safe distance. He told me that Glock has become a drug addict with not too many years left to live, and Feldman has become private detective with his own agency.

135

Quite a successful one, hardly in need of an inheritance, but Mr Norris disapproved of his profession and would have left him nothing whether he had been rich or poor. Mr Clancy gathers all unto his honest breast.' Quiddick smiled at them. It was not a smile designed to warm the heart – just something for his mouth to do to signal the end of the sentence.

'You say you "inherited" Fred Norris from your late partner. Didn't you know Norris yourself?'

'Not really, no. I had just the one interview with him here when he got out of jail – he dictated his will and waited for it to be typed so he could sign it. While he waited, we chatted. He said something about having written a book while in prison, so I sent him along to Eustace Millington, whom I knew to be in the market for that sort of thing.'

'And how did you know that?'

'Millington and I belong to the same clubs and occasionally meet over the bridge table. This firm also handles the legal affairs of the Millington Foundation.'

'I see. And that was the only time you had any contact with Fred Norris?'

'As I said. Just the one meeting here, when he got out of jail.'

'And you have no idea where his papers and things might be?'

'None whatsoever.'

'I see.' Jake hesitated, glanced at Joe, then stood up. 'Well, thank you for seeing us, Mr Quiddick. I know you're a busy man, and we appreciate it. We may have to be in touch again.' He took a step back, bumped into a rubber plant, apologized to it and exited. He said nothing until they were downstairs and out of the building. Then he glanced at Joe.

'It's worse than I thought,' he said.

They drove back to the Hall of Justice and parked in the underground section allotted to the Police Department. As they crossed the first-floor lobby, they met Molly Pemberton.

'Hello, Jake,' she said. 'And Joe – how are the children?'

They discussed families for a moment, and then she glanced sideways at Jake. 'I see they've arrested Mrs Corelli, Jake. Didn't I tell you she did it?'

'You did,' he agreed. He always had time for Molly, whose late husband had been the first sergeant he had worked under. The man had been simply the best cop Jake had ever known, and he'd treasured every moment of the time the older man had given him. A lot of the men felt the same way, which was why Molly was always welcome downtown or in any station in the city. 'I was nearly ready to close the case, but Stryker got there first.'

'Lieutenant Stryker is a good man,' Molly said.

Jake sighed. 'I know he is, dammit. I wish it had been somebody I hated. Would have made it easier.' He smiled down at her. 'Dropping in for coffee, are you?'

'No, no,' Molly said. 'Just paying a parking fine.'

'I'm shocked,' Jake said in mock horror.

'Lots of people get parking tickets,' Molly protested.

'I know. I'm shocked you didn't bring it to one of us to lose for you.'

Molly smiled. 'You know I wouldn't do any such thing, Jake Chase.' She glanced from one to the other. 'What are you working on now?'

'We're not really sure yet,' Jake said. 'Supposedly it's the Norris killing, but it seems to be spreading out a little.' He regarded her thoughtfully. 'You know anything about Gurney Lightfoot, Molly?'

'Oh, my – do I ever,' Molly said. 'Dan used to go on about Lightfoot for hours. He said he was a dangerous man with his own peculiar sense of honor. Why?'

'I'm not certain yet,' Jake said. 'I've got an itchy brain just now and I don't know where to scratch.'

Tears glittered briefly in Molly's eyes. She knew where Jake had gotten that phrase – it had been one of Dan's. 'Well, if I can help, just let me know.'

'I may just do that, Molly. Thanks.'

She watched them go, then went slowly out into the street. She knew she should have mentioned her problem to Jake – the real reason she'd been standing in the lobby for the past half hour, trying to make up her mind. She knew what Dan would have said – you must report suspicious circumstances. But she also knew that the official response would be guarded.

After all, lots of old ladies imagine that people are trying to break into their apartments at five in the morning. It was almost a joke, wasn't it? And five a.m. is the standard time for the insomniac's plague of squeaks and bumps to strike. Also for nightmares. But she had never slept poorly in her life, and her nightmares had ended when Dan died – for nothing could ever haunt her the way the dangers of his job had done.

Mr Braithwaite had heard the noises, too, of course, but a cat would hardly be considered a reliable or useful witness. He'd sat up on the bed, then jumped softly down and padded into the sitting room to investigate what might have been a tasty mouse but had only proved to be a shadow on the curtains.

A shadow that had disappeared when she'd turned on her bedside light. A shadow that had made definite noises going down the fire escape.

Would they believe her?

She'd looked at the window, of course. But only in the morning, after she'd laid awake for hours, then gotten up, washed and dressed and had breakfast. She'd kept putting it off, not really wanting to know how vulnerable she was.

And there was nothing there. Not a smudge or smear on the glass or frame, no indentations caused by crowbar or pocket-knife, no scratches from a glasscutter. Nothing.

There *had* been some mud on the metal grid of the fire escape platform which she had, rather self-consciously, scraped into a small plastic bag.

Could have been there for days, of course.

But she'd let Mr Braithwaite out for a bit of exercise last evening when she'd come home, and she was sure it hadn't been there then.

Well, reasonably sure.

Nearly certain.

Molly sighed. During her lunch hour she'd go along and buy the best window lock she could find, and perhaps some kind of burglar alarm. She'd meant to do something like that for years, but it was such a nice neighborhood, and she'd always hoped that the crime that haunted so much of the city would somehow miss out on Riverview.

Now it seemed its time had come, too.

There were no safe places anymore.

TWENTY-ONE

'I knew it!' Jake said triumphantly an hour later. He was crouched over the shoulder of Hal Dubrowski, one of the criminal records clerks, who was crouched in turn over the keyboard of the computer. Dubrowski wouldn't let Jake near the computer.

Not since the last time.

'Let's have that printed out,' Jake said, reaching over to punch the appropriate buttons.

Dubrowski slapped his hand. 'You want to lose me my job?' he said. 'Listen, Chase, it's not only this computer that's got a good memory. Did you know they use you over at the school as a Horrible Example?'

Jake straightened up. 'Well, that's damned ungrateful of them. If it hadn't been for me they'd have never found that particular glitz in the system.'

'It wasn't the glitz,' Dubrowski said, activating the printout. 'It was the way you found it. There are still two people working full time just to relocate and input those lost files.'

'There you are – I'm a boon to job creation,' Jake said. 'It's all in your point of view.'

'Well,' Dubrowski said, rolling his wheelchair over to the printer, which had begun to chatter, 'all I know is, I'm not to let you near *anything* in here. Sit down. *NOT THERE!*'

Jake looked down. 'Stupid place to put a floppy disk,' he muttered. Dubrowski had wheeled over with quite a turn of speed. He snatched up the disk, glared at Jake and took it over to his desk, where he put it into a drawer and locked it.

'You're so cute when you're mad,' Jake said.

'See?' Jake flipped the pages and pointed to the relevant portion of the printout. 'It's there in black and white. Interviewee – Charles Edward Porter. That's the connection.'

Joe leaned back in his chair. 'I'm slow, Jake. Explain me already.'

Jake sat down on the corner of the desk, catching the ashtray before it hit the linoleum and shoving it back next to the telephone. 'That is the computer file on the Ariadne Finch case. Still an open file, you notice, on deposit downstairs. I had Dubrowski pull this because I just couldn't figure why somebody as important as Quiddick would even say *hello* to a guy like Norris, much less write his will for him or admit any connection with him to somebody like Millington. There had to be some pressure from somewhere – and there it is. Porter.'

'The ex-mayor?'

Something seemed to be buzzing in Jake's ear. He put a finger in and shook it around, then went on. 'Oh, come on, Joe, you know Quiddick is Porter's man, for crying out loud. And you know that Porter and Lightfoot have been deadly enemies for donkey's years. I don't know why – but they hate each other's guts.' He banged the side of his head gently to dislodge the buzz from his ear. 'Damn.'

'You what?'

Jake sighed. 'Porter hates Lightfoot and vice versa. Porter is retired from politics, but his son Tony is chief city planner now, and I hear he's a holy terror, a real crusading fire-eater, out to build a New Tomorrow. As part of his plans to revitalize the entire city and probably the universe after that, young Tony Porter is doing his damnedest to tear down Gurney Lightfoot's headquarters on Federal Street. Today the building, tomorrow the organization – and I'll bet Charley Porter is behind his son all the way,' Jake said. 'Are you with me so far?' His gaze wandered away from his partner as he seemed to search the room for something.

'Yeah, I think so,' Joe said. He couldn't figure out what Jake was looking for, and started his own survey of the room while Jake continued his explanation.

'Lightfoot's boy is set to take over *his* kingdom, too. And Rocky – well, little Rocky is Gurney Lightfoot all over again, but *without* the laughs.' Jake turned his head sharply, a puzzled look on his face. Where the hell was that buzz coming from?

'OK, OK, I'm with you now,' Joe said. 'The feud goes on, Grandfather Red Ned Porter hates Grandfather Digger Lightfoot, Father Charley Porter hates Father Gurney Lightfoot, and Son Tony hates Son Rocky. Or, at least, I suppose he does?'

'He might. They went to the same school – dear old

140

Grantham Old School, where money gets you everything except an education. I don't know what their relationship was there but I can't imagine they moved in the same circles. Rocky was a wild kid. Tony was probably class president. That school has had its share of saints and sinners, believe me.'

'So – how does this all tie up, then?' Joe asked.

'Well, the way I see it, Porter was probably behind Norris and his book. I don't know whether he actually made him write it or not, but he sure as hell sicced him onto Lightfoot. Look, Casey said that when Norris talked about why he'd written the book, the lines "didn't ring true" – like he'd *memorized* them, right? So maybe somebody gave him those lines – somebody like Porter, by way of Quiddick. She also said he went on and on about the money side of the book – but he *had* plenty of money. So I reckon the whole book thing was planned by Porter.'

'Why would Norris work for Porter?'

Jake shrugged. 'Either he was blackmailed into it, or he was paying off a favor – or he really hated Gurney Lightfoot. I reckon mostly it was hate, and Porter picked up on it. Remember, it was one of Quiddick's partners who messed up the Norris defense and got him sent to the slammer. Maybe it goes back as far as that. Porter is supposed to be quite a chess player – maybe he moved Norris off to one side as a pawn-in-waiting or something. Whatever it was, Porter couldn't be connected, so he had Quiddick handle it – as usual – and somehow Quiddick got Millington to agree to publish it. Maybe Millington owed him a favor, too. The guy has lines out all over the city – a real little spider is our Stanley Quiddick.'

'But what harm could it do Gurney Lightfoot to be charged with murder? He hasn't got much more than a year to live anyway, and it would take that long for the thing to even get to pretrial arraignment, what with new investigations and—'

'Not Gurney Lightfoot, dummy – Rocky Lightfoot. While I was tossing and turning last night, it came to me that maybe it was little *Rocky* who knocked off Mrs Finch, not dear old Dad.' He was still looking around the room as he spoke, trying to locate the source of that irritating buzz.

'But he would only have been about seventeen then.'

Jake nodded. 'All the best ones start young,' he said.

'But I've read the damn manuscript now,' Joe protested. 'It

doesn't say a thing about Rocky. Norris claims Gurney himself did the killing.'

'Maybe that's what he thought,' Jake said. 'But my bet is he's wrong. Gurney knows the truth. Gurney is protecting his *son*, not himself. And when Gurney Lightfoot decides to do something, he does it with all the brakes off. Do you remember the bomb he put into—' He stopped suddenly, a terrible suspicion washing over him like ice water. 'Oh, shit!' He jumped off the desk and looked around wildly. 'Bomb, *BOMB!*' he shouted, diving for cover.

Everybody jumped up and started to yell, 'Bomb!'

Papers flew high, chairs scraped back, and there was a scuffle as people jammed in the doorway of the detective squad room.

Joe started to get up, then stopped, reached forward and replaced the phone receiver that Jake had knocked off the hook when replacing the ashtray a few minutes before. The buzzing stopped.

'False alarm,' Joe called in a bored voice.

There was a moment of silence, then the grumbling and muttering began as the other on-duty detectives filtered back into the room. 'Hey, Jake! Count to ten and take a deep breath next time, for God's sake!' Pinsky shouted.

'Even better, take a running jump,' Neilson suggested sourly as he limped back to his desk and began to gather up his notes on the Corelli case. He'd twisted his ankle getting out of his chair, and had a date to go to a disco that night. Jack Stryker, leaning against the doorpost of the corner office, was laughing too hard to say anything.

Jake stood up and brushed himself off. 'The point is,' he said to Joe, ignoring the catcalls, 'Gurney Lightfoot wouldn't waste time, energy or manpower on a lost cause. No, it's *got* to be his son he's protecting, he doesn't care about anything else.'

Jake picked up a couple of papers that had flown past him from Neilson's desk and started to hand them back. Then he froze for a moment, staring at one. 'Hell's teeth,' he said.

Neilson looked up and reached out for the papers. 'What is it?' he asked, looking at them. One was a quote from a company for putting a new kitchen in his apartment, the other was a memo from the coroner's office about the Corelli interment. 'This is nothing,' Neilson said. 'What the hell?'

'From the desk of,' Jake said, pointing to the memo from the coroner's office. 'From the desk of.'

Neilson and Joe exchanged a glance. 'Sit down, Jake,' Joe said. 'You didn't sleep good last night.'

Jake ignored them and reached for the phone that had so recently betrayed his trust. He called a number, identified himself and asked for the supervisor. Neilson and Joe leaned back in their respective chairs, watching him.

'Yes, good morning, Mrs Hrmmrsmmm, I hope you can help me. I want to know if you have a telephone listed in the name of Norris, Frederick.' He waited. 'Yes, we have that one. Is there another, by any chance? Perhaps an unlisted number?' Jake listened, and then a smile lit his face. 'Thank you. And can you give me an address, please?' He grabbed a pen from Joe's desk, sending the ashtray flying again. There was a crash of glass from beyond the desk as Jake scribbled on the corner of the nearest piece of paper. 'Thanks. Thanks very much.' He hung up the phone. 'Hey, Joe—' He looked around. 'Joe?'

Joe emerged from beneath the desk, shards of ashtray and cigarette butts cupped in his hands. He leaned over the wastebasket and dropped them in with a clatter. 'Yes?' he answered in a dangerously quiet voice.

'Norris had no papers in his apartment because he kept them all at his office,' Jake said triumphantly.

'What office?' Joe asked dutifully.

'Don't you remember that set of keys we found in his place? His office – number four-seven-four in the Burnley Building.'

Joe had leaned forward. 'What is this, Jake?' He was pointing at the paper on which Jake had scribbled the address. His voice rose to an outraged crescendo. 'What is this you've written indelibly and forever on the front of the expensive anniversary card I spent an hour looking for to give to Becky tonight?'

'It's Norris's office number – four-seven-four. Like on the key,' Jake said in an apologetic voice.

'Hey, Kaminsky,' Neilson said, leaning toward Joe's desk. 'Do us all a favor. Shoot this guy in the ass and make them put him out to pasture. He's a public danger.'

Joe sighed. 'I can't kill him – he still owes me fifty bucks for the barbecue he blew up in my garden last July.'

'It was only twenty-five you said,' Jake protested.

Joe glared at him. 'I decided to charge interest.'

'Do you think Jake Chase is an honest cop?' Casey asked Sylvester.

'Honest? Oh, yes, he's straight all right,' Sylvester said, looking out the window for the two hundredth time that morning. 'He's a good *man*, and he has good *instincts*, but he's a little crazy. Also, he has a problem.'

'I know – Joe told me. He falls over things,' Casey said.

Sylvester turned and raised an eyebrow. 'So do you,' he said pointedly. 'I still have the bruises.'

'Not the same,' Casey protested, smiling.

'Uh-huh. What time did you say the police were coming?'

'They *said* right away.' Casey got up and joined him at the window. He glanced sideways at her. She had shadows under her eyes and was very pale.

'You OK?'

'No. Both of you snore. I hardly slept at all.'

'Nice to know somebody was watching over us,' Sylvester said dryly. He knew he didn't look well himself. Drying out had been a more than sobering experience, and the triple effort of thinking intelligently, acting reasonably and speaking coherently was beginning to wear him down. He hadn't had to behave like a grown-up human being for some years. The pain it was producing within his body and soul was simply a reminder of why he had abandoned it in the first place. Nevertheless he was determined to continue the attempt. Somewhere within were vague memories that tugged at him, indications that being an adult had had its compensations once and might again.

He could not at the moment catch firm hold of these memories, but he had a kind of blind faith that they would eventually surface. Meanwhile, he had an assignment.

Watch the girl.

Joe had left with his wife about ten thirty the previous evening. Eustace and Richard Armbruster had tried to last the distance, but eventually had given in and left.

Jake and Sylvester had spent the night in the apartment, 'guarding' Casey – much to her annoyance. This activity seemed to consist mostly of glaring at one another, dozing off, snoring,

144

waking up, walking around, opening the bedroom door and checking to see if she was still there and all right, looking out the window, making toast and coffee, more glares, more snores and so on. All night long.

'There they are,' Casey said suddenly. Below the window the white top of a police car pulled into the curb.

'They certainly took their time,' Sylvester grumbled. 'Jake said they'd be here within ten minutes after he had to leave.'

'Maybe they had another call,' Casey said.

'Yeah – and maybe they stopped for a second breakfast or a doughnut break on the way,' Sylvester grumbled as he watched the caps of the two uniformed officers disappear below them as they entered the apartment building. 'You let me answer the door.'

'Oh, for heaven's sake,' Casey muttered, but went into the kitchen and began washing up the frying pan. She heard Sylvester answer the door and demand to see identification. There was a low-voiced exchange, and a moment later one of the officers appeared in the kitchen door.

'Ma'am?'

She turned. 'Yes?'

'The lieutenant, he says he wants we should take you downtown to see his captain,' the uniformed officer said. 'Right away, he said.'

'Oh. Did he say why?'

'Something about identifying somebody, ma'am.'

'Oh – very well.' She dried her hands and came out into the sitting room. 'Where's Mr Crump?'

'He went down already with my partner. You want to take a handbag or a coat or anything, ma'am? It's kind of chilly out.' He was a large man, and his hat and uniform seemed rather tight. Maybe Sylvester was right about the doughnuts.

'Thanks – maybe I will at that.' Casey went into the bedroom.

The officer looked around the apartment with some bewilderment. It was not the kind of decor he was accustomed to – not one piece of furniture matched another, and—

There was the sound of a window opening.

Moving quickly into the bedroom, he found Casey halfway out onto the fire escape. 'Hey!' he shouted, going for her.

Casey shrieked and tried to scramble over the sill onto the metal rungs of the balcony, but the man was large and too strong for her. Slowly, inexorably, he dragged her back into the bedroom. When he had her, he locked her arm behind her and tried to frog-march her out, but she kicked and struggled, escaping him once, only to be thrown down again.

'What gimme away?' he panted into her face. 'Hey?'

'Brown shoes,' Casey gasped. His massive weight was bearing down on her chest. As he twisted around to verify her observation, she wriggled out from under him and was nearly on her feet when he grabbed an ankle and held it. Wildly, Casey shrieked for help and tried to grab furniture to help herself, but though she reduced several chairs to splinters, she could not escape the big man whose face was vaguely familiar, and eventually she was brought to her knees. Literally.

Fritz, for it was he in a 'borrowed' uniform, grinned down at her. 'I got cleaned up,' he said.

'Oh, no,' Casey moaned. She recognized him now. In the melee of the Piggy Wiggy Wondermart she'd only had a quick glimpse of his face under a different hat, and then he had become covered in flour. Why hadn't she noticed the shoes more quickly? It had only been when she was in the bedroom and caught sight of him in the mirror over her dressing table that she had seen he was wearing nonregulation shoes with his uniform. The window had been the only way out – and she'd taken it too late.

Fritz was pleased with having his second chance. 'He was gonna send Burpee, but Burpee had a dentist appointment, so he sent me. And Knapp. Let's go.' He pulled her to her feet, not ungently in the circumstances. He got her through the door, despite her trying to brace her feet on either side of the frame, and they started down the hall.

Mrs Agnes Rooney, who had the next apartment and had heard all the yelling and crashing, was standing in her doorway.

'Help, Mrs Rooney!' Casey shouted as they passed her. 'I'm being kidnapped! Call the police! Call the FBI!'

'She's under arrest,' Fritz improvised sweatily. 'For suspicion.' He specified no further because he couldn't think of anything, but instead gave Mrs Rooney a big reassuring grin. There was one thing about Fritz – he had a good grin. All his own teeth, and no fillings.

Mrs Rooney regarded them sourly. 'I'm not surprised,' she commented. 'Showers in the middle of the night, men in and out at all hours. I had *my* suspicions all right.'

'You don't understand, Mrs Rooney! Call Jake Chase – Lieutenant Jake Chase, the police depart—' Casey's desperate voice faded as she and Fritz started down the stairs. Then it stopped altogether as he put his hand over her mouth.

Mrs Rooney sniffed. 'I understand all right, young lady,' she said, and slammed her door good and tight behind her as she returned to the peace and quiet of her own tidy apartment and the strange and gripping symptoms of the newest patient in *General Hospital*.

TWENTY-TWO

'Can you get together some social background for us on Ariadne Finch?' Joe asked Molly Pemberton. He had gone around to the library while Jake was still reading through the old reports on the Finch case.

'Who?' Molly was startled. She had been thinking about where to go to buy her window locks and whether she could get Mr Niforos to put them on for her before tonight.

'Ariadne Finch – she was a society dame who disappeared about ten years ago. We've got all the case files, but what we need is newspaper stuff, gossip, you know.' He checked his notebook. 'Presumed date of death November 29 1977, date of birth October 12 1930. Maiden name, Ariadne—'

'Gossart. I remember,' Molly said. 'Dan was in on some of that, I know. Very frustrating case – they found signs of a struggle but no body. Never did find a body, as I recall.'

'That's right – so the case is still open.'

She nodded knowingly. 'I remember Dan saying there was a lot to the Finch case that never came out – and that Gurney Lightfoot was mixed up in it, but they could never prove it. He's mixed up in the Norris killing, too, isn't he?'

Joe raised an eyebrow. 'What makes you say that?'

'Well, it was common knowledge that Fred Norris was working for Lightfoot when he was arrested on that extortion charge some years ago. Dan told me at the time that Lightfoot pulled the plug on Norris and let him go down the drain. Norris was really bitter, but he kept his mouth shut and took his sentence.'

'Well, he wasn't keeping it shut anymore,' Joe whispered.

Molly leaned forward over her desk, glancing around to make certain nobody was near enough to overhear them. 'Tell me,' she whispered. 'You know *I* can keep my mouth shut.'

'Norris wrote a book, telling all about Lightfoot's involvement in the Finch case. It was going to be published.'

'No!' Molly sat back and looked at Joe for a moment. 'I bet that's why Lightfoot framed him – because he knew too much about what happened to Ariadne Finch.'

'Maybe. Although, if that had been the case, Norris would have probably offered what he knew to the DA at the time in some kind of plea bargain.'

'That's true enough,' Molly agreed. 'Maybe he found out something while he was in jail?'

Joe nodded. 'That's what Jake thinks – although we don't know what it is yet. Maybe somebody arranged it, knowing how Norris felt about Lightfoot.'

'Are you serious? Who?'

'Somebody who didn't like Lightfoot.'

'That's a long list.'

'Somebody with clout.'

'Ahhhh – our esteemed ex-mayor, Mr Charley Porter?'

'Norris's lawyer was a late partner of Stanley Quiddick, that's all I can say.'

'That's saying it all, Joe,' Molly nodded. 'This is really fascinating. Who was going to publish the book?'

'Millingtons.'

Molly sat back in surprise. 'That's not the usual Millington type of thing.'

'Needed the money, apparently.'

Molly looked puzzled at that, then shrugged. 'I guess times change,' she said. 'Are they still going to publish it?'

'I don't know. The killing seems to have thrown a scare into dear old Eustace. He says he won't publish, but with all the publicity about the murder – well, I don't think he'll be able to resist the temptation, myself. Once she gets it cleaned up, that is.'

'Who?'

'A girl named Casey Hewson. She's a Millington editor and she'd been working on the manuscript with Norris to make sure nobody can sue them for libel if they do publish. Somebody tried to steal the manuscript from her the other night.'

'Really?' Molly was interested. 'You know, Joe, I could swear somebody tried to break into *my* place the other night, but the next morning—'

A shadow fell over Molly's desk and they looked up. A sweet little old lady stood there, beaming at them. 'I wonder if you have *The Midnight Slasher Strikes Again* by Scarlett Gore? It's her latest, but I can't find it on the shelf.'

'It's on the reserved list,' Molly said, standing up. 'Are you certain it's what you want? It's very . . . violent.'

'Of course I'm sure I want it,' the little old lady said self-righteously. 'I've read all her stuff: *Bonecrusher*, *The Bloody Bludgeon*, *The Disemboweled Debutante* – just everything. She really calls the shots, you know?'

'I know, I know,' Molly said tonelessly. She turned to Joe. 'I'll drop by with whatever I can find later on.'

'Right, Mrs Pemberton. Thanks.' As he left, he heard Molly enlightening the old lady further.

'Scarlett Gore writes under another name, you know.'

The little old lady was thrilled. 'No, *really*? Do tell me.'

'She's also Thistle Windrush, author of *Moonlight Magic*, *The Gossamer Glade*, *Love's Lacy Wings* and *Be Still My Trembling Heart*.'

'No shit?' said the little old lady.

When Joe got back to the office, Jake was just replacing the phone. 'No answer at Casey's apartment,' he said. 'And she's not at the office either.'

'Probably halfway between the two,' Joe said, glancing at the clock. 'Or maybe they stopped for lunch on the way. It's about that time,' he pointed out, and added a small, meaningful belch for emphasis. 'You remember what lunch is, don't you?'

'Yeah,' Jake said, but made no move to get up. He looked down at the Finch case printout. 'She was some dame.'

'The presumably late Ariadne Finch?'

Jake nodded. 'Finch himself was a rich but sickly widower. He was content to have her as an ornament and gave her a free hand and a private entrance and obligingly spent most of his time accumulating yet more money for her to spend. Then he ends up outliving her. According to this, he died a few years after she disappeared.'

'Guilt?'

Jake shook his head. 'No, he had an airtight alibi, and besides, by all accounts he was absolutely nuts about her.'

Joe was leafing through the case reports. 'How many guys did they pull in for questioning when Mrs Finch disappeared?'

Jake forced his attention back. 'About a dozen. Mrs Finch had a suite of rooms overlooking the pool at the back of the house, well away from the servants' quarters – and there was a small gate in the wall through which her various visitors could enter without being seen. I gather there was quite a well-beaten path from the gate to the spiral staircase that led up to her bedroom. Different man every month, according to her personal maid – sometimes more than one, although never more than one at a time.'

'Of course not. A lady of dignity,' Joe said sarcastically.

'A woman of healthy appetite, according to her loving husband. An appetite he couldn't satisfy – although by all accounts he'd given it the old college try at the beginning. Had a heart attack in her bed, and his doctor said that was the end of his sex life or the end of his life – he could take his pick. He was sixty-three – he chose to go on making money. That was when they put in the spiral staircase. Again, according to the maid, the lady couldn't sleep unless she'd had an "adventure" – presumably why most of them only lasted a month or so. She'd been fond of Finch and went on being fond of him, I gather.'

'You're kidding.'

'Nope. I asked a few of the women here, and they agreed with me. They said if she had this terrific sex drive, and didn't want to risk getting emotionally involved with anyone else, then she might just have kept herself sort of locked up inside and just satisfied her body. It's a kind of fidelity, they said. The kind prostitutes sometimes have for their pimps. One is "love", the other is "business". In Ariadne's case it was a psychosexual need rather than a monetary one, but the theory is the same. What do you think?'

'I still think it's nuts.' Joe had standards. He wasn't going to give Ariadne Finch the benefit of any doubts.

Jake shrugged. 'Whatever. The fact is, she favored certain types. Men of power. Not necessarily physical power – but the ones who were a little . . . dangerous. Like Gurney Lightfoot.'

'Sounds like she needed a hefty dose of barbiturates and a good psychiatrist,' Joe said.

Jake raised an eyebrow. 'Why?'

'Well, I mean, all that—'

'According to our tame psychiatrist she'd made a "good adjustment" to her particular problem. He says she sounds like a manic-depressive personality, which can sometimes take the form of obsessive sexual desire. Particularly in a beautiful woman who is growing older and hates it. She was rich, her husband understood and looked the other way, and there was no lack of partners – even at forty-seven she was still a real beauty apparently.'

'And totally immoral.'

'Amoral. Without any morals, good or bad. About this aspect of her life anyway. According to her husband, she didn't think it was right *or* wrong, it was just a physical craving and she got on with it and had a good time.'

'I think that's terrible.'

'The hell you do – you think it would be great.'

'No, I don't – really,' Joe said seriously. 'At the very least it was unemotional lust. At the worst it was damn risky. She could have caught VD, she could have got—'

'Killed?'

'Exactly.'

Jake shrugged. 'Women are allowed a little lust, you know, Joe. It's the New World, it's Liberation.'

'It's crap,' Joe said firmly.

Jake looked at him with a little wonder in his eyes. 'You know, Joe, I don't think I've ever seen this side of you before. A Catholic Father Speaks. Nothing to do with your three daughters, is it?'

'Probably.' Joe had the grace to grin. 'First little snot-nose twerp gets out of line with them, I bust his chops.'

'Well, Ariadne made her own choices. Among them, such rough diamonds as Gurney Lightfoot, a trumpeter named Sugarmouth Thompson, a boxer named Gorgo and a Teamsters organizer named Hooley. She also bestowed her favors on a professor of business studies, a high-school gym teacher, a jockey, an insurance broker and – get this – Charles Edward Porter.'

'That's quite a mixture.'

'Not when you check out their pictures. All attractive men in their own way. Even Lightfoot had a certain snaky charm before he got sick. Presumably variety was the spice of her life. During the year before she disappeared she slept with both Lightfoot and Porter.'

'You think that's why they hate each other?'

Jake shook his head. 'From what I can gather from old-timers around here, their feud goes way back, long before Ariadne

152

Finch decided to launch her all-comers indoor events.'

'You listed Porter last. Was he there the night she was killed?'

'No. He had an alibi – he was playing chess with Stanley Quiddick.'

Joe raised an eyebrow. 'Oh, really? How convenient. And Lightfoot?'

'Out of town – alibi verified by California police.' He checked his notes. 'The maid says a jockey was due, but he canceled – he was in a race the next day. So much for life in the saddle, I guess.'

'Just the same old round – horse to whores to horse?'

'Yeah. Anyway, it was the maid's night off, and when she left, Ariadne was on the phone. When she came back, she could hear a man's voice in her mistress's bedroom, so she didn't knock or anything – just went on to bed. When she went to wake Ariadne the next morning, she wasn't in her room. The place had been turned upside-down, but there were no clothes missing other than the negligee she had been wearing the night before.'

'Well, if nobody else has solved the Finch case in the past ten years, what makes you think Norris had the answer?'

Jake smiled. 'Ariadne had two books beside her bed, bound in red leather, tooled in gold. One was an address book and the other was a diary. According to the maid, both were there when she left that night, and both were missing the next morning.'

'And according to you?'

'Two years after her mistress disappeared, the maid retired to Florida,' Jake said. 'Bought a nice little condo near the beach, apparently. The maid knew Norris – it was him she'd gone out with that night. The condo cost twenty thousand. What do *you* think happened to the diary and address book, Joe?'

When Fritz had wrestled Casey down the stairs and out into the street, he shoved her unceremoniously into the back seat of the squad car at the curb. Sylvester was already in the back seat, next to Knapp, who had a gun pointed at his stomach. The old man had his hands held unnaturally high, and looked at Casey with a sad, defeated expression on his face.

'Sorry, my dear – I should have done something constructive to protect you.'

'Nonsense,' Casey said, with more assurance than she felt. 'A gun is a gun.'

'Is a gun – as Gertrude Stein would say.' Sylvester nodded. He glanced at Knapp, who stared back. 'Fond of poetry, are you?' he asked.

'Pull into that alley there,' Knapp said to Fritz, who was driving.

'Nobody appreciates the finer things anymore,' Sylvester said sadly, and looked out the window. Fritz pulled into an alley and from that into another, which was just a dark notch between two buildings.

'Cover the girl,' Knapp said to Fritz, when the latter had turned off the engine. He put his own gun away, and produced a handkerchief. He folded it carefully, then reached for Sylvester in order to blindfold him.

Sylvester brought his raised arms down swiftly, his hands locked together, and hit Knapp on the top of the head. 'Run, Casey – run!' he shouted. But she tried to help – and that was a mistake.

Fritz swiveled in the front seat and grabbed for Sylvester. Casey grabbed the stunned Knapp, only to discover that he wasn't as stunned as all that. He grabbed back – and so she turned to open the door next to her and discovered the reason for the stop in this particular alley. It was so narrow that none of the doors would open.

Sylvester was struggling manfully, but he was no match for the other two men, and the entire episode was brought to a sudden and terrible stop with the descent of the billy club that came with the borrowed uniform. Fritz brought it down hard on the old man's head.

The sound reminded Casey of the sound the melons in the supermarket had made when they fell. And split.

'Sylvester!' she screamed, and began to pound Knapp on the back. She kicked, she scratched, she howled, she sobbed.

But it was no good.

No good at all.

This time they had her.

TWENTY-THREE

'What do we have on young Rocky, anyway?' Jake asked.

He was restless, edgy. They were waiting for a search warrant on Suite 474 of the Burnley Building. Most of the other detectives were out to lunch – all except two, sitting on the far side of the room, finishing up some paperwork.

Joe consulted the latest information. 'Well, you were right about the trouble when he was going to Grantham Old School. Three arrests – one attempted rape while under the influence, charges dropped; one for destruction of private property, charges dropped; another attempted rape, charges dropped. Just before he went off to college there was another bit of trouble – a drug bust at some girl's Sweet Sixteen party.'

'Charges dropped?'

'Charges dropped.'

Jake sighed. 'What it is to have a father with a handy checkbook and a few big mean guys on the payroll. Anything else?'

'Not since he came back from college. You want me to wire for anything that might have happened while he was away?'

'Yeah, I think so. Just to get the whole picture.' Jake leaned precariously back in his chair. The two detectives across the room looked over and, putting aside their boring paperwork, sat back and decided to wait for the inevitable crash. Joe, too, was nervously watching the legs of Jake's chair on the linoleum. Two or three more degrees off the perpendicular and down he'd go.

'Tell me, does it give ages on that sheet? Ages of the women concerned in those two attempted rapes?' Jake asked as he teetered back and forth.

Joe reluctantly took his eyes from Jake's chair and looked again at the list of charges. 'The first was a kid, about fourteen to his fifteen, the second was a neighbour's wife, about thirty.'

Jake brought the chair back down. 'Ha – you see? Getting older all the time.'

The other detectives looked disappointed at Jake's safe return to the vertical, and Joe grinned in relief.

Jake went on. 'I mean, have you ever seen Rocky Lightfoot? He's not good-looking. Skinny, like a kid. And then he *was* a kid. The kind older women want to mother, you know? Maybe that was it. Maybe she wanted to mother him, and he wanted to lay her. Conflict of interests. Although she doesn't sound the type who'd ask to see a driver's license.' Jake's chair went back again as he considered various possibilities, and the two detectives across the room exchanged a glance. One held up two fingers, and the other nodded. There was a minute of silence, during which Jake began to hum to himself, rocking back and forth, and the two detectives began to smile again in anticipation.

'Hey, wait a minute!' Joe said suddenly. He'd been reading on through Rocky's file. Jake's chair came forward safely with a thump, and the two detectives looked disgusted. 'The party girl, the place where he and some others got busted for possession of pot – the girl's name was Finch, Jake! Kathy Finch! She was Ariadne's stepdaughter!'

'No kidding! Let me see that!' Jake reached over and grabbed the file from his partner. 'And the address is the same, too. Maybe that's the connection. What's the date on it? Nearly a year before the murder. Maybe that's why nobody made the connection at the time. Rocky had just turned seventeen, and he was still a few weeks short of eighteen when Ariadne Finch disappeared. Still a juvie. But he must have met her then – at that party – when there was all that trouble.' He leaned back in his chair again, at an even more precarious angle than before, tapping his chin with the case file and looking reflective. One of the detectives across the room held up five fingers, and the other shook his head. The tension was obviously getting to him. They settled on three, as Jake continued to rock and think. 'But there was no mention of a daughter during the investigation of her stepmother's disappearance a year later. None at all. What the hell happened to her? We'd better check that out.'

'Right.' Joe was making notes.

'And that stuff Mrs Pemberton was gathering, we'd better ask her to hoik out anything on this mysterious stepdaughter, too. So maybe little Rocky wasn't *boffing* Ariadne – she did seem to favor older men, after all. Maybe he was boffing the daughter, and Ariadne objected. Or maybe he killed Ariadne for some other reason – something connected with what happened at the daughter's party maybe, or the girl herself.'

'If he killed her at all,' Joe said pointedly.

Jake shrugged. 'It's just a theory, Joe. But nothing has knocked it out so far, has it?'

'No,' Joe agreed reluctantly. The phone rang and he answered it. While he was talking, Jake reached over to use Neilson's telephone (causing considerable excitement on the far side of the room as his chair tilted sideways as well as backward). He and Joe hung up almost simultaneously, but Joe spoke first. 'The warrant's ready – we can pick it up on the way out.'

'Right. Great.' Jake straightened up abruptly, brought his chair back down on all four legs, stood up, grabbed his jacket and made for the door. Joe followed. Across the room, the two detectives stared after them glumly. One held out his hand to the other for his three bucks.

Out in the hall Jake turned to Joe and started to speak when there was a loud crash from within the office. Joe, in the doorway, looked back, then joined Jake.

'What was that?' Jake asked.

'McNally fell out of his chair,' Joe told him.

Molly Pemberton found the locks she wanted at the third shop she tried. As it was quite close to her apartment building, and she had the time, she caught a cab back and asked him to wait while she took the locks down to Mr Niforos.

Victor Niforos answered her knock on his door with some difficulty, as he was covered in filth up to his elbows, and faced her with a combination of pleasure, embarrassment and shock. 'Mizz Pemberton – is something wrong?'

'Not really, Mr Niforos. I just dashed back on my lunch hour to ask if you could do me a favor.'

'Of course,' he said. 'What you want?'

'You're so kind,' Molly said. 'I hate to impose, but do you think you could put these locks on my windows before tonight – especially the one that opens onto the fire escape?'

Gingerly, he took the brown paper bag in his grimy hands and peered inside. 'These good locks,' he said approvingly. 'Sure, I do. You afraid of burglars?'

'Well, yes, as a matter of fact, I am. I thought somebody was trying to break into my apartment the other night. It was probably nothing, but I was very frightened.'

He looked hurt. 'You should have call me!' he said. 'I come right away, don't you worry.'

'I didn't like to wake you – and there was nothing there in the morning. I expect it was my imagination, but I'll feel safer with these locks on the windows. I suppose you think I'm silly.'

'No, never, not you,' he said. 'I never think that. You come in for coffee?'

'Oh, thank you, I'd love to, but I asked the taxi to wait – I have to be back at the library. Maybe next time?'

'Sure, sure.' He beamed at her.

'Well, thank you.' She started back up the steps to the upper hall, then turned. 'How is the table coming?'

'Oh, is fine. That is what all this is,' he said, indicating the stains and sticky mess on his hands. 'I strip back to the wood, start fresh, make right this time. Slow work, I hope you don't mind to wait.'

'Of course not – especially since I keep coming down with other things for you to do – I can hardly complain, can I?' she laughed.

He watched her go up the stairs and heard her run down the hall to the front door, which thumped shut gently behind her. Such a nice lady. His heart swelled with anger that she should have been frightened in *his* building. He would put these locks on as soon as he cleaned up. The desk had to dry anyway before he started treating the abused wood, but already the glow of it was a pleasure to behold.

Like the lady herself.

Smiling with purpose and dedication, Mr Niforos closed his door. After a while he began to sing, his voice rising to fill his basement apartment with its resonance.

Which is probably why he didn't hear the other steps in the upper hall, or the second closing of the front door.

The Burnley Building was one of the older structures on the west side of the downtown area. Built in the 'thirties it had an abundance of decorative motifs without and marble within. Fat pink-and-black-veined marble pillars marched through the lobby, and brass-framed store windows surrounded it, looking inward. Drugstore, cafeteria, shoe repairs, dry cleaners – every small necessity catered for. An office worker need never leave the building during the lunch hour to fulfill those annoying little errands.

Jake preferred this old, cozy way. A cigar stand where a girl knew your name and kept your newspaper for you every morning, an elevator operator who smiled at you, a barber who could give you a shave on those occasional mornings when your hand wasn't too steady, and where you could hide under a hot towel to avoid bill collectors and ex-wives. He expected to see William Powell or Alan Ladd appear in a snap-brim any minute.

Strangely enough, the Burnley Building seemed to have survived the onslaughts of time with dignity. True, the brass was wearing a little thin here and there, but somebody was looking after it right. He didn't blame Fred Norris for choosing it – he would have, too.

The name listed for 474 was Kickback Inc.

'Very nice, Fred,' Jake murmured. 'Very appropriate.'

There was no elevator operator, and Jake felt a fleeting sense of disappointment. He'd wanted an old man in a brown uniform sitting on one of those round drop-down seats and ready to turn the handle of the control, to lift them up and align the floors and open the doors and call the numbers. An old man with bright eyes, ready to talk.

But there was only a panel of buttons.

He pushed number 4 and the doors closed.

No. 474 consisted of an empty outer office, a washroom and a very cluttered inner office. The desk was stacked with papers, as were the two chairs, and there was a four-drawer filing cabinet in one corner. 'I give up, already,' Jake said, looking around. 'It will take us hours to go through all this.'

Joe grunted his acknowledgment of this observation. They took off their coats to begin the search. The filing cabinet was empty, save for a bottle of bourbon in the top drawer. On the desk were all the things they'd not found at his apartment. The foundations of the book – the first jumbled notes, then a rough draft of the manuscript, heavily annotated, and a second draft, rough but clean. They found personal letters, business letters, bank statements and so on.

But nothing that looked like a diary.

It was only when Joe got desperate and began looking at the backs of the pictures on the wall that the reason for Norris taking this particular office in this particular building was revealed.

It had a safe.

'Oh, swell,' Jake said. 'That must be the key that Hack replaced on the key ring. It's still sitting in the lab, I suppose?'

'No,' said Joe. 'It's sitting in my pocket.'

Jake grinned at him. 'It's times like these I notice your natural charm and good looks.'

Joe opened the safe. In it was a collection of stock certificates, an insurance policy and a red leather-covered book. 'Aha!'

It was the address book.

No diary.

'The little weasel!' Joe said, slamming the book down onto the desk and causing a whirl of dust to fly up. 'Where's the goddamn diary?'

Jake shrugged and began leafing through the pages. 'This isn't just an address book, Joe. It's more like a score sheet – all men's names and phone numbers, and some kind of code beside each one. There are at least four kinds of marks against each name. I wonder what for?'

'The mind boggles.'

'There are hatch marks – presumably for the number of sessions with each.'

'It's kind of painful to cut notches in your thigh, I suppose,' Joe said reflectively.

'And then these are – what? – performance ratings? Five, nine, ten-plus?' He suddenly looked glum. 'I probably would have fallen out of her goddamn bed and gotten a one-minus,' he grumbled, and went back to thumbing through the pages. 'My God – some of these names are hot stuff. This is a blackmailer's charter, Joe, even without the diary.'

'Oh, no,' Joe moaned. 'You don't suppose that's what this is, do you?' He held up a small black notebook that had been lying between two blocks of stock certificates. 'See if any of the names match.' He handed the book to Jake, who opened it and also groaned.

'This explains all those recent deposits on his bank statements, the little bastard. Quiddick said his "investments accumulated" – my ass. Yes, some of the names match all right. And this gives us a whole new set of suspects. It will take days to check out these guys – we're going to need more help.'

'What about Pinsky? He's finished on the Corelli thing,' Joe suggested.

'Worth a try,' Jake said morosely, and started to look for the telephone. Four stacks of papers slithered to the floor before he found it. He dialed downtown and got Pinsky at last.

'Christ – why didn't you leave us that number?' Pinsky complained. 'You know the black and white you sent over to that girl's place earlier?'

Jake sat up suddenly, and something metallic snapped in the chair mechanism beneath him. 'Yeah – why?'

'We just found it in an alley, with the two officers who drove it tied up in the trunk in their underwear.'

'Oh, Jesus—' Jake looked stricken. 'I *knew* I should have waited – but Klotzman said I should report—'

'Yeah, well. From what I can make out, they were on their way to stand guard on her when they came across a hit-and-run – which wasn't one, needless to say. When we found them I sent another black and white to the apartment. They just reported in a few minutes ago to say the place was kind of a mess. The door was open, a couple of chairs and a table knocked over, and blood on the floor. According to a neighbor, Casey was arrested by a nice big policeman about an hour ago.'

Jake stared across the desk at Joe. 'They got Casey,' he said in a ghastly voice. Slowly, very slowly, his chair was tilting sideways, its altering angle accompanied by a grating, scraping sound. Jake braced a foot against the desk to keep himself upright, and the desk started to slide toward Joe, who stood up in some alarm and began to back away.

At the other end of the line, Pinsky frowned. 'Did you hear that, Jake? They impersonated officers, the creeps.' There was a peculiar noise from Jake's end of the phone, and Pinsky shook the receiver a little. 'Jake? Jake? You there?'

There was a pause, during which Pinsky heard a number of peculiar and unidentifiable noises, not least of which was the voice of Joe Kaminsky pleading for someone to get something the hell off of him.

Pinsky frowned. He shouted down the phone. 'Jake? The girl's gone, disappeared, vanished.' He listened – listened hard. 'Did you hear me, Jake?'

But at the other end of the line, there was only silence.

TWENTY-FOUR

Casey was cold, hungry and extremely angry.

This was an advance on her situation when the door had first closed behind her. Before that she had been merely terrified.

The room was about ten feet square. The walls were covered floor to ceiling in white tiles, some stained, a few cracked or missing altogether. There were three narrow windows just below the ceiling – grimy, heavily barred and well out of her reach. Some light came through them – not much.

It had obviously been a bathroom. Against one wall stood a big, old-fashioned bathtub. It was covered over with a heavy board, and on this had been placed a thin mattress and a couple of brown plaid blankets, quite clean. No pillow. There was also a toilet and a washbasin. There was no soap on the basin, but there was a new, wrapped roll of toilet paper on the floor.

The room was not particularly dirty, although it had a musty, mildewed smell. There was a large, unpleasant stain on the cracked, green linoleum floor near the tub. It was shaped like a comet with a long, diminishing tail, about ten inches across at its widest point, and dark. After about an hour she was certain it was blood, that someone had died there and been dragged away.

From the sound it had made when they'd banged it shut, the door was both thick and solid, and the lock looked extremely strong. There was one light bulb in a caged fixture in the center of the ceiling, but no amount of flicking at the switch produced any illumination.

The building felt dead above her.

Sitting on the edge of the makeshift bed, hugging herself, she went back over what had happened. Despite her best intentions, tears welled up and she wiped them away with her sleeve. She picked up one of the blankets, wrapped it around herself and began to compose a letter of complaint to the management.

'*Dear Sir – I would like to protest at the lack of pillows in my room . . .*'

They had backed the stolen police car out of the narrow alley into the wider one, pushed Sylvester's limp body out and then driven away, very fast. She had twisted around to look back through the rear window. As they had moved off he'd looked smaller and smaller, lying there, so still, like a heap of rags beside an overflowing garbage can.

'The heating system seems to be out of order, and there is no television . . .'

The smaller man had grabbed her shoulder and turned her forward again. He had bent her down, tied her hands behind her and then jerked her roughly upright in order to put the blindfold back on. His hands had been strong and she hadn't resisted. The small man hadn't spoken a word to her. Just done his work. The last thing she had seen had been his eyes, so close to her own, the irises flat brown and dead, the whites discolored, the lashes short and stubby, and a mole, a tiny mole, in the shiny, sweaty skin beside the bridge of his nose.

'The decor is definitely uninspired . . .'

They had driven for a long time after that, turning corner after corner. She had listened for any odd sound, sniffed for any unusual smell, but could remember nothing now. Eventually they had stopped, jerked her out, made her walk a few steps and go through a door. The change in the quality of sound – outdoor to indoor – was clear enough. Outdoors there had been a lot of noise, distant shouting and what sounded like the roar of heavy machinery. Indoors, only echoes. She'd been frog-marched across a big room – high-ceilinged, from the sound of it – and then through a door and onto stairs that went down. Across another room, a pause and then a scraping noise.

There had been the sound of a key in a lock. Then she was pushed forward. One of the men – the big one, she thought – untied her blindfold and her hands. The door had been slammed shut behind her, leaving her in semi-darkness. After a while her eyes had adjusted, and she had seen the room.

'Also, through some oversight, the bellboy seems to have forgotten to leave me a key . . .'

Soon somebody would come and she would find out what they wanted. She would wait until then to feel anything. In the meantime it was necessary to stay calm and quiet, and keep her mind clear.

She'd had plenty of practice at that, over the past few years.

Meeting her husband at college, their two happy years together – that had been fine. His death had been ghastly. The shock of the diagnosis, the hope, the destruction of hope, the long sad lingering, the agony, the loss. Work had been the only anodyne. She'd taken another degree to blot out the emptiness, but even her new career, varied and complex as it had been, hadn't been enough. Then the chance to come to Grantham – to start again, to feel again, even if it was the renewal of pain from an old sadness – had seeemed the right course. To face the past, to face the truth, like an acid bath, would strip away the accumulated crusts and shells she had built around herself.

And what had been the result?

This.

Well maybe, like Nat, it was time she was buried, too. 'I don't give a damn anymore,' she said aloud. But even as her words echoed off the tiled walls, she knew it was a lie. She *hadn't* given a damn – until that totally impossible man had pushed himself into her life and made things so difficult. Jake Chase, professional idiot. Saying silly things about curtains (she and Nat had never argued about curtains), falling over things (Nat had been a wonderful dancer), insisting on protecting her (Nat had always said she should stand on her own two feet), telling her she was in danger . . .

Well, he'd been right about that.

She rolled herself up in the blankets, lay down and stared at the ceiling. There was another stain there, almost like a face looking down at her. If she squinted her eyes nearly closed, it might almost be the face of Jake Chase. Or a crazed kumquat.

After a while she fell asleep.

'Why doesn't he come to see me?' Gurney Lightfoot said irritably. 'For the past two days, nobody comes.'

'The doctor said you must have rest,' the nurse purred. 'You know you upset yourself the other day, and nearly started another hemmorhage.'

'I want to see Ronald,' he snapped. 'Go out there, find him. Tell him I want to know what's going on. If you can't find Ronald, then get Littlewood for me. Or Knapp. Or even Friedlander, for Christ's sake. Anyone, dammit!'

The nurse was uncertain, her expression flickering between annoyance and appeasement. 'Perhaps tomorrow morning, when you've had a good sleep—' She stopped as Lightfoot, with a monumental effort, began to throw back the coverlet. 'All right, all right!' she squeaked. 'I'll see who I can find. Just lie back down and rest.' She tucked him back in, felt his forehead, frowned and looked down at his wrinkled, yellowing face.

'I'll bring someone,' she promised quietly. 'The first person I can find.'

He watched her go out the door and then angrily felt a tear sliding out the corner of one eye. He wiped it away, then stared at his hand, wrinkled and clawlike, a stranger's hand. It was shaking, and he could see a faint gleam where the tear had smeared its back – then the brief moisture disappeared.

'Bastards,' he whispered. 'They're all bastards.'

Now the routine began. The description of the two men who had stolen the police car and the uniforms was circulated. The car itself was taken for forensic examination, in the hope of finding fingerprints of the men. Two hours later there was a call from the hospital.

Sylvester Crump had been found lying in an alley about a mile uptown from Casey's apartment house. He was unconscious from a severe blow on the skull, and his chances for lasting the night were poor, because of his general physical debility.

Jake went to sit by the old man's bedside. Joe remained at Headquarters, sat stoically by the phone hoping for a lead to materialize, and filling in forms. He also spent an hour explaining everything to Captain Klotzman. Again.

He told Klotzman that Jake was at the hospital because otherwise he would probably kill Klotzman with his bare hands. He had threatened to do this because he considered the entire thing to be Klotzman's fault for having pulled him away from protecting Casey Hewson before the uniformed officers had arrived, just because Klotzman had had an appointment with the commissioner.

Klotzman agreed that the hospital was probably a really good place for Jake to be.

He could rest his nerves there, Klotzman said.

'You mean better him as a visitor than you as a patient?' Joe said wryly.

'Something like that,' Klotzman muttered. 'Look, Joe, I'm sorry about the girl. This morning it looked like a really thin connection, you know? I thought it was another attack of Jake's Jinx, that's all.'

Joe evaded Klotzman's eye, jamming his hands into his pockets and gazing at the first-aid box on the wall. He sighed. 'All right, all right. But he's a good cop in the long run, Captain. You know he is. You *know* that.'

'He'd have been selling his horseshit to fertilizer dealers long ago if I didn't,' Klotzman agreed benignly, starting to look over a stack of reports on his desk. 'OK, so I was hasty. I'm sorry. Tell him I'm sorry. We'll let him run with this thing on the girl for the moment. I'll put somebody else on the Norris killing.'

'But I told you, the two are connected,' Joe said doggedly. 'Whoever killed Norris was after the proof about the Finch case, because probably he also killed the Finch woman, or was involved somehow.'

Klotzman shook his head. 'That Chase, he's some salesman. He gets you going every time, doesn't he?'

'We usually get there in the end,' Joe said pointedly.

Klotzman signed something, put down his pen, folded his hands and looked up. 'So, run it by me again.'

'It's in the evening paper,' Molly Pemberton told Mr Braithwaite when she came in. 'Some poor girl, snatched in broad daylight, and an old man nearly killed trying to protect her. Jake's name is there – contact Lieutenant J. Chase if you have any information.'

She hung up her coat, put her books for the evening on the table beside her reading chair and then went into the kitchen to start her meal. Turning on the television, she saw that the news had just finished, and sighed.

Her whole timetable was off tonight. If it hadn't started to rain she would have been home sooner. As it was she'd heard the phone ringing as she came up the stairs, but it had stopped before she could unlock the door. She didn't get many calls these days and was extremely disappointed to have missed it. Even somebody selling something would have been a friendly voice. Why a bit of rain should make traffic slow down to a crawl was beyond her – you'd think it was something they'd never seen before. She looked down at the cat, who was walking back and forth from the kitchen to the sitting room, making odd, growling noises. 'Whatever is the matter, Braithwaite? You seem upset.'

She watched the cat for a moment, then went with him to the sitting room. He went into the bedroom and over to the window.

'Oh, is *that* it? I know Mr Niforos was here. He put new locks on the windows, didn't he? Well, thank you for telling me. I'll have a look at them later. Come and have some dinner.'

She returned to the kitchen, and after a moment the cat reappeared. It sat down in its usual position, seemingly content at having drawn her attention to something unusual, and waited for her to spoon the food into a bowl. As she put it down, there was a knock on the door.

'Excuse me,' she said to the cat, and then, to herself, 'I must stop doing that.'

Her caller was Victor Niforos. 'Good evening,' he said rather formally when she opened the door.

'Well, hello,' she said, smiling. 'Thank you for putting on my new locks.'

He looked puzzled for an instant, then embarrassed. 'No, no, I come to say I have finished him for you.'

'Yes, thank you, I know.' She looked at him briefly, then her face cleared. 'Oh, you mean my table, not my locks, is that it?'

'You call table?' He shrugged – this language was so difficult. 'Yes. You like to see him now?'

She glanced over her shoulder at the kitchen, from which was beginning to emanate the odor of burning onions. 'Well, not just now, actually – I'm just cooking dinner. Perhaps later on? Will you be at home later on?'

'I . . . yes . . . sure.' He was overwhelmed by her friendly tone. Taking courage from it, he said, 'Maybe you like to have some coffee with me?'

She was startled momentarily, and then remembered that his wife was away and he was probably lonely. That was something she knew about only too well. 'That would be very nice, Mr Niforos. I'll be down in about an hour or so, all right?'

He beamed his agreement and was still nodding as she closed the door. He stood staring at its blank panels for a while, confusion in his eyes and the first faint flags of triumph beginning to rise in his heart.

He turned and went back down the stairs. From behind the other doors of other apartments came the sounds of humanity –

arguments, laughter, the blasting overtures of various television programs.

Who knows what each moment will bring? he told himself. She will come, we will drink coffee, and something may happen. But I will be very, very careful. She could be a dangerous woman, perhaps a fatal female like in these soap programs on the TV. Niforos, he warned his romantic soul, do not get yourself in a web. Do not make naked your chest to her in case she steals your heart and then eats it. He went through the main lobby and back to the door that led to his basement domain, trembling faintly with anticipation and cautious delight.

Jake sat quietly beside the old man's bed, watching his face. There were no answers there – only the spreading black and purple bruise edging the bandage.

From time to time Jake jerked himself awake from a doze, lulled by the quiet hiss of the oxygen feed valve and the distant footsteps and voices of the hospital beyond the closed door. On the opposite side of the bed a monitor beeped hypnotically, green waves rolling across the tiny circular screen in time to the electronic noises from within. It was the most boring – and reassuring – program Jake had ever watched.

He glanced out the window. Rain streaked the scene into an impressionist's delight, each new drop wavering down the windows to join others in tiny rivers, glowing with reflections, moving and darting in ever-changing patterns, drawn by gravity, blown and smeared sideways by an erratic wind.

Beyond this glittering web, the city lights twinkled, long strands of headlights and taillights weaving between towers striped with random ranks of lit and unlit windows. The black band of the river divided the scene abruptly, crossed by the looped diadems of the two bridges.

The curtains framed a gift from the night he was in no mood to appreciate. Perhaps Casey could see the same scene. Or perhaps she was in darkness, afraid and alone. Even worse – afraid and *not* alone.

He knew that back at Division Joe and Klotzman were sorting out the deployment of those men that could be switched to the case. They, in turn, would be contacting snitches, making street sweeps and checking known addresses and hangouts for the two men. In addition to all official alerts, the word was going out on the street, favors were being called in, pressures applied. He also knew Joe would be doing his damnedest to get a tap on Lightfoot's phones, but that could take hours and Lightfoot wasn't dumb enough to give orders over the phone – assuming he was giving them at all.

He also knew he should be at Division himself – he was the ranking officer on the case – but had been sent here to cool off and keep out of trouble for a few hours. Knowing that didn't help much, but it helped. Take a breath, Jake, he told himself. Take another. Get yourself together.

As a working cop he should have been accustomed to this feeling of helplessness and frustration. (Things being what they were, he had more of these moments than most cops.) It was the bitter realization that you were only one man and the world was large and mostly against you. It came at some point in most cases, especially the ones that dragged on past the 24-hour mark. You were told to expect it, and you were taught how to deal with it – even how to make it work for you.

But this one hurt more. This one was personal. He knew it shouldn't happen, he was trained and experienced and knew better than to let it get like that, but it *was* like that and there wasn't a goddamn thing he could do about it now.

From a professional point of view, he'd been right to want to protect her – all the signs pointed to it being necessary – and wrong to back off when ordered to do so by Klotzman. Maybe he should have told Klotzman about Casey's furtive phone call to Richard Armbruster, or her theft of the key from Norris's apartment. Would it have made any difference? Probably not. Once Klotzman got the bit between his teeth, there was no turning him. Especially after the Piggy Wiggy debacle.

He stood up and walked around the room, jingling the keys and coins in his pocket for company, wanting to shout, wanting to sock someone, most of all wanting to kick himself in the ass.

There was a clatter as he turned and walked into the bedside table. Maybe he should go back to that psychologist for more tests, he thought as he rubbed his side, picked up the aluminum kidney dish, put it back beside the water pitcher and dropped the broken bits of Sylvester's drinking glass into the wastebasket. He was so sick of picking up pieces of things, including people.

Tests, hell. Maybe it was time for a room with rubber wallpaper.

The noise of the falling metal dish and shattering glass hadn't brought any response from Sylvester, which pitched Jake deeper into gloom. Maybe the old guy wasn't going to make it. Maybe this time Jake's Jinx was going to be fatal to somebody.

He sank back down in his chair and put his head in his hands. What the hell was he going to do?

The door opened and Joe came in.

'How's he doing?' Joe asked Jake, nodding at Sylvester.

Jake shrugged. 'No change.' He looked at Joe hopefully. 'Any word on anything?'

'Yeah – we found Armbruster. Or rather, Armbruster found us.' Joe glanced uneasily at the door and moved a little closer to Jake. 'There's a problem, Jake.'

'Oh?'

Joe was embarrassed – an emotion Jake had rarely seen in his partner. Joe cleared his throat. 'He's a fed, Jake. He's *Agent* Richard Armbruster.'

'Agent?' Jake asked.

'Yeah – but that isn't the bad part, Jake.'

'So tell me the bad part.' Jake was getting edgy. He had the feeling he was failing some kind of secret and unannounced test. 'Well?'

'Casey,' Joe said.

Jake felt cold all over – cold and afraid. 'My God – is she dead?'

'No . . . she . . . well – Armbruster just told me.'

'Jesus – told you what?' Jake shouted, unable to bear it.

'Casey is a federal agent, too, Jake.'

Jake stared at him. As he opened his mouth to speak, there was a strange, rhythmic, rasping sound in the room. Startled, they turned toward the bed.

Sylvester was laughing.

TWENTY-FIVE

Sylvester's return to consciousness was sudden and complete. Too complete. He kept shouting, 'I knew it, I knew it,' alternating this with 'Where's my goddamn pants?' The doctor, summoned by Jake, had examined Sylvester and pronounced him a survivor.

However, when Jake had tried to get a statement from him concerning what had happened to Casey and to get a description or any detail that might help them trace the men or the car, Sylvester grew sly. Finally, when he insisted that he was only prepared to 'spill the beans' if given a bottle of whiskey, they'd had to give up. Resignedly, the young doctor sedated him into a peaceful sleep.

'I think he might be a bit more coherent in the morning,' he said. Jake, who had been feeling quite guilty about Sylvester's injuries, was now more than ready to add to them, given half a chance. Joe and Armbruster led him away gently.

He eyed his two escorts grimly. Especially Armbruster. 'I don't believe this about Casey,' he growled.

'I assure you, Lieutenant Chase, it's no lie,' Armbruster said.

'I never figured it,' Jake said morosely. 'I had a hundred theories – but that wasn't one of them.'

'She said she had a law degree,' Joe said. 'Maybe that should have told us – but I didn't find her in the records, so I figured it was just hot air.'

'Oh, Casey *did* study law,' Armbruster said. 'But her main qualification is as a certified public accountant. A lot of us are CPAs these days. She was initially sent here to get a line on Eustace Millington. Or, more specifically, the covert operations of the Millington Foundation,' Armbruster was saying. 'We heard he was looking for an editor, and we set her up with references and all the rest of it. Naturally, he hired her.'

'Naturally,' Joe said, trying to ease the situation. 'Who wouldn't?' He wilted slightly under Jake's glare.

Armbruster was trying. 'Well, we had to get her in somehow. We didn't want him to suspect it was the Foundation finances

172

we were interested in, so we took this rather oblique approach. But it was working – he was taking her more and more into his confidence—'

'I'll bet he was,' Jake growled.

Joe was avoiding Jake's eyes as they left the elevator and walked toward the exit. The night air was cold, with the last rags of the rainclouds being torn from the sky by a brisk wind. Jake hunched into his jacket, feeling the chill after the hothouse warmth of the hospital room. Armbruster was still talking.

'Anyway, Casey happened onto this business with Norris purely by chance. Millington gave her the manuscript to edit and she saw immediately that it might be of interest to us,' Armbruster went on after a pause to negotiate their way past a couple of parked cars.

'It would have interested *us* even more,' Jake growled.

'Yes, I know. I'm sorry about that,' Armbruster apologized. 'We just didn't want the one to mess up the other.'

Jake gritted his teeth. 'Oh, really? Did it ever occur to you that maybe it wasn't "chance" that Millington gave her the manuscript? Maybe he suspected her – or someone did. Maybe she was set up.' It would be easier to think that than to think she had been let down – although he knew that was true, too.

They were passing the emergency entrance and had to step back as an ambulance roared past, siren blaring, followed by a police car. Armbruster looked concerned at Jake's suggestion that Casey's cover had been transparent to Millington. He stopped and considered the possibility.

'I hope not – although when she told me about the theft of her briefcase I must admit my first thought was that it must have to do with her original assignment. But she assured me there was nothing in it to connect her with us.'

'Yeah – we heard the call.'

Armbruster regrded him with interest. 'Did you? Then why didn't you confront her?'

'I wanted to see how far she'd run with it. Did she give you that key?'

'Yes, she gave me the key.'

'Any good?'

'You know damn well it wasn't.' Armbruster's voice was neutral.

'Yeah, well – Hack will be glad to get it back. His old lady's pissed off at him because of the grass.'

'Hey, Chase!' It was Jack Stryker, jumpy and electric as ever, pacing back and forth outside the emergency entrance.

Jake went over to him. 'What are you doing here?' he asked. 'Not one of ours, is it?'

'Only in a manner of speaking. Molly Pemberton. I was on my way home when the call came in. You see that guy in there?' Stryker pointed through the glass doors at a large man in a plaid shirt with curly dark hair and a heavy scowl, who was pacing back and forth, wringing his hands. Occasionally he smote himself on the forehead, and he appeared to be muttering at and cursing his shoes. 'Name of Niforos, Victor Niforos. He's the caretaker at her apartment house. He found her and made the call. She was attacked and beaten up in her own place, about an hour ago.'

'Oh, hell,' Jake said. 'Is she bad?'

Stryker shrugged. 'Pretty bad, but more from shock than anything else. Whoever it was knocked her around some, broke her nose they think, maybe concussion. Thing is, this Niforos keeps saying he did it – but there isn't a mark on him. I think it's just a language problem. We can't get much sense out of him. We *think* he was expecting her to drop down to see him or something – he's a good-looking guy but that doesn't sound like our Molly – and when she didn't appear he went up to her place, found the door open and there she was – lying on the floor unconscious.'

'Signs of a break-in?'

Stryker nodded. 'Sure. Broken window in the bedroom, but as far as we can tell nothing was taken. He – Niforos – keeps going on about some locks she asked him to put on, but he didn't get around to it.' Stryker shrugged. 'Maybe that's what he means about it being his fault – he's not too coherent right now.'

Joe and Armbruster had come up to join them, and Jake explained. Armbruster said, 'Why don't you get somebody down here who speaks Greek?'

'On his way,' Stryker said, giving him an odd glance.

'When I was at the library this morning, Molly said something about someone trying to break into her place,' Joe said thoughtfully. 'That is, she *started* to tell me, but some old fruitcake came along and she never finished. How about old offenders who might have had a grudge against Dan and have maybe just gotten out?'

Stryker nodded his head and rubbed his scalp vigorously, as if charging up his brain for action. 'I thought of that. I've asked for a computer run, but, Jesus, Dan must have put away a million guys in his time. It would have to be a real nutter to carry a grudge even after Dan was gone.'

'It only takes one. If he – or she – was harassing Molly, then maybe that was the reason for the locks,' Jake said.

'Yeah, maybe. She was conscious, but I didn't like to press until she'd been made more comfortable. I'm just waiting for them to check her out before getting a statement. If I can get past that big Greek, that is. He seems to see himself as some kind of Cerberus at the gate.' Stryker was currently living with a lady college professor, and his conversation had become peppered with literary allusions. It had raised the tone of the Division considerably, but God knew where it would lead. Somebody had even caught Pinsky reading *Moby Dick* the other day. Next week, *East Lynne*, Klotzman had said.

'I heard about the girl getting taken. Tough one,' Stryker said, shifting from one foot to the other, like a boxer waiting for the bell.

'Yes,' Jake said grimly.

Stryker nodded. 'And she's tied in with the Norris thing, which isn't just a mugging but maybe has to do with the old Finch murder? Your case is growing branches, Jake.'

'And roots and leaves and little acorns, too,' Jake growled. He liked Stryker, but he was in no mood for bonhomie.

Stryker shrugged and glanced up at the high clouds racing across a pale moon. 'Halloween's still a few weeks off, but it seems to me like we're already getting haunted by old crimes and old ghosts. Today is hard enough to deal with, but this just-for-old-times stuff . . .' He gave a shiver. 'I don't like it.' He glanced through the glass doors and seemed to spot some encouraging sign within, because he started for the door as if a gun had gone off. 'I'll let you know about Molly,' he said over his shoulder.

'Appreciate it,' Joe called as the automatic doors swished open and then shut behind the sprinting Stryker. He glanced at Armbruster. 'Sergeant's widow – kind of a special lady.'

Armbruster nodded. 'They all are,' he said. When they looked

175

at him in surprise he smiled thinly. 'My mother is a cop's widow, too,' he said.

Eustace Millington was pacing back and forth in the lobby of the Hall of Justice when they got downtown. He was the only person visible in the vast marble expanse, and when he spotted Jake he came straight over to him. 'Have you found her yet?' he demanded. 'Is there any news?'

'No. sorry.' Jake was terse and started to walk past.

Millington grabbed his arm. 'Why aren't you out looking for her? Isn't it obvious? It must be Lightfoot's people who took her. Why haven't you brought him in for questioning?'

Jake looked down. 'Cut yourself shaving?'

Millington let go of Jake's sleeve and thrust his bandaged hand into his pocket. 'Two of my cats got into an altercation and I had to part them. Would you like to have me make out a report on it?' he added snidely. 'You all seem to *thrive* on reports.'

'Not unless you want to charge the cats with assault,' Jake said evenly. 'And reports are necessary if we don't want to walk all over each other and waste time. We're doing all we can to find Casey, as you damn well know. How did you find out, anyway?'

'It was in the evening papers,' Millington snapped. 'Or didn't you notice?'

'No, I didn't notice,' Jake said quietly. 'As far as Lightfoot is concerned, we have no hard evidence on which to question anyone except the two men who actually took her.'

'Who are they?'

'As far as we know, just a couple of goons with records.'

'Who work for Lightfoot,' Millington said flatly.

Jake raised an eyebrow. 'You know that, do you? What have you got – paychecks? Contracts of employment?'

Millington sneered. It seemed to come naturally to his features, as if they had been bred to it. 'It's obvious.'

'Obvious isn't enough to satisfy a judge. Why don't you go home and put some iodine on those scratches?' Jake suggested. 'Leave us to do our job.'

'I would if I thought you were doing it,' Millington snapped.

Jake looked at him in disgust. 'What do you expect us to do, search every building in the city? Arrest every man on the street? Believe me, if I could, I would. But there are rules, Millington.

It's our job to enforce them, so we have to go by them, as annoying as that may be. Go home. Read a book. Give yourself a perm. Rinse out a few things. Or, better still, send Sylvester some flowers.'

'Don't be ridiculous.'

'Ridiculous? You think someone getting his head bashed in trying to protect the girl you're suddenly so worried about is ridiculous, do you? I can think of a few things that are ridiculous, Millington, such as your moustache, your necktie and your goddamn attitude, but one of them isn't Sylvester Crump. You want to throw your weight around, fine, but do it on somebody else's time, not mine.' He started to walk away.

'I have important friends in this building, Chase. One word from me and they could break you,' Millington called after him.

Jake stopped, turned and started back. 'Then why don't you say that one word? Go on. Say it.'

Millington, after one look at his face, began to back away. As Jake came closer, Millington opened his mouth, closed it and then broke. He didn't run – not quite – but he went.

Joe and Armbruster hadn't moved during this encounter. Armbruster reached into his jacket, got out his tobacco pouch and began to fill his pipe. They watched the revolving door spin round and round and round after Eustace had shot out the other side and disappeared.

'I clock that at about fifty r.p.m.,' Armbruster said to Joe.

'Easy,' Joe agreed. 'Maybe more.'

'Shame we haven't got a full churn attached to it,' Armbruster said, striking a match. 'I sure could use a pound of butter.'

Jake glanced at him. 'Tell me more about how and why you want to get the dirt on that gasbag.'

Armbruster smiled. 'My pleasure,' he said, and glanced at the elevators. 'Your place or ours?'

HE DIDN'T KNOW WHAT TO DO.

When the desk hadn't been delivered, he'd known what to do. He'd broken into the basement offices of the Lecomber Galleries and gotten the delivery list. He'd felt pretty clever, doing that.

And when he had the list he'd known what to do. He'd spent

most of the day on the telephone and after a number of verifications and eliminations (and not a little abuse from dissatisfied customers who thought he worked for Lecomber Galleries) he'd thought he had it straight. Just a matter of using his intelligence.

He, as 'Mr Pilkington', had bought a desk. Molly Pemberton had bought a table. A Mr Tiverton had bought a bureau. And the Rev. Merton had bought some chairs.

But, thanks to bad handwriting or gross stupidity, the delivery men had given Molly Pemberton's table to Mr Tiverton, sent Mr Tiverton's bureau to the Rev. Merton, deposited the Rev. Merton's chairs in the empty apartment of 'Mr Pilkington' and sent 'Mr Pilkington's' desk to Molly Pemberton.

Fine. When he knew who had the desk, he'd known what to do.

Except the desk hadn't been in Molly Pemberton's apartment.

And she had been.

He had rung the apartment and there had been no answer. He hadn't seen any lights on. It wasn't until he'd gotten in through the window that he saw her sitting there in the chair, one small shaded reading light beside her.

AND HE HADN'T KNOWN WHAT TO DO.

So panic had come over him again.

He should have killed her.

What did one more matter now?

He should kill everybody.

EVERYBODY, HE SHOULD KILL—

Calm down! he told himself. Think. Think hard.

He'd overheard a conversation between the Pemberton woman and the caretaker, about her table. He'd therefore crossed her off the list of wrong deliveries – until a process of elimination had made her the only possible recipient of the desk. The caretaker had talked of refinishing – but what if it wasn't a table but the *desk* he was working on?

In which case, the desk was in the basement.

Of course.

The desk was in the basement, and the caretaker was refinishing it.

And if he was refinishing it – he'd have taken out all the drawers.

And if he'd taken out all the drawers – he'd have found the knife and the monogramed handkerchief . . . and the key.

Wouldn't he? *Wouldn't he?*

WOULDN'T HE?

TWENTY-SIX

'What do you come under?' Jake asked. 'I didn't exactly read the fine print on your ID.'

Armbruster again produced the Gucci leather folder and tossed it across. Jake opened it and read it through, front and back. 'I thought your bunch had their offices over on de Quincy.' He tossed it back.

'I'm a floater,' Armbruster said with a boyish grin. 'I believe the British would call me an "ombudsman". When there are a lot of interests involved, someone like me steps in. Just to keep things neat. I can give you a few names and numbers for reference, if it would make you happy?'

'It would make me happy,' Jake said, and noted them down. He then handed them to Joe. 'Mind checking these out on your way down to Hack's office?'

'Not at all,' Joe said, standing up. 'I'll see if there's any fresh news while I'm down there.' He went out.

Jake leaned back and stretched his arms wide. A button pinged off his shirt and shot past Armbruster's ear, making him flinch. It hit the window behind, bounced off and landed in a wastebasket. Armbruster chuckled. 'They said working around you was dangerous, but I guess your aim is better than they know.'

Jake shrugged. 'Lucky shot.'

'I didn't mean hitting the basket, and you know it.' There was a moment of silence, during which both men acknowledged the other's excellent camouflage, intentional or not. Then Armbruster got on with it.

'The main point is this: Little Eustace had most of the bowl and handle of his particular silver spoon taken away from him by the Millington Foundation, over the years. By the time his father popped off, practically everything old Augustus had made was transferred into that damn Foundation. But is Eustace sulky? Is he cross? No, he's not. What's more, he's never even *tried* to break the arrangement – and you'd think anybody with any brains at all would have tried to long ago. So why isn't he kicking? They say the publishing business is going down the tubes – but Eustace is still afloat. Why? How? There doesn't seem to be any sense to it. Not yet, anyway. Casey was sent to find some.'

'Suppose Eustace is really Mr Nice Guy, patron of the arts and one of life's charitable gurus?' Jake suggested.

'Let's just get on with this, shall we?' Armbruster said dryly. 'Up front Eustace gets nothing but his salary as the co-administrator, twenty thousand a year, which is hardly a fortune considering that he's managing assets of close to twenty million.'

'Jesus, I had no idea it was worth that.'

Armbruster nodded. 'The advantages of knowing the law, my friend. Private companies, charitable institutions – they're all very well protected, even in this age of the Freedom of Information Act. All *that's* done is to drive the real secrets further underground.'

Joe returned and handed Armbruster's list of numbers and names to Jake. 'They all say he's Clark Kent.'

'Yeah,' Armbruster agreed. 'You ought to time me in a phone booth, it's a real revelation.'

Joe gave him a brief smile. 'I also talked to Bill Irvine.'

Irvine was a local FBI man they'd worked with before. 'He says he's the real thing, but to watch him. He's been here before, but they aren't sure how many times, because he doesn't always leave a calling card. Or if he does, it sometimes doesn't go off until years later. Bill says he likes him, but he wouldn't trust him more than a few inches.'

'Thank you, Bill,' murmured Armbruster. 'It takes one to know one.'

Joe went on. 'They've finished going over the stolen squad car, by the way. The kidnappers had wiped it over pretty good, but our guys found a few marks they must have missed. Most important – Sylvester's. On the roof lining. Both hands, nice and neat, for the record.'

'Let's hear it for Sylvester,' said Armbruster. 'That was good thinking.'

Joe was carrying a manila envelope, which he handed to Jake. 'Molly Pemberton left this for us on her way home tonight.'

'Isn't that the woman who was beaten up in her apartment?' Armbruster asked, leaning forward. 'That's too much of a coincidence, surely.'

181

'There are eight million stories in the naked city,' Jake said. 'Sometimes they cross – big deal. The funny thing would be if they didn't. Molly is always helping us out on cases. She knows the kind of thing we need, saves us a hell of a lot of time.' He opened the envelope and drew out a cream-colored file which proved to contain a great number of photocopies of articles about Ariadne Finch, her life, her family, the mystery of her disappearance. The latest of these was only a year or so old – an article in a local newspaper about famous 'disappearances'.

'This ought to keep us off the streets for a while,' Jake said, shuffling through them. Armbruster got up and came around to look over his shoulder. 'There's the beautiful, sexy and ever-available Mrs Finch – no wonder she had them lined up. There's the "anything you want, dear" husband, Frederick J. Finch – poor bastard. And there—' He stopped, stared and nearly choked.

They were looking down at a photocopy of a women's magazine article published a year before Ariadne's disappearance. It had many photographs of the Finch Family at Home (Mom and Dad and lovely daughter before a huge fireplace, with several large dogs at their feet), the Finch Family at One of Their Famous Poolside Parties (everybody who was anybody was there), Fred and Ariadne Finch at the Opera (Ariadne beautiful in clinging velvet, Ariadne ravishing in mink), at Mayor Porter's Charity Ball (Ariadne looking very cozy between Charley and his son, with poor Fred stuck to one side), at a Millington Foundation Concert (Augustus looking fragile but game, and Eustace kissing Ariadne's hand), and the Finch Family Attending Church on Sunday (with the vicar looking the other way).

'Oh, shit,' Jake said.

'I'll be damned,' Joe said.

'Son of a bitch,' Armbruster said.

Casey had managed to get some sleep, off and on, although she was never quite warm enough. They had taken her handbag, so there was no convenient nailfile with which to tunnel out, nor any handy hairpin she could use to pick the lock. All she had were her teeth (which occasionally chattered) and her wits (which seemed to have gone into suspended animation). All her fieldwork had been in offices – the worst situations she'd ever faced were snagged tights or running out of red ink.

She was awakened from her fitful night's sleep by the sound of a key in the lock of her cell. Pale light came in through the high windows. A glance at her watch told her it was eight thirty.

There was a long and terrible pause as the door swung slowly inward, and then two figures appeared. Two figures she remembered only too clearly from the night (about three hundred years ago) when they had chased her, robbed her and knocked her out. The two men Jake had told her far too much about.

Obediah Smith and Tanker Jones.

So it *was* the Lightfoot bunch.

Why didn't she feel relieved?

'My, my, little lady, you *do* look chilly,' said Obediah Smith. His black skin gleamed in the harsh light. He was wearing an immaculate white suit, with a red shirt and a white tie. On his feet were red patent-leather brogues. He was beautiful.

Casey swallowed. 'It's my blue eyes,' she said.

He smiled a broad, white smile that made his own brown eyes crinkle at the corners. He was a handsome man, with regular features and a well-set-up body. She didn't know why that made him more frightening, but it did. What had Jake said – torturer for the Ton Ton Macoute? Somehow it would have been better if he'd had a hump and lots of scars. 'Blue eyes – very amusing,' he said. 'Isn't that amusing, Tanker, my friend?' His singsong accent was even more pronounced now than it had been the other night.

'Real funny,' Jones agreed. He was dressed in the same scruffy suit and battered cap he'd worn the last time she saw him. He didn't smile. Just looked at her steadily, without expression, as if waiting for something.

That was scary, too.

In fact, neither of them did anything at all. After a minute passed Casey was almost ready to start screaming, simply from tension. Only name, rank and serial number, of course. Oh, God – when they'd recruited her in Washington she'd *told* them she was no good against pain. Why had she agreed to all this?

She sat up straighter. Actually, upon reflection, she *hadn't* agreed to all this, had she? Only to investigating the Millington

Foundation and, indirectly, Eustace. She hadn't much liked Eustace, but she liked these two even less. Perhaps if she asked them nicely they would smuggle out a letter to Dick Armbruster with her resignation in it, and then she could go back to her original career goal.

Circus clown.

They were still just standing there, watching her.

'Looks like rain,' she said brightly. No response. 'Broken any good bones lately?'

'I don't do bones,' Smith said.

'He does skin, mostly,' Jones told her in a businesslike tone, rather like an agent touting a new act. Or, in this case, a very old one. 'He's brilliant with needles and razors. An artist.'

'I like to think so,' Smith agreed, beaming at her. 'It *is* an art, you know, getting the balance right, between the agony and the information.'

'He don't like it to come too easy,' Jones kindly explained.

Smith nodded. 'One is always suspicious if it comes too easily,' he agreed. 'And, of course, when one is disappointed, one is apt to be abrupt.'

'Not much choice for the victim there,' Casey said.

'No,' Smith nodded gravely. 'Not much.'

Casey swung her feet over the edge of the bed and smoothed her skirt. She busied herself folding the blankets she'd been huddling under, and placed them neatly at the foot of the bed. 'Well,' she said. 'Shall we start?'

'Start?' Jones asked.

'The torture,' Casey said chirpily. 'I'll hold out as long as I can – I'd hate for you to be disappointed – but I expect I'll tell you things eventually. Of course, they may not be the things you want to know, because I don't know anything you want to know – as far as I know. But I know a lot of good cookie recipes, and there's all the dirty stuff I did behind the gym with Roscoe Lakeland when I was fourteen, and taxes – my *God*, the things I could tell you about tax evasion – I hope you have a notebook – and then there's my marriage – don't ask me about my marriage – well, maybe you could ask me a little bit—'

Smith turned to Jones. 'Did you bring any spare socks?'

'Yeah, why?'

'Put one of them in her mouth.'

'They're in the car.'

184

'Damn.' Smith looked at Casey. 'Lady – would you shut up? I have a migraine. I've had it all day and all night, and I'd appreciate some quiet.'

'I'll try not to scream,' Casey said.

'Good,' Smith said. 'Very good.'

They continued to stand there.

Casey was puzzled. 'Aren't you going to torture me?'

'I hope not,' Smith said. 'Not until I get something for this head.'

'Then – what are you doing here?'

'Watching you.'

Well, that seemed fairly obvious. 'And – nothing else?'

'Waiting for someone,' Jones said. 'We're waiting for someone.'

'And *then* you'll torture me?'

Smith rubbed his temples. 'I don't think I can take much more of this.'

'He's not very good about pain,' Jones explained. 'Or blood. When he was working, back home, the sight of all the blood always made him puke. His victims used to resent that, he told me.'

'Well, I guess it could give a person a feeling of rejection,' Casey agreed. 'Maybe you'd feel better if you sat down, Mr Smith. There's plenty of room here.' She patted the bed beside her.

She could see he was torn. 'Well – just for a minute,' he finally said, giving in. He came across the room and sat down beside her, rather gingerly, so as not to jar his head. He smelled wonderfully of fresh lime aftershave.

'Mr Jones? Would you like to sit down, too?'

'Why not?' Jones came over and thumped down next to her. Smith held his head and moaned. 'Sorry, Obie.'

Casey cleared her throat. 'I had quite a headache the other night, after you hit me.'

'You would,' Jones agreed. 'That was a good sap – imported from New Jersey, that was. I gave it to him for his birthday last year, didn't I, Obie?' Smith grunted in agreement. 'And he gave me a tattoo.'

'A tattoo?' Casey asked.

'I told you he was good at skin. A special snake, each scale so nice and detailed, you wouldn't believe it.'

'I've never seen a really good tattoo,' Casey said.

Jones blushed. 'I can't show you. It starts on my chest but it ends up in what you might call an intimate area.'

'Oh.' Casey was disappointed. 'I only got a pair of earrings and a new calculator for my birthday last year.'

'Boring,' Jones opined. 'Next time, ask for a tattoo. Obie could recommend somebody, I'm sure, although you might have to go to New York or something.'

'I could do that, I could go to New York,' Casey said eagerly. 'I could leave right now.' She started to get up, but both men grabbed an arm and pulled her back.

'No,' Jones said.

'No?'

'No.'

'I thought perhaps an early start . . .' She watched him shaking his head. 'Oh, well.' She looked at her watch. 'Who are we waiting for anyway?'

'Mr Lightfoot.'

'Who?' she squeaked.

'Mr Rocky Lightfoot. He won't be long – but I wouldn't try to be funny with him. He didn't get much sleep on account of he was out most of the night, somebody told us, and came back in a real bad mood. He has these moods apparently from time to time. We never worked for him before, we're mostly out of New York these days. It was always his father gave us our orders, you know? But the old guy is dying. Shame. He had balls, the old man did. *Cojones*, as the spics say.'

'Don't be racist,' Smith muttered darkly.

'Sorry, Obie,' Tanker said. 'No offense.'

'People of Spanish extraction,' Smith went on.

'Right. As people of Spanish extraction say,' Jones said carefully.

'Rocky has balls, too, believe me,' Casey whispered.

She stiffened between the two men as a step sounded outside the door. Rocky Lightfoot came in, accompanied by a large pear-shaped man. Both were wearing overcoats, but only Rocky was wearing a hat – a very beautiful wide-brimmed pearl gray trilby that almost suited him. He looked around the bleak little cell with an expression of distaste and sighed. His eyes came to rest on the trio seated on the bed, and his mouth tightened. 'Cozy,' he snapped.

186

Smith and Jones got up quickly and moved aside. Rocky gave them each a long, level stare, and then turned to Casey. He frowned for a moment, then stepped closer and looked down at her. His eyes widened suddenly, and he smiled, revealing small white teeth and very pink gums.

'Well, well – if it isn't little Miss Finch, the prize prick-teaser of Grantham Old School,' he said softly. 'Hello, Kathy. Welcome home.'

TWENTY-SEVEN

'What do you mean, you didn't know?' Jake demanded.

Armbruster raised his hands. 'I mean I didn't know. She was assigned to me as Mrs Hewson. I'm a field man, I don't vet and recruit. It would be on her personnel file, but I didn't go into that. I just asked for a good, reliable agent specializing in legal and commercial procedures, and she was seconded to me. Normally she runs for either Treasury or IRS, not us.' He looked from Joe to Jake. 'Jesus, you take what you're given, guys. Somebody issues you a gun, you don't look at it and say, "Where were you last Tuesday?" Do you?'

Joe sighed. 'Listen—'

'It's coming through now,' Dubrowski said. He had been less than pleased when Jake had burst into Records before he'd even had a chance to put sugar into his first cup of coffee. Leaning forward, he watched the green letters parade across the screen, hemmed in on three sides of his wheelchair by Jake, Joe and Armbruster.

'There it is,' Armbruster said. 'Born Katherine Charlotte Finch, here in Grantham. Mother Ariadne, father Frederick J., no siblings. Married Nathaniel Scott Hewson in 1982, widowed in 1984.' He sighed. 'I knew Nat Hewson – hell of a good agent.'

'She married a government agent?' Jake asked.

'Looks like they married while they were in college. He would have been recruited after graduation, probably. She wouldn't have been recruited at the same time, they don't like husband and wife teams much – ah, yes, there it is. Recruited after he died. Worked in Washington before that – yeah. It's all there.'

'It doesn't say there why she would lie to me about being born in some little town in—' Jake stopped himself. 'Cover?'

'Sure,' Armbruster nodded. 'For all she knew, you might have been one of Lightfoot's tame cops.'

'Thanks a lot,' Jake said, deeply insulted.

'Come on – give the girl credit,' Joe said. 'She was just doing her job.' He paused. 'The thing is, if it's Ronald Lightfoot who's got her—'

'Maybe not *just*,' Jake said.

'What the hell is that supposed to mean?' Armbruster asked.

'Who assigned her to you?' Jake asked.

'Zipkiss – my director of field operations,' Armbruster said.

Dubrowski looked up at him. 'No kidding?'

Armbruster was surprised. 'You know Zane?'

'Zane? His first name is Zane?' Dubrowski demanded, reaching for a red looseleaf notebook. 'This is for sure?'

'Yes, that's right, Zane Zipkiss,' Armbruster said, slightly nettled.

'You know if he's got a middle name?' Dubrowski demanded.

'I have no idea. We call him Crackers because he's always putting—'

'Oh, I don't take nicknames,' mumbled Dubrowski, writing furiously in his notebook. 'Zane Zipkiss. Terrific. Beautiful.'

Armbruster looked at Jake and raised an eyebrow. 'He collects names,' Jake explained, with a shrug.

'I'm worried about something . . .' Joe began.

Dubrowski, still crouched over the book, spoke absently. 'It's because my mother and father named me Hal.'

Armbruster looked puzzled. 'That's a perfectly good name,' he said. 'I have a cousin named Hal.'

Dubrowski smiled at him. Here was a new audience for his obsession. 'Short for Harold or Henry?'

'Halloran, I believe. A family name.'

'Uh-huh. That's nice. *My* Hal is short for Halloween Trickortreat Dubrowski,' he said flatly, defying them to laugh. 'I was born on October 31st, and my mother said it was no treat giving birth to a baby that weighed fourteen pounds, and my father said that, on the contrary, *he* thought it was quite a trick. They thought that was *real* funny. My mother used to tell me she laughed so much she nearly burst her stitches.' Hal's voice was bland. 'So, every time I find a name as odd as mine, it makes me feel better. Has to be a real, verified name, of course – no show-business stuff or anything like that. My favorite is Cigar Stubbs – but I got others. Crystal Shanda Lear, Larry Derryberry—'

'Hal – could we have a printout of that information from Washington, please?' Jake interrupted, before Hal got to Bunyon Snipes Womble, Gaston J. Feeblebunny and Hugh

Pugh. He'd heard them all during the two disastrous weeks he'd been assigned to Records. 'We're kind of in a hurry.'

'Sure.' Dubrowski reluctantly put the red book away, and did the necessary, handing the tear-off to Joe, who began looking through it with a worried expression. 'Anytime.'

'You made his day,' Jake said as they went down the hall.

Armbruster looked grim. 'The sins of the fathers,' he murmured, shaking his head sorrowfully. 'I take it you want me to call Zipkiss and ask whether Casey was a random choice or if she volunteered to be sent here?'

'You got it,' Jake said.

It took about twenty minutes, but Armbruster got the answer. He put the phone down and said in a flat voice, 'She asked for the job.'

'It looks like she's been asking for it all along,' Jake said angrily. 'And now she's got it.'

'Yes, but what was she asking *for* exactly?' muttered Joe, who had been scrabbling through the papers on his desk. 'Maybe she asked for the Norris job, too. I mean – there's more than one thing going on here.'

Jake ignored him, ignored Armbruster, ignored all the bustle around them of incoming duty detectives shouting and talking to one another. He felt emotions welling up in him, conflicting and confusing. Casey wasn't Casey, she was Katherine Charlotte – K. C. Finch. Fine. Great. She had lied to him, to Armbruster, to everyone. She was rotten, she was wonderful and brave, she was stupid and in danger, he was an idiot, she was an idiot, she was rich and he was poor, her mother had been murdered, Norris had been murdered, maybe even Casey/K.C./Kathy herself had been murdered by now. If she hadn't been he would kill her with his bare hands when he caught up with her.

Except that he couldn't find her, didn't even begin to know where to look. It was a big city with a long history, full of nasty people with a thousand axes to grind. He was helpless to do anything about any of it. He was Jake Chase, the schmuck who broke things, wasn't he? Maybe he deserved this. Maybe he deserved it all. He picked up an empty dirty coffee cup from somebody's desk and threw it hard against the floor.

It didn't break. Instead, it bounced sideways and caught Captain Klotzman on the knee.

Klotzman had just come on duty. He hadn't been in the

building more than eight minutes, and he hadn't been in the Homicide Division offices more than forty-five seconds. He bent at the waist and looked at the trickle of cold coffee that ran down his clean trouser leg and dripped onto his freshly shined shoe, then straightened up, shook his leg slightly and sighed.

'Good morning, Chase,' he said in a dull, resigned voice. 'Put your socks on the wrong feet again this morning?'

He walked on into his office, closing the door very quietly behind him. After a while it opened again, and he pointed to Armbruster. 'Who's he?'

'It's not easy to explain,' Jake said cautiously.

Klotzman sighed. 'No,' he said, beckoning them into his office. 'Somehow I knew it wouldn't be.'

After breakfast Molly Pemberton went into the large, sunny day room and glanced around. She knew she looked a sight, with her two black eyes and her hair sticking up around the bandage, but she couldn't stay in that room and listen to the woman in the bed next to hers droning on about her bowels for a minute longer.

The day room had bright yellow curtains. A choice of either chintz-covered armchairs or more supportive straight chairs were dotted around in groups. She selected a deep armchair that faced the windows looking out over the little park behind the hospital. She was half-dozing, looking at the lovely fall colors of the leaves, when she sensed someone coming up beside her and gave a little yelp of fear.

It was a man of about her own age, gray-haired, very pale, with a bandage similar to hers and two black eyes to match, too. He was very unsteady on his feet.

'I'm sorry,' he said. 'I certainly didn't mean to startle you.'

'No, of course you didn't – I was just being silly,' Molly said in embarrassment.

'Do you mind if I sit here?' the man asked. 'I was on my way across to the television set, but I find it's beyond my capability.'

'Of course I don't mind. I only just made it here myself,' Molly said. 'But I was determined to get out and about.'

The man sank gratefully into the chair next to hers. They gazed at one another for a painful, hazy moment – and then Molly began to giggle. 'We look like twins,' she said. The man stared at her for a moment, then half-smiled.

'Fraternal, of course.'

'Of course,' Molly agreed. 'Were you mugged?'

'In a manner of speaking, yes,' he said. 'Were you?'

'Burgled – I think. I really don't remember much about it,' Molly had to admit. 'One minute I was sitting there reading about the evolution of the Dracula legend, and the next minute there was a voice behind me demanding to know where I'd put the key.'

'What key?'

'I don't know. When I tried to turn he grabbed hold of my shoulders and held me down. He was very strong. Then he started asking me about a desk being delivered from Lecomber Galleries, and about a key. He *insisted* I had a key that belonged to him. I think he was a dope addict or something – he sounded half-crazy anyway. I tried to scream for help, and that's when he hit me. They said he didn't take anything, and I'm lucky to be alive.'

'You are. We all are.'

Molly smiled. 'How true.'

They sat in companionable silence for a while. Then: 'Do you often read horror stories at night?' he asked her.

Molly laughed. 'Heavens, no. This was actually rather a scholarly work evaluating the psychological aspects of Dracula. It was most interesting. The author was postulating the theory that we respond so strongly to the legend because we all know vampires. Indeed, that there are vampires everywhere – people who suck the emotional lifeblood of others to feed their own needs or obsessions,' Molly said. 'I had just gotten up to a comparison of Barry's play, *The Silver Cord*, with Coward's *The Vortex* when this voice spoke to me out of the darkness . . . most alarming.'

'Your husband wasn't there to protect you?'

Molly smiled reminiscently. 'No, I'm a widow. There's just Mr Braithwaite.'

'A live-in lover?'

She chuckled. 'You flatter me. No – just my rather elderly cat.'

'Ah.' He nodded understandingly. 'Like you, I relish the company of cats. But they do have one drawback in comparison with dogs, and that is their lamentable inability to bark when required. A loud purr is really not the same, is it?' He smiled, a wistful, charming smile, despite his missing teeth.

'No.' She warmed to him. He didn't look at all like Dan, and yet there was something about him that reminded her of her late husband. 'There seems to be an epidemic of senseless violence these days,' Molly said mournfully. 'I mean, look at the two of us.'

He nodded gingerly. 'I'm afraid the senselessness in the attack on me was all my own.'

She saw that the subject depressed him, and decided to try and cheer him up. 'I was thinking of taking a class in karate,' she said brightly. 'I just love the thought of being able to toss some rotten mugger head over keester into the nearest garbage can – we old folks have got to stick up for ourselves, you know.' He gave her no answer. 'My name is Molly,' she said. 'Molly Pemberton.' She looked at him expectantly.

He seemed to hesitate, then took a deep breath, as if fortifying himself for a plunge into unknown waters. 'How nice to meet you. I have very few friends here in Grantham. My name is Crump – but do please call me Sylvester.'

TWENTY-EIGHT

'You're a bad girl, Kathy,' Rocky Lightfoot said with a very unfriendly smile. 'You're still holding out on us. I don't like that.'

'I'm *not* holding out on you or anybody else, *Ronald*,' Casey said, sticking her chin out.

Obie looked at him. 'Ronald? Is that your name?'

'Shut up,' Rocky snapped.

'His name isn't Rocky, it's Ronald,' Obie told Tanker.

'You might have guessed,' Tanker said.

'Norris never showed me anything or told me anything about his so-called "proof",' Casey went on. 'He may have showed something to Eustace – I think he must have, or Eustace wouldn't have gone ahead with the book. But he never showed anything to *me*. I was just the editor.'

'He claims my father killed your mother.'

'Stepmother,' Casey said firmly. 'That's right, he does. Did.'

'He claims my father was jealous of her because of all the other men she slept with.' He spoke the words with some relish.

'Ronald – I can't get over it,' Obie marveled loudly.

Casey kept her voice even. It wasn't easy. 'That's what he *said*, all right. Was it true?'

'Don't you know? Didn't you see the rest of the manuscript?'

'No. Norris died before he finished it.'

'Oh, come on – do you expect me to believe that?' Rocky asked, walking to the far wall and back. It didn't take him long. 'Let's have the truth now, Kathy, or I shall be forced to ask these gentlemen to use certain skills they possess to help you to talk.'

'I knew it,' Obediah groaned.

Rocky looked at him, frowned and then went on. 'Naturally, I'd like to avoid this – as I'm sure you would.'

'We *all* would,' Obediah muttered.

'And it's so simple.' Rocky beamed at her. She'd seen that smile before – on her sixteenth birthday, when he and some other boys had brought her a 'special present' and lured her out to the boathouse to get it. The offer of a reefer was a powerful

194

lure to a sixteen-year-old girl anxious to appear grown up and sophisticated. 'All you have to do is tell me what Norris knew and turn over the proof.'

Casey pressed her lips together. Rocky slapped her hard across the mouth. There was no expression on his face, but his eyes were burning. 'You just hate giving things away, don't you, you smug little bitch?'

'Here now, Ronald,' murmured Obediah, scowling at Rocky. If there was going to be anything done to the girl, he was going to do it. There was such a thing as demarcation, after all. He was a professional, and he demanded proper working conditions.

Casey turned to the big black man. 'Did you know what your boss and some of his friends did to me at my sixteenth birthday party? They got me high on pot and got me to take all my clothes off. Some of them tried to make me have sex with him while they watched but I wouldn't, so they poured garbage all over me, took me back to my own party like that and made me sing and dance. They said they would beat me up if I didn't do what they said. Everyone laughed at me. Then they tore up the gardens driving my father's car through the flowerbeds and dumped it into the swimming pool. That's when the police came.' Tears came into her eyes and she wiped blood from the corner of her mouth.

'That true?' Obediah asked Rocky.

'Do you really want to know?' Rocky asked in a dangerous voice. He turned to Casey. 'Look, I know what Norris had on my father, and I want it now.'

'I don't like men who hurt women,' Obediah said.

'Me neither,' Tanker said. 'Not unless that's their *job*, of course.'

Rocky glared at them, his narrow face going white and red and white again with the pressure of the memories. 'They never said anything about hurting her or humiliating her in front of everyone else. They'd found out I had a crush on her and they said they would "help" me get her to like me. They said they would lure her out to the boathouse and get her drunk or high enough to do it with me, and then she would be my girl. But she wouldn't – not even when she was high as a kite. She was such a stuck-up little bitch—' He turned to Casey. 'You were, weren't you?'

Casey nodded. She hadn't known he liked her at the

195

time – and fair was fair. 'Yes, I was.'

Rocky seemed momentarily balked by this flat admission of her own weakness, then went on, his voice filled with bitter pain. 'I never wanted to get into trouble, but because I was Gurney Lightfoot's kid they figured I was bad news. I had to act tough the best I could, or they would have laughed at me. They did anyway, some of the time. But some of them – rich men's kids – they were worse than I ever was.' Rocky's voice had grown defensive and shrill. 'Worse than any of my father's people would ever be. One especially. They told me she would love it – that she was hot for it, secretly hot for me, and I believed them. If I'd known what they were really planning, I wouldn't have done it. Especially since afterward they said it was all my idea. It wasn't – but I took the blame so I'd look big to them.' He was quite pale now. 'But that didn't work either. They just went on as before. Nothing changed, except my father turned against me because of her stepmother going off the deep end about everything. All right. I was a stupid kid then. I'm not stupid now. For Christ's sake, you knocked her out the other night yourself.'

'Yes – I knocked her out, neat and clean. It was business.'

'Well then, you *stick* to business,' Rocky said angrily. 'That's what you've been brought here to do. That's what you've been paid for.'

'He hasn't been paid yet,' Tanker said. 'So far it's been strictly spec. We don't usually work on spec, only seeing as it was your father asking, we came along.'

'You'll be *paid*, dammit!' Rocky shrieked. 'Do things to her – make her tell me what I want to know.'

'I don't *know* what you want to know,' Casey said desperately. She appealed to Obediah. 'I don't *know* where Norris kept his proof, if he had any. I don't *know*.'

Obediah turned to Rocky. 'She says she doesn't know.'

'I believe her,' Tanker said.

'Me, too,' Obediah agreed. They stared at Rocky.

'This is ridiculous,' Rocky stormed. 'Do what I tell you, *now*.'

'I don't feel like it,' Obediah said. 'I have a headache.'

'Of *course* somebody rolled the dead guy's fingerprints and checked,' Klotzman said, slamming the phone back into its cradle. 'It was Norris all right, dead as a doornail. Boy, you really had me going for a minute there.'

'Me, too,' Joe said.

'It was just a thought,' Jake said irritably. 'Don't worry – I have others.'

'That's what I'm afraid of,' Klotzman said.

Armbruster returned from making his calls. 'Nobody is admitting anything, but I get the feeling that Quiddick is behind some string-pulling that started about six months ago – maybe longer.'

'Six *months* ago? *Before* Norris got out of jail?' Klotzman asked in an astonished voice.

'Looks that way.'

'We seem to have a chicken-and-egg situation here,' Armbruster said, settling back down in the chair between Jake and Joe. 'Chicken – Ariadne Finch; egg – she disappears, probably murdered. Chicken – Norris being dumped by Lightfoot; egg – Norris decides to get his revenge by writing a book claiming Lightfoot killed Ariadne Finch. Chicken – the proof; egg – *Norris* is murdered by Lightfoot who's trying to get hold of the proof – whatever it is – and destroy it. Chicken – my operative, who is working for Millington on a different assignment, and who happens to be Ariadne Finch's daughter . . .'

'*That's* the first chicken,' Klotzman interrupted. 'Ariadne's daughter getting suspicious about Rocky Lightfoot; egg – she gets herself assigned to come back to Grantham—'

'Wait a minute,' Armbruster put in. 'It was *well* before that that Quiddick started up the hare about getting Millington investigated so he and Porter can put on the pressure—'

'How did rabbits get into this?' Klotzman asked.

'Hell – there's an earlier chicken than *that*,' Joe shouted, standing up and waving his arms in his excitement. 'What about the reason Porter and Lightfoot have always hated each other, hey?' He looked around at them all in turn. 'Beat *that* chicken,' he said smugly, and sat down again.

TWENTY-NINE

'Well, has Rocky come back yet?' Gurney Lightfoot rasped.

'No.' Evelyn's voice was soft, and she looked around the room cautiously.

'The old bitch has gone out to do some shopping,' Gurney said impatiently. 'Come closer, girl, I can hardly see you if you stand over there.'

Evelyn was an obedient girl – she came closer. She was also a soft-hearted girl, and when the nurse had grabbed her by the arm the previous night saying that the old man was in a state, she had readily gone with her to the sickroom, thinking she might help. When she found Gurney only wanted company and information, she regretted the impulse, but it was too late by then.

And anyway, Ronnie had been irritable all afternoon because his shirts hadn't come back from the laundry, and the old man was kind of pathetic, lying there all sick and thin and alone, except for the bossy, silly nurse. Gurney had told the old biddy to get out, and after extracting a promise from Evelyn that she'd be called if necessary, she had left them alone together.

'He's told them all to stay away from me,' Gurney had confided to Evelyn in a gravelly croak. 'All the men are afraid of him, they know he's going to be the big bazoomba around here when I kick it, and they want to stay on his good side. How about you, sweetheart? Are you afraid of him?'

'No,' Evelyn said frankly. 'Ronnie is easy to manage if you know what he likes.'

Gurney grinned, exposing big, strong yellow teeth, all his own. It was small consolation to be able to chew anything and digest almost nothing. 'So you've learned that, have you? I remember the day you arrived. I spotted you for a good operator right away.'

'Thank you,' Evelyn said demurely. 'He needs a strong hand.'

Gurney cackled to himself. 'He does indeed. There is everything wrong with him that there could possibly be wrong with anybody, and yet he's my son. I love him. I can't stand the sight of him, but I love him. You have to look after your own, no matter how obnoxious they might be, that's how I was brought up, that's how I believe and I'm stuck with it. Also with him, the little nerk.'

'He's that all right,' Evelyn agreed. 'But I love him, too. I can't help thinking that deep inside that bitter little pill there's a sugar lump wanting to get out.'

'Are you serious?' Gurney demanded.

'No,' Evelyn said with a sigh. 'Not really. Sometimes it's easier to pretend, though.'

Gurney laughed. 'He's been pretending all his life. He may be silly – he may even be a little crazy, like his mother was – but he's not dumb. Believe me, he's not dumb.'

'Oh, I know that,' she said, almost to herself. 'Neither am I – although he thinks I am. *That* smart he isn't.'

Gurney nodded, as if his own opinion had been confirmed. 'Here – come closer.' When Evelyn hesitated, he smiled without humor. 'I'm no danger to you, girl. I'm not going to ask for anything you don't want to give.'

Evelyn came over and sat on the nurse's chair. 'What *are* you going to ask me for, then?'

'I want to know what he's up to.'

'Oh.' She looked down and made small folds in her long pale blue velvet lounger, piling them into a little mound on her knee and then letting them slide off again. Her hair was a golden cascade that ran down her neck and nestled in the curve of her shoulders. Her huge eyes were half-hidden behind thick, dark lashes – you could be forgiven for not seeing the glint of intelligence there. The boy may have no sense, Gurney thought, but he has good taste in women. 'I don't think I could do that,' Evelyn finally said. 'He'd be very angry.'

'Oh, yes, he would be. Very angry indeed – if he ever found out, that is,' Gurney nodded. 'Go over and look in the top drawer of that big bureau over there. Go on – do what I ask.' Evelyn got up and went across the room. She moved with a sinuous grace that Gurney appreciated – but only academically.

'That's right,' Gurney said. 'Now reach into the back – there's a little latch – flip it and pull the drawer right out. Good girl. Now reach into the space. That's good. Wotcha got, baby?' Evelyn turned toward him, holding out a green leather box. 'Good girl. Put the drawer back and then bring that box over here.'

He watched as she did what she was told and then returned and sat down with the box on her lap. 'Open it,' he directed.

She lifted the lid and looked down on a dazzling collection of diamonds and emeralds set in gold – earrings, necklace and two bracelets as heavy as shackles. 'Ohhh,' she breathed. After a time she looked up at him. 'Have I got this right?' she asked.

'I think so,' Gurney said softly.

Carefully, Evelyn closed the box and placed both her beautiful shaped and manicured hands on its top, as if holding it down on her lap. 'He's kidnapped a girl,' she began.

That had been last night. All morning he had fretted, waiting for the nurse to go out on the errands he'd thought up for her. He'd laid awake most of the night going over all the things Evelyn had told him – from Obie and Tanker knocking the girl out to the Great Shoot-Out at the Piggy Wiggy Wondermart. He'd been looking for a pattern – but every time he thought he saw one, it slipped away like a dream. He didn't know whether that was because of his illness . . . or because there was no pattern to find.

'Did you find out where he's holding her?' he asked Evelyn when she came again.

'I'm not sure – I think I heard Littlewood say something about the Magnolia Hotel? Is that right?'

'Jesus – what a place to choose,' Gurney said. 'Typical – he's playing Capone again.'

'He did have that big gray hat on,' Evelyn agreed. 'And he took a silver dollar – although he's not much good at flipping it.'

'Capone *and* Raft,' Gurney muttered. 'What a combination.' He sighed in exasperation, precipitating a coughing fit. Evelyn poured him out a drink of water and held his shaking shoulders while he sipped it. Then he lay back on his pillows, exhausted. 'He's after the rest of the Norris stuff?'

'Yes.'

'She don't have it. She's been palsy with the cops – she would have given it to them by now if she had anything. But does he see that? Oh, no, not him. My son, the head case.'

'He sent for Smith and Jones,' Evelyn said uneasily. 'Aren't they the two men who do tortures?'

He gazed at her, astounded. 'He plans to *torture* her? Why?'

'I don't know. Maybe he's frustrated.' She looked down and

smoothed her dress. 'I haven't been well lately,' she murmured shyly. 'Just a temporary problem.'

'I see. He had that nasty streak where women are concerned, but I thought he'd grown out of it since college,' Gurney murmured. 'He's got to be stopped before he goes too far – he's done it before. I saved his bacon each time, but I don't know if I can do it again. I figure he killed Norris – well, he deserved killing, the little snipe, so we have to handle that. I think we can handle that. But kidnapping is federal. The local cops can bring in the FBI on this, see? That's where he's gone too far. Aside from Prohibition, I never went up against the feds, Evelyn, that was my code. And I never affiliated either. I don't like big organizations. Strictly local was good enough for me – occasionally state, but mostly local. I am not greedy.'

'I can't stop him,' Evelyn said. 'I'm not supposed to know anything about anything.' She was alarmed.

'No – no – I understand that.' He rubbed his fingers absently on the sheet. 'How did they look, by the way?'

'The emeralds? They looked great.'

'Where did you hide them?'

She looked at him. 'They're safe,' she said levelly.

He chuckled. 'Good girl – keep me from temptation.' He frowned again. 'Who's in the house at the moment?'

'I don't know for sure. Maybe Fritz and Knapp?'

'Oh, God,' Gurney moaned in a defeated voice. 'Well – see if you can find them for me.'

'I don't think I can—'

'Say you were passing the door and heard me yelling and you think I'm dying but you're afraid to go in and find out,' Gurney suggested.

'Oh.' She considered this for a while. He could see her mind working on it. Well, a girl should take her time, consider all the angles, he admired her for that. Also, it gave him time to build up a little oxygen. Eventually she smiled at him. 'OK,' she said. 'Start yelling.'

'My God – hasn't anyone turned up anything?' Jake demanded fretfully. He'd slept in the chair behind his desk, dozing off every once in a while as they went over the material they'd collected from Norris's office in the Burnley Building. Joe and

Armbruster had done the same. As the long night hours had passed, the rustle of paper had been regularly overlaid with the fine buzz of somebody's involuntary snore. Klotzman had claimed Captain's Immunity and had gone home at nine o'clock. Now Jake looked blearily around the room. 'Pinsky,' he shouted, as the detective came in. 'Where's my girl?'

Pinsky shrugged. 'Sorry, Jake – still nothing. We've been working the street all night – but nothing yet.'

'That's the third time,' Armbruster said.

'What?' Jake looked at him.

'I've been going over this rough draft again,' Armbruster said. He sounded hoarse. 'And every once in a while he has a note in the margin – I mean he has lots of them – but three times now he's had "check box". What box?'

'Beats hell out of me,' Jake said despairingly. He knew Pinsky was being kind. He knew they'd all been checking their street contacts yesterday and last night. He also knew this morning they'd be checking the river, and the morgue.

'Look higher,' Joe mumbled from where he lay with his chin on crossed arms. 'About halfway up on the left, in among something about railway tickets.'

Armbruster squinted at it. Jake pulled over the desk lamp for better light. The ashtray fell off and smashed on the floor. Nobody even glanced up. 'It says . . . "check daily",' Armbruster finally decided.

'No, it doesn't,' Jake whispered. 'It says "check *diary*".' His voice rose. 'Dammit – it says check *DIARY*! He did have the goddamn diary, then!'

'Yeah,' Joe mumbled.

'Why the hell didn't you say this before?' Jake demanded.

Joe lifted his head. 'I just saw it when he held it up,' he yawned, and began rubbing his eyes. 'Through the back of the paper you could read it easier.'

Armbruster turned the page over. 'Oh, yeah. He must have written it down first, then written all that other stuff over it.'

'So he *did* have proof,' Jake said. He sat back, gratified.

'Yeah,' Joe said sarcastically. 'And according to Armbruster here, he also had a box. Now we know everything, right?'

Jake stared at him. Joe was right. They'd sat there all night, waiting for something on which to move concerning the kidnapping. They'd whiled away the time scrabbling through these papers looking for clues. No word had come on Casey, and all the paperchase had done was to confirm what they'd already suspected – that Norris had bought the diary from the Finch maid, or gotten it from someone else who had. There was still no indication of where the diary was. There was still no explanation of where Ariadne Finch was, alive or dead. There was still no word on where Casey was, alive or dead. There was no coffee left in the coffee machine. There were no cigarettes. There were no doughnuts. And there was no Santa Claus. 'I want my mommy,' Jake said plaintively.

'Wake her up,' Rocky Lightfoot said.

'No good – she's out for the count,' Obediah Smith said.

'Put some water on her,' Rocky snapped.

Smith and Jones looked at one another. 'I don't do water,' Smith said finally.

Rocky looked from one to the other. He took a deep breath. 'Damn you,' he said through clenched teeth. 'Damn you both.' He turned and walked out of the room.

'Is that it?' Jones asked.

'It'll have to do,' Smith said. He bent down and pulled the blankets up over the unconscious girl. Now the little piss-ass would have to let her go, he thought. He'd stood there for two hours while Rocky badgered the girl, demanding information. It was pathetic. Obediah had been disgusted by the entire thing – ashamed to have had any part in it. Despite hysterical threats from Rocky, he had refused to do anything to Casey.

Obediah Smith had had quite a reputation in Haiti. He was a professional and, as a professional, he had standards. There was a point in every interrogation when he knew whether or not there was any more to get out of a victim. Obediah had reached that point about two minutes after hearing Casey protest her ignorance.

'She's telling the truth,' he'd said. 'She doesn't know anything about this.'

Rocky had refused to believe that but in Obediah's presence he had apparently been afraid to do anything to her himself. Littlewood had offered to break her arm, but Obediah had looked at him out of those dark, liquid eyes and the idea had lost its appeal suddenly. Littlewood hadn't said much after that.

Gradually Obediah's dark, brooding disapproval of the proceedings had had an effect on Rocky, too. He became edgy. He pretended to become bored. It was apparent to everyone that he'd gotten himself into a corner on this. Eventually Littlewood had been inspired from some dim recess of his brain to give him a way out by reminding him that it was getting late and that he had a dentist's appointment.

Throughout the ordeal Obediah had watched the girl. He admired her. She had guts. And she had understood about his headache, which by now was considerably worse – mostly due to Rocky's regular screams of rage and frustration.

Obediah Smith didn't like Rocky Lightfoot. He didn't like taking orders from Rocky Lightfoot. Old Gurney was a crud – all bosses were cruds – but he never pretended to be anything *but* a crud. Obediah had never minded coming along to do a job for Gurney, the old man always played it straight and paid what was asked. He'd thought *this* job was for Gurney when he'd left New York. But it had turned out to be for Rocky.

Now, going up the filthy stairs from the sub-basement, he was entirely sorry he'd come. He gazed at Rocky's skinny back and the heavily padded sloping shoulders. He had the feeling that Rocky was not cut out for the criminal life, no matter how he dressed himself up. He was not a professional. There was considerable malevolence in Obediah's brown eyes. He would have liked to kick Rocky's ass, but Littlewood was there. Obediah was not a fool. He knew Littlewood was fast with a gun and devoted to Rocky. So he trudged on. But that didn't stop him from thinking.

As they stood outside the condemned hotel, they heard the distant sound of heavy machinery and the machine-gun rattle of pneumatic drills. The old neighborhood was changing fast. It looked to Obediah like the whole setup here in Grantham was changing – and not for the good.

'When are you going to let her go?' Tanker asked, reading Obediah's mind, as he often did.

'I am not going to let her go,' Rocky snarled. 'I can use her to bargain with, if nothing else.' He turned and started down the street. When Obediah hesitated, thinking maybe it was time he and Tanker got back to where crooks were crooks and a man knew where he was, Littlewood drew his gun.

'I think you should join us,' he said.

When the reached the front of the Lightfoot residence, Arthur Burpee was standing in the entrance, waiting for them. He looked at Rocky.

'Your father wants to see you,' he said.

'Too bad,' Rocky said, pushing past him.

'He wants to see you *now*,' Burpee said. He seemed to have lost his earlier fear, and looked Rocky straight in the eye.

Rocky was suddenly alarmed. 'Is he dying?' he asked.

'Could be,' Burpee said.

Rocky hurried up the stairs and down the hall to his father's room. He opened the door and went in.

Gurney Lightfoot was propped up in bed. His eyes were clear and his hair was brushed and he had on his best silk pajamas. On either side of the bed were ranged all his men – Nipsy Friedlander, Fritz and Knapp, Bumbo, Kretzmer, Cyril, Bippy, even Thrushwood, the garage man. 'Hello, Rocky,' Gurney said. 'I've been waiting for you.'

Rocky Lightfoot swallowed. Obediah Smith, looking down, almost felt sorry for him. It looked as if his little flush was busted. 'You look better, Father,' Rocky said. His voice squeaked briefly.

'I understand you've been running things pretty well while I've been sick,' Gurney said. 'The men say you've got things running so smooth, they haven't got anything to do.'

'Oh?'

'Yes, indeed. And I want you to know, Rocky, that I appreciate your efforts.'

'Oh.' Patently, Rocky was puzzled. 'Thank you.'

'But now I think it's time I took the reins back again.'

'But you might – I mean, you wouldn't understand my system – that is – the doctor says—' Rocky was babbling.

'About this girl, Rocky,' Gurney interrupted.

'Girl?'

'The girl you've taken and put into the Magnolia Hotel.'

'Oh – *that* girl. She's not Casey Hewson at all, you know,' Rocky said quickly. 'She's really Kathy Finch.'

'Is she?' Gurney said. 'That's interesting. As I recall, you and she are old school friends, aren't you? She was Ariadne's girl.' Gurney's voice was thin and breathy, but it had a dangerous edge to it.

'Yes – this whole *thing* is about Ariadne Finch.'

'Is it?' Gurney Lightfoot looked at his son and sighed. The boy had never been handsome, and now, in his fear and his pinstripe suit and big hat, he was even more unprepossessing than usual. Evelyn must be extremely nearsighted, he thought to himself. She certainly has remarkable staying power.

'Norris was writing a book about Ariadne Finch's murder.'

'She only disappeared,' Gurney corrected him.

'That isn't the point,' Rocky said.

'What is the point, Rocky?' Gurney asked.

Rocky was getting exasperated – the old man looked better, but it was obvious his mind was gone. 'She is Ariadne Finch's daughter,' Rocky said, as if explaining to an idiot child.

'Stepdaughter,' Gurney corrected his son wearily. 'Ariadne couldn't have children – it was the great sorrow of her life. For my part, looking at you, it doesn't seem such a tragedy, but it bothered her. Some women – they're funny like that.'

Desperate to please, even to divert some attention from himself, Rocky burst out. 'Evelyn is pregnant, Father. We're going to have a baby – I'm going to be a father!'

'Jesus,' Gurney said. It took him a moment to assimilate this improbable piece of information. He smiled briefly, realizing at last why Evelyn was still hanging on. 'Congratulations,' he said.

Taking the smile for encouragement, Rocky went on. 'If it's a boy we'll name him after you, of course.'

'Of course,' Gurney said. 'I want you to let the girl go, Rocky.'

'What?' Rocky said, startled into another vocal squeak. Tanker Jones glanced at Obediah Smith and raised his eyes to the ceiling. Obie had been right, the guy had lousy footwork.

'I said I want you to let the Finch girl go,' Gurney repeated. 'This is kidnapping. You are risking some nosing in our affairs by the FBI. I don't like that. She can tell us nothing. We will have to get the information some other way.'

'But – there isn't *time*,' Rocky said. There was panic in his voice. 'The police are all over the place—'

'Looking for the girl,' Fritz pointed out. He was enjoying himself. He hadn't enjoyed himself at all since Gurney had first fallen sick.

Ever since Rocky had started taking over, things had been bad for the boys. When Gurney had called them in, a while ago, they'd told him how nobody knew what was going on anymore. They were confused, they said. For a start, they hadn't collected for numbers or beat anyone up for months. Rocky said the computers were handling it. The money came in, apparently, because they got paid. But what the hell? they said. Paid for what?

Well, it was gonna be OK now. Gurney Lightfoot valued loyalty – he always had. People like Gurney didn't forget. What he had just promised each of them in the past hour was proof of that. He said he would divide the kingdom – they could each run their own rackets and not have to put up with little pipsqueaks who didn't know their ass from their elbow. He gazed at Gurney's son with some gratification. Rocky was sweating. Fritz knew how that felt.

'Yeah, looking for the girl,' Knapp echoed. He was enjoying himself, too.

'Not just the girl,' Rocky protested desperately. 'They're after the proof Norris had about who killed Ariadne. We can't let them find it. We have to get to it first and destroy it, or you'll die in jail.'

'Me? Why should *I* die in jail?' Gurney asked.

'Because . . . because . . .' Rocky swallowed hard. 'Because it was you who killed Ariadne Finch,' he said at last.

Gurney stared at him. 'No, it wasn't,' he said. 'I didn't kill Ariadne Finch.'

Rocky stared back. 'But I thought—' He stopped.

'Is that why you've been running around like a blue-assed fly – because you thought I killed Ariadne Finch?' his father asked him in a curious tone.

'Well – yes, as a matter of fact,' Rocky said awkwardly. 'I had to protect you, didn't I? You're my father – and you couldn't protect yourself, being sick and all, could you?'

'That's nice, Ronald, that's very nice. I'm touched,' Gurney Lightfoot said. 'But I didn't kill her.'

Rocky looked around the room, and then back at his father, confused. 'But – if you didn't kill her, who did?'

'I don't know,' Gurney said. 'I thought it was you.'

THIRTY

Casey awoke slowly. She felt sick, and it was a long time before she tried to move. Bit by bit, she was remembering what had happened.

Rocky, that was it, Rocky had been yelling at her, and yelling, and yelling. And the big black man, Obediah, had been beside her. She was crying and he put his hand on her shoulder, as if to comfort her. Then darkness.

'Good heavens!' she said aloud. 'The Vulcan neck pinch!'

Well, something like that anyway. She felt sure of it – Obediah Smith had made her lose consciousness. In all his 'studies' of torture he had no doubt come across many esoteric little items of that nature. She remembered something about it herself – something about the vagus nerve or the carotid artery or something. Dangerous, unless you knew exactly what you were doing.

She had the feeling Obediah did.

But why?

Because he had believed her? Or because his migraine had worsened?

She stood up, and nearly fell down again. Little by little, she worked feeling back into her legs, which had gotten cramped in the chilly room. She felt weak and exhausted – but she was afraid that Rocky would come back at any time. Wherever she was, he might not be far away. She'd changed – had he? Had all that rage been a front? His eyes had been different – not the spiteful eyes of a frustrated boy, but the calculating and intelligent eyes of a man with a purpose.

Which might be even more dangerous.

Depending on the purpose, of course.

In this instance, the purpose seemed to be an implacable or even hysterical obsession with the 'proof' about Ariadne's disappearance and/or death.

– Oh, Ariadne, she thought. Why did you go away like that, without a word, breaking my father's heart at last? Did you run away – or did someone destroy you? That's what I'd hoped to find out. That's why I volunteered to come back to Grantham on the Millington job. But I didn't get anywhere, until Norris walked in with that manuscript. Of course I knew about the men, but as Daddy said, it didn't seem to really touch you. It was a sickness, that's all. By night you were one thing, but by day you lit up his life and mine with your beauty and your laughter and your madcap way of running at everything full tilt.

And you loved me, too, I know you did. I remember how angry you were when Rocky's friends hurt me. I didn't understand why you called a crook like Rocky's father by his first name. I understand now.

He was one of your men.

Was that why everyone told me to forget? Why Daddy sent me away to the boarding school, and kissed me goodbye without meeting my eyes? Had your midnight life finally touched our daytime brightness? And is that why you went away? . . .

She was away at boarding school when Ariadne disappeared.

She had been at college when her father died.

Grantham had become a dark world, full of dragons and memories, a place to stay away from, until she had gathered up enough courage to face it and light up the corners.

Fred Norris had sensed her fear and her curiosity, without knowing the reason, and it had pleased his rather sadistic nature to play on it. He claimed to know the truth about what happened to Ariadne, but he had played a little game with her. Held it out, like some kind of carrot, always promising to explain it in the next chapter, or the next, always promising to show her the proof.

But he never had.

And now he never would.

Whoever had killed him had silenced him forever, and his so-called proof probably had never even existed.

She looked at the door. Could Obediah's kindness (if that's what it had been) have extended that far? she asked herself, crossing the room.

No.

The door was locked.

She was still a prisoner of both the present and the past.

Victor Niforos felt terrible about Molly Pemberton's being attacked in her own home – and in *his* building. He should have been there to protect her. He had failed her, he was a worm, a fool, an idiot. He should have known, when she told him to fix the locks on the windows, that she was afraid of someone. And he had *forgotten* to fix the locks. He had been so engrossed in finishing the desk that the time had flown by. And he knew this was because of his terrible pride.

He had wanted her praise for the thing well done. He had wanted to strut before her, to have her be impressed, admiring. Grateful.

Now she was in the hospital, alone, hurt and frightened and had no one to console her.

He had made up his mind to visit her that afternoon, and had purchased some beautiful flowers to take to her, roses and other things he didn't know the name of, but which were very expensive. He knew, in his heart of hearts, that he was trying to buy his way out of his guilt, but he didn't know what else he could do.

Then his eye had fallen on the desk, gleaming so beautifully under his workshop lights. And he remembered the little camera that Sophia, his daughter, had sent him for Christmas. Of course! He would take photographs, he would have them developed at that special place that did them in an hour, and he would take them down to her at the hospital so she could see how lovely it was, and know that it was waiting for her when she came home!

Quickly he went to his apartment and fetched the camera. Busily, he took the entire roll of film, showing the desk from this angle and that, drawers open, drawers closed, the grain on the top, the dovetailing of the joint he had repaired – everything. He ran the three blocks to the photography shop, and they said the prints would be ready in an hour.

He ran back to his apartment, took a bath and put on clean clothes. As he was leaving the building, a man approached him. 'I wonder if you could help me—' he began.

'I'm sorry, I'm on way to hospital,' Victor apologized. 'No apartments for rent here.'

'No, no – I have an apartment. I'm looking for a desk.'

'A desk?'

'Yes. Delivered to Mrs Pemberton.'

'Oh. That desk.'

'You do have it, then?'

'Yes, it is here – but Mizz Pemberton, she is not.'

'Oh. I had hoped to see her about it. You see – I want to buy it from her.'

Victor was instantly suspicious. 'Why you want to buy this desk?' he asked in a growl.

'Well, my wife and I saw it in the shop and had intended to come back to get it, but when she returned it was gone. They told me it was sold to a Mrs Pemberton. My wife was very taken with the desk, and we thought – well, I thought that perhaps Mrs Pemberton might consider selling it. At a profit, of course, for her trouble. My wife was so disappointed – it was just what she wanted.'

'Mizz Pemberton, she not want to sell this desk. Not now.'

'What do you mean, not now?' The man seemed puzzled.

Victor Niforos glanced at his watch. There was a moment or two to spare. If this man had seen the desk as it was before, he could appreciate what he, Victor Niforos, had made of it. 'I show you,' he said proudly. 'Come with me.'

Charles E. Porter stood on the sidewalk opposite the Lightfoot building. He'd been standing there for a long time. His presence had been noted and communicated to Headquarters by the officers covertly watching the place. They had been told not to approach him.

After a long time, he slowly walked across the street and mounted the ten steps to the door. He rang the bell and waited.

It took some time, but eventually the door opened and a girl stood there. She was beautiful, buxom and blonde. Dressed in an expensive gown, it was obvious that she was not the maid.

'Good afternoon,' Charley said, with his best smile. 'My name is Porter. I would like to see Mr Gurney Lightfoot.'

'He's sick,' she said. 'He doesn't see anyone anymore.'

'I appreciate that he's unwell,' Charley said. He reached into his pocket, got out his wallet and produced a card. 'He might make an exception for me. Tell him it is very important – although I would think he would probably realize that for himself.'

The girl sized him up. He was class and money, no doubt

211

about that. 'OK,' she said. 'Wait here.'

'There's this guy downstairs,' Evelyn told Gurney, when she had finally been admitted to his room. She looked around at all the men gathered there – and saw Rocky, looking pale, among them. 'Hi, honey,' she said. When he didn't answer her, she shrugged and went closer to the bed. 'Regular army you got here, Mr Lightfoot,' she said, handing him the card.

'This better be good,' Fritz said. 'You're interrupting something important here.' He glared at Rocky. 'We're discovering some interesting stuff here.'

'I got a right to visit my future father-in-law,' Evelyn said. 'Don't I, Mr Lightfoot?'

'Yeah, you have,' Gurney said. He was staring at the card hard and kept blinking as if clearing his vision. 'This guy downstairs, Evelyn. What does he look like?'

She considered this. 'He's big, handsome in an older-guy kind of a way, gray hair – what I could see under his hat – and is money all the way.'

'What kind of a hat?' croaked Rocky.

She looked at him in concern. 'You sound like you have a cold coming, honey. You should do something for that throat.'

Gurney spoke. 'And he said he wants to talk to me? Personal?'

'That's what he said, yeah. He knows you're sick, Mr Lightfoot, he didn't look like he would be any trouble. He was kind of – I don't know – kind of humble, you know?'

Gurney looked astonished. 'Humble, hey? This I have to see for myself. Bring him up.'

'OK.' She turned and started for the door, then looked back. 'I think he wants to see you alone, Mr Lightfoot.'

'Yeah – all you guys, disappear,' Gurney said. 'Rocky – she's right. With a cold like you just gave to all of us, you should be in bed.'

'I feel fine,' Rocky protested.

'Evelyn – put him to bed,' Gurney said. 'He doesn't seem to know what's good for him anymore. We have to look after him now – he's going to be a father, right?'

'But this guy – he could be trouble, Gurney,' Friedlander said in a worried voice.

'I know this guy,' Gurney said. 'He's trouble all right, but not like you mean. It'll be OK.' They all stood there, looking at him. 'Dammit, it'll be OK,' Gurney said irritably. 'And if it isn't, I

212

can always use this.' He produced a small gun from under his pillow. 'All right?'

'But I did not trust him!' Victor Niforos said proudly. 'His spectacles they were false, his moustache it was false, his words they were false. A bad man, a man of lies, I knew right away, this. He comes to ask me, as if it were not important, if I found anything in the desk. So I tell him yes, and I could see he becomes excited. "What?" he asks me. So I tell him a knife and a dirty handkerchief – a knife with blood on, I was sick by it, and threw it in the incinerator, and I tell him this. He look angry for a minute, then he is calmed down. "How odd," he say, and then after a minute or two more, he goes away.'

'You found a bloody knife in the desk?' Sylvester asked. 'Are you certain it was blood?'

Mr Niforos ignored him. 'I tell him I throw all into the incinerator, but, of course, I do not. This, Mizz Pemberton, I save for you!' With a flourish, he produced from his jacket pocket the highly polished little brass acorn and its attached key.

Molly Pemberton was staring at the photographs in a bewildered fashion. 'But I don't understand this,' she said finally, accepting the acorn without really looking at it. 'I bought a dining table at the Galleries, not this desk.'

Victor stared at her. 'What you say?'

'I said I bought a table – a large drop-leaf table, not a desk. I mean this looks like a beautiful desk—'

'It was not so beautiful when it arrives,' Victor said.

'But it's not mine,' she finished.

'May I see that key, Molly?' Sylvester asked. Victor looked at him and scowled. He had expected to find Molly Pemberton alone, pale and glad to see him. Instead he found her pink-cheeked and laughing in the company of this nearly toothless gray-haired man. He calls her 'Molly', fumed Victor. Me, I know her for five years, still I call her Mizz Pemberton. He has a nerve, this dreadful man.

Molly handed over the key on its broken gold chain and Sylvester inspected it. 'Where did you buy this desk? Or rather, your table?'

'From the Lecomber Galleries,' Molly said.

'Where might that me?'

'On Lincoln Avenue, just down from Madigan Square.'

Sylvester's eyes gleamed. 'Holy shit,' he breathed reverently, looking at the acorn. He held it up to the light. 'Holy shit,' he said again.

Victor Niforos frowned. 'I do not like this language in front of a lady,' he said. 'This is very disrespectful.'

'What is it, Sylvester?' Molly asked.

'Norris,' Sylvester said, hitting his fist into his palm in triumphant emphasis. 'Norris was killed in the lobby of his apartment building, which is right on Madigan Square. He was stabbed, and the killer ran off. Suppose he went down Lincoln Avenue? Suppose he works in this gallery place? Or maybe he just ran in there to get away from the police. You said the man who attacked you last night was asking about a key, didn't you? Suppose it was this key, and it got stuck to his bloody handkerchief without him realizing it? When he did realize it, it was too late. The desk got delivered to you by mistake and he's only just now tracked it down.'

Molly stared at him with wide, wondering eyes. 'Holy shit,' she said.

Casey was examining the room. There was nothing else to do, and it kept her from thinking.

The door was hopeless. Thick and solid, it presented an insurmountable obstacle. If she'd worn long hair and had the requisite hairpin, she might have attempted the lock. Where was the mysterious armorer who was supposed to outfit secret agents with all kinds of magic tricks to get them out of tight situations? All Washington had ever issued her was a calculator and an unlimited supply of leaky ballpoint pens.

Big deal.

First of all she counted the tiles. The room was fifty-two tiles high, and one hundred and twenty tiles square. She tried multiplying that in her head, but found she could not. 'Too dependent on modern technology,' she said aloud.

She stood on the toilet and tried to look into the ventilator, but all she could see was dust. There wasn't much air movement through the thing either. She wouldn't suffocate anyway.

At least she had water to drink. She ran water into the basin and scooped a little up to sip. As she reached for the faucet to turn it off, the water flow slowed to a trickle and then stopped altogether. She frowned at it, then turned the other faucet on – with a similar result. Worrying. She sat on the toilet lid and looked around. Distinctly lacking in possibilities.

'Come on, girl, think of something,' she said to herself. 'Be creative.'

She went over and, with some considerable effort, took the heavy board off the bath and tried to carry it over to the wall under the windows. If she could prop it there at an angle, wedging one corner against the base of the toilet, she might be able to climb up high enough to reach the window, and perhaps get a hand through the bars to smash the glass and scream for help.

The board was just wide enough to be difficult to grasp, and very heavy. Struggling with the weight of it, she began to lose her grip and her balance. At the last minute it slipped from her fingers and crashed against the rear wall. Cursing, she went to retrieve it, and found that it was standing at an angle.

'That's funny,' she said, her words echoing off the tiles in a way they hadn't before. She took hold of the heavy board and started to slide it sideways. As she did, it caught on something, then moved on.

Wavering for a moment, fighting the weight of the board, she looked beyond its edge at the wall. There was a line there – a line between the tiles. She let go of the board and it fell with a deafening crash behind her, but she ignored it as she went forward to take a closer look at the wall.

In falling, the topmost corner of the board had hit hard against a tile about halfway up the wall which was a slightly different color than the rest. Not enough to notice at a quick glance, but more apparent now. She poked at it curiously and found it had a spongy feel to it. She poked it harder – and the wall began to move back.

Or, at least, part of the wall did. As it moved, there was a sudden whoosh of air past her.

'Oh, come on,' she said. 'I thought this kind of thing went out with Nancy Drew.'

The wall now stood in two sections, one about a foot back from the other. Casey went forward and peered into the opening.

It was very dark in there.

Maybe it was just a way of getting at the plumbing, she thought suddenly. Access to pipes and stuff. Of course – that had to be it. How else would they repair things?

On the other hand . . .

Why conceal the mechanism?

She wished she knew how old the building was that stood above her. Was it like one of the really old houses, say, that lined the River Drive? Several of them dated back to before the Civil War – and she'd come pretty far down. What about this being part of the underground railway that had been used to help fleeing slaves?

The building just didn't feel that old.

And it had felt a lot bigger than a house, or even a mansion, when she had been led across the first room off the street. An office building, then? There were plenty of those downtown. But there had been nobody around when they had arrived – and it had been in the lunch hour. A deserted building, then.

Which got her nowhere. She'd only been back in Grantham for a few months, and she hadn't exactly haunted the downtown area when she had been a teenager. If this dark space wasn't a bit of the underground railway, and it wasn't a plumber's access shaft, what was it? And did she really want to find out?

She decided to sit down and think about it. Crossing the room, she sat down on the closed toilet again and stared at the opening in the wall.

For all she knew, it could be full of spiders.

It was hardly likely to be full of pirate treasure, was it?

On the other hand, if it opened on this wall, it could open on another. It could be a way out.

She stood up. If Butch Cassidy and the Sundance Kid could do it, so could she. 'Oooohhhhhhh shiiiiiiiit!' she shouted, and ran into the black pit beyond the wall. After three steps she crashed into another wall on the other side. Staggering back, rubbing her forehead and nose, she turned – and saw the opening through which she had come slowly narrow and disappear.

Now she *was* in trouble.

This was the result of seeing too many movies and watching too much television. This was what happened to girls who thought working as Jane Dope, Secret Agent, was going to be fun. Would Cagney and Lacey have gotten into this? Would

Magnum have done such a dumb thing? Would Clint Eastwood? Betrayed by Hollywood.

'Somebody call the Equalizer!' she shouted.

Terrified and enraged, she banged at the wall. Something clicked. After a moment, and very slowly, yellowing light began to rise around her. It went from yellow to pale yellow to dim white.

She turned around.

It was a narrow corridor in which she stood – a concrete-lined corridor lit by a string of bulbs that hung from a wire along its roof. Many of them were burned out – but there was sufficient light to see where she was going. The tunnel went about twenty feet to the right and then turned a corner. Casey went along it slowly, cautiously – after all, this movie might not be *Alice in Wonderland*.

The corridor opened onto a large room, also concrete – floors, walls, ceiling. There was a light layer of dust on the wooden crates that were stacked against the far wall. Casey was aware of these only peripherally, for her attention was taken by what stood in the center of the room.

It was an enormous, old, dark-blue Packard limousine.

She went over to it, looked through the open window on the driver's side and jumped back. There was someone in there. Or some*thing*. Taking a deep breath, she looked again.

Slumped in the driver's seat, a little to one side, were the desiccated mummy-like remains of a man clad in the dusty rags of a dinner suit, the front of which displayed a large hole and heavy staining. Its hand was in its lap, and clutched in the leathery claw Casey could see the tarnished gleam of a gun.

The face was very like pictures she had seen of Tutankhamun, closed and secret, the skin tight to the skull, the teeth prominent behind the shriveled lips. One thing about this modern mummy was rather odd, however.

On its taut and dusty skull were the remains of a fine head of red, curly hair.

THIRTY-ONE

Sylvester was frustrated.

He had been waiting for several hours for Jake to return his call, and it hadn't come. He called back several times, only to be told that Lieutenant Chase was 'out'.

Out of luck, he thought to himself, staring at the shiny brass acorn and key. He knew, he just *knew* that this key would give them the answer they were looking for. It was obvious – whatever proof Norris had had about the fate of Ariadne Finch lay safely locked in a deposit box in some bank. Finding the bank would take some doing – but Jake could do it, if Jake would only call back.

Tired of pacing his room, he went back to the day room and found Molly sitting alone and staring at the pictures of the desk which Niforos must have left with her. He sat down beside her. 'He's still out,' he said morosely. 'Damn, I feel so *useless* sitting here.'

'So do I,' Molly said.

'I mean – it's just a matter of tracking down the bank,' Sylvester said. 'They've got people who can do that. Wouldn't take any time at all.'

'May I see the key again, please?' Molly asked. He handed it to her and she examined it closely. 'You know,' she said, 'I think each bank must have an individual way of numbering their boxes. To someone who knows, this number is probably as good as an address.'

'Sure – like I said, Jake has people to do that.'

Molly's cheeks were getting pink. 'People who know things usually learn them from books, you know,' she said. 'Information is always written down somewhere.'

'Not the formula for Coca-Cola,' Sylvester said. 'Only three men are supposed to know that.'

'All right, but everything else is written down somewhere,' Molly said. 'Isn't it?'

'I suppose so.'

'Somewhere like a library, for instance,' Molly continued.

218

'Or City Hall or wherever. So?'

'*I* work in a library,' Molly said. 'And I know a lot of people at City Hall, too. They like me there.'

Sylvester was looking at her with the dawning of hope. They stared at one another from beneath their bandages, their eyes bright within the panda bruises. 'We're supposed to be sick,' he said. 'We're supposed to be recovering from shock and injuries. We were attacked and beaten, remember?'

Molly stood up. '*You* might be beaten, but I'm not,' she said firmly.

Sylvester stood up, took her arm and put it through his own. 'You're a game girl, Molly,' he said, beaming.

'No, I'm not,' Molly said as they headed toward the door. 'I'm just so damn mad I could spit.'

'Well, looks like it's just you and me,' Casey said to the dead man in the front seat. After the initial shock of finding him, followed by some rather pointless screaming, she had settled down to the situation. He looked kind of jaunty, sitting up there – almost like an ancient Charon, ready to drive her across the bridge over the River Styx.

Not that she had any plans to go that way.

Propped on the dashboard of the limousine had been a folded note. With a whisper of apology to what appeared to have been its writer, she had opened it.

To my dear wife Myra and my son Charley –

All the money is gone, my darlings, and even Digger can't dig me out this time, although he's offered to try. I am a bad man and a bad father not to have provided for you and I am sorry for that because I love you both very much. Digger says he will look after you if you will let him. Please let him, Myra. Forget your hate and your pride – and forgive me for being such a coward. I cannot face a life of nothing, when we had so much – together.

All my love – Ned.

The names stirred memories from her childhood. Why,

'Digger' Lightfoot had been Rocky's grandfather, hadn't he? And Ned? She looked at the wisps of hair on the skull.

'Red Ned Porter!' she said aloud, making herself jump.

For a heart-lurching instant she almost expected the corpse to answer her. She wished she could remember more about the stories her father used to tell about the old days, the wild days of Prohibition in Grantham. After a while she replaced the note and began to investigate the room. She wasn't certain how long the lights would continue to burn – already one had gone out with a frightening 'pop' – and the wiring looked very dodgy. It went down the wall and disappeared behind the crates. She moved a few, revealing a door, but when she opened it there was only dirt and rocks there.

She had found the latch to open the concealed door back into her previous cell, but had left it closed for the moment. For all she knew, Rocky and his 'friends' could come back any time, without warning.

What she was hoping was that on finding her gone they would assume she had picked the lock or something and would rush out to look for her, leaving the door to the white-tiled room open. Then, when the coast was clear, she planned just to walk out.

Alternatively, there was a well-equipped tool box in the trunk of the limousine, with which she could virtually dismantle the door of her cell. She didn't do it now because, if they came back and caught her halfway through this operation, the whole effort would be wasted. They'd just stick her someplace else.

She glanced at her watch. Just after three o'clock in the afternoon. OK. If they hadn't come back by midnight, she'd go to work on the cell door. Meanwhile, she was sitting pretty – literally. Ensconced on the luxurious leather upholstery of the wide and deep rear seat of the limousine, she was enjoying a picnic. Along with the tool box, the trunk had contained a basket full of canned biscuits – with an opener thoughtfully provided. And in the crates that lined the walls of this macabre little nook, approximately 240 bottles of the finest French brandy – every one of them without a tax band, which was no surprise.

For she knew exactly what she had stumbled on – Red Ned's hideaway and escape tunnel, stocked against a nasty encounter with the Revenue agents. The double doors that faced the limousine had been a disappointment, too. The mechanism that opened them still worked after a fashion. After much grinding and grumbling they had opened about a foot, only to reveal a solid wall of earth. Presumably the tunnel – for there must have been a tunnel once – had long since collapsed. The room was a dead end, in more ways than one. She hoped it wouldn't be hers as well.

She vaguely remembered reading they had found something similar in Chicago – said to belong to Al Capone himself. Well, there had been plenty of bootleggers in Grantham, too. With Canada so close, why not?

Well, things weren't too bad after all, Casey decided.

She applied the corkscrew she had found to one of the bottles of brandy and opened a can of biscuits. It wasn't fancy, but it was filling. And all she had to do was wait.

One way or another she'd get out of this place tonight.

No problem.

Mr Niforos stood at the back of the hall and watched Molly and Sylvester climb the stairs to her apartment. He sighed. His heart was heavy. All his hard work, all his hopes, had come to nothing. What was worse, she had brought this terrible old man home with her, choosing him over Niforos! It was unthinkable.

But Niforos, he told himself, also unthinkable was what has been in your wicked heart. Did you not have the evil thoughts? Did you not have the bad hunger? And how much of this was simply because you are getting old? Do not be sad that she has chosen this other man. Be happy that she has *not* chosen you.

It could have meant bad trouble.

As it is, you can hold up your head. You still have your soul. You still have your honor and have not given in to temptation. You have used your old skills to make an ugly thing beautiful again. You have bravely protected the lady from pain.

And your daughter has given you a handsome grandson.

He opened the envelope that had arrived that morning and looked again at the photograph his wife had sent. Only one day old but he could see there the Niforos nose, the Niforos chin.

Some things come and go.

Some things last forever.

Niforos, he told himself, you put on your hat, you put on

your coat and you go down to buy the airplane ticket. The apartment house can go on without you for a day or two.

This grandson you must see *now*.

Upstairs, Molly heard the front door slam below and glanced at the clock. 'Come on – they'll be closing soon,' she said impatiently. She surveyed Sylvester, now arrayed in one of Dan's old suits. He looked very respectable, as long as he kept the jacket buttoned to cover the fact they'd had to roll the waistband of the trousers to keep him from tripping over the cuffs.

'Yes – but what if the clerk knows Norris by sight?' Sylvester demanded.

'Possible, but unlikely,' Molly said. 'Anyway, they had his picture in the paper when he got killed. You could be him, under that bandage and black eyes.'

'But they'll know he's dead,' Sylvester protested. They'd found out in which bank Norris had the safety deposit box easily enough. Getting into it was, however, a knottier problem. At least so it had seemed to Sylvester, but Molly had an answer for everything.

'You don't think he used his own name, do you?' Molly demanded.

'Well then, what name did he use?'

'I'm taking a gamble on this—' Molly began.

'*You're* taking a gamble?'

'All right, we are. I think he used the name Finch,' Molly said. 'Now, have you got the story straight?'

Sylvester nodded. 'Car crash, need to get insurance policy,' he said. Molly had bandaged his right hand, so nobody would expect the signatures to match.

'Right,' she said. 'Let's go.' She was full of hustle and bustle, having found a hat that nearly covered her bandaged head, and having put on fresh clothes and makeup. Mr Braithwaite had been pathetically glad to see her and had taken Sylvester on approval. She had organized everything efficiently and speedily in the two hours since they'd walked out of the hospital. Now they were ready for the last and trickiest step.

'You're enjoying all this, aren't you?' Sylvester asked her.

'Aren't you?'

They gazed at one another for quite a while, the question in

222

the air between them. Other questions hung there, too – questions that would have to be answered later. Meanwhile, they had a job to do.

'Let's go,' Sylvester said.

THIRTY-TWO

'Well, Charley – it's been a long time,' Gurney said. He lay back on his pillows, exhausted by his efforts that morning to temporarily retake control of his empire. His voice was very weak and hoarse, and he knew his face was gray. The nurse had taken one look at him on her return and demanded that the doctor be called at once. When he told her to shut her face, she had refused to take further responsibility for him. At present she was sulking in the hall, telling everyone who passed that whatever happened it wouldn't be *her* fault.

'Many years, yes,' Charley agreed coldly, sitting down on the chair vacated by the nurse. 'How are you?'

'What you see is how I am,' Gurney said philosophically. 'What do you want?'

'First, I want to explain some things,' Charley said.

'What things?'

'Fred Norris and his book, for example.'

'You mean how you set him up to cut my legs out from under me?' Gurney's laugh was like the crinkle of burning paper. 'How you got to him in jail, promised him money to dump everything he knew about me – like that?'

'You knew?' Charley was astonished.

'I knew.'

'It got out of hand,' Charley admitted. 'In the beginning I only intended it as a bit of leverage to get you out of this place. But Norris had other ideas. He was a bitter, vengeful little man. I didn't expect him to actually produce a book, but he got carried away.'

Gurney nodded. 'He was like that, the little creep. Always looking to sell out for a step up – that's why I dumped him, years ago, before he could dump on me. So he saved it up for you. Did you kill Ariadne, by the way?'

'No – I was as mystified as anyone else when she disappeared. I hadn't slept with her for weeks.'

'Me neither. Somebody else had come along – I never knew who, though. She was funny about him. He must have been

224

something new.' Gurney's voice was reflective.

'Norris said he knew, although he wouldn't tell me, or Stanley—'

'Quiddick.' In Gurney's mouth the name was a curse.

'Yes.'

'You don't suppose it was *him* she was going with, do you?' Gurney asked suddenly.

'You know, that never occurred to me,' Charley said in some astonishment. 'It's possible, I suppose. She liked variety.'

'She liked a lot of things,' Gurney said, smiling. 'She was some crazy broad. I wonder what happened to her?'

'Maybe the same thing that happened to Red Ned,' Charley said bitterly.

Gurney looked at him with some pity. 'You've always hated me because your ma taught you my old man killed Ned, didn't she?'

'He did.'

Gurney shook his head against the pillow. 'I'm older than you, Charley. I remember things I saw and heard that you never saw or heard. Your ma neither. *We* never killed Red Ned. My old man and yours – they was friendly enemies, Charley. They met in secret, the two of them – made their plans. Your ma, she was uptown stuff, she didn't approve of Digger, but he and Red Ned got on fine. Digger used to say Red Ned figured the feud was good for business, so they laid it on thick. He was around here a hell of a lot. My old man built a couple of tunnels between this place and your old man's hotel, did you know that? That's why they called him Digger – he was always at it. He'd been a construction man before Prohibition, and he loved to build.'

'I always thought it was-short for Gravedigger,' Charley said.

'Nah – Digger, like a mole. I remember the tunnels. Real well built, they were. Digger never did anything halfway. Some lit from this end, some from Ned's. The guys would shunt booze back and forth on trollies, depending on who was doing better business. Maybe other things went back and forth, too – like a dame or two. He loved your ma, but he was a man of appetite, a real high-life guy, your old man.'

'You remember him?'

'I remember him laughing all the time, yeah. But when Repeal came, he had nothing left. He stopped laughing then.' Gurney sighed. 'Digger tried to help your ma after Ned went off, but she wouldn't take a thing from him. Proud. And she could hate – my God, how that woman could hate. Those tunnels nearly killed my old man, you know. Last one went when Digger was looking for your old man. He had an idea Ned might have had an attack or something down there – but the roof came in on top of him before he could find out. The fall caved in Digger's chest, and he was never the same after that. Without Ned to buck him up and laugh him out of it, Digger just faded away. That's the truth, Charley. I got no damn reason to lie now, have I? And what happened? She taught you to hate me, and you learned good. You got to be mayor, and I got to stay a crook.' There was bitterness in his voice now.

Charley was floundering, trying to reconcile this story with what he had always heard as a child. But Gurney was right – he had no reason to lie now. Charley thought of all the years in between. 'I did a lot of things to you.'

Gurney shrugged. 'And I did a lot of things back. Maybe over the years we just about came out even.'

'That doesn't excuse—'

Gurney waved a thin, almost transparent hand. 'Forget it. Dying changes your perspective, Charley. Let it go.' He regarded his caller with wry curiosity. He could see Porter was reeling. It was always good to move in when your opponent was on the ropes. 'So, what do you want from me, Charley? What can I do for you?'

Charley sighed heavily – letting go. 'Cards on the table?'

'Lay 'em out.'

'I want you to kill a man named Millington.'

Gurney looked disappointed. And sad. 'You don't mean that, Charley. I can tell you don't mean that.'

'You had Norris killed—'

'I didn't have Norris killed,' Gurney said in exasperation. 'Goddammit, some pretty old pigeons are coming home to roost today. I haven't had anybody killed in years, Charley. A few guys in the beginning, sure, other crooks – never family men – that was enough to keep everyone in line. My own son thought I killed Ariadne – so did you, I guess – and now you say you think I killed Norris. Jesus, what it is to have a reputation. I don't have people killed anymore, Charley. I ain't got a man who could handle the job. They're all old and stupid or old and slow. Sometimes I think I got more people pensioned off than General Motors. I can't help you.'

'I see.' Charley started to get up.

'Don't rush away – you look terrible. Rest a minute.' Gurney regarded his old enemy. 'This cost you – coming here like this.'

'Yes.' There was no point in pretending otherwise.

'It was so important, what this Millington was going to do?'

'Yes. It would ruin something I've been working on for years.'

Gurney settled back against his pillows. 'Tell me.' He watched Porter's face and smiled. 'Consider it ransom, Charley. I want to know. What the hell harm can it do, the way I am? Despite the years, despite the battles, I got nothing against you now. And there's not a hell of a lot you can do to me either.'

So Charley told him about the big new park that was going to replace the rotten center of the city. How it would incorporate a small sailing lake, a restaurant, a museum, all kinds of amenities that would give a beautiful green heart to Grantham and make it a very special town.

'You see, with Tony being city planner, I got to know about this new project very early. I knew where the boundaries would fall, because I helped him choose the site. He's a good boy, he listens to his father.'

'Lucky you,' Gurney said with heavy irony.

'The site I got him to settle on included land and property belonging to a company called Red King Investments.'

'Nice,' Gurney said approvingly. 'Ned would have liked that.'

'Yes. I see you're ahead of me.'

'Not always, Charley – just enough, over the years,' Gurney smiled.

'Well, you're right. I own half the stock in Red King, and the other half is owned by Eustace Millington, through a holding company based in the Bahamas.'

'So?'

'Eustace bought his shares with Foundation money. He put in a grant application under a false name and got the trustees to approve it.'

'Uh-oh.'

'Yes. He called me last night, in an absolute panic. Said Stanley Quiddick had told him that the girl who had been working with Fred Norris on his damned book was actually a federal investigator sent to find out about the Foundation finances.'

'If you mean the girl named Casey Hewson, that's not all she is. She's also Kathy Finch, Ariadne's stepdaughter,' Gurney said. 'She may be investigating the Foundation, but I have a feeling she's also raking up old mud.'

Charley stared at him. 'What the hell is going on here?'

'Beats hell out of me.'

Charley leaned back in his chair and thought for a moment. 'Stanley still handles the Finch estate. He would have known who she was all along.'

'Maybe. Does that mean something?'

Charley nodded. 'It means I was right. Eustace said that if *I* don't buy him out of Red King in the next twenty-four hours, so he can replace the money he stole, he's going to sell his Red King shares to Stanley Quiddick. When I called Stanley, he said it was just good business – that he was helping out an old friend. But if Stanley knew who the girl really is, then he's been working both ends against the middle for a long time. Damn! I should have seen it. Eustace is a fool and he's weak. Stanley is good at using weak people. He's done it often enough for me.' Charley's voice was bitter. 'Once Stanley gets hold of those Red King shares, he'll have something on me he can use, and will use, believe me.'

'What good would killing Millington do?'

'If he *dies*, his shares revert to me.'

'Ah.' Gurney lay back on his pillows. 'But killing isn't the answer, Charley.'

'No – it was a crazy idea. I'm sorry I even asked you about it.'

'Are you?'

Charley looked up at the older man. 'Yes, I am. It was . . . disrespectful.'

Gurney sighed. His ransom had been paid. 'What kind of money are we talking here?' he asked after a pause.

'Two million five,' Charley said morosely. 'I could get it in a month, but not in twenty-four hours.' He glanced at Gurney. 'The thing that really upsets me is Tony finding out I used information from him to make money. He's such an idealist.'

'So I hear,' Gurney said neutrally.

'I suppose you'll laugh, but I promise you, I didn't just do it for the profits.'

Gurney gave him a look. 'You did it *mostly* for the profits, Charley.'

'Well, yes – but I wanted to leave something to the city, too.' He hesitated – and then it burst out. 'Something . . . well – something with my name on it.' Charley was down to bedrock now. Gurney was dying, he would understand about wanting to leave something behind to show you'd been there. Of all the people in the world, he suddenly realized, Gurney Lightfoot would understand. 'Tony said he could get them to name the park after me,' Charley whispered.

Gurney nodded but didn't speak for a while. 'Sounds nice, this park thing,' he finally said slowly.

'It will be.'

Gurney gave a rasping struggle of a laugh. 'You should have come to me in the first place, Charley, you should have come and told me the truth. I could have got you a better deal on a lot of those places – because most of them were mine.'

'No!'

'Yeah. In other names, of course. I noticed you buying here, buying there, I wondered what you were up to. Lying here, I didn't have much else to do but wonder what you were up to. You have afforded me hours of good, clean fun, as they say, Charley. I never figured a park, though. A park is a nice thing. I thought maybe a casino, maybe a shopping mall—'

Charley smiled. 'Maybe a castle with a drawbridge.'

'Yeah. That's why I held out against selling this place to the city. Hell, I don't need all this, I could have moved to the country a long time ago, would have been better for me. I hardly use half the rooms here anymore. You go downstairs, you find maybe one, two rooms used. Rocky's computers do most of it. But I didn't want to sell until I found out what you were up to, see?'

'You alway liked an edge, Gurney,' Charley said, feeling laughter, weak but irresistible, trying to get past him.

'True.' Gurney chuckled. 'Which is why I am going to loan you the two million five to buy out Eustace Millington. Then you can transfer his shares to me.'

Charley's jaw dropped. '*What?*'

'Why not? I have the money, you need the money, and it's a very good proposition, business–wise, as they say uptown. In fact, if you'd come to me in the first place you could even have avoided getting involved with that Foundation stuff. We could have made a good profit on it together – kept Millington right out of it.'

'You and me? That's a hell of a combination.'

'I suppose you think I'm not respectable enough?'

'I didn't say that, dammit.'

'Let me tell you about respectable. You know what I just found out my little prick of a son Rocky has done to me? He's made me so goddamn respectable, *I* could be mayor, I should live so long. With his college brain and his computers he's turned all my hard-stolen and grafted money into legitimate businesses! I own the Monaco Bowling Alleys – all three of them! I own the Socrates Bookshop *and* the Poetry Corner, for God's sake!' He was counting on his bony fingers. 'I own Merrythought Ice Cream. I own the Little Pavlova Ballet School. I own Twinkle Bakeries. I am a corporation, he tells me! I am called Bigbrain Industries, would you believe? I am worth maybe sixty million. I have social responsibilities and obligations to my employees, he says.'

'That's quite an . . . unusual name,' Charley choked.

'It's not only unusual, it's nuts! *Bigbrain Industries!* When he told me I could have had a heart attack if I hadn't been so sick already. Get this! We have an active payroll of fifty, we have twice that on pensions, we have hospitalization, the works. He's been letting all my old gonzos and their families live across the street rent-free and is only charging them cost prices for their groceries and stuff at the "company stores". He runs the movie house here on the block, and he lets them into the movies for twenty-five cents. He says they're company dependents – so it's good, tax-wise. *Tax-wise*, for Christ's sake! That's how he talks. All this he does behind my back when I trusted him to be out there busting chops and making collections and running things. No wonder my boys are always hanging around here looking miserable – they got nothing to do! He says Bigbrain Industries is planning a retraining program for them. Great God Almighty! He's learned nothing from me – nothing at all. I tell you, Charley, I'm ashamed of him.' Gurney fell back onto his pillows, exhausted by his outrage.

Charley was trying not to laugh. 'That *was* rather sneaky.'

'Yeah – the little shit. And as if that weren't bad enough, I'm also going to become a grandfather now.'

'I don't believe it.'

Gurney smiled. 'Well, I didn't exactly do it *myself*, you know.'

'That's nice, Gurney. I envy you.'

'Hah! I can't believe you said that.'

The laughter was coming, he couldn't stop it, neither of them could. 'Maybe I should become a loan shark,' Charley choked.

'No – according to Rocky, it's not cost effective,' Gurney said rather grimly. 'He also says crime doesn't pay because it is not technologically oriented. Too labour intensive or something like that. He clicks when he walks, that boy. If it wasn't for the hats, and the fact that the little slimebag actually likes me, I'd shoot his balls off.' Suddenly he brightened. 'Tell you what. There's some writing paper over there. You're a lawyer – write this up. I'll *give* this place to the goddamn city for five cents. Five lousy cents. I'll show him social responsibility. That'll get him where it hurts, he's been holding out for three million.'

'Done.'

'There's a string.'

'Dangle it.'

'I want a bandstand named after me.'

'Done and done.'

'Concerts every Sunday – a tradition.'

'Gilbert and Sullivan?'

'Why not? Also a public toilet named after Quiddick. Just so *he'll* know what it feels like to be pissed on.'

'Wonderful, wonderful. I'll bring Tony's model over so you can tell us exactly where to put him.'

The door to the bedroom opened. Evelyn stood there, staring at the two men who were laughing together to the point of tears. She had never seen Gurney Lightfoot laugh before, and she wondered if it would kill him. She wondered if she should call Rocky. Maybe not yet.

'There are some men downstairs, Gurney. They say we have to get out of the building because they're going to blow up the Magnolia Hotel.'

THIRTY-THREE

'Anything more on the stakeout at the Lightfoot place?'

Pinsky sat down next to Jake's desk. 'One of the men just came through to say they'd seen Charley Porter going in.'

Jake and Joe stared at him.

Joe spoke first. 'What are those guys putting in their coffee these days?'

Pinsky shrugged. 'That's what they said.'

'When they spot Judge Crater, let me know – I've been trying to get his autograph for years.'

'What about the tail on Millington?'

Pinsky flushed. 'They lost him.'

Jake sat up. 'What the hell?'

'Well, all we had left was those two rookies and they hadn't done any real tailing before.' Pinsky's voice was defensive. 'We can't pull guys off other cases, Jake – not until we get something solid. We have to use who's in the pool, right?'

'Hey! Joe! Line five!' Stryker shouted from across the room.

Joe reached out a long arm and dragged the telephone across the desk. He lifted the receiver. 'Detective Sergeant Kaminsky,' he said. Then he listened to the voice at the other end, a succession of expressions flickering across his face. 'Thanks,' he said when the voice stopped, and he replaced the receiver.

'That was Sylvester Crump,' he said.

'What does he want us to do – send him in a fifth of scotch?' Jake asked.

'He's not in the hospital,' Joe said. He had a faraway look in his eye, and his voice was almost dreamy. He looked rather like a middleweight after a hard ten rounds.

'Where is he?' asked Pinsky, who had yet to encounter Sylvester face to face.

'He's at the Washington Avenue precinct station. He's with Molly Pemberton,' Joe said in a distant voice. 'They've been arrested trying to rob a bank.'

Jake leapt to his feet, and Pinsky joined him. They looked at Joe. 'Aren't you coming?' Jake asked.

'No. I think I am going to put in for a leave of absence,' Joe said. 'I'm tired, Jake. I can't take anymore. I keep hearing little birds twittering and the sound of elvish laughter—'

'Bring him,' Jake said to Pinsky.

Pinsky, who was large and had been through a lot lately, picked up Joe and slung him over his shoulder. Joe hung there, quite limp, and watched the floor go by.

'And sometimes, Jake . . . sometimes I think I hear my mother's voice, singing those old Polish lullabies she used to sing to me when I was a kid.'

Jake held the door open for Pinsky to pass through. He looked down at Joe. 'You always said your mother had a lousy voice.'

'She did. That's why I know I need a rest, Jake. She's beginning to sound good to me.'

Richard Armbruster faced Stanley Quiddick across the desk.

'You've been busy, Stanley,' he said.

'I don't know what you mean,' Quiddick said edgily.

'You've been pulling private strings again. We've told you about that before, haven't we? You get a quiet retainer for pulling the strings we tell you to pull – not your own.'

'A man has to live.'

'When did you tell Casey Hewson – or Kathy Finch – about Norris – and why?'

'Did I?'

'I'm waiting for an explanation, Stanley. Our employers are not happy with you. What am I going to tell them?'

'I don't care what you tell them. They won't believe you.'

'Oh, I think they will. It's such a neat little chain you forged. Continually feeding Charles Porter's hatred of Gurney Lightfoot so he would persecute him – and taking backhanders from Lightfoot to keep Porter off his case. Coming across Norris in your old partner's file, and suggesting he might be the man who could help Porter destroy his enemy. Priming Norris, sending him to Eustace Millington. Encouraging Millington to get in over his head by tying him to Porter and then letting the dam burst on both of them. All that. Probably more than that. I've been watching. I've been impressed.'

'Go to hell.'

'I expect we both will. We're in a dirty business. Once you

233

had the situation primed, you got in touch with Casey – sorry, Kathy. She was the queen on your board, wasn't she?'

'I have nothing to say,' Stanley muttered in a sulky voice.

'You opened a few cracks in the Millington Foundation and anonymously invited a federal investigation. When it looked ripe, you told her about it, and of course she volunteered for it.'

'Nonsense. You have no proof.'

'But something went wrong, didn't it, Stanley?' Armbruster's voice was deceptively soft.

'I tell you, I don't know what you're talking about.' Quiddick was beginning to perspire, and his fingers left damp marks on the gleaming surface of his desk as he grasped its edge.

'What you really wanted was for the killer, whoever he was, to think that Kathy knew the truth – you wanted him to murder Kathy Finch the way he had murdered her mother, am I right? Because you've had your fingers in the honeypot, haven't you? Kathy was due to come into the Finch estate on her twenty-ninth birthday, wasn't she? There would have been an accounting, and your thefts would have been revealed. So she had to die.'

'That's preposterous!' Quiddick blustered.

'Maybe you had some other victims lined up for this shadowy assassin – you have a lot of people on your little list. But the gameplan went wrong, didn't it? Norris tried to get some money for himself – it was an old habit of his – and the killer murdered him instead of Casey – or Kathy.'

'No.' Quiddick shook his head. 'No!'

'I've seen the Finch account books.'

'You can't have, I—'

Armbruster chuckled. 'We didn't mind when you played some small games, took a rake-off here and there. Perks of the game. As long as you did what we wanted when we wanted something done. But not murder, Stanley. Not murder.'

'I never killed anyone!'

'Not directly, no. But you tethered a goat, didn't you? You set her up, didn't you?'

'There's no evidence, it's mere conjecture . . .'

Armbruster was shaking his head. 'Who said we need evidence? Evidence is for courts. Anyway, trials are such tense things, aren't they? The excitement could be too much for you. You could have a stroke, a heart attack—'

'You wouldn't! You can't – I have papers placed in readiness should anything happen to me—'

Armbruster nodded. 'With someone in another country, presumably? London? Yes, we thought that might be the case. Still, we have many friends in London – should we choose to call on them.'

'You bastards!'

'Now, Stanley – calm down. There's probably a way out of this that would suit everyone. For example, the Finch money. You'll have to replace that, I'm afraid.'

Quiddick's eyes widened. 'That would take all my personal resources!'

'Perhaps we could arrange a loan.'

'Why should you do that?'

'To keep things in the family. Lower profiles all around, you could say. Of course – with a loan of that size there must be a few strings attached. And there would be interest to pay, of course.'

Quiddick went quite pale. Then his eyes narrowed, and he sat back in his chair. 'Go on.'

Armbruster smiled and went on. 'Oh, there are a few other things to clear up, naturally, but they will be taken care of in their time. The main problem is you, Stanley. What the hell are we going to *do* with *you*?'

'I've been framed!' Sylvester said. 'This is a fix.'

'Oh, for heaven's sake, hush,' Molly snapped.

'Go on about the key,' Jake said.

'You never answered my calls!' Sylvester shouted. 'I got sick of waiting around in my goddamn pajamas, while Casey could be in real danger somewhere—'

Molly's cool voice broke in. 'We thought if Sylvester pretended to be Fred Norris we could get the box opened and—'

'We did get the box open,' Sylvester grumbled.

'And get the proof for you,' Molly went on. 'And we did.'

'We just couldn't get out the door with it,' Sylvester said. 'They locked us in and called the cops. They said I was a dangerous character,' he finished in an injured voice.

'I think it was the way he shrieked "Holy shit! We've got the son of a bitch!" that aroused their suspicions,' Molly said mildly.

'Mere youthful exuberance,' Sylvester said. 'Anyway, we have, haven't we?'

'So it would seem,' Joe said. He had been looking through the red leather-covered diary of Ariadne Finch. 'Her style is a bit over the top – "my golden darling" and all that.'

'Have you gotten to the part about him being "a glowing young stallion full of sun-blazed joy" yet?' Molly asked. She leaned forward and began to read the pages upside-down. 'No – next one along. That's it.'

'Christ,' Jake muttered.

'It is a bit rich,' Molly acknowledged. 'I think she read too much Anais Nin and not enough Jane Austen, myself.'

'As far as I can see she never had the time,' Joe commented. 'I'm going to be an hour in the confessional after reading this stuff.'

'It's not a sin if you don't enjoy it,' Pinsky observed, as he returned to the interrogation room and began to read over Joe's shoulder.

Molly looked sad. 'And to think that her own daughter introduced them. It's hard to believe.'

Jake glanced up. 'Have you got the warrant?' Pinsky held it up, his lips moving silently as he read the diary. 'And have they located him?' Jake persisted.

Pinsky nodded absently, absorbed as he was in the life and times of Ariadne Finch. 'He's down on Federal Street.'

The last remaining block of Federal Street was empty.

All around it stretched the bleak muddy devastation that would one day be transformed from yellow-and-gray mud flats to a lush and lovely park. But not yet.

There was still work to do.

Everybody had been moved out of the buildings on this last block. Everybody except the Lightfoot family, who refused to budge. Since their building was at the opposite corner of the block from the Magnolia Hotel, it was decided to leave them in place rather than delay the demolition any longer. If the workmen didn't hurry, the light would begin to wane.

Tony Porter made the final decision to go ahead. He was on site, his yellow hard-hat in strong contrast to his well-cut suit, overseeing the beginning of the end of this annoying obstruction to his plans for the park. After such a long battle, it was going to be eminently satisfying to see this last bastion fall. And anyway it had been his grandfather's – it was only right that someone from the Porter family should be in attendance.

Huge yellow bulldozers and diggers were drawn up across the sidewalks on either side, revving their engines to show their readiness, and men were milling around, talking and laughing, as if waiting for an order to form up and attack.

'Tony?'

Tony Porter turned. 'Dad! What are you doing here? Come to see it go down at last?'

'Yes, of course.' Charley smiled at his son, grateful for this excuse for being seen on Federal Street. It would never do for Tony to know why he was really here, or who he'd been with. To ever know, for that matter. 'Is everything ready?'

'Just about. They've just finished making a last check of the rooms. Don't even want a stray cat in there when it goes down.'

'Porter – can we talk?'

Tony and Charley turned as one. Eustace Millington stood just behind them. His face was pale, and there was a wild light in his eyes. 'Can we talk *now*?'

'Excuse me a moment, Tony,' Charley said, and taking Millington's arm he walked away from the barriers. Tony watched them go, a speculative expression on his face, and then turned back to the street. The project engineer, Boscabelli, was coming back down the street followed by four men in hard-hats.

'Well?' Tony asked, as Boscabelli mounted the temporary earth barrier that had been thrown up for protection from the blast and slid down toward him.

'All clear – basement to attic,' Boscabelli said. 'A few cockroaches is all. I didn't figure you wanted them out.'

'Let them take their chances with the rats,' Tony said grimly. 'I guess you'd better wire up, then.'

Joe, Jake and Pinsky pulled up behind the wall of huge yellow bulldozers, scrapers and diggers and got out of the police car. 'What's going on here?' Jake asked the nearest man.

'Oh, demolition. You'll have to go around—'

'What's coming down?' Joe asked.

'That building at the far end – the old Magnolia Hotel,' another construction worker told them. 'It's been wired for days. We've been held up waiting for somebody to sign some damn paper or other – hey! You can't go in there! Hey!' he called after them as Jake, Joe and Pinsky vaulted the sawhorses and started down the street.

As they approached the temporary earth barrier, Rocky Lightfoot burst out of the building next to them and began running. Instinctively, they bolted after him, only catching up when he skidded to a halt and grabbed Tony Porter's sleeve.

'There's a girl in that building!' Rocky shrieked over the roar of a bulldozer that was backing and circling impatiently around them.

'The hell there is!' Boscabelli said, before Tony could speak. 'We just been through it.' He was crouched on his knees in front of a square box with a large red button, attaching wires.

'The basement – she's in the basement!' Rocky said frantically.

Boscabelli paused and looked at him. Was he serious, or just another nut? That he was a crackpot would have been an easy assumption to make – Rocky's hair was standing on end, as if he'd just gotten out of bed, and he was wearing a woman's lacy flowered bathrobe over old khaki trousers. The robe was Evelyn's – the first thing he'd grabbed when the noise of the earth-moving machines had woken him and she'd told him about the demolition. 'I been through the basement myself,' Boscabelli said. 'Nothing.' He turned back to his box of tricks.

'No, no, no!' Rocky was literally jumping up and down with frustration. 'You can't *see* the door unless you know where to look! It's a secret door, hidden behind some wine racks!'

Tony Porter looked concerned. 'Did you see any wine racks, Ray?'

'The whole damn basement is full of wine racks,' Boscabelli said wearily, standing up.

Tony turned to Rocky. 'How do you know she's down there?'

'Because I *put* her there!' Rocky shrieked. He peered at Tony. 'Oh, my God, it's Pushy Porter. It would have to be you, you smug bastard. You've got to get her *out*!' Rocky suddenly took hold of Tony's lapels. 'It's Kathy Finch, you bastard! You can't let her die in there!'

Tony stared at him in horror. 'Who?'

A big Negro had followed Rocky out the house and now plucked him from Tony Porter's lapels and set him down gently. 'That's the truth,' Obediah Smith said. 'He's telling the

238

truth – there's a girl down there all right. She's probably asleep, that's why she didn't hear you.'

'Keep out of this,' Rocky snapped.

'I'll show you where she is,' Obediah continued, unperturbed.

Pinsky and Joe came up, followed by a muttering Jake, who'd nearly lost a toe under the tread of a bulldozer.

'Tony Porter?' Pinsky asked formally.

'Yes?'

'You've got to get her out!' Rocky shouted. 'Dammit!' He grabbed Boscabelli by the back of the shirt and tried to drag him away from the detonator. 'You can't just blow up the place on top of her!'

'On top of who?' Jake demanded.

Pinsky took the warrant out of his pocket. 'I have a warrant for the arrest—'

'Wait a minute, wait a minute,' Boscabelli said, shaking Rocky off like a flea. He was a short, stocky man with a naturally belligerent manner. 'Get the hell off me!'

'Call the police!' Rocky shouted suddenly, desperately, for the first and last time in his life. 'You've got to stop this, somebody has to *stop* this!' He began to jump up and down again in a frenzy of frustration.

'Take it easy. We're the police, what's the problem?' Joe asked.

'. . . of Anthony Charles Porter for the murder of—'

'Is it Casey?' Jake shouted over Pinsky and the roar of the bulldozers.

'Yes, yes . . .' Rocky nodded, pulling the flowered lace robe tighter across his chest as a chilly breeze caught him. He sneezed suddenly. And again. 'I shouldn't be out here without a sweater,' he sniffled.

'*Casey* is in that hotel?' Jake asked aghast.

'. . . Ariadne Gladys Finch and Frederick Norris. I have to advise you that—'

'What's going on here?' Charley asked in his best mayor's voice. He looked into his son's face with concern. Tony Porter's mouth was opening and closing soundlessly, and his skin showed chalk-white beneath the yellow hard-hat.

'We're about to blow up this hotel when these guys—' Boscabelli began.

'Don't blow it up!' Jake and Rocky shouted simultaneously.

239

'All right, all right!' Boscabelli shouted back. 'But I looked all over that goddamn hotel, I tell you, and there's nobody—'

'Tony?' Charley asked suddenly, terribly afraid.

'No, no – he burned the handkerchief and threw away the key,' Tony was babbling. 'He told me he burned it—'

'He didn't,' Pinsky said. '*We* have the diary now, Porter. *And* you.'

'Stop the blowing up! Stop the dynamite – don't press the – I have to – you can't—' Jake and Rocky were screaming at Boscabelli.

'Keep your shirt on, buddy,' Boscabelli said, backing away from Jake's wild war dance. 'OK, OK – yeah, I see your badge, OK – whatever you say—'

'. . . and you have the right to legal representation. If you choose not to—' Pinsky raised his voice over Jake's screams. He reached out to take hold of Tony Porter, for Tony had begun to back away, his arms out before him, shaking his head.

'Tony,' Charley said. 'It's all right, son. There's obviously been some mistake—'

'Where is the door to the room?' Jake screamed. 'Which room? Where is it? Where is she?'

'I'll show you, man,' said Obediah.

'Turn it off, turn it off, unhook it, unfix it!' Rocky screamed at Boscabelli.

'I'm turning it off, I'm turning it—'

'No, don't touch me, don't touch me!' Tony Porter screamed over the revving engines of the bulldozers that surrounded them. 'You can't touch me. Nobody can touch me. Nobody. Nobody!'

He backed away from his father, from Pinsky, from Eustace Millington, from Rocky, from Joe. His eyes were wild, unseeing. His foot slipped on the loose earth of the barrier and he lost his balance. Obediah reached for him and missed. Tony righted himself by pushing against Boscabelli's hunched back, then clambered up the earth bulwark and began to run wildly down the street.

Staggered by the unexpected blow from behind, Boscabelli went down hard across the detonator.

Jake screamed, 'No!'

Rocky screamed, 'No!'

Charley screamed, 'No!'

Boscabelli screamed, 'Son of a bitch!'

And at the far end of the street the old Magnolia Hotel gave a start – as if she had just seen a mouse.

First came the noise – a series of sharp ear-splitting explosions, a brief instant of impossible silence, followed by deeper internal rumblings. Then the invisible globe of sound grew and swelled outward until it overtook and deafened them.

Everyone stood frozen for a moment, caught and held by sheer horror, then threw themselves to the ground. Beyond the earth barrier an invisible fist seemed to hit Tony Porter, and he fell back, arms flung wide and face to the sky.

Clouds of brown and gray dust billowed outward from the base of the hotel, followed by smaller clouds from the floors above. The entire structure seemed to shimmy and then to hang unsupported above the dustcloud below, before starting to collapse, settling lower and lower as the noise and the dust and the debris continued toward them, borne on a whirlwind of destruction, blown outward and upward on the shoulders of the unending thunder that rose from the ground to the blue sky. In a last moment of grace and elegance the fourteen stories of the Magnolia Hotel seemed to rise briefly into the sky, and then it disappeared behind the tornado of its own dusty destruction.

The noise seemed to go on for a long time.

Then it stopped.

What followed seemed like silence, but wasn't. Behind the barriers men were cheering and whistling, and the drivers of the bulldozers were revving their engines, ready to start work. But over all this there came a weird groaning and screeching that sounded like a giant in pain. As the dust settled, they saw why.

The Magnolia Hotel was still alive.

It had only half-collapsed. The right-hand end had fallen completely, but the heap of broken timbers, twisted steel and crumbled masonry sloped upward to the remaining structure. The half that was left was cracked, tilted and crumbling – but it still stood. From the sounds that came from it, its dying was not going to be easy.

'Jesus, Mary and Joseph,' Boscabelli moaned. Only half the charges had gone off. If anyone had ever asked him what was the worst possible situation he could think of in a demolition job, he would have described this one.

And here it was.

241

'The entrance is still clear!' Jake shouted, staggering to his feet, dust obscuring his features but not the triumph in his eyes. 'Come on!' He started forward, but Boscabelli was on him in an instant.

'You dumb bastard!' he shouted. 'That place is unstable – it could go down any second. What's more, it's full of goddamn dynamite.'

'Disconnect it!' Jake said, pointing at the box.

'That won't make any difference,' Boscabelli said. 'The detonators were fired – some of them went off, some of them didn't. I don't know why, and I'm not about to go ask them. They're unstable, too. The least shift and any one of them might go off. We've got to leave it for at least twenty-four hours, and then—'

'The hell with that!' Jake said, pushing Boscabelli aside. He looked at Obediah. 'You said you'd show me where she is.'

Obediah just looked at him. 'Sorry, man,' he said softly. 'That was then.'

'Hey – he's getting up!' Pinsky shouted, and started toward the fallen figure of Tony Porter, who was struggling to his feet. Porter took a step, looked back over his shoulder in a dazed way and then began a lurching run toward what was left of the hotel.

The men had stopped cheering. One by one the engines were turned off. As Tony Porter disappeared through the broken entrance of the hotel, it became very quiet.

'OK.' Jake reached over, took Boscabelli's hard-hat and put it on. Boscabelli just looked at him, shaking his head in pity and horror. Jake's voice was thin and tight. 'That makes two that have to come out,' he said. He sounded like a demented dentist.

'Jake, for God's sake!' Joe said in an agonized voice. 'Let them call the Army, the Fire Department rescue guys, the goddamned Boy Scouts – anybody but *you*!'

But Jake ignored him and started forward.

There was a murmuring in the crowd. Rocky looked at Obediah. Obediah shook his head. Rocky looked at Tanker. Tanker shook his head. Rocky looked at Charley, at Boscabelli, at Joe and Pinsky. Then he turned to Evelyn and sighed. He took off the lacy flowered robe, and his pale exposed flesh flinched as a cool breeze struck it. He handed the robe to Evelyn.

'Hold my coat,' he said.

They were nearly at the entrance. The ornately carved lintel had fallen down on one side, leaving a triangular opening, through which came the terrible sounds of masonry falling, beams groaning and the occasional manic shriek of metal twisting under unimaginable stress. There was also a rat-like scuttling, which was almost worse.

Jake looked at Rocky again. There was a bright light in the smaller man's eyes. 'Feeling big and brave, are you?' he asked.

'I feel like a goddamned jerk,' Rocky snapped. 'OK?'

Jake nodded. 'OK.'

They stepped inside.

The huge front windows of the abandoned hotel had been boarded over for years, but the explosion had knocked out the old slats, so that some light came in. Through its bright shafts swirled a drifting, eddying fog of plaster dust and dirt. Its hazy luminosity contrasted with the deep slashes of shadow in the momentarily petrified forest of debris.

The once magnificent vault of the Magnolia Hotel lobby was cracked in two. On the right a mass of rubble stretched high, its clotted face broken here and there with cracks through which the sky could be seen. On the left was what remained of the reception desk, leaning against the side wall. Beside it the door to the basement hung crookedly on its hinges, exposing an angled oblong of pitch darkness.

Straight ahead of them, curving upward to an abrupt and jagged end, rose the grand stairway. Halfway up its cracked marble treads Tony Porter stood, watching them.

'Welcome to the Magnolia Hotel,' he said, sweeping his arm upward in a grandiose gesture. 'We are temporarily undergoing renovations, but there should be some rooms open soon, one way or another.' His hair was hanging in his face, and there was a blank smile on his handsome features. 'Would you care to register, gentlemen?'

'He's snapped his cap,' Rocky said in horror.

The stairway suddenly settled slightly. As it lurched, Tony threw his arms back against the wall and clung there, smiling.

'You'd better come down now, Mr Porter. It's dangerous in here,' Jake said quietly.

From above them came the sound of a staccato ricochet, growing louder. Abruptly it stopped. Silence. Then, without further warning, a huge jagged block of concrete and plaster, still bearing here and there an elaborate frieze of decoration, burst through a gaping hole in the ceiling and fell between them, shattering at their feet.

Tony Porter giggled. 'Ooops!' he said.

'Jesus,' Rocky breathed, and choked suddenly on the fresh rise of dust that filled his throat. From the broken ceiling and the breached floors above it, rivulets of sand and crushed plaster flowed like water, creating small heaps and mounds or sliding away again into invisible gaps under the floor. From everywhere around them came the sharp syncopated snapping of fragile laths, the stealthy slither of shifting beams and supports and the agonized moaning and groaning of the dying hotel.

'Of course, you'll be staying on for the grand opening,' Tony Porter continued ebulliently. 'I have planned a spectacular green heart for the center of Grantham, you know. Planning and details are my strength, my life. I am brilliant at planning things, everyone says so.'

'Did you plan to kill Ariadne Finch?' Jake asked abruptly.

The smile left Tony's eyes, and his happy expression twisted suddenly into something quite different. 'She laughed at me,' he said. 'I told her she must divorce her husband and marry me. We would run away. I had brought my father's car. I had everything worked out. Everything, to the last detail. I'm good at that. But she laughed at me. She said I was a beautiful boy, but only a beautiful toy. Nobody laughs at Tony Porter. Nobody!'

'You've laughed at plenty of people,' Rocky shouted suddenly. The startling vibrations of his harsh voice echoed around the shattered space, and a tattered sheet of wallpaper detached itself and sailed across the gap beneath the stairway like a gliding bird. In the darkness from which it came there was a brief, gravelly crunching. 'You always laughed,' Rocky whispered. He glanced at Jake. 'I guess it's funny when you think about it – I spent my life trying to look bad, and he spent his life trying to look good.'

'He doesn't look so good now,' Jake muttered.

Tony beamed down at both of them. 'I stopped her laughing,' he said. 'And I gave her a lovely memorial, built with my own fair hands. She liked my hands.'

'Can you get downstairs and find Casey?' Jake whispered.

Rocky paled as he glanced across the lobby toward the black opening. Then he grimaced, squared his narrow shoulders and started toward it.

'Where's he going?' Tony demanded suspiciously.

'To get some wine,' Jake said.

'What for?'

'To celebrate this project of yours. The great plan,' Jake said. There was another rumbling, from above this time, and he looked up. Through the hole in the ceiling he could see floor above floor of the old hotel, stretching upward like a doll's house, the beautiful old wallpapers stained and faded. A blue room, a pink room, a green and gold room. Thrusting out into the gaping hole was a beam, like the hand of a clock. The noises and crashes were growing louder, more frequent.

Time was running out.

'Maybe you'd like to see the model?' Tony suggested from his precarious perch on the disintegrating stairway. 'Come up to my office and I'll show you.'

'Why not?' Jake said, and put his foot on the first step.

'Because it would be stupid,' Tony said in a new and vicious voice, launching himself suddenly and landing squarely on top of Jake with a spine-jarring thud. Everything went dark for a moment, and then into the dizzy circle of Jake's vision came the triumphant face of Tony Porter, haloed by the gaping hole in the ceiling above them.

'I thought if I went on playing dingbat you'd eventually come into range,' he said, and there was no madness in his eyes. Only clear, cold intelligence and implacable intent. Jake was gasping as Tony's weight pressed down on him. 'You wanted to know what I did to Ariadne? It was something like this,' Tony said, and his fingers closed around Jake's throat.

The hazy graying light became darker and darker. Jake was losing the light. Suddenly there was a loud crack, as if a giant pistol had fired, and the entire building lurched briefly. Tony smiled and pressed harder. 'Her back's broken,' he said. 'It won't be long now. For either of you.' The crack was followed by a steady rumbling that did not stop this time but began to grow in intensity. Fear entered Tony's eyes for a split second, and in that instant Jake heaved his body upwards, breaking the choking hold on his throat. He went for Tony's throat in turn, but before he got his hands on him there was another crack, and his quarry was knocked back, sprawling onto the broken black-and-white marble floor like a doll.

Rocky stood with a length of freshly splintered wooden joist in his hand, ready to strike again if Porter moved. But Porter didn't move.

There were streaks down Rocky's dirty face that might have been sweat or tears. Bloodstreaks ran from a dozen scratches on his thin chest, and a large red area was already darkening on his bony shoulder where something heavy had fallen on him. His eyes were wide, and he was wheezing with effort, the words gasping from him. 'All the wine racks have fallen against the panel. I can't move them, I'm not strong enough. A lot of stuff has fallen down there, Jake. I think it's too late.'

'Never too late,' Jake croaked. He was crawling across the floor. He levered himself up at the edge of the old reception desk and looked down at the unconscious body of Tony Porter. He bent and clicked handcuffs onto the muscular wrists that had nearly been the end of him, then rose and started toward the basement door. But even as he took the first step, the floor beneath his feet moved.

'Oh, Jesus,' Rocky shrieked, dropping the piece of wood and grabbing hold of Jake's arm. 'It's going, the floor is going. The whole place is going!'

And it was.

From overhead a growing crescendo of cracks, crashes, thuds, screeches and bangs resounded. The floor rocked and buckled, the wall ahead of them seemed to bulge and recede and bulge again. Fresh cascades of dust and plaster and wood fragments showered onto their heads and shoulders. A huge length of timber beam fell across the opening to the basement, and a whoosh of black dust billowed out at them.

'She's dead already, Jake – she must be. Come on!' Rocky screamed. He clutched at Jake's rigid arm, tugging it, willing him to come away. 'It's the living or the dead, Jake . . .'

Jake was bigger, but Rocky had the manic strength that flows from sheer unreasoning terror. They strained against one another as the Magnolia Hotel collapsed around them.

And then Jake went limp.

Rocky was right.

She was dead.

Between them they dragged the inert body of Tony Porter out through the broken entrance and across the street. Sirens sounded in the distance as the Magnolia Hotel screamed and groaned behind them, imploding into itself, convulsed by its last terrible death throes.

Jake refused to look back.

When the noise finally stopped, he fell to his knees beside a fire hydrant. Joe found him there, his clothes torn, his hair encrusted with dust and debris, his face buried in his hands. When he looked up at his partner, Jake's eyes were filled with a terrible emptiness.

'It fell down, Joe,' he whispered. 'It all fell down on top of her. But it wasn't my fault. Honest, Joe – I never even touched it.'

THIRTY-FOUR

'Seems to be a day for digging,' Joe said to Armbruster, as they stood in the grounds of the Porter mansion, watching them excavate beneath the ornamental fountain.

'Yes. Has he stopped talking yet?'

Joe shook his head. 'No. His father has lined up all kinds of psychiatrists and lawyers. I notice his old faithful, Quiddick, isn't among them, by the way.'

Armbruster looked up at the sky. 'I believe I heard he was retiring from active practice. Something about writing a book on jurisprudence.'

'Oh. Anyway, Tony Porter just goes on talking. The lawyers keep trying to say it's not confession but concussion, but they aren't getting very far.'

'And does he say why he did it?' Armbruster asked.

'Killed Ariadne? Apparently she thought he was wonderful to screw but wouldn't take him seriously. She laughed. Nobody laughs at Tony Porter – or at least nobody ever had up until that point in his golden young life. He strangled her, he said, so nobody else could ever have her after him. Then he brought her body back here in his car and buried her under the foundations of a fountain he'd been building all summer.'

'This fountain here,' Armbruster said, pointing with his pipe.

'This very one you see before you, yeah. According to her diary – you've *got* to read that diary – she particularly loved the fact that he was tanned from working outside all that summer.' Joe's voice was neutral.

'Porter is taking it hard, I hear.'

Joe shrugged. 'Mostly he just can't understand. It's the old story of "but he's always been such a wonderful son" and so on and so on. I feel sorry for the poor bastard, although I can't say I ever voted for him.' Joe looked around and saw the newsmen in the distance, watching through the bars of the big double gates. 'Anyway, if they can't put him away for killing Ariadne Finch, they've got pretty Mr Tony Porter cold on killing Fred Norris. I don't know how he expected to get away with that one. He runs around like a madman looking for the safe deposit box key, desperate to find the damn diary, and then is surprised when all kinds of people can identify him. He says he didn't want Norris to ruin the family name. Some family name – his grandfather was a bootlegger, for crying out loud.'

Armbruster turned to look around at the bright colors of the autumn leaves around them. The Porter gardens were particularly rich in maples and beeches. 'Tell me, is it true that Porter was seen going into the Lightfoot place shortly before we arrived?'

'Unconfirmed, although he was there when the hotel went up all right. Probably a coincidence – they've been enemies for years. Must have been someone else.'

'Mmmmm. I wonder?' Armbruster said.

'What are you going to do about your investigation into the Millington Foundation now?' Joe asked curiously.

'I expect somebody will put it on a shelf someplace,' Armbruster said carefully. 'When I called they said they were "reconsidering" their approach. *Somebody* pulled some strings.'

'Quiddick?'

'I don't think so.' Armbruster looked slightly puzzled. 'Zane Zipkiss told me it was somebody new on the scene. He said they were a really tough number. I thought he said something like "Bigbrain Industries", but that couldn't have been it. Must have been a bad line. I've never heard of any company called Bigbrain Industries – have you?'

Joe shrugged. 'Can't say I have.' He turned at a shout. 'Sounds like they've found something. Let's take a look.'

'Would you like more duckling, Sylvester?' Molly asked, holding her spoon over the casserole dish.

'I couldn't eat another bite,' he told her, sitting back. 'Ah, this is good. You're very kind to put me up like this.'

'Not at all. Mr Braithwaite and I are glad to have company. I won't be able to go back to work for another week or so anyway, so we can enjoy the time together.'

'I don't want to impose,' Sylvester said.

'It's no imposition, and you know it,' Molly said firmly. 'The spare room is there, and I know Dan would have wanted you to stay here. I feel it somehow.'

'I shall have to find a place of my own,' Sylvester said carefully. 'Did I tell you I intend to write my memoirs?'

'No – really?'

'Oh, yes. I talked to that chap Millington about it last night. Dear Eustace. He seemed quite unnerved by my suggestion that he give me a grant from the Millington Foundation. He huffed and puffed quite a lot about it. But I told him everyone's life is full of interesting surprises. For example, I told him, what about those entries in Ariadne's diary about his late father stealing those oil claims, and getting Ariadne to dance naked for him when he was nearly eighty? Plus a few other choice items. I said I was sure that *my* life was just as interesting as his old man's had been – and that if he wouldn't publish me, *somebody* would. I've led quite a varied life myself, you see.'

'Oh, yes,' Molly smiled. 'I see.'

'He seemed pretty keen after that.' Sylvester gazed around the apartment, avoiding her eye. 'Yes, it's very kind of you to look after me like this, Molly. If it's all right, I'll stay until the funeral.'

Molly's face filled with sadness. 'Poor girl – I wish I had met her. What a terrible way to die. I don't think Jake will ever get over it. Poor man.'

The bulldozers moved steadily in and out of the wreck of the Magnolia Hotel, and the cranes dipped and lifted their heads, jaws laden with debris, which they dropped into the waiting trucks. It had been going on all night. Boscabelli had had lights rigged, and they had brought in machines from all over the city to speed up the work, on the off chance that the girl might have survived.

The noise was terrific.

'You can't just stay here like this, Jake,' Captain Klotzman said, putting his hand on Chase's shoulder. 'You haven't had any sleep, your hands need attention.' He looked down at Jake's hands, roughly bandaged over. They'd had to drag him away yesterday – masonry was falling all the time, and an unstable timber had nearly taken his head off.

'I want to be here when they . . . when . . .' Jake took a deep breath. 'When they find her body,' he said in a firm voice.

Under his hand Klotzman felt the muscles tighten, felt the shiver go through Jake's bones. 'I should have just stayed with her—'

'That was my fault, Jake—'

'No, it was mine. I could have ignored you, I've done it before,' Jake said. He swayed slightly, then steadied himself. 'But I wanted to solve the Norris killing. I wanted to be big because Stryker got there first on the Corelli case. I guess I wanted to impress her. Instead, I got her killed.' He looked up at the sky. His face was still filthy from the dust of the afternoon before. The air was cold, but the midday sun was warm.

Boscabelli came up. 'We've uncovered part of a white-tiled room in the basement, Jake.' He looked awful, almost as bad as Jake himself. He'd never had a fatality on a job before, and it had shaken him considerably. 'We must be close now. You said you wanted to know.'

'I'm coming,' Jake said.

'I'll come with you, son,' Klotzman said. The three of them walked across the street toward what was left of the Magnolia Hotel. The bulldozers had stopped, and men were working with picks and shovels at the near corner of the lot. They stood at the edge of the pit, watching. Suddenly one of the men straightened up.

'Hey!' he called. 'Over here!'

'I guess they've found her, Jake,' Klotzman said. 'Take it easy.' Following Boscabelli they scrambled carefully down the side of the pit and went over to the man who had shouted.

'Well?' Boscabelli demanded, looking at the ground. 'Where?'

'No – I ain't found her. But listen – do you hear that?'

'What are you – crazy?'

'No – listen. I keep hearing a horn blowing. You know – the kind of old-fashioned car horn where you squeeze the bulb, like. There – did you hear that? What did I tell you?'

They stared at each other.

'Over there – look—' Another man went over to a piece of tiled wall that was projecting above the debris. 'There's a gap – there's a space behind there that leads out under the road.'

They all went over. Jake knelt down and listened.

Far away, beneath them, regularly punctuated by blasts from a 1932 Packard limousine bulbhorn, a voice was raised in a loud and extremely drunken aria. Occasionally it would stop, and if

251

you listened closely you could hear the sound of gurgling – as from a tipped bottle and a swallowing throat. Then the song would begin again, with horn accompaniment.

'Someday my PRINCE will come,
SomeDAY my prince will come—'

Grabbing the nearest shovel, Jake began to dig.